A
LUSH
AND
SEETHING HELL

Two Tales of Cosmic Horror

JOHN HORNOR JACOBS

HARPER Voyager

An Imprint of HarperCollins Publishers

A LUSH AND SEETHING HELL. Copyright © 2019 by John Hornor Jacobs. Foreword copyright © 2019 by Chuck Wendig. All rights reserved. Printed in the United States of America. No part of this book may be used or reproduced in any manner whatsoever without written permission except in the case of brief quotations embodied in critical articles and reviews. For information, address HarperCollins Publishers, 195 Broadway, New York, NY 10007.

HarperCollins books may be purchased for educational, business, or sales promotional use. For information, please email the Special Markets Department at SPsales@harpercollins.com.

Harper Voyager and design are trademarks of HarperCollins Publishers LLC.

FIRST EDITION

Designed by Joy O'Meara
Interior illustrations by Jeffrey Alan Love

Library of Congress Cataloging-in-Publication Data has been applied for.

ISBN 978-0-06-288082-6

19 20 21 22 23 LSC 10 9 8 7 6 5 4 3 2 1

CONTENTS

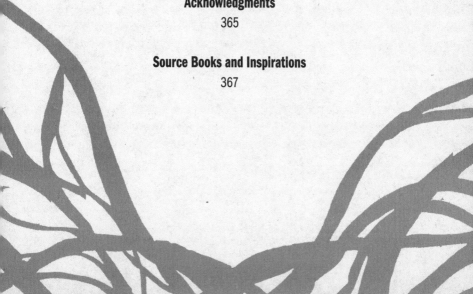

FOREWORD

What you have before you is a pair of novellas. (Okay, one may be a smidge closer to a novel, but that's a feature, not a bug.) They're excellent, though you probably already guessed that, or at least you hoped. They may be compared somewhat to Lovecraft, but there is perhaps a better relationship to a more modern master, Clive Barker, who has none of the bigoted trappings of Lovecraft and whose view of madness and descent is stranger and more nuanced, as they are here. Though it's also folly to try to compare John Hornor Jacobs to either author, because he, and his work, are singular. Without giving away too much, you will find two protagonists who—by a mix of situational happenstance and professional merit—find themselves in receipt of found history. In one, a woman meets a one-eyed, half-mad, bon vivant expat poet from a (fictional) country lost to a dictatorial regime, and she discovers not only his writings but his translations of a grotesque and forbidden work. It is a tale of resistance, both politically *and* personally, against an encroaching, sinister reality. In the other, a man besieged by love, loss, and lust finds—in the purview of working for the Library of Congress—century-old recordings of folk songs and murder ballads, which carry with them a deep and peculiar cost. It would be tempting to say that in each tale the characters *unearth* this found history, but that's not exactly right. It's that each piece of the discovered past has a kind of gravity to it—the translation is not simply a translation, not of Latin, not of deep holler blues. Rather, each is a labyrinth—or the center of a labyrinth—and the protagonists are doomed heroes compelled to walk the maze in order to find the monstrous heart of truth and authenticity. And in that walk, each character loses something of themselves, and gains something, too.

The only questions are: What is lost? And what is gained?

Does each lose a vital part of themselves, or are they discarding pieces that never truly belonged? Some trapping of civilization, some false bit of human pretense? Or is what they lose the thing that marked them as human, as part of this world and its cosmic order? Is it about their coming to terms with that or utterly destroying the balance? They lose emotional and intellectual pieces; they also lose physical parts of themselves. (Interior and exterior.) Are these sacrifices to a greater truth? Or prices to pay for sin?

You'll have to read the stories to find out.

Again, they're excellent novellas written by a storyteller and writer working at the top of his game.

But enough about him; let's talk about me.

———

I didn't want to write this foreword. I hesitated. And the reason for that is woefully simple: I am fucking jealous as fuck of John Hornor Jacobs.

Like, seriously. It is puzzling to me that his work hasn't broken out yet in a major way—it should, and it will, because it's just that good.

Here's the thing. I expect it is true of most writers that it gets harder and harder for us to read fiction because, simply put, we know how the sausage is made. We have internalized the beats. We can hum the tune even before it hits our ears. A story is a lot of front-facing artifice, and behind the scenes is a world of hidden architecture. Most readers don't see and cannot detect that architecture, but writers and storytellers usually can and do (whether we want to or not). It's not that it diminishes the experience or makes it seem amateurish—it's just that it takes us out of the weird wonder of reading, a little bit. We're too busy subtly detecting the seams or figuring out the magic tricks.

But I can't detect the seams in this man's work.

His magic tricks remain pure fucking magic.

These murder ballads are ones we have not heard before.

And *god*, I hate that. I love it! But I *hate* it. Because I read his work and he is so good, there's no artifice, there's no architecture, it's just great storytelling. The kind of stories in which you lose yourself.

The kind of stories that are, in their way, labyrinths all their own. Each a story with gravity. A story that compels.

A story of descent.

And that's where I get it. It's where I find myself relating to these characters—Isabel, in the one, and Cromwell, in the other—as people compelled by a narrative, pulled down into it. Lost to it, in a way. It's hard not to read these two novellas without a similar feeling of maze walking, a wander into the dark. I'm Isabel, swept up in the narrative of The Eye and his journey, and his translations. I'm Cromwell, tying himself to the journals of Harlan Parker, lost in the hollers, searching for the crass modalities of "Stagger Lee." Maybe they resist at first, but it gets them. It holds them, hooks them, drags them down.

For me, at least, it's a good thing. (I can't necessarily say the same for the characters in these novellas; that's for you to figure out.) My jealousy is a healthy one, thankfully. I feared I'd read these stories and want to take my own novel and chuck it in a ditch, because fuck it, I'll never write like JHJ does. That last part is true, but unlike Isabel and Cromwell, I didn't have to give up anything to read these stories and write this foreword. I've still got my jealousy of a writer and storyteller operating at the top of not just his game but all the damn games—but I've also got my work, too. I can aspire to be better than I am now. Like Isabel and Cromwell, wrestling with some vision of what came before and some reckoning of the now. Regarding the stories seen and heard, trying to find a way out and through.

Maybe one day I, too, can write like John Hornor Jacobs.

All it'll cost me is my eye, I'm told. And maybe my soul . . .

—Chuck Wendig

A
LUSH
AND
SEETHING HELL

THE
SEA DREAMS
IT IS
THE SKY

*There once was a time when poets were famous
and their words could set whole countries aflame*

I have walked in the mountains,
And beneath the shadowed trees.
I have touched the altars of night
And will always carry them within me.
Should you seal me away for a thousand years
I will still remain there
Eternally revived, steaming in the dark.
I am an eon rising in man,
I am a thousand tomorrowless days.

—Guillermo Benedición, *Nuestra Guerra Celestial* or *Our Heavenly War*

The perception of time and the experience of being rooted in
temporality becomes dilated during torture . . . Fernándes examines
the relationship between spatial dissociation, chronological experience,
and the subjectivity of memory. For those who experienced torture
within the Pinochet regime, he explores not only how torture
deconstructed the victim's humanity, but how it lessened the torturer's
humanity as well, and, acting as proxy, the state's . . .

—Cristiána Reyes, *The Rivers Flow Red to the Sea:*
State Violence in Chile and Magera

1

Málaga, Spain
1987

I can recognize a Mageran in any city of the world. Violence leaves its mark, and horror makes siblings of us all. A diaspora of exiles, dreaming of home.

On the streets, they called him "The Eye," for obvious reasons—the eyepatch, of course, but also his wary, sleepless demeanor. He would sit in the afternoons in the Parque de Huelin in the shade, a wide-brimmed straw hat on his head, a Bali cigarette hanging from his lower lip. The patch made him look like a veteran, and I guess we both were, though he was much older than I was then. I remember the scent of cloves around him, and the smell of the sea that we could hear but not see. It hissed and murmured at us from beyond the Paseo Maritimo. At the time, I was teaching writing and poetry at the Universidad de Málaga. In the evenings I would ride my Vespa down to the park to catch a breeze from the sea, to drink in the cafés and watch the young, bronzed women, happy and glowing, and forget about Magera. And Pedro Pablo Vidal, the cruel. And my family. I was young and very poor.

We became used to the sight of each other. Him, a watchful yet benevolent Polyphemus, attired in rumpled linen suits and bright-colored shirts, ash-mottled at the cuffs. Me, a pale, bespectacled ghost, clad all in black despite the heat: dress, blouse, hat, hair, sunglasses. An affectation, I guess, toward the grave.

For weeks, we engaged in what other people—other people who were not Mageran—might think of as a mating ritual. He would approach, face shadowed, newspaper tucked under his arm, and take a seat at another table, but always facing me—not too close, though never very far away. He crossed his legs and tilted his head so that his one good eye was directed toward me. He was a man who could make crossing his legs seem an outrageous indolence. When he would nod to me, it was as a king acknowledging a rival. Or a brother. There is very little difference between the two, after all. He seemed very familiar, not as if I had met him before, but as if I had seen him somewhere, in a play, or a television show. I resolved to speak with him and satisfy my curiosity.

The night we finally spoke, though, it was not of my doing. Instead of observing me from afar, with only a nod, he approached and sat at my table without as much as a word of greeting, ordered a pisco, and turned disgruntled when the waitress apologized that they did not have any. I was so used to the sight of him by then, it was almost expected. There are a million allowances and rudenesses even the most banal man will permit himself. And The Eye was most definitely not ordinary. I put down my book and gave him my attention.

"Coffee and fernet, then," he said to the waitress, a little peevishly, after she assured him they had no pisco for him to drink with his coffee. His singular gaze returned to me. "Santaverde," he said.

"No," I said.

"Las Palas, then. Most assuredly."

"No."

He frowned. I began to speak but he shushed me.

"Concepción or nothing and nowhere."

"No. I am from Coronada."

"Ahh!" He raised a finger as if making a point in a philosopher's salon. "I was very close!"

"You were getting farther away with every guess."

"You are very acute," he said.

"They call you 'The Eye' around here. Did you know that?"

He shrugged. "It is as good a name as any. Would you like to know my given name?"

"I somewhat prefer 'The Eye,'" I said.

He laughed. I could see the silver fillings in his molars. When he was through, he gestured at my clothing. "Are you still in mourning?"

The question startled me. I looked down at my garb and then back to him. "I didn't think so, but—"

"It was a trick question. As Magerans, we will always be in mourning." He reached out and touched the cover of the book I was reading. It was Léon Felipe's *Goodbye, Panamá*. "You are quite the bookworm, are you not? I always see you nose-down in some book or another."

I shrugged, used to intrusive men commenting on my studious nature. "I am a lecturer at the university."

"And what do you lecture about?"

"Poetry. Modern South American writers. I teach composition to first-year students."

"Do you like your work?" The Eye asked.

I might have been more taken aback if he had said, "Do you have a lover?" but not by much. It was such an intimate question for someone I had known—and to be fair, not actually known other than to say we'd seen each other—for such a short amount of time.

"It is work," I said. "We all have to work, do we not?"

"There is work that tunnels inward. There is work that tunnels outward," he said. His choice of words was quirky. I wanted to write down "tunnels" for later and think about why he might have used it.

"My turn, now, for the—" I almost said "interrogation," but stopped myself. There was a real chance that might not sit well with him. "Questions," I finished, lamely.

He withdrew a Bali cigarette and lit it, pluming clove-scented smoke into the air. Cars and pedestrians passed on the street. A mother with a squealing child. Lovers arm in arm. The summer sun had set and the air had cooled, still smelling of salt and sea. Later, musicians and dancers would busk in the streetlights, hoping for a drunken coin and a laugh. The Eye took a sip of fernet, then of coffee, and then a drag from his cigarette. He remained quiet.

"What happened to your eye?" I asked.

"It had seen too much," he said. "So I plucked it out."

"Plucked?"

"Removed it."

"Surely you're joking."

"Am I?" he said. "Do you like the cinema?"

"Of course. But I rarely have the money for it."

"Would you like to go to the cinema with me?" He drank his fernet down and shifted in his seat—the motions of a man preparing to depart. "My treat."

It was a sharp turn in the conversation. Maybe due to the

complete and inadvertent honesty I gave to him when admitting my poverty.

"Yes," I said. I could not say I liked The Eye. I think I disliked him the way one dislikes a cousin or uncle. But he was interesting. And so familiar. We agreed on a meeting time.

He stood, drained his coffee to its dregs. "I will be up all night now," he said. He placed far too much money on the table. When I indicated it was ten times his share, he said, "Go, buy yourself a book. I've enough to spare. Allow me to spend my money on young women in ways that won't get me chased out of town."

We were to meet at the same café the following evening, a Sunday. Throughout the morning, I couldn't shake the feeling I had met him or had seen him somewhere before, not in Spain. We met at the Café de Soto then and wandered to the Calle Frigiliana, where, at that time, there were many small cinemas and nightclubs. I was interested in Almodóvar's *La ley del deseo*, but The Eye sniffed and on his insistence, we walked on to the Cinema la Playa, a run-down venue that played only Mexican films, mostly luchador and horror. He chose *Veneno para las hadas—Poison for the Fairies*—and led me into the atrium, where he bought us both beers and popcorn. The movie was a disjointed story of two little girls becoming initiated into the powers of witchcraft, and it did not end well. The Eye laughed raucously at inappropriate moments, making me nervous. When one of the children locked the other in a barn and set it ablaze, he hawed like a donkey. I thought he might be choking.

Afterward, we had drinks at "our" café.

"Well, what did you think?"

"Gruesome," I said. "I don't understand how you can enjoy such fare, with all we've been through."

He fixed me with his stare, surprisingly more powerful with one eye than two. For all that, I could tell he was in a good mood, but he did not intend to apologize or be cowed at his enjoyment of the film. "You do not know what I've been through," he said. "And I do not know what you've suffered. There is a *beyond* to every woman and man. There is a *beneath*. There will always be misery in the world. Right now, countless children are dying." He gestured at the city around us. "Some even here. Each night could be the end of all nights." He looked up at the canopy of trees wreathing the café's outdoor seating area. It was a faraway look with a faraway eye, like the Rolling Stones song that a girl-friend used to always sing me in broken English when I was in school in Buenos Aires. Marcia Alavedes, her name was. I had not thought of her in a long time. She had been a total disaster, but sometimes I missed her, as one does with fondly remem-bered mistakes. I missed her mostly at night or when I wanted to clean the smell of Málaga from my nose. She used to take me on long motorcycle rides in the countryside; in those mo-ments, arms around her stomach as we barreled down Argentin-ian highways, head pressed to her strong back, cocooned in the sound of motor and wind, she was something wondrous. But when the movement stopped, she was a figurative wreck. The Eye simply looked up at the trees as if witnessing some dawn-ing and not wholly welcome vista. "Misery is a condition that we are all promised," he continued. "On the screen, painted in light, that misery is very small." He made his fingers dance on the table. "Little witches! Next time, we will go see wrestlers fighting vampires and maybe you'll understand."

We drank enough to be unsteady and I took my leave of him. The next Sunday, we watched a film about a musician who knew a song that could kill vampires. And the next, a masked wrestler fought a golem. The next, a story of an auditorium haunted by the ghost of a vicious luchador. And on and on, week after week. The Eye laughed through all of them. We had grown comfortable with each other. Our relationship—I cannot call it a friendship—grew. What lay between us was more than friendship. We were outcasts, together.

Only when he left his wallet at the table one night did I learn his Christian name. I took it and opened it and withdrew his Spanish driver's license.

Rafael Avendaño.

2

Rafael Avendaño is a name every Mageran knows. While no South American poet is more famous than Pablo Neruda, no poet is more *in*famous than Avendaño. A son of extraordinarily wealthy parents, he once stabbed his wife with a paring knife at a cocktail party when he discovered she had been having an affair. It being a paring knife, she lived to make him regret it. She took his daughter and forbade him to see her ever again.

A tamer moment for him.

Avendaño wrote of outrageous sex acts, French whores, and Indonesian courtesans. He drank heavily and smoked marijuana and loudly proclaimed the benefits of cocaine. He glorified boxers and the false masculine ideal. He admired American writers like Bukowski and Mailer and traveled to New York and Paris and kept the society of artists and bohemians. He dressed handsomely and was in the newspaper social sections. It's reported that he once had a fistfight with two literary critics at a book event in Mexico City and beat them both soundly. They sued him as vigorously as he had assaulted them. He thumbed his nose at the Mexican legal system and in an interview in a Mageran newspaper—*La Sirena*—

vowed never to return to Mexico, calling the whole country the "shit stain between the asshole of America and the cunt of Colombia." In response, Mexican president Ordaz declared him an enemy of Mexico and banned him, specifically, from returning. Thousands of Mexican patriots vowed to kill him if he was ever seen in their country again. In a follow-up editorial, Avendaño reveled in his new status.

For my part, I had never liked his writings very much. The poems were self-indulgent and misogynistic. If they did not celebrate drunken womanizing, then they were pensive and shallow explorations into the most rudimentary and puerile existentialism. I was conscious of the fact I did not claim him in my curriculum. My first thought at knowing his identity was if he would ask me of that omission—a completely irrational fear, on my part, but there nonetheless.

A beneficiary of Esteban Pávez's socialist programs—the hallmark agenda of our deposed Mageran president—Avendaño had reputedly committed suicide along with his friend on the day of Vidal and his junta's coup.

"You know who I am," he said, after he'd returned from the restroom. He looked to his wallet. "I can see it on your face." He smiled.

Like many older men, he dribbled when he urinated, for there was a discoloration at the crotch of his tan linen suit. It was quite prominent. Avendaño did not seem to care. I half considered him as a Zorba that, through some alternate fate, became an artist and scholar. He loudly ordered another pisco and sat down, at peace with the world.

"It was becoming hard to think of you only as 'The Eye,'" I said.

He nodded. "Of course. I would have just told you." He shifted and lit a Bali. "I think I offered on our first night together."

Knowing his history, "our first night together" made me uncomfortable.

"You did," I said. "The world thinks you are dead."

He shrugged. "It's a big world. I'm not, nor have I ever pretended to be dead." He paused. "Well, except once, but that was dire circumstances." He looked at me. "You are reevaluating me now. I am no longer the jolly old fool who pays for things because he's smitten by your beauty."

"I'm not beautiful and you're not smitten," I said.

He looked sad for a moment. "True." Part of me had wanted him to say, *yes, yes, you are beautiful*, but real life doesn't work like that. "I pay for your drinks because you're Mageran and friendless. Because you are young and very poor. And because my kindness is infinite."

Almost everything he said made me want to respond with profanity. Or laugh madly.

A thought struck me. "Did you know who I was before we became friends?"

"No," he said. "But after *El mundo de los vampiros,* I visited the university, searched for Isabel Certa, and read your writings. You are very good. A little dry for my taste. I especially enjoyed your paper 'Neruda as Prometheus: The New Poets of South America.' I liked the mention you gave me, but you seemed to not appreciate my genius. I hate academic papers that get too pretentious in their titles. So . . . cheers." He took a drink.

I waved that away. "I don't know what to think. About this. About you."

He shrugged again. He made it look so effortless. He was old, but for an instant, I could see what women might find attractive in a younger version of him.

"What really happened to your eye?" I asked.

"I plucked it out. That is true," he said.

"That is shit."

"No, it's not shit. It is the truth." He paused, thinking. "Put out your hands."

"Bah," I said.

"Put them out." He put out his. Their mottled backs were specked with liver marks.

I put mine out. He took them in his.

"When you throw a ball, which hand do you use?" he said.

"The right one."

"And when you shoot a rifle?"

"I don't have a rifle."

"Surely you've shot a gun?" His hands were warm, dry. Like the cover of a cherished leather-bound book.

"No." I looked at the people in the café, certain they were all staring at us. They weren't.

"A bow and arrow, like Artemis?"

"The right one."

"Ahh," he said. It was an exhalation. A pregnant pause, signifying nothing except delay. He was thinking, his single eye shifting in its socket as he studied my face very closely. "There might come a time when your eyes see too much. Or too little."

I pulled my hands away. "This is nonsense."

He laughed, sitting back in his chair as if it were all a joke. "Look with the lesser eye."

"Both of my eyes are lesser. The ophthalmologist in Coronada said I have weak eyes."

Avendaño laughed again. It was a phlegmy laugh, thick in his throat. He often wiped his nose and eyes, hocked up wads of yellow sputum. He was like my grandfather in that way. Men of a certain age cease caring about the impression the fecundity of their bodies makes on others. It's a selfishness and privilege that has always rankled. Yet it was almost impossible to stay disgruntled with The Eye, despite his indifferent narcissism.

I laughed with him. He could be very charming when he had a mind to be.

He withdrew an envelope from his inside jacket pocket. "I have to go away." He placed the letter on the table. "I need you to take care of some things while I'm gone."

I stammered. The Eye laughed and ordered more drinks.

I opened the envelope. It contained a key, a slip of paper bearing an address, and a check from the Bank of Barcelona for a hundred thousand pesetas—more than a whole year of my teaching salary. I placed them back in the envelope and set it between us on the café table.

Questions filled my head, and my mouth could not catch up. "Why? Why me? Where are you going?" I held up the envelope. "What is all this shit?"

"Money for you. An address and the key to my apartment," he said. "I do not know how long I will be gone, and I've made arrangements for my rent to be paid for a long while. All of my books and papers are there and need some organization. You can leave them as they are, if you wish. But, should you have an urge to tidy up or—"

"Where the *fuck*—" I realized I had raised my voice. I lowered it, leaning closer into the table, palms flat on the surface. "Where the *fuck* are you going?" I whispered.

"Where do you think?" He withdrew a piece of paper from his shirt pocket and threw it on the table. I unfolded it and picked it up. It read *-19.5967, -70.2123*. The scrawl of a woman's name in pencil. *Nivia*.

"What is this?" I asked, but I already knew, just as I had always known where he was going. It was a simple enough cipher. Longitude and latitude.

He was going back to Magera.

3

He tells me about a letter arriving from Santaverde, a slip of paper within, and the name of his ex-wife at the bottom. No message, no plea for help. The Eye did not know who had sent the numbers and did not think anyone in Magera even knew he was still alive, though he had never tried to hide it. However, he had not published anything since Pávez's fall.

"Poetry's been burned from me. You need two eyes for that," he said.

"You can't go back to Magera," I said. "You will be shot. Vidal is a beast now that Los Diablos's assassination attempt failed. He won't have forgotten you."

"I was never a friend to Marxists," he said.

"But you *were* friends with Pávez. And look what happened to him. Do you think anyone there makes such distinctions?"

"Still. I must go. I am old and have nothing to lose," he said. His brow furrowed, a craggy landscape. Thoughts crossed his features, like the surface of a dark, silted river, hiding danger beneath. "My daughter is there. She would be grown now. She might still be. And I fled. At some point every exile must return home."

"Not every exile," I said. They had jailed my mother when I was eight. She held meetings in our little house in Coronada, and later, when we moved to Santaverde. Fiery meetings with many young, unshaven men carrying books and smoking. The soldiers came and arrested everyone in our house. Mama locked herself in a bathroom and put me out a window before they took her, and I ran to the home of Puella, our kind neighbor who would give me milk. Mama never came home. When my father returned, haggard and bearing wounds all over his body, he spent the following years drinking himself to death from anger and guilt. And fear. Fear they would take him again and do whatever ANI—the secret police—did. When I enrolled at the University of Buenos Aires, I think he decided to die. A week after matriculation, he emptied a handful of painkillers into a bottle of vodka.

I would never go back; there was nothing there to bind me.

Avendaño sighed, looked pained, as if a great, invisible yoke pressed down on him. "At the end, there were things that—"

"That what?"

"Defied comprehension. Or my attempts at it," he said.

He pushed the envelope at me. I pushed it back.

"What is the location on the paper?"

"It's an area on the coast in the northern part of the country. Past Cachopo."

"That's nowhere and nothing," I said, using his own words. A game we played. Saying things we'd said before back to the other.

He shrugged. "It's not nothing." He pushed the envelope at me once more.

I racked my memory. A barren area, even on the shore— blue salt to the west, brown scree and sharp hills to the east. They mine things up there, in that barren land. I looked at The Eye closely, trying to penetrate him as if by the force of my gaze alone. His ever-present and indolent mirth failed. Something in his demeanor changed. The ease and arrogance, like a pattern of light on a bedroom wall at night, became the figure of a real man, made of pain, and a history of suffering. The rumors that surrounded Avendaño were simply a cloak he pulled about himself. He might have been the rake, the sot, the womanizer, but that was when he had two eyes.

"Take the envelope," he said. "I need your help."

"I don't want you to go," I said. A hard thing for me to admit. The movies, the walks in the Parque de Huelin, the long discussions of Magera and poets and the meaning of art—he had filled a part of my life I did not even know I had been missing. "Who will teach me about luchadores and buy me dinners?"

He smiled and took my hands in his large warm ones and squeezed. Then he pressed the envelope in them.

I kept it, though it was difficult.

———

The Eye flew from Málaga to Barcelona the next day, and from there to Paris and then west, across the Atlantic to Buenos Aires. He told me he would rent a Jeep and drive across Argentina to Magera because he wanted to check in with some of his ex-wife's family in Córdoba and in order to avoid any trouble with Vidal's men at the Santaverde airport. I wished him well and told him I would make sure no thieves pilfered his papers, and that, as they say, was that. The next day, after I was through with classes, I went to his apartment.

Opening the door, I found a note left in the small atrium. *There is a cat, for your protection. Feed him.* He had signed off with a rudimentary drawing of an eye.

It was a spacious if cluttered three-room affair stuffed to brimming with books and papers. It possessed a well-appointed kitchen and even-better-appointed bar, but the most striking part of the whole area was that every counter doubled as a workspace. Three typewriters—an Underwood, an Olivetti, and an IBM Selectric—sat in a jumbled palaver on a dining room table as if communing with one another, stones standing in a tide of loose paper, ribbons, pencils, and notebooks. Each typewriter had unfinished writing in carriage and under platen. In the Underwood, a segment of a long blank-verse poem about, surprisingly, a subject that was either a young woman or a hoary old tomcat. It was hard to tell. I enjoyed it more than most of his earlier work. In the Olivetti, a letter to the Mageran Minister of Workforce and Social Security, asking if the minister or any of his agents might have record of Bella Avendaño, who might be living under the name of Isabella Avendaño, or even Isabella Campos, which I assumed was his ex-wife's family name. I couldn't help but connect the similarities between his daughter's name and my own. In the Selectric, typed notes accompanied a sheaf of distressed and rumpled photographs of a pamphlet in Latin that, from all appearances, was titled *Opusculus Noctis,* and seemed quite gruesome. Having studied Latin intensively in my Catholic youth and roseate stained-glass undergraduate years, I could see quite a few errors in his translation, but it was done well enough that I knew I didn't want to read more.

There were books, though not as many academic volumes as one would think, for a lettered man his age. The Eye's tastes ran toward fiction rather than poetry, and he enjoyed thrillers and crime more than stories of a "literary bent." There were bestsellers sandwiched among esoteric novels by writers I had never heard of before. Kilgore Trout stood near Archimboldi. A Spanish copy of *The Osterman Weekend (El caos omega)* leaned into an English copy of Seamus Cullen's *Walk Away Slowly.* Many dictionaries—Spanish, Portuguese, and English—and a Latin grammar book ostensibly for his efforts at translation. Among his shelves, he reserved a single full one for his own books of poetry. All slim volumes—*La orilla verde* (*The Verdant Shore*), *Sobre las mujeres y sus virtudes* (*On Women and Their Virtues*), *La carne de Huasos* (*The Meat of Huasos*), *Cabeza, corazón, hígado* (*Head, Heart, Liver*), *La indiferencia del gobierno* (*The Indifference of Government*), *Nubes oscuras sobre Santaverde* (*Dark Clouds over Santaverde*), *El Mapocho negro* (*The Black Mapocho*), *Fantasma de Pizzaro* (*Pizzaro's Ghost*)—and many dissimilar-size literary magazines and collections of poetry from regional and communal competitions that, with their different and irregular dimensions and standing sideways to my perspective, looked like a wild thatch of hay.

I withdrew *The Indifference of Government* and flipped randomly to a page.

I dreamed the earth was finished, cinders and ash, and the only
man left was a man who had not loved dogs. He had kicked them
when they begged, ignored them on the streets.

But now, his wife and child lay dead and great brooding clouds
  loomed
overhead, noxious mushrooms fruiting on the rot of land. He
  walked
the streets, calling ¡Quinque! ¡Quinque!

But his dog would not come. It had died when he was a boy.

There was more like that, but I did not pursue it any further. I had remembered him from my undergraduate years being more jovial in his verse, and this was darker than I recalled, however shallow and poorly executed. Behind his books, I noticed a curl of yellowed paper. I pushed the books aside and withdrew it. A manuscript, dated 1979. Written during the first decade of his exile. I withdrew the brittle rubber band that encircled it and read the title. *Below, Behind, Beneath, Between: Being an Account of the Circumstance of My Torture and Transformation by Rafael Avendaño.* It was not thick, maybe thirty or forty pages. And as I riffled through the curled stack, at first blush it seemed deeply personal and intimate, and I think I wasn't ready for that sort of closeness—letting his words inside my head. I'd been resistant to them even before I knew him.

I set the manuscript aside and continued to examine The Eye's apartment. From the small balcony, a glimpse of the Alboran shone sparkling and I was elated with the knowledge that as the line of sight flew, there stood northern Africa in the dark distance: Morocco. The lights of ships winked and flickered on the water. The breeze was cool and fresh. I estimated the apartment's rent—it had to be at least ten to fifteen times mine. The Eye's kitchen alone was bigger than my own meager dwelling.

There were two more rooms off the kitchen and dining area, one with a large bed with many pillows, decorated in what Avendaño obviously considered a "Moorish" style—tapestries and walls festooned with gauzy fabrics, candles and teardrop-shaped hanging lanterns, ottomans and curving and mosque-shaped electric lamps draped with more fabric—surely the man was entranced with legends of Sir Richard Burton (not the actor married to Elizabeth Taylor, but the partner of the discoverer of the headwaters of the Nile) and Saladin, and the mystique of perfumed lovemaking among Arabic geometries and expensive tiles. It was the bedroom of a man forty years his junior. A man with a high estimation of his own sexual prowess. He might have been old, he might have lost his eye, but he was not dead. Or so the room seemed to be screaming at me.

The other bedroom was full of boxes—books, trinkets, papers, old clothing, a toaster, a radio, what looked like a black-and-white television. Under the boxes, a single bed. I saw no cats, anywhere.

I poured myself a brandy from his bar, sat on the balcony's single chair, and watched the ships sail in and out of the Málaga harbor. The Eye had left no instructions as to the apartment's upkeep other than to tidy up his books if I felt like it. I didn't. I finished my drink and went home.

─────────

It was almost two weeks later before I returned. I'd been seeing a teacher's assistant fresh out of university in Madrid and after one of our dates (when she asked how I could afford the meal—wine, *frutti di mare, chocolate y churros*) I hesitantly told her of The Eye and our agreement. Claudia insisted she see the "famous poet's" apartment and after a walk on the beach, I took her there.

A pile of mail awaited me just inside the door.

"Oh my," Claudia whispered, looking about. She walked farther into the space. "This is amazing."

"What, the books?" I said, flipping through the envelopes.

No bills. Various correspondences from far-flung postmarks—two letters from America, one from France, two from Germany, three from the UK. There were two from Magera. Those were addressed to Rafe Daño, which made some sense, though I got the impression from everything I knew about Avendaño that it was an uneven and one-sided subterfuge. The Eye was a man too proud of himself to hide behind an alias. I was tempted to open them—to pilfer his private life—but I already felt somewhat intrusive being in his apartment, despite the fact I obviously was enjoying the money he'd already paid me to be there. Sometimes I make less sense than the greater world around me.

"Holy Mary, Mother of God," Claudia stage-whispered.

I looked up from the letters, half expecting her to be holding some rare book, or piece of ancient pornography. Instead I found her opening the dry bar and withdrawing a bottle of tequila.

The next morning, I had a more intimate understanding of The Eye and his worldview.

I woke up in his bed, with Claudia beside me. Head pounding. It was a very nice bed, and the sheets felt luxurious just to the touch. The Moroccan tile was both more and less pleasing to me from that vantage. Claudia (who had been vigorous and receptive by turns and all at once and more than I can express with any clarity, since my memories of the night before were brilliantly muddy and opaquely full of pleasure) did not stir when I rose and went to find coffee.

I had not rummaged through many cupboards by the time I found a tin of cheap coffee and a percolator and began brewing. Head ripped asunder. The half-empty bottle of tequila glared accusingly from atop the dry bar. I banished it below. There was a single egg in the refrigerator and cheap bagels in the rimed icebox. I put them on the counter and then found it all too much to heat the bread or fry the egg.

I waited, grimacing, until the coffee had brewed and poured a cup; went back to the refrigerator and smelled the cream to see if it was acceptable. It was, I hoped. Once my coffee was the proper color, I slunk out to the balcony and peered out at the sea and the threatening clouds scuttling across the sky to deal with my conflicting emotions of elation and fright that Claudia was still here with me.

I could almost sense The Eye laughing at me, halfway across the world. It began to rain.

After an hour of staring at the rain-speckled sea and listening to Claudia's faint snores, I put on clothes, found an umbrella, and left. I visited the local grocery and bought the stuff of life—butter, eggs, fresh bread, milk, *jamon,* pasta, rice. At the market: rosemary, thyme, garlic, onions, lettuce, cabbage, tomatoes, antennae-spiked prawns, shining mackerel. Twine-bound bundles of crocuses and narcissus blooms.

When I returned to Avendaño's apartment, Claudia was still asleep. I placed the flowers in jars and pitchers I found in cupboards, placed the food in the refrigerator. There was a turntable and vinyl albums below the bookcases. The Eye seemed to favor jazz, and classical music, so I put on an ebullient Charles Trenet album at low volume and began cooking breakfast.

Claudia, when she woke, greeted me tentatively, which was, as I was coming to understand, not precisely part of her makeup—timidity. Finally, she kissed me and we became distracted until it grew obvious we would have all the time we wanted for that. Our stomachs worked on different timelines.

I served her toast and butter, ham and eggs, and tomato slices with olive oil and basil. She fell to the food with much enthusiasm and we listened to Trenet's trumpeting voice and chatted about school and the vagaries of being cogs within the great machine of trivium and quadrivium. In this I had more experience than she and offered her recommendations in ways to navigate the currents of faculty and administration. But there was something of her that reminded me of The Eye—she was so assured in her own importance and knowledge, you could not tell her anything. I sighed. She'd have to find out for herself.

Claudia rose, poured herself more coffee, and took one of Avendaño's books of poetry down from his shelf. She moved away from the dining table—I had hastily rearranged the typewriters and shoved papers aside to make room for our breakfast—and placed herself in an overstuffed and well-used chair near the stereo. She lit a cigarette and flipped through the slim volume. I began looking through The Eye's papers on the table.

"I like him!" she said. "He's got a real hard-on for authority."

"He's a lovely old codger. But I don't really care for his poetry," I said. Our relationship was so newborn as to be tenuous still, and I did not want to argue. But I saw no reason to lie to please her.

"It's shallow. I can't help but think half of the poems are odes to his dick."

"Listen to this," she said, ignoring me, holding the book in her hands. It was *Dark Clouds over Santaverde*. "It's titled 'We Stand Beneath an Enormous Sky,' and begins like this: 'You dress in a sweater against the chill, and we watch the clouds drift over the barren plain. The Atacama rusty and lifeless, abandoned by all except us. Are you hungry, I say. There is lamb. And you say, no, touching your flat belly, then your hair.'" Claudia flipped pages. "He understands subtext, at least."

She stubbed out her cigarette and rose. She looked in the fridge. "Did you get tomato juice?" Something about the question irked me. There had been no thanks from her, for anything. The breakfast. The date. The lovemaking—not that I demand assurances. But she was ungracious.

"I think you should go," I said. "I've got work to do here."

She turned to look at me, incredulous. I ignored her, picking up the manuscript of *Below, Behind, Beneath, Between*. "Okay," she said. She disappeared into The Eye's bedroom. When she emerged, she had her purse and was putting on her earrings. "See you at school," she said, and left unceremoniously.

I sighed. I felt as if a great weight had lifted. Surely, Sartre had it right. Hell is other people. I found myself holding Avendaño's secret manuscript.

I opened it and began to read.

AVENDAÑO

I was sleeping with a student activist at the time. Alejandra Llamos, I think her name was, though it has been so long and, as they say, so much water underneath that particular bridge. I suspect I've blocked full memory of our relationship and her, purposefully. And I was not with her for her name—I remember her hair, her silhouette backlit by sunshine and lamplight. Her form is indistinct, but the taste of her skin still burns on my tongue, when the salt-sea air would cool upon it. The flavor and feel of her body, *soixante-neuf*. I vaguely recall, like a boy at his mother's bosom, her breasts. They were modest. I recall the timbre of her voice raised in anger. She reminded me of Nivia, my wife. My ex-wife. Which is probably why I treated her so poorly. If I were a moral man, and not Avendaño, I might feel bad about admitting that. But there it is. Her name, though. I'm sure it was Alejandra Llamos. It's what I shall call her, anyway.

Do not think poorly of me. You will see.

I could say that it was my relationship to her that brought Vidal's men to our door. That is what they said. But it wasn't true. The Vidalistas were always going to come for me. Because Pávez was my friend and patron, as he was to all poets and writers. I never bought, wholesale, the socialist agenda, though my sympathies tended toward that direction, but they at least respected the written word, and knew writers, poets, journalists were a part of the fabric of commerce, of culture. My mistake was that I had praised him too highly in op-ed pieces in *La Sirena* and *La Trompeta*. Pávez was a man strong enough for dissent, though he and I did not agree on routes for the common man's empowerment. I praised the arts, and education, and while he supported them, his focus was on industry and the collective power of men unified against the interests of the wealthy. Now, in the remove of years, I know how this drew the attention of Nixon, and even worse, Kissinger, and their minions, their money, their influence. The whiff of Communism distasteful to them. Their noxious pressure moved in vast, invisible arteries in the atmosphere. They plotted to overthrow my homeland.

And they were always going to come for me.

Because I open doors without knowing why.

I open doors without understanding the possible consequences.

My publisher had just paid me for my last book, and I had taken a house for the summer in Santo Isodoro on the southern Magera coast, near Chile, in a small fishing village called Nazaré near a little river of the same name. November to April, through the temperate summer months. I was to write my novel, the one I had been planning. The great novel of Avendaño! Oxblood prose, steaming in the night air! My Argentinian publisher was excited. My lover was happy, if lonely for the company of other students, adrift without the firebrands to whom she preached Marxism and the Gospel of Guevara.

It was heady . . . but for me, the words would not come.

The distractions were too easy, or too intriguing, to pass up. When Ángel Ilabaca, my predecessor as the chair of history and literature at the Universidad Católica de Santaverde, died unexpectedly—and since he considered me his protégé—he left me the lion's share of his books, many of which were rare and very old. His widow brought them to me in Santaverde, crying. I took them solemnly, promising to uphold his legacy. She did not know what to do, telling me if I found something valuable, to please bring it to her children. I said I would.

The boxes of books came with me south, to the shore, and at night I found myself preoccupied with reading and indexing their contents, instead of writing. During the days, Alejandra and I would sleep in, eat sardines, and drink the rich, dry Argentinian wines and smoke the reefer we had bought in Santaverde before our three-day drive south.

And then I'd read.

"He loved Neruda," Alejandra said, the second night in Nazaré. She flipped through a box of books.

"Who does not?" I said. "He is a treasure and the father of us all."

She shrugged, sniffing. "He's an imperialist puppet."

I said, "There has never been a greater voice for South America!"

"For Chile, maybe. But not for everyone."

She closed the box, and moved to sit by me, relighting the joint we had partially smoked earlier. Living with Alejandra was like living with a big cat—loving and playful one moment, biting and clawing the next. She handed the joint to me and I inhaled the smoke, holding it in as long as I was able. She pulled a book from the box I was rummaging through. "Tomás Lago." She flipped it open, riffling through the pages. She tossed it aside and withdrew another. "Nicanor Parra. I have always loved him." Also tossed aside. "*The Magus. Dune. Cosmicomics. The Cherry Orchard. The Death of Artemio Cruz.*" Each book tossed on top of a growing pile. "Odd. This one is unmarked, as is this." She flipped the first open, wrinkling her nose at the smell of mold. "I can't even read this shit. *The Lesser Key*? What nonsense." She took up the other volume, holding it as she might an occupied rat trap. She opened it with a look of pure disgust on her face. "Something something, *Eibon*," she said. She tossed it on top of all the others and wiped her hands on her thighs. "It's a whole lot of rotting wood pulp."

"Look at this," I said, withdrawing a thick leather-bound portfolio.

Opening it caused Alejandra to snicker. "Now we get to the good stuff."

Pornographic photography, developed in a home darkroom, judging by the irregular sizes of the prints. Black and white. Men fucking women, women fucking women, men fucking men. The letting of blood. The consumption of bodily fluids. Buggery, sodomy: men and women going back and forth between god and the devil. A long series of photographs featuring a hermaphrodite fornicating with all sorts. Aesthetically, all of the photographs were poor examples of composition and lighting, except for those prints that focused on sexual organs or seed spilled on face, chest. Judging by their wear, most of the photos had been well loved, and pored over.

Alejandra placed her hand on my crotch.

"Your reputation precedes you," Alejandra said, rubbing. "This must be why he left you his books."

"Most likely," I said. "He knew I could be relied upon to not be outraged. Or make any noise about it at the university."

"Maybe a little noise," Alejandra said, her mouth close to my ear.

"Look at this," I said, holding up a photo.

"It's a picture of what?" she said. "A book? That's hardly stimulating."

"A manuscript, I think. Many pages," I said, shuffling through the photos. There were fifteen to twenty photos, roughly eight by ten inches, each featuring a relatively well-lit manuscript. The mottled appearance of the paper or vellum seemed to indicate a great age. "Written in Latin and Greek. Why would he hide them within a trove of pornography?"

"He either wanted them found desperately, or never found at all," Alejandra said, her hand insistent. "I prefer the fucking."

After our lovemaking, later that night, I drank wine and examined the photos of the manuscript without distraction. In a pocket of the leather portfolio, a sheaf of typewritten pages contained Ángel Ilabaca's beginning passes of a translation of the manuscript. Notes on Latin words, their definitions. Like me, he possessed no Greek, though I found in his notes references to three scholars who could assist in translation to Spanish.

Ángel's work was hastily begun and shoddily pursued and followed for only a short time judging by the dearth of research. I went to find my spectacles and returned to the photographs. I held them near the glossy surface of the first image so that the glasses functioned as a makeshift magnifying glass. I began copying the Latin for translation later, working late into the night. When my eyes finally grew so weak as to become blurry, I joined Alejandra in our bed, the sound of the Atlantic a soft hush beyond the stucco walls.

It was days before I had taken down all of the original text, and once that was complete, it felt extraordinarily good to begin typing my handwritten copy on the Underwood. From there I would begin a translation. It had been many years since my youth, when the abuses of the Catholic clergy were fresh, as were their lessons: The streets of Rome and antiquity seemed immediate; the declensions of verbs sprang easily to mind. Once as a young man in a single fevered summer, I had translated Ovid's *Metamorphoses* to Spanish, whole. It was my first attempt at verse, listening to a ghost's echoes from millennia before.

Other creatures crawl the earth on all fours, looking downward, only Man lifts his head, majestic, and raises his eyes to the sky and the bright stars above.

But I am Avendaño! I am an inveterate poet, drawn to the mystery of language. I would never be content to remain simply a translator of verse. I would become a master of it. I would storm heaven and supplant Ovid himself.

I was precocious and so very young.

That was then. Now the novel did not budge and *this* manuscript gave me some satisfaction. Of progress. I was a vehicle mired along a muddy track, taking a different road for progress's sake. I ignored what Ilabaca had written and started anew, something wholly my own. From everything I could tell from his notes and the photographs the manuscript was titled *Opusculus Noctis*, which I translated into Spanish as *A Little Night Work*.

When I puzzled it out, I laughed, reminded of *Eine kleine Nachtmusik*.

I do not know what the mental block was that made me focus on this rather than my novel, but I would have gotten in far less trouble in my life if I understood exactly what drove me toward action and inaction. I am a mystery, even to myself.

Weeks passed. I spent the nights in the study, nose down, and the days either sleeping or drinking. Alejandra became short.

"You're manic," she said. "And smell terrible. Let's visit Buenos Aires. Or Castuera. Someplace with a nightclub and a restaurant. I've grown tired of cooking for you." It was early evening, when the shadows began to lengthen toward the sea. She stood in the study door, light behind her, so I could see the outline of her body in her peasant's dress, but not her face.

"I'm sure you can take any lover you might wish," I said, gesturing to the door. "Even one who knows how to cook."

"I can find another man, very easily." She cursed then, quite eloquently. "All you do is stare at those photos and that manuscript and drink yourself to death. I worry about your liver."

"Every night it is torn from me, and every morning when I wake it is renewed, whole once more," I said. Ovid must have been weighing on me.

Alejandra and I fought, and fucked, and fought again. She became unhappier, and it was only when her sister came to visit that her demeanor changed. They packed her things into a Volkswagen and drove north to Castuera and left me with my pursuits. I was not sorry to see them go. I drank too much rum and scotch and wine and ate too many tortillas and cheese and lamb dripping with fat, packing on weight, a Lord Byron at the shore. I did not sleep well, despite the ocean only paces from my back door. When slumber totally eluded me, I would go down to the waves and wade in, head full of desperate and dark images, hoping the old cure, salt and foam, would wash away my shadow. But the thoughts remained.

Sometimes I felt abandoned on a vast, starless shore, waiting for the seas to rise up, or the sky to crack and distend, spilling forth the heavens to drown the world. I heard whispers at night, even when the house was empty. The weather changed. We were far south. For two weeks, bright autumn days became dark and stormy. I bought another woolen sweater, long johns to wear beneath my trousers. Still, I would swim in the sea, searching for the old cure. And fretted at the translation like a terrier with some dead thing he's found in the forest.

The more I read, the more I translated *A Little Night Work*, the more restless I became. I'd walk to the village and drink beer with the fishermen, home from the sea. The old men in the *cervecería* would discuss the weather, and the size of the swells of the ocean as if they were the breasts of a woman—the size of them! Their great bounty! It's a thin, wind-scraped land, Santo Isodoro, with no real trees or growth until you travel miles inland, and this lack of biologic diversity is mirrored in the people. But they were attuned to the wind, and weather. The fishermen would say when the sky turned dark, *"El mar sueña que es el cielo." The sea dreams it is the sky.* And I immediately decided it would be the title of the novel I was most obviously *not* writing.

My days were filled with puzzling out sections of *A Little Night Work*. I kept returning to the photographs. The challenges the endeavor offered sparked in me a dogged and inexorable determination. My vision became clear in my mind and I thought the vision might meet the execution, if I was diligent.

I wanted the translation to illuminate and expand upon the illustrations that sometimes felt like macabre ciphers. There was a man on a field with thirty coins and men with faces like wolves around a corpse where a crowned man wielding a sword climbed out of the body cavity. There was the figure of a man with his hand chopped off, and a great serpent made from a great conglomeration of human body parts, possessed of gleaming and intelligent eyes. All of the illustrations were executed in a rough, primitive style—but so very expressive!—that seemed like something from a stone wall at Lascaux, rather than an illustration on yellowed vellum. At night, in dreams, I could see myself holding the true object in my hand—the manuscript of *A Little Night Work*—and turning the pages. The fecund smell of the paper blooming in my nostrils. Eyes swimming with images drawn by a malevolent but genius child. Each photo, crooked Latin crowded around horrors in dark skeins. I ignored the Greek, the scribbles, the spatters of ink and intaglios of an unsteady hand. I pored over the drawings: a bird splayed open, suspended in the sky, swimming in what looked like leeches; a corpse rising from the earth, hollow-eyed, pointing an accusing finger at a small house on a mountain; a woman wearing a crown looking upon an infant's desiccated corpse in a bassinet, a phial in her hand; a group of soldiers with spears, a black cloud with a wicked animalistic tail hanging above their heads. Brutalist cave paintings. Yet how close the translation came to poetry. I half fancied myself taking the passages and publishing them as *The Sea Dreams It Is the Sky,* my novel abandoned once and for all. This idea became firm in my mind. I began my real work then. How to not just translate this from Latin, but elevate the ancient words to art?

I gave myself the answer: Through pride. Through ego. *Night Work* would become art by passing through the portal that is the poet. Me. And my genius would transform it. I burned then, I became incensed and electric.

The photos became words. The words became poems. The poems became frameworks for elements of my soul. "The Revenant" and "The Severed Hand" were followed by "Reckonings and the Elements of Reclamation." Through me the Latin scrawls became a window into the human experience.

One passage—the passage nearest the many soldiers and the

wicked-tailed cloud—became a poem called "On the Miasma of Soldiers and the Beacon of Cruelty." It went:

The soldiers come, without knowing,
bearing the mantle of the unnamed:
the vast prodigals, destroyers of heaven,
and from their spear tips to sword hafts—
from their ill intentions to their cruel thoughts—
a rich smell rises.
Blood calls to blood,
bad calls to bad,
and through pain and sacrifice,
we draw the gaze of hidden eyes,
of titanic movements beyond the stars.
It is a lure, a sweet aroma,
the killing and
the letting of blood.
The pain becomes an offering
and sacrifice becomes a beacon.
The beacon becomes a door.

It was not half-bad. I would clean it up, fix the repetitions, clarify the muddy thoughts, and make it more applicable to the Mageran spirit. My focus would be on it, solely. The novel was, by then, totally forgotten. I was energized and excited for the future and what my new book of poetry would become.

Except that I had bad dreams.

Alejandra returned from Castuera, bid farewell to her sister Ofelia, and convinced me to put work aside. Now that I had some progress, I could breathe once more. We resumed our endless cycle of fighting and fevered lovemaking. I took her out on Perón's skiff and down long walks on the beach. An old fisherman at the *cervecería* whom everyone called Ballo invited us to a festive New Year's beach *asado*, where many of the young and old people of the town would be gathered for drink and dancing. We happily joined.

Alejandra and I held hands near the fire where musicians strummed guitars. Laughing men filled our cups with wine. The sun set, the burning wood sent sparks swimming upward to the heavens. Torches and lanterns were lit and hung from poles. Young men and women laughed and kissed in the flickering yellow light. No one else acted surprised when Ballo casually led a sow forward, placed a pistol to her head, and fired. The pig thrummed and pitched over. The music stopped and all of the partygoers gave a great cry in exultation. Men and women rushed in, grabbing feet and rearranging the stiff-legged body of the animal.

"It will take more than a popgun to kill her," Ballo said to me, his grin showing great gaps in his teeth. The light from the torches and the bonfire, at such an inferior angle, shadowed the whole revelrous crowd's features in a hellish cast. Ballo's mouth seemed black, his eyes pools of oil, and his smile absolutely ravenous. "But thank Mary the Mother, no squealing." From nowhere, he withdrew a knife and, hands digging into the jowls, cut the sow's throat. Impossibly red gouts of blood rushed from the wound and nut-brown local women collected the blood in a tin. Ballo began singing "Noches de luna" as they raised the sow and tossed her body onto the fire to char for a few moments, and then dragged it off once more to scrape it with battens, removing all of the bristles. Afterward, Ballo's real knifework began. Viscera spilled in blue-white coils and were placed in a large wooden bucket to be cleaned in the surf. Ballo took the liver, the stomach, the heart. The lungs, no one wanted—they looked like a drowned pink bird—and he waded out into the sea, lungs in one hand and knife in the other, backlit by moonlight shattered on the ocean's wave, and tossed them as far as he could, washing his bloody arms and knife afterward in salt water.

Alejandra watched avidly, afraid of nothing. Ballo returned, dripping, to stand over the now-empty body cavity of the pig, grinning, his avid expression mirrored in the men's and women's faces all around. I had this uncomfortable feeling. The pig lay splayed out on the rocks and pebbles of the beach, gaping, gleaming wet and red in the center. I could not look away. The terrible figure of a man, wearing a crown and bearing a sword, drenched in blood, wormed his way up out of the cavity, into the world of men . . .

"Are you all right?" Alejandra asked, placing a cool hand on my arm.

I broke from my reverie and led her away to leave Ballo to the slaughter. And to find something stronger to drink. I could not bring myself to eat any of the *asado* cooked that night.

The translation was calling to me once again, seething in my subconscious, but now there was a reluctance to answer its call. Alejandra was my anchor. Alejandra Llamos, that was her name, I'm sure of it now. Every time I closed my eyes, I saw my hands, and in them was the manuscript of *Night Work*. My mind was a chorus, caught in a refrain of Latin phrases, Gregorian echoes—so similar to Spanish. Just reading the untranslated words, I felt I could ascertain their meaning. Alejandra took to slapping me during moments when I would fade away, thoughts bound up in ancient poetry. Or sinking to her knees and unbuckling my belt. Other days we spent on Perón's fishing boat, drinking rum and casting metal-tipped lines and screaming when the silver, thrashing fish were pulled aboard. I grew a beard (then coming in white for the first time) and ate my weight in mackerel. Each night, I fell into bed stinking of sun and sea and fish. But I began seeing shadows moving, even in the day. No amount of sea and foam and drenching myself in the waves could make them go away. I began to take long walks to wear myself out, doing hundreds of push-ups and sit-ups to exhaust my body. Sleep eluded me.

I was bleary. And worse, I was unaware of what was happening in Santaverde.

I have tried to put it together, to assemble the puzzle of how they could have located me, since I was so far away in Santo Isodoro. My housekeeper? My publisher, who helped arrange the rental of the house in Estancia las Violetas?

In the end, it does not matter.

Four men found us one evening as the shadows were growing long over the beach at our backs, the sky bluing. They looked, in my mind, like American GIs from the movies *Battleground* and *Tora! Tora! Tora!* I thought of the soldier holding stolen eggs in his helmet, constantly whipping them to keep them from congealing. Van Johnson. But these soldiers called for me in Spanish.

"Avendaño!" they said, outside the door. A man on the street told them in a tremulous voice that I was not there, I was fishing and far out to sea, but I was foolish and did not want any man to lie for me. I was no coward. I was racked with bad dreams, and no soldier could frighten me.

I threw open the door, saying, "Here I am, what do you want?" The soldiers looked at each other, amazed at my brazen appearance. Then one of the men struck me in the face with the butt of his rifle. It happened so quickly, I had an impression of movement and something growing in my vision. A pain blooming in my face and the peculiar sensation of falling. Peculiar because falling has always been a weightless freedom punctuated by a harsh reminder of gravity. The descent of Lucifer writ small. The soldiers bellowed something, but I cannot remember what. I do remember Alejandra screaming, and them dragging me to a rattling truck and the smell of diesel. I passed out of consciousness then so I do not know what horrors they might have inflicted upon Alejandra. I never saw her again, at least not in the waking world.

Once I became transformed, once I had the greater sight, I did not return to look for her. I did not fight to find her. Alejandra Llamos, I am sure her name was.

I was, and remain, a coward after all.

4

Avendaño in prose was even more frustrating than Avendaño in person. I put aside his manuscript, tidied the kitchen and his Moorish bedroom, and left the apartment.

The next day, I called Claudia from my office, leaving a hesitant message on her answering machine. *This is the Clod, leave words after the beep.* The machine chirped, an unforeseen stage call. Performance anxiety in the least likely of places, my own office.

"Hey, it's Isabel. I'm—"

What does one say? Other people, people who just blithely wander from situation to situation, talking, laughing, interacting, would know exactly what words to give voice to. Like a confidence man, throwing out a convincing line of patter. We are animals and much of communication is just soothing vocalizations, soft glottals and plosives, that indicate to other animals we do not intend harm, we consider them part of our tribe. Any meaning layered on top of that is just . . . *extra.* I found I could not make those animal sounds. "Sorry I didn't catch you. I wanted to talk," I said, and then hung up. I gathered my notes and then went to class to lecture on Yesenia Pinilla and the pastoral imagery in her poems. Yesenia was from La Coronada, Magera. My home.

Two days later I was reading in the Parque de Huelin, sitting at the bench where I first noticed The Eye. The day was bright and lovely, the scents of the sea fresh, and I felt at any moment Avendaño might stride right up and sit down, smoking a Bali cigarette, and begin a discussion of religious imagery in luchador films, or discuss the best part of a chicken to eat. (He says liver, I say thigh.) I watched mothers walking strollers, young men smoking. A guitarist busked somewhere out of sight, singing Elvis and Beatles songs in a very poor American accent.

I was distracted. Two things warred in my mind. The first was Claudia. Our night together had been wonderful, and I wished I could talk to her without the complication of what I had begun to think of as a mating pressure. After sex, I had noticed (though I was not, essentially, a sex-driven person) that the other person in the equation often takes on a possessive demeanor, and something in that rankled me. Claudia, with her brazen ways, seemed brutish the morning after. I reacted instinctively, I think. I am a solitary being, though Avendaño would argue with me about that for hours. *How did you know I was Mageran? How did I know you are? You're part of a bigger fabric than you know, Isabel.*

And Avendaño's testament kept popping up in my awareness during random moments. I might be on the beach, taking in sun, and look to the light shattering on its surface and think, *The sea dreams it is the sky.*

When the sky dreams, what does it become?

In quiet moments, I wondered what Alejandra might look like, how she walked or the sound of her voice. In my mind, she began to resemble Claudia. At night, in those moments lying in bed and desperately trying to sleep when the mind turns to every terrible thing you've said, or done, and every terrible thing said and done to you, I would think of his poem "The Miasma of Soldiers." I would think of the Vidalistas who came to take The Eye from his idylls and labors. *Blood calls to blood, bad calls to bad, and through pain and sacrifice, we draw the gaze of hidden eyes, of titanic movements beyond the stars.* I did not know what it meant, or its significance, but part of me wanted to look at the Latin, and see if I could find a better meaning there than Avendaño did. I was exceptional in church, and school, and university—I was sure I could offer a better interpretation than The Eye.

Such were my thoughts when Claudia appeared on the park's far path, strolling along manicured flower beds and lush ferns. I raised my arm to hail her but stopped, seeing the woman she was with. A tall, gangly girl with bad posture but lustrous hair. Claudia spotted me, grabbed her companion's hand, and dragged her forward.

"Hello, Isabel!" Claudia said, entirely too bright. "Catching up on your studies?"

When I was young, I spent weeks looking into the mirror, coaching reluctant muscles into arching my eyebrows. I thought, if they were going to be so prominent, why not learn to use them to great effect? "What else would I be doing? Football?" I knew Claudia had played at the Universidad de Barcelona on a scholarship. "Every week brings new classes, with new lessons. How is your assistant teaching coming along?"

"Wonderful! I have hammered home the Krebs cycle, and now we have moved on to aerobic and anaerobic pathways."

The woman with Claudia said, "Thirty-four ATP!"

Claudia shook her head, frowning, and said, "No. Thirty-eight."

Ignoring Claudia, I put aside my Pinilla collection and stood. "Hello," I said, extending my hand to the new woman. "I'm a friend of Claudia's." She was three, maybe four, inches taller than me, tall enough that I could look up her nostrils and see the fine cilia crossed in a weave like the crown of a leafless tree. A peculiar enough view. She smiled, which made her face soften and her whole countenance brighten. She had sad eyes and I could see why Claudia was in her company. I felt as if a radiologist had just laid a heavy leaden vest upon me.

"I'm Laura," she said, taking my hand and shaking.

"We're going to Manuel's for drinks," Claudia said, still holding Laura's other hand. Looking dead at me, she raised it and kissed the back. "Would you like to join us?"

"No, thank you," I said. "I have to prepare for class tomorrow." I hastily packed my book into my bag and fled, wandering down the streets and alleys until, before I knew it, I had returned to Avendaño's apartment.

When I opened the door, I saw the tomcat. He sat in Avendaño's reading chair, one leg up, licking his balls. On my entry, he looked up from his testicular occupation and stared at me with one large, yellow eye. The other was milky white. There were notches on his ears—due to territorial battles with other males, most likely—and his fur possessed a latticework of bare stripes, more testament to his bellicose nature. His tail had been gone for years. He was quite large and I stopped in my tracks once I saw him.

Eventually, he looked away and, rising, he stretched and hopped down from the chair and padded toward me. He brushed past my leg, pressing into me, his back rising to lean on my calf with his full weight. Silent. He circled me once and then walked back into the apartment, out onto the balcony. I followed, so I could keep him in view. He leapt up, onto the narrow cast-iron grating, and vaulted onto a nearby roof covered in red ceramic tile. The tomcat gave one last glance and then, with an absolute insolent stride, walked up the roof, out of view.

Bemused, I turned back to the entryway. There were only two

new pieces of mail, one obviously an advertisement. The other was addressed to me. I opened it.

Dearest Isabel,

I've arrived safe in Buenos Aires, and have bought a cheap Volkswagen Beetle like one I had long ago, before the heavens fell. I thought I might rent a Jeep, but no one here in Argentina will rent to a one-eyed man intending to travel to Magera. There is much anti-Vidal sentiment and very dark rumors of ANI and the influence of Vidal's secret police extending beyond borders. Ever since Alfonsín took over after the junta government, Argentina has come to its senses and eyes its neighbor with great suspicion.

I'm writing you now from Córdoba, where my wife's family is from. They have not heard from her since the coup, so many years ago. I have a rather mixed reputation here in Argentina, and am not very welcome, so I must continue on. I leave tomorrow for the push into Magera. I must decide whether to try and cross near Santaverde or take a more northern route and cross over the mountains near Cascavel. I am favoring the latter, since word has it that the border near Santaverde teems with carabineros with a direct line to the secret police.

I would like to schedule a phone call with you for November 12, at six P.M. I will call my apartment. If you would be there to answer, I would appreciate it. There is a telephone beneath my bed, and a jack for it in the kitchen.

Whatever mail you find, please open. I'm expecting some checks from my publishers, and you may deposit them in the Bank of Barcelona on the Calle Passasuego. Just bring your identification; I've left word with them you will be acting as my agent.

I miss our conversations and our time together.

*Feed the cat, for your protection. If you read my books,
do not be too hard on me. There are manuscripts in my
apartment that should remain unread, now that I think
about it. Some knowledge is better off unknown.*

Your friend,

The man was outrageously annoying and endearing by turns,
I decided, but I worried for him. ANI was rumored to have killed
thousands and tortured ten times that. And he was driving toward them.

I went through his other mail. My English is passable, my German weak, and my French deplorable. However, it was not hard
to make sense of the correspondences. One of the letters from
America was from another Mageran exile, a poet and scholar
who obviously had a great friendship and familiarity with the
supposedly dead Avendaño, writing for advice on how to advance
his career. The second letter was friendly as well. Possibly overly
friendly. It came from a woman who was quite explicit in the
erotic actions she wished to perform upon The Eye. From con-
text I inferred they had a long and robust correspondence. Her
heartfelt and lascivious entreaties were working toward a meeting, if Avendaño would only see it. He probably did. There were
three checks from publishers nestled among labyrinthine sales
reports—one from France, one from Germany, and the other
from Britain—totaling over twenty thousand pesetas. More ad-
verts and promotions.

The two letters from Magera, addressed to Rafe Daño, I opened
last. The first was a response from the Magera Minister of Licenses
and Business Permits, a José Blanco, stating there was no record

of Bella Avendaño, Isabella Avendaño, or Isabella Campos. But, Señor Blanco wrote, he would love for Rafe Daño to come to his office so they might discuss his interests in missing persons more in depth.

I shivered. Something about the phrasing affected me on a physical level.

Putting that aside, I opened the last letter. It contained a single slip of paper.

-20.518097, -67.65773

Alejandra

———

I never really returned to my life before meeting The Eye, such as it was. With the arrival of his letter, my connection to Málaga, the university, and everything else in Spain became tenuous. I taught classes, but just as a way of marking the days until the twelfth of November. I found myself spending more and more time at Avendaño's apartment and less at my own. I bought tuna and kibble for the cat; I withdrew the phone from under his bed and plugged it in in the kitchen. I deposited his checks and was surprised when the teller directed me to a handsome woman's office, where I was greeted warmly and handed ten thousand pesetas (roughly one thousand American dollars) in an envelope, stating it was the standing instructions of Rafael Avendaño that his agent receive a monthly stipend.

"Trust me," she said. "Mister Avendaño can afford to be generous." I took the money. How easy it was to travel down that road. Had The Eye dressed up in a scarlet suit, pitchfork aloft, leaping to a rooftop to be illuminated by fire and twirling his mustache, he could not have corrupted me more easily. Hell must be filled with poor academics.

On the twelfth, I waited in his kitchen, watching the hands of the clock slowly turn. At six, the phone remained silent.

I called in sick to work the next day and remained at Avendaño's, waiting expectantly for the phone to ring. I went to the landlord and arranged for him to telephone the apartment while I was there, to check and see if the ringer worked. While I was out, I had an anxious dread that the phone would ring while I was gone. When I returned, even though I had arranged the call with the landlord, I nearly screamed from the sound of the rotary's bell, I was wound so tight. My unease regarding my friend increased.

Part of The Eye must have leached into his apartment. I began smoking more frequently—something I rarely did—and drinking even in the day. I bought a message machine for when I left the apartment to teach classes. I rarely went to my office at the university and returned to my own room only to pack my belongings and move them into Avendaño's. I warred with myself: agitated yet distracted, worried yet conflicted, lonely yet connected to this strange, foolish old man.

Again and again, I found myself returning to his writings. I continued the translation Avendaño had begun, since my Latin was fresher than his, despite my having never translated *Metamorphoses* whole. I searched his apartment for his Ovid manuscript but, failing to find it, settled for reading The Eye's poetry and *A Little Night Work*. The latter was gruesome and disturbing in ways I cannot, even to this day, put into words. Of the themes contained (as far as I could tell) in that work, two stood very prominent:

The first was that of sacrifice, of blood, of life, of innocence. Of value. I began to understand why it had been hidden inside a sheaf of pornography. I am no dullard; I recognized this was a profane book, a book that would have been destroyed or locked away by the Catholic Church (or any other) if they had come across it. Those with it in their possession would have found themselves excommunicated, swiftly and without any red tape. *A Little Night Work* hid its true nature in oblique verse, and stilted and antiquated Latin, but it was most definitely a book of witchcraft, or black magic. The stories contained within, and their rudimentary yet evocative illustrations, were more like primers for bargaining with unseen forces rather than spells.

And while sacrifice was the predominant theme, the secondary theme was that the fruit of sacrifice was one of *entry*. "*Ingressus*" was used over and over. As was "liminal." The descriptions of violence, and incest, and self-mutilation became like wounds in my mind, festering. At night, I could not sleep, and in the day, I moved through the streets of Málaga in a dreamlike state, as I had not slept the night before, cotton-headed and dull.

I found myself wondering how Avendaño had come by the photographs of the prints of *A Little Night Work*, since he'd been arrested by the Vidalistas on that night so long ago.

One thing leads to another. By resuming *A Little Night Work*, I was led back to *Below, Behind, Beneath, Between*, Avendaño's strange testament. I needed to understand how the two manuscripts were related to each other, and to the man who had introduced them to me. And he had not called when he said he would. A pressure was building inside me, and I could not express it properly without knowing the full story.

I began to read once more.

AVENDAÑO 2

Take down my name, write it with obsidian ink
Like the black waves upon stone shores of Magera
Where the sea meets the land

And the sky teems with terns and gulls
Gliding upon the currents of air.
No man stands tall in such a prison,
And his weakness is on display
For any creature that passes by.
         —Guillermo Benedición, *Nuestra Guerra Celestial*

There are poets who think they are angels, that their words are sent from some divine power greater than themselves. Other poets feel they're daemons, giving voice to the molten words of the subconscious, spewing the hot stuff of psyche out into the world. As I passed in and out of consciousness, my face swelling, the words of both angels and daemons came to me—Camila Araya, Guillermo Benedición, Yesenia Pinilla, and, above all, our great father Neruda—whispering to me as I lay in the twilight between lucidity and oblivion. *Warm socks, the appearance of the hordes, fixed ideas that make me read with obscene attention a few psychologists, our heavenly war, I do not love you, I love the jealousy I have for you, the breaking clouds, the breaking sky.* A thousand voices caromed in my head. From such a remove, I can see now it was just the tugging of the flesh, trying to find something to grasp on to to protect itself, the quivers of an organism in distress sorting through experience and conditioning. My life up until then was just a fabric of verse and poems.

Now my life was no longer mine.

The soldiers stripped me to my underwear, bound my hands and feet with duct tape, and placed me on hard wooden planks in the back of a truck. I knew there was unrest in Magera, and a great hatred of Pávez by the rich, elite men who had made their fortunes on the backs of the poor. And our distant northern neighbor, that looming storm front—Estado Unidos, the American vastness—hated socialist and Marxist movements. They had killed Guevara.

It might have been Bolivian *carabineros,* but certainly shadow-men stood by them and their rifles were made of metal cast in America. At that time, I was apolitical, concerned solely with the ways of the flesh and the soul. Yet I was not an ostrich; I was aware of some of the hidden currents of unrest in Magera, thanks to Alejandra. And so, as I rattled in the back of the truck for hours, those periods when I was awake, I was filled with great foreboding and disturbing thoughts, not just for myself, not just for Alejandra, but for my country.

The soldiers smoked American cigarettes and spoke in hushed voices over me. The smell of their smoldering tobacco came as a burnt offering, ash and cinder, falling lightly on me as if I were a bound sacrificial lamb. The stink of the cigarettes—Pall Malls, or Winstons, or Marlboros, shipped south out of Texas on some cursed diesel container-barge to brave the gulf and then the Atlantic down the coast to Argentina, off-loaded by sun-drenched stevedores in Buenos Aires beneath wheeling seagulls shrieking at the sky and loathsome shore; crates of cartons loaded unceremoniously on truck beds by calloused hands and then driven west over mountains to finally bring their cancerous stench here, to me, in the hands of soldiers; a gift maybe, from an American governmental operative; a bribe, a lagniappe for doing business with the anti-Marxist blond-haired, blue-eyed giant looming so far north, its breath stinking and foul—the smell settled upon me, lying raw and delirious, as the truck rattled north and west, away from the shore. After some interminable time where I floated, insensate, suspended within the cloud of pain, we came to a stop. I was awake then and aching. Of all the pains my body endured, my head was the worst, but the skin of my legs, arms, and chest was bloody and abraded by the planks. Worse, the outrage to my pride and security. What had become of Alejandra? My nostrils were full of caked blood and the salt-sweat smell of men and stale cigarettes. The soldiers made crude jokes about my belly, poking me with the bores of their rifles. The skin on my face, especially near my eye, felt as sausages cooking over a fire, full of juice and ready to spit. They removed me from the truck without binding my face or covering my eyes, and this terrified me—*they did not care if I knew where I was*. For an instant, I had fresh air filling my nose, the scent of foliage and plant life blooming, sunlight streaming—I caught sight of a building, its roof and courtyard wall, beyond that a tree, even farther than that a sliver of sky and mountain. Magera. Guillermo Benedición called my beloved country a long petal of sea, wine, and snow. I knew the sky. I knew the snow-peaked mountains. If I wasn't in Santaverde, I was very close. Even if I had been blindfolded, I would have known. I could smell the brown shallow water of the Mapacho River, running to the thick Palas, itself running to the sea.

I am a Mageran and I did not require sight to know I was home. And the *carabineros* did not care if I knew. What terrible things had occurred since I had left?

They took me into the building. It was full of the silence that comes from the cessation of loud, painful noise. A hush. Two soldiers hefted me by the armpits, and my bare feet, still bound, dragged behind. It was cold here; thick stone walls provided some insulation, but not enough. They carried me through an eerily quiet room full of people, all nude, who stared at me with hollow eyes. *Carabineros* watched them silently, their weapons unwavering. The abruptness of soldiers' laughter echoed loudly down the stone halls.

The soldiers placed me in what appeared to have been an office, except that where there once was a window, it had been mortared with brick. A metal chair with a plastic seat sat near an administrator's desk. A single caged lightbulb on the ceiling cast distorted squares of yellow light. The space smelled of urine and fear, though had I been asked then to define the latter, I would not have been able to answer. And afterward . . .

Well, we all would be able to.

I cannot say how long they left me there. I sat in the uncomfortable metal-and-plastic chair. I paced. I pressed my swollen eye to the stone walls, cooling it. I needed to void my bowels and bladder, and was desperately eyeing the corner, when keys clanked in the door and a man entered the office, a *carabinero* hefting a rifle. He scanned the room and gestured with the bore of his weapon that I was to sit in the chair. I did. Once I was seated, another man entered the office, head down, peering at a clipboard. He read the cover sheet without looking up. He shuffled to the second page and then glanced over his spectacles at me, like an aged professor—except this man wore a Mageran army uniform, not heavily decorated, but with the rank of lieutenant colonel. A stocky man, with a heavy black mustache and deep-set, sleepless eyes. The nametag on his breast read SEPÚLVEDA.

I thought of lunging at the *carabinero,* gouging his eyes, wresting his gun from him. But I was not young, even then, and near naked. I felt very small.

"Rafael Avendaño?" he said.

"Where is Alejandra?" I managed to say.

Sepúlveda glanced at the soldier. He approached, lifted his rifle, reversed it, and struck me in my already-wounded eye with the weapon's stock. Such a casual movement. The pain blossomed, so outrageous, the sensation of the blow expanded to suffuse my whole body. It was as if my toe and my palm and my calf and forearm; every pore, every tooth, every hair; my bones and sinew; every bit of me felt the outrage done to my eye, simultaneously. Pain was the sum of my body. I could no longer think of my body in parts. All was one. The air vibrated, electric. I felt all my blood being pushed through the maze of my body's corridors and passageways, pulsing. And then I felt nothing. I picked myself up off the floor and retook my seat in the chair. It was no longer uncomfortable. A dislocation came with the blow.

"Rafael Avendaño?" he said.

It was easier to speak than to nod. "Yes."

He made a small mark on his clipboard. "Welcome home," he said.

"What—" I said. Sepúlveda raised his eyebrows quizzically in response. "What is going on?"

"Ah, yes," he said. "I imagine you would have some questions. There has been some unrest throughout Magera. The *resistance* has been very active in recent days." He removed his spectacles and cleaned the lenses with a white handkerchief. "I'm afraid they managed to kill President Pávez."

Despite the pain, my first inclination was to laugh at the absurdity of his statement. Pávez was a socialist! Most regarded him as an ally and Pávez's nephew was an early firebrand in the socialist movement. It was ridiculous.

Yet I kept my expression still and did not laugh or exclaim.

Sepúlveda returned his glasses to his face. "Currently, our generals have reestablished order."

"Who is in charge?" I asked.

"It is a commission of equals, of course. But General Vidal is the eldest," Sepúlveda said.

"A junta, then," I said.

Sepúlveda frowned. "I was hoping that as our guest—*a laureled and renowned poet!*—you would offer more substantive commentary." He sighed. "Let us earn a crust, then." He flipped a page on his clipboard. "Alejandra Llamos has a sister, does she not?"

Alejandra's sister? Why would they want—

"Answer the question, please," Sepúlveda said. The soldier stepped closer to me.

"Yes," I said. "Ofelia." It is so easy to fall when one is hurt, afraid, and naked. These are things I tell myself now, rather than "Where is she now?" as Sepúlveda asked then.

"I have no idea," I said.

"Yet she visited you in Santo Isodoro," he said.

"She visited Alejandra," I said. "And I am sleeping with Alejandra. Where is *she*?" I said before I could stop myself. The soldier raised his rifle to strike me again, but Sepúlveda shook his head imperceptibly, stilling the other man.

"You will be reunited in time," he said. "If you are cooperative."

"I am a son of Magera," I said. "You cannot hold me."

"You'll find we can do whatever we want to sons and daughters of Magera, if they are enemies of the state," he said. "Or their allies." He made a half gesture with his pen and peeked his head out the door. "Marcos, Jorge, be so kind as to give this prisoner some *asado*. But not too spicy, understand? He has information," Sepúlveda said.

"I don't—" I began, but the soldier placed his boot on the chair and pushed it over. I flailed backward and ended up on the ground. My vision went white—another dislocation—and I smelled molasses, orange zest, and freshly slaughtered rabbit. My mind made strange connections. When I regained my vision, two more soldiers accompanied the first and they bound my hands and lifted me up.

"*La parilla*," the first soldier said to the others. *The grill.* They took me down stairs, through corridors. I was near insensible from fatigue, from pain. They brought me into a windowless stone room with a bare metal bed frame. The space stank of feces and urine, stale cigarette burns, human sweat—and something worse. My eye and face felt as though a dull knife had worked its way into my ocular cavity.

They moved me to the bed, cut away my underwear, and strapped me down. They prodded my genitals with their guns; they extinguished their cigarettes on them as well. They attached jumper cables to car batteries and the other clamps to me in places. Sepúlveda asked, "Where is Ofelia Llamos?" and "What do you know about the whereabouts of MIR?" but the questioning seemed perfunctory and the lieutenant colonel did not seem to care what I answered. I told him everything I knew, which was nothing. I told him things I did not know, where I thought the MIR guerillas might be located. Sepúlveda assiduously wrote down everything I said. And then instructed them to hurt me more. To insert things into my anus, my penis. To make me less than meat. But this part is not my testament. Now, as I write this, this isn't what I want to tell. All I can say of my experience on "the grill" was that inside me something stretched and broke and my mind dissociated itself from my body, as if time itself fractured. I was infinitesimal in the face of the pain, and so I became less than human. In this I matched my torturers.

It went on and on. Over hours. Over eons. I became aware of something more. Something there, hanging in the air. A haze, dark and pulsing, like storm clouds over the sea, clouds piling up on the peaks of the Andes. A hallucinatory presence, filtering through the room. And for an instant, I felt like it saw me, recognized me.

But it did nothing to help me.

In the end, they were disappointed. Sepúlveda had them douse me with water—I had soiled myself, more than once—and they carried me back to my earlier cell and dumped me on the floor. It was a long time before I could move. But the body wants to live, even if the mind has given itself over to despair and has vacated its integuments. A crust of bread, an apple core, and a paper milk carton half-full of water sat on a flea-bit woolen blanket. All could have been scavenged from a Santaverde alleyway trash bin. But I ate the bread and drank the water that tasted like sour milk and devoured the apple core to the pips. I wrapped myself in the blanket—a large section of it was sticky, and it stank of dead things I do not like to think about even now—but it provided me with enough warmth that I soon slept.

When I was awoken, Sepúlveda had returned with different soldiers. He asked me two questions. "What are the whereabouts of Ofelia Llamos?" and "What do you know of the location of the resistance guerillas?" with that same disinterested expression on his face. He ignored my protestations of innocence.

"His eye looks very bad, does it not?" Sepúlveda said to his soldiers. They murmured assent. "And the rest of him is not much better." The cigarette burns on my chest, legs, and genitals had suppurated and were now leaking. "Get him some clothes," Sepúlveda said. "If only so I don't have to look on his nakedness." A soldier left and returned with some semi-clean linen pants and a woolen tunic. My body did not move easily—it was a shamble of pains and seized like a car driven hard with no oil—but I managed to dress myself as Sepúlveda and his men watched me, implacable.

"Today, Rafael Avendaño," Sepúlveda said, "you bear witness."

They led me through the building, to a different room than before, but just as desperate and dreary. It began with a young man, a student, who they placed in an oil drum that was set upon a metal grate. Somewhere below chittered the avaricious voices of rats. Dripping water. The man thrashed and fought, but in the end he slipped in the barrel like a snake into a drainage pipe. Black water sloshed over the rim and the man vomited. One of the soldiers tugged on rubber gloves and forced the man's head beneath the evil liquid. From the smell, I realized it was full of human waste. I retched.

And then the questioning began.

They used his name, and had I been of a better mind, or if that part of me that will never die was stronger, I would have remembered him. I would have etched his name into my memory. But I am a coward. I have forgotten it and everything about him except for his pain.

He was just the first. Another man they took to the grill; a woman, they hung like beef in a restaurant walk-in cooler. Another woman they . . .

No, I cannot think of it. I cannot think of them.

I am not strong enough.

They tortured me again, and again, but in the times between, they made me watch.

I do not know what they did to Alejandra, or if I do know, it is not accessible to me now, in the halls of my memory.

I have locked those doors.

When you are sunless and less than human, time changes—it expands, it contracts. It passes and you understand its passage, but with only an animal understanding, the tug of the moon on the sea of body, the fall of temperature indicating night. You exist outside of time, in near-time. A stilled fermata. The moment when the wave crashes, but frozen. The point the sparrow falls, floating. All moments now singular. Collapsed upon each other. And pain is the door to near-time.

I was delirious, aphasic. Soldiers collected me from my cell, led me to horrors, or led me to moments of pain. It became unclear to me which I found worse. They stopped asking me questions, I think. Or maybe I stopped being able to understand them.

And then *he* came.

————

I do not know how long he was speaking before his words filtered into my consciousness. I was on the floor, wrapped in the tattered, stinking blanket, while he sat in a chair, at the desk. The swelling in my eye had become an overwhelming pressure. Something was wrong, and I only needed my hands and fingertips to comprehend that, without a doctor, I might not live to see again.

I might not.

There were papers in front of him, and he held a single sheet in his hand. The caged bulb burned brightly above, but this man held the paper so that its shadow fell across my face. As I looked up at him, the sheet became a luminous thing, glowing, with the faint intimation of the words inked on the other side. Somehow, I knew they were words I had written.

"'. . . from their spear tips to sword hafts, from their ill intentions to their cruel thoughts a rich smell rises. Blood calls to blood, bad calls to bad, and through pain and sacrifice, we draw the gaze of hidden eyes of titanic movements beyond the stars. It is a lure, a sweet aroma, the killing and the letting of blood. The pain becomes an offering and sacrifice becomes a beacon.'"

He paused, moving the paper, allowing the light to fall upon my face. A fractal expansion of pain, intricate and myriad. It felt like a physical blow. I winced and closed my eyes.

"Are you with me now, Señor Avendaño?" the man said. His voice was deep, rich. The voice of a man that might be able to sing, if he wished. Become part of a choir. "Please, join me. I have water here for you, and some wine, if you will take it. Aspirin. Food."

Even if he was lying, I was at least going to see to what extent this man was a liar. And something was wrong with him, sideways.

American.

I do not know if it was because of my deep thrall to the collapsed-time of torture, but he terrified me. I feared Sepúlveda. But in this man, I could feel my end. I could feel *all* ends. I could not tell if it was his accent, or the lack of it. He spoke Spanish in a cultured, easy voice. His resonant tones and perfect pronunciation seemed out of sync with the visual information I could glean from him—each was separate from the other—possibly an effect of the torture, perhaps my ears along with my eye had been injured. I was becoming a haphazard collection of sensorial injuries. His voice seemed to be everywhere, behind me, below. Coming from beyond. I could not apprehend it, and for me—where language was everything—that was frightening.

I did not know if I still existed in collapsed-time, but everything moved slow. Pushing myself up, I felt as if I forded the Mapacho, made sluggish by rushing water tearing at me, wanting to drag me to the sea. To the wide salt desert, sky full of sharks.

There was another chair in the cell now, I assumed set in place by Sepúlveda's men. But Sepúlveda and his cohorts were nowhere to be seen.

"Sit," he said. And gestured to the chair. I sat.

My one eye fixed on him. He appeared to be a handsome man, dressed in a very nice blue suit, immaculate white shirt, and blood-orange tie. A pressed handkerchief peeked from the jacket's pocket, a bit of elegant sartorial geometry. His face was bland, if somewhat angular. He wore spectacles a size too small for his face. His hair was dark, and oiled away from his brow. He was clean-shaven, but the bluish tint to his jaw made me think he might have a heavy beard if he allowed it to grow. When he reached into his jacket pocket to retrieve cigarettes, polished onyx cuff links glinted at his wrists.

"My name is—" he said, lighting a cigarette and then passing it over to me. I took the burning thing in my hand, wondering what it was for a moment. He reached over and drew a tray holding a plate, a carafe of wine, and a small pitcher of water between us. "Wilson Cleave. I am an emissary."

I looked around me. The room was empty except for myself

and this man. I considered standing, going for his throat. Slamming the pitcher against his head, cutting his throat with the shattered glass. Knocking him down and stomping all upon his head and neck until he was dead. I considered if I could even do any of those things.

I thought I might be able to, now.

He leaned back in his chair and watched me as my gaze wandered, my mind conjured phantoms of violence.

"You are understandably disturbed," he said. He poured some water into a glass. "Start with this."

I was loath to accept anything from him, but I did anyway. I drank. I took food into my mouth and discovered I had far fewer teeth to chew it with. One was shattered, and my tongue worried at the fragments protruding from my outraged gum line. I drank wine and tried to ignore the pain. Cleave watched implacably.

When I was finished, he offered me another cigarette and this one I smoked, unspeaking. We sat that way for what seemed a long time, but, as I have said, time expands and contracts in places and circumstances like this.

"You will hate yourself now," Cleave said.

"Who are you and what do you want?" I managed, my throat still raw. Either from screaming or lack of water, I did not know. Large portions of my mind had been scoured clean.

Cleave shrugged. "My role is one of liaison."

"You said 'emissary,'" I said. "For the American government?"

He gave a small inclination of his head, as if we played a guessing game and he wanted to indicate a partial correctness. When I was a child, my cousins and I would hide items from each other, and then run around my parents' house, yelling "*Caliente!*" when a child got near the object and "*Frio!*" if they moved away from it. A toy gun, a spinning top, a bit of candy, a magazine. Finding it, we would squeal with laughter.

Cleave's head tilt was *caliente*.

"The army?" I asked.

He pursed his lips and gave an imperceptible shake of his head.

"Central Intelligence Agency," I said in English, thinking of the American branch of government that James Bond's American counterpart—*Felix something?*—worked for. "CIA," I said.

Cleave smiled. He sat forward, placing the papers he'd been reading aloud when I awoke between us.

"Whatever acronym accompanies my role doesn't matter." He settled himself. A strange movement, like squaring one's shoulders. The light overhead winked out and then came back on. A power surge. The electrical grid in Santaverde at that time was unreliable, though I wasn't sure until later that it *was* Santaverde. A strange expression crossed Cleave's face. "Think of me as an envoy from the exterior brigade, if that helps," he said.

"The exterior brigade? What is that?"

"You should know, Señor Avendaño. You've been desperately signaling us for quite some time."

"I have no idea what you're talking about," I said.

He tapped the paper. "What can you tell me about this? Your *A Little Night Work*?"

Here was a man versed in misdirection. My attention was suddenly on the papers in front of me. Typed sheets. Familiar to my eye, my hand. I picked one up. He lifted his briefcase from where it sat beside him on the floor and placed it on the desk. He popped the latches. The sound pinged and echoed brightly off the stone walls.

He lightly tossed the sheaf of photos on the desk. Ángel Ilabaca's photos from Santo Isodoro, and the house Alejandra and I rented there. He'd taken the effort to remove the salacious photographs, leaving only the prints of *Opusculus Noctis,* but it was no longer clear which were the more troublesome.

"This, Señor Avendaño. Your great work."

"It's nonsense. Old, vile nonsense. Expressions of the id before the world knew what to call it," I said. *Old, vile nonsense.* As I said it, I realized how much of my life, my career—*my poetry*—was old, vile nonsense.

"Is that so?" Cleave said. He stood. "I did not know you had such a keen interest in psychological fads." He pursed his lips once more. He looked down at his manicured hands, which he held out, fanned, nails facing him. He picked at a cuticle. Shifting his attention, he picked a piece of lint from his suit. It was a very nice suit. There was a time I would have asked him about it. "Finish your translation and you'll not have to bear witness to torture anymore. Not in eye, not in body."

He walked to the door, knocked on it. A soldier opened it and Cleave gestured to the man. He brought in a single pencil sitting atop two legal pads. "When the pencil needs sharpening, slip it under the door and it will be replaced. With every photograph translated, you'll be rewarded, as long as you're good. Food. Wine. Vodka, if you wish. Even a girl, if you so desire."

"Alejandra," I said.

"Alejandra?" Cleave said. He laughed. It was absolutely mirthless, the sound. For a moment, Cleave seemed a marionette whose puppeteer was very far away and a poor emulator of human emotion. "I'm afraid we cannot do the impossible. Do you not remember?"

"Remember?" I said.

He *tsk*ed and shook his head. "We have been unkind." He buttoned his jacket and smoothed its front, hand touching each button lightly. A man taking inventory, checking his appearance for performance's sake. He moved his arms in such a manner that his white cuffs shot out. "Alejandra is gone. But surely another woman would suffice. No?" He waited just a moment while I stared at my hands, trying to remember. "Translate, Señor Avendaño. And you will be fed. Maybe we will even find a doctor to tend to your face. You are quite a mess, after all."

"My glasses, I can't—"

He snapped his fingers. He said a few words to the soldier, who disappeared and then returned. He had a tin bucket—a makeshift latrine, it seemed—and a magnifying glass. He placed the glass on the table and the bucket in the corner. "You might break the glass and consider using that to attack a guard. Or me. You are, of course, welcome to try. It would be a fruitless endeavor." He put his hands in his pockets. The gesture was such a casual insolence, it almost passed unnoticed. He could assume a familiarity with this prisoner, because he did not fear me. He did not pity me. We simply occupied the same instant of collapsed-time.

He stood there, framed in the door. Behind him, darkness. I thought I saw figures moving in the gloom. But I was tired and very weak, and lacking use of an eye. The mind conjures phantoms when the senses fail. Yet . . . these strange figures, wet and glistening. Myopia conjured the illusion of distance beyond, a mountain wreathed in smoke, obscured by streamers of effluvium. It moved, massive and intricate and cold.

I rubbed my face as best I could without aggravating my swollen eye and picked up the magnifying glass.

"If you use it on yourself, Señor Avendaño," Cleave said, "try to bleed on the paper. Much more effective that way."

He stepped back, into the darkness, and shut the door. A moment later I heard the bolt being slid home.

———

Collapsed-time expanded. The pulsating haze of pain and terror receded some. My heart was not always blood-spiked and panicked. It seems the human body cannot maintain a level of fear indefinitely.

Becoming familiar with terror, the flesh and mind breeds if not contempt then a weary, wrung-out simulacrum of it.

I spent the rest of that waking time with the photographs, finding where I'd stopped my translation of *A Little Night Work*. *Un pequeño trabajo nocturno*. I could not discern if it was day or night, still. I had no recollection of how long I had been there, in the confines of the building. I could not recall once going to sleep—only ever waking, fevered and disoriented.

The photographs were life, then. A tether to the world I once knew. I smelled the prints, bringing them to my nose to inhale their scent. Alejandra had held these once. Her molecules were here, an infinitesimal piece of her. Her perfumed breath— exhaled water vapor as she laughed—had condensed in the air and settled on the glossy surface, maybe. We'd had sex in the office one afternoon, on the rug in the shadow of the bookcase, and the photos were nearby. The window was open and my breathing and her coos mixed with the cries of seagulls over the surf. The essence of her steamed off, like smoke, to fall as microscopic rain in her vicinity.

I inhaled . . . but could perceive nothing of her. Cleave had asked me, "Do you not remember?" and I hated him for that. More than the burns, the shocks, the torture they put my body through, that question was worse.

It pained me even when Cleave was absent.

———

Sobre el excremento y sus usos. On Excrement and Its Uses . . .

One-eyed, peering through a monocled glass, hunched over photographs.

La madre venenosa se convierte en regente. The Poisonous Mother Assumes Power.

I finished translating a photo, tore the handwritten sheets

from the legal pad, and slipped the paper under the door. Minutes later, the bolt rattled and slid back with a wooden *thwock,* and two soldiers entered and placed on the desk a tray bearing two boiled eggs and a bottle of wine. I drank the wine, stuffed the eggs in my mouth, and stumbled around my cell, screaming at the walls until I could stand no more.

Los grados variantes de sacrificio. The Varying Degrees of Sacrifice . . .

Apprehension of the divine through subtraction. I begged walls for cigarettes, for more wine, but neither Cleave, nor Sepúlveda, nor the soldiers answered. I sat at the desk, poring over a particularly hideous Latin passage. On my bloody knees, I placed my mouth at the gap at the bottom of the door and whispered hoarse pleas for a Latin-to-Spanish dictionary. It did not open.

Racking my withered brain for declensions, definitions of words, I managed to get through the photograph. In this picture, there was a shadow, half falling upon the cramped page of the *Opusculus Noctis,* and I assumed it was that of the photographer. I found myself at odd times wondering what he might have been wearing. What he had in his pockets. Bali cigarettes? A flask full of Glenlivet? A wallet with American dollars? Or Belgian francs? Were there pictures in the wallet? He was a photographer, after all. Was there an aproned, smiling wife, beaming from a stamp-size picture? An apple-cheeked, fat and roly-poly child? Or did he know what it was he photographed?

A hand was more than a finger. An arm, greater than a hand. A testicle was less than the phallus itself but greater than an ear. Both testes would yield much power. Lips, nose—the concentration of senses—those were weighty. An eye was close to titanic. A heart or head or full sex—berry, twig, root, and stem—trumped them all. But that was just if you had no . . . subjects. *Pretium.* The author was very sad at this recipe. How to make bread when you have no flour—cut off a finger. When I was finished, I didn't bother recopying the verses, cleaning up the marked-out failed starts or multiple guesses at words I wasn't certain about. I ripped the pages from the pad and stuffed them under the door and waited.

This time, a carafe of water and a small bottle of vodka. A pack of American Pall Mall cigarettes and five strike-anywhere matches. A tin of sardines. A sleeve of crackers. A withered orange. Paper napkins. A Latin-to-Spanish dictionary. I consumed all of the food quickly, and began a furious session of chain-smoking and sipping the vodka.

La voz de los muertos. The Voice of the Dead . . .

The dead lie inert, like rocks, waiting to be picked up. Whatever passage they might have after life takes a long time and they can answer questions with the right *pretium.* The speaking with the dead, all in all, is a bargain, really. A finger, a toe. A pint of blood. The right phrase said with the correct intention. Though there's a footnote—a sentence boxed in blood—that intention outweighs iteration and recitation.

Before I finished, the door opened, and soldiers entered; Sepúlveda, and another man, one I'd never seen before. He had a black leather bag. The soldiers took my arms, held me to the floor. The placid man, the new man, he withdrew a long needle and filled it from a phial and injected it into my arm. You would think that with all I'd been through, I wouldn't wince. They forced open my mouth, shoved in acrid-tasting pills, and held my mouth shut until I had to swallow. As I struggled against the soldiers, the doctor probed my eye with cold fingers.

"*Puede que nunca vuelva a ver fuera de él, pero no lo perderá,*" he said. *He might not ever be able to see out of it again, but he won't lose it.* "*Sin sangrado en el cerebro.*"

He patted my head as if I were a good dog, or an obedient and genial child. The soldiers allowed me to rise. I had run out of matches, but had cigarettes left. They ignored my begging for fire; Olympians denying humanity before Prometheus stole the flame.

La dulce bruma del dolor. The Sweet Miasma of Pain . . .

We are bits of meat in a watery broth. Sweet-tallow candles waiting to be lit. Pleasure makes us numb, stupid, inert. Pain sparks our wicks. The light and scent of pain—the greater the better—draws the attention of the mighty. The prodigious. The vast and numberless. And that frisson, between the pain, the effluent release of it, and the intention of the deliverers and emissaries, brings forth the miasma.

I shit in the bucket, used the paper napkins to clean myself. The stink of it made me gag, retch. I wondered, amazed, at how unused I was to discomfort, despite my situation. The tooth they had shattered on *la parilla,* it caused my whole body to writhe and shudder with pain. Cleave's doctor missed that, or more likely, didn't care. Like a deranged homeless man, *desposeído,* I shouted at the walls for a dentist, a masseuse, a podiatrist. Laughing, I begged for my ophthalmologist.

They did not come.

Las manos de los fantasmas. The Hands of the Fallen . . .

Under the door and waiting.

They did not come.

El señuelo de la inocencia. The Lure of Innocence . . .

At the door, nothing but silence.

Sobre el poder del incesto. The Power of Incest . . .

I stopped translating. Wadded up the photos and tossed them aside. I bellowed my refusal to translate any more. Curling into a ball, I nested under the desk, aware of my cowardice—I did not tear the photographs into tiny pieces. I sobbed until unconsciousness took me. When I returned, absolute darkness. Careening questions rattled in what was left of my brain. Was I asleep? Had time utterly collapsed? When I could reason once more, I stood, and blackness hung all around. I touched my face, to see if my other eye was swollen shut as well, but found my injured eye had improved, the swelling had subsided and I could make out the ridges and contours of my ocular cavity. I took a step, barking my toe on something.

In the dark, there is no time, just one moment, stalled out, breathless, that goes on forever. I counted the rising and falling of my chest until I reached a thousand. I held my breath, in hopes of hearing a footfall in the outer passage. A scream from some poor soul on the "grill." Something to let me know I was still alive, and on the earth.

Nothing.

I don't know how long I was like that. Five minutes. A month? All was dislocated. I tested the limits of the room blindly. I felt corners, the door. I gathered crumpled photos from the floor. I returned to the desk.

Sitting down, my hands found the legal pad, the pencil, and a photograph. I said into the empty darkness, "I will return to work now."

The light flicked back on.

Un pasaje a los sueños. A Passage to Dreams . . .

Other places than these, shining with light from other suns. Flesh-filled worlds are a palace, a villa with many chambers, and with the right *pretium,* the most valuable *pretium,* one can extend oneself into the far halls and galleries by giving part of oneself up. An act of self-negation, closing oneself away from the living world purposely. Sacrifice of the seat of a sense.

I tested the only exit, listening. I tried to peer underneath into the hall beyond. I could hear no patrol. It was as if I was alone in the building.

"Cleave," I said. "We need to talk."

"Not now, poet," a voice immediately whispered on the far side of the door. So very close. "You have work to do."

El emisario requiere un recipiente. The Emissary Requires a Vessel . . .

One shall prepare the way, chosen and marked, to cut through night. He will draw minions to him. The first bargain. The sunderer of veils.

El mar se convierte en el cielo. The Sea Becomes the Sky . . .

A tide, sweeping in, scouring the shore. A freedom for the mountains beneath the waves, inverting the sky, the darkness between stars. All will be loosed. Tearing the last sheets from the pads, I went to the door and slipped them underneath.

Immediately I heard the bolt slide back. The door opened up, and Cleave stood before me, fresh as ever.

"Come with me."

———

I followed him through the building. I saw no soldiers, but there was such a presence about the man—a powerful remoteness—that I never considered attacking him. Instead of tunneling downward, he led me up myriad stairs, rising higher and higher, until I found myself coming into a half-lit, blue-gray world. A high stone patio, far above a city. Santaverde. The mountains stood at our back. Tattered wisps of clouds tore across the sky, driven by relentless wind from the sea. It was cold. Even though the outer world was dim, I blinked my good eye furiously in the blooming of light.

"Poet," Cleave said. "You have done good work, though some of your early translations were inelegant. Nevertheless, my counterparts are pleased."

"Your . . . The American president?" I said. "Nixon?"

"Noooo," he said, drawing it out. Then laughed. "Even my employers have masters. And they, I assure you, are well satisfied," he said. "For now."

Something about that chilled and relieved me, all at once.

"I have a place for a man of your . . ." I thought he was going to say "weaknesses." He did not. He said, "talents."

"What about Alejandra? Can she—" I began.

"Rafael," Cleave said. He withdrew a cigarette and a lighter, cupped his hand around the end, and lit it. He took a long drag and then offered it to me. "May I call you Rafael?"

"I don't care, I just want—"

"Alejandra is dead, I'm afraid," he said. "I'm sorry it happened how it happened and I hope you're not too traumatized by the—"

"Traumatized? By what?" I said. "What could've traumatized me?"

"You do not remember, and that is understandable. Our work has certain—" He withdrew another cigarette and held it in his hand, unlit. He gestured with the tan-speckled filter. "Amnestic effects." He indicated Santaverde, which was spread out below us like a map on a table. The sky was dark and I could not tell if it was night or day. The lights of the city glowed in a feeble electric grid with large areas of blue-black darkness. Fires burned, and pillars of dark smoke rose crookedly up to higher altitudes where wind streams caught them and sheared away the tops of the plumes. From the city a haze rose, undulant.

"What happened to Alejandra?" I asked. "What did you do?"

No answer.

"What did *I* do?"

Cleave walked to the edge of the patio, rested his hands on the waist-high stone wall there. He looked out over Santaverde. "You see it, don't you? The haze. The scent."

"The *miasma*," I said without thinking.

"Yes," Cleave said. "Yes! It is pleasing, is it not? Think of the amount of suffering. We are almost there." Cleave snapped his fingers and something changed, the world tilted. It was bright now, and a watery sun shone above. I could hear cars honking and the crackle of what sounded like gunfire below. Smells of sewage and burning tires filled the air. We had come out of collapsed-time. The sway of the *miasma* was broken. For the moment.

Cleave turned. "Sepúlveda."

The lieutenant colonel stood near the passage we had come from, waiting. Two soldiers flanked him. "Señor Cleave," he said. "The helicopter is ready."

"Perfect," Cleave said. "And the sarin canister?"

"On board," he said. "The facility is ready in the north."

"Wonderful." He turned back to me. "What do you say, Rafael? Are you with me?"

"I don't—" I said. "I don't know what—"

Cleave allowed himself to grin. "This is where I promise you things—things you want—and then you yield to temptation."

"Alejandra," I said.

Cleave sighed. "Anything except that. There is no bringing her back. Especially not for you, after what you did. Anyone else, we could—" He paused, thinking. "Work something out. Your mother. A sister? No?" He shrugged. "I'm very sorry, but we're bound by certain rules and the hand that kills cannot be the hand that resurrects." He gestured to the guards. "Think about it, Rafael. We have time, do we not?" He drew a huge draft of air into his nostrils. "Within the *miasma*, there's all the time in the world." He lit his cigarette. "Take him back to his cell. Give him food, drink. Let him think about it. Right, Rafael? You'll think about it?"

The soldiers looked at me dubiously. Maybe it was my lost, dumbstruck expression. Maybe it was that I didn't move until they raised their rifles and nudged me back into the villa.

The hand that kills cannot be the hand that resurrects.

What have I done?

What did they do to me?

In the cell, once the guards were gone, I found they had not removed the photographs of the manuscript. An oversight, possibly. Another avenue to torture. They were valuable to Cleave, obviously. And they were what kept me alive and useful.

I felt sick at the uncertainty of my role here, but ate the food and smoked cigarettes anyway. I pretended to sleep, but then slept. With no clock, no way to tell the passage of time, no indication that Cleave or the soldiers watched me in my cell—I was out of the *miasma*, the collapsed-time of torture, I had to assume Cleave's frightening immediacy and surveillance had ended—I took up the photograph I had been thinking of since looking out at Santaverde, the thick haze rising up under the dark skies.

Un pasaje a los sueños. A Passage to Dreams.

From sojourner to journeyer, the pretium *is dear; for the one rich in flesh, a measure of beloved filial blood, a hymen, a punctured ear. For the one poor in flesh, the egg, the eye, the stone, and nothing less.* In girum imus nocte et consumimur igni. *We turn in circles in the night and we are devoured by fire.*

So much more, long passages, swimming in my failing sight. Markings, Aramaic, Greek, Gnostic symbols. Rough drawings painted in blood: the hanged child, a man mounting a girl, a needle in an ear, a dagger in the eye. Blood-streaked phalluses slipping through viscera. Tongues split to the root. Images writhed and danced in the photograph.

I stood, taking the magnifying glass in hand. I cast it down, on the floor. The brass ring around the looking glass pinged and broke, a spring suddenly releasing its tension. The glass skittered across the floor like a skipped stone and hit the wall. *Scarred but unbroken.* In my mind, with the impact, it would fracture into shards, but it remained whole. I snatched up the glass and placing it on the floor, raised the desk's corner-leg up, nudged the glass forward with my toe, and let the desk's metal foot fall, slamming down on the glass. I thought it would fracture into knifelike shards. It did not. The blow reduced it to glass powder.

Sobbing, I beat the table until my hands were raw. I screamed and clawed at the door until my fingers were bloody tatters. I drank the vodka and swung at phantoms, bellowing for Cleave, for Sepúlveda. I cursed god, I cursed myself. I screamed for Alejandra. I screamed for any memory of what they made me do to her.

Delirious, my gaze fell upon the brass ring that once held the looking glass. Picking it up, I tested the edge with my thumb.

The hardest part was prying down the swollen lower eyelid so that the lip of brass could slip under the eye, into the ocular cavity. It met some resistance, gristly, tenacious sinews and fibers. Occipital ridge, blood welling, unraveling of the woven tissues, the tearing of the fabric of blood vessels and capillaries. I mouthed the words, over and over, backward and forward. The shock of pain spread. Yawing, I pitched forward, the floor flashing in my one good eye. I righted myself, unsteadily, working the piece of brass into my socket. A soft sucking pop, as the eye came free, dangling upon its bloody stem. My brain sparked and flashed with occipital nerve death. *Will I see things still, through those dead ends?* The light overhead flickered and went out. I put the bloody eye on the desk, to stare balefully at any who entered. The pain was gone. I looked down at the stark contrast of blood on my chalky white skin. Shock. *I am become a phantom.* The walls stood indistinct. The cell, though dark, was not pitch-black—a pulsing scintillate haze floated through it, like a ghost's trail. And . . . the door stood open.

I took up the photographs in white, unsteady hands, and

clutched them to my chest. I walked through the doorway, out into the far landscape beyond, mountains shifting in the distance.

I wandered through lands I could not tell you of now; lands made strange by impossible geometries and vile arcologies my mind could not comprehend. I knew not how long I was there, how long I roamed that land, but when I was conscious again, I felt rough hands on me and I was being pulled from the cold, black shore of the Mapacho.

———

Men lifted me from the ground, dried my skin with rough woolen blankets. Pried loose my frozen hands from the sheaf of photographs. For days, my tongue failed me, aphasic once more, so close to the *miasma*. They took me to their fishing village, near the sea. A veterinarian tended to the ruins of my eye, silently. He'd seen men and women like me before—state-gnawed bones coughed up by the junta's dogs and Vidal's men, once their usefulness was over, cast into the Mapacho or the Palas. *You are lucky to be alive*, the men said. Laborers, stevedores, fishermen. Those workers who dallied with socialism, but never took up a book or attended any meeting. The hard memory of Pávez's end was fresh among them.

They took me into their houses, among their wives and children. *This is Avendaño? The Avendaño?*

I do not know. I saw him once on the television, and he was fatter then.

He can't be Avendaño. Look at his face.

Mary, Mother of Jesus, they hate poetry. Pinochet kills Neruda and Vidal mutilates Avendaño. Will all beauty in the world be extinguished?

Surely not Avendaño. He can't be Avendaño. Look at him. A shadow of a man.

This is not Avendaño.

And I wasn't. Avendaño was gone. That wastrel man, so full of pride, died in his cell.

When I could talk, I sent the men to my old flat near the university, to retrieve my checks, and what money I had there. They came back with the checks, but no cash. A locker full of clothes. Vidal and his generals did not have the foresight to confiscate the belongings of enemies of the state. At least not then. I told the men there was nothing in my possession they could not have. I left them a small fortune. They laughed and fed me lamb stew and salmon and poured wine into chipped glasses in their small houses. The sea called outside. A reminder. The junta and Vidal seemed very far away.

They placed me, clad in rough-spun laborer's garb, on a container ship, holds full of copper wire, bound for Cape Town, then Nouakchott, and then Lisbon. I spent those yawing days at sea wondering if I still inhabited the *miasma,* or if I'd ever left.

I found, eventually, warmer shores.

Now I am well, and my family money—I never had much want—has been transferred to me here. My publishers know I'm alive, but not many others. I have kept few contacts in Magera. To what end? Vidal's arm is long. I dare not return home, I dare not publish again. I don't think I can write poetry anymore.

A poet sees what the world offers and gives voice to its wonderful strangeness. We look at the world, and all those who move within it, with frank stares and brutal words. It was not just an eye I gave up, in that cell on the mountainside. It was so much more than that.

This manuscript will remain secret, until the time comes for all to be known.

I am content. As content as I can be.

Some knowledge forbids happiness. Some knowledge makes action impossible. I spend my days trying to find what pleasure I can. They're filled with garlic prawns and polenta and lovely rich wines, and my nights are replete with aromatic smoke and pisco and sweets, soft music, and the smell of the Alboran Sea.

And forgotten dreams of the things I have done. And what was done to me.

Forgive me for forgetting your name.

Forgive me for forgetting.

Forgive me, Alejandra.

5

The Eye was, most assuredly, insane. Possibly the stress of being an exile had driven him to this particular psychosis. As Magerans, we are all prone to paranoia, by either experience or necessity. And this manuscript—apparently the only writing Avendaño had done since the coup—stood as testament to that. The man's demented imagination was prodigious and disgusting by turns. Whatever injury that had occurred to his eye during Vidal's coup (and I do believe that part, at least, the injury), it could have resulted in an infection that spread to his brain, leading to a fevered perception of reality. The rampant horde of imagery: body parts, blood, outrage, loss, guilt, mutilation, fecal matter, chiaroscuro, food. The terrifying realization of madness crept in as I read—breathless and stunned, galloping down dark paths, a pornography of excruciating psychic pain—if not by him, then by me, as his audience.

The stress of being a fugitive alone would have broken most men and some women. His time in the hands of Vidal's secret police had shattered him—left him with a burden of guilt it was not wholly clear he deserved. It became muddy the further along the testament went. But despite all that, it did give me an idea of what might have happened to my mother. And for that, I was grateful, however much it hurt.

One thing was clear, he could not be abandoned and forgotten. If I abandoned him, left him to whatever end he found in his enfeebled and deranged mental state, I would be forsaking any right I had to return home. Avendaño was like an infection—I had spent many years not thinking about my homeland, and now it was forefront in my mind. Mother came to me unbidden, and my father, before the drink took him, had become mingled in my mind with The Eye. Avendaño would vanish back into that forgotten landscape. One of the *disappeared*. I could not allow it, for my own sanity's sake.

I had to find Avendaño and help him.

———

Claudia did not call.

The semester had wound down to its inevitable end—papers, grading, wheedling students, the desolation of faculty offices, vacant cafeterias, and eventually a two-week stint of barren campus before it was all to start up again. And I came to a conclusion regarding The Eye. He had never contacted me, nor had he contacted the bank. Something would have to be done.

"I have to take a leave of absence," I said to Matilda Orés, my faculty head. "Just for the summer."

"You won't come back," she said, shaking her head.

"What do you mean?"

"Word is you've got some patron keeping you in style now. An old lech," she said.

Whatever contortions my expression went through, she realized I was not taking that well.

"I'm going back to Magera. A family emergency," I said.

"Magera?" she said. "*Santa Maria,* you're really asking for it."

"I just want to know if I'll have my position when I return," I said.

Matilda shrugged. "Filling your classes this summer—even though it's a light load—will be difficult. What's the emergency?"

"My uncle is dying," I said. "Cancer. I'm the only living family member." I can lie with facility if I have enough preparation.

"I'm sorry to hear that," she said. She didn't sound it.

"We're all sorry," I said.

She produced an official Universidad de Málaga faculty absentee form, sat me down, and had me fill it out. When I was finished, she picked it up, looked at it, and slipped it in an envelope, addressed it to the board.

"Your advisees need to be shifted to someone else, and any clubs or groups you supervise will need to be adjusted. Are you on any committees of master's or doctoral candidates?"

"No," I said.

"Let me be honest. You don't have any close friends here who could take up your slack. If you were beloved by the faculty, they'd jump in, but—"

"I'm not," I said. I looked down at myself. "I eat alone. I wear black."

"That is apropos of nothing. Yet it *is* true," Matilda said, nodding. "I can't tell you much other than your job probably won't be here when you get back. If we have to replace you for a summer, we might as well just replace *you,*" she said, shrugging. "Not a lot I can do about it. But you're young," she said, as if that meant loss, or change, did not affect me as much. And maybe she was right. "And it's possible we won't find a replacement. So check in. If things go sour sooner than you expect—" She realized what she was saying, shook her head, and then nervously began packing up her papers and stuffing them into a briefcase. "Call or send a letter.

You've got my number." She stopped and looked at me. "You're a good teacher and I don't want to lose you, but more and more, this university is run like a business and I have people I have to answer to. So . . . I'll do what I can."

Afterward, I went to the bank. "I need to withdraw all of my money." A hundred thousand pesetas that Avendaño paid me, and more. I never managed to burn through my own pay plus the monthly stipend. It was the first time in my life I was flush.

The bank manager counted out more money than I had ever seen or held before, and I signed for it. I found myself clutching my bag to my chest on the way home.

Back at the apartment, I checked the message machine. There were two calls, both around a minute of crackling silence. No Avendaño. No Claudia. I erased them. After calling information, I contacted a local travel agent about a flight to Buenos Aires and she said she could have an itinerary by the end of the week.

That night, I turned my attention to the photographs of *Opusculus Noctis,* since they figured so prominently in Avendaño's testament. I compared my translations with his writing in the testament and continued on, focusing on the photo I had come to think of as *A Passage to Dreams*. His "doorway" out of his cell. Maybe the photograph held some inkling as to the source of The Eye's madness. Knowing it, I could know his mind. Still Claudia did not call. I worked through the Latin, *Quam alibi, ex solis luce refulgens. Caro referta regia mundi et villae multa cubicula iure pretium, pretium clarissimae licet adhuc in atriis gallerys paris . . .* there are other worlds than these, and with the right payment, one can move through the universe's rooms and halls. The *pretium* is dear.

After setting out tuna for Tomás, as I began to think of him, I poured vodka over ice for myself, sat at the kitchen table, and began smoking, poring over the photographs, surrounded by typewriters.

The night wore on. I boiled eggs, ate them. I made coffee, found it bland, poured myself more vodka. I picked up the phone, recalling Claudia's number, hand poised over the rotary dial. I hung up without calling her. Reread sections of *Below, Behind, Beneath, Between,* the ones focusing on Avendaño's translation. I found myself in that same strange state in which long periods of study for my doctorate left me—dissociative, sleepless, and wrung out. The rucks and runnels of my mind blank except for that which I focused on. Pinching filters from the cigarettes, I twisted their ends until they were puckered little white sausages, stronger now than normal. Their smoke burned when I took it into my lungs. I searched The Eye's room, looking for I don't know what. Returning to the kitchen, I found *A Little Night Work* before me, both The Eye's typed Latin and the rumpled photographs. The vodka tasted like water, the cigarettes, even filterless, as plain as air. *I should be thinking about packing,* I thought. *I guess I am. What will I need? Warm clothes, boots, gloves, lots of money. Nothing else.* I felt some sort of kinship with Avendaño, laboring for Sepúlveda and Cleave, if that really happened—I entered a soporific waking-dream state, head full of grammar and declensions. But also, displaced, lost. I was leaving home, to go home.

I rolled the Latin over my tongue like a bitter lozenge, sounding the words out. Scribbling over a piece of paper, I took down my interpretation of the words, in Spanish. You can only enter the river once, they say, and I was in it. I placed a Louis Armstrong and Ella Fitzgerald disc on the turntable and in some Latinate oblivion, began singing foreign words to "They Can't Take That Away from Me" that must've sounded deranged to the cat if he lurked about, or someone strolling on the street below, passing my open windows.

I did not notice when the black-clad figure appeared in the

room. Holding a photograph of *A Passage to Dreams,* hunched over, looking at it so closely that my hair fell down on either side of my face, to me the figure was simply a darker lock, a tress hanging indistinct in the corner of my vision. It was this photograph, these words, he read before taking out his own eye. There is a shadow of the photographer, the foot of a chair captured at the image's corner.

I was smoking too much, my throat ached, and I was at a state of drunkenness where I felt elated, sober. The room was hazy with blue smoke. The French doors leading to the balcony were cracked, the air was warm, and I could hear conversation from passersby coming from outside, the buzzy honking of mopeds and cars, the cry of cart vendors down off the Paseo Maritimo below, near the shore, mingling with the strains of Louis Armstrong's pealing horn.

The record ended, the needle taking its final plunge to the record's center. The tone arm, through some sensory mechanism, detected this and rose from the vinyl, and seated itself back in its cradle.

Silence.

The music, the world outside, the sea, the cars, the passersby. All quiet, as if they never existed.

My eyes shifted in their sockets; I was arrested with fright yet straining to see. The lights in the apartment flickered and, somehow, I realized all of Málaga's lights were flickering. Or maybe it wasn't Málaga's indecisive and irregular power supply—possibly it was something else pushing in. I could not tell.

Awareness filtered in. My breath caught, and I turned my head slowly away from the photograph. A cigarette sat with an inch-long ash in the tray, spooling out thin blue-white smoke to the ceiling. Behind that smoke, indistinct and defocused, a man. He seemed as though I observed him through a camera with a long lens, and he was outside my depth of field. At any moment he could snap into focus. Despite the vodka, my heart began to skitter in my chest. My hand found a pencil; I gripped it like a dagger.

I tilted my head to get a better look, pushing myself away from the table. His appearance warped and wavered, like a shadow puppet from a candle. Somehow, he remained behind smoke. The room darkened and filled with his presence, hazy, muddied. A flash of water, over my head, full of sediment and silt, hair floating in a benthic halo. Then it was gone. Yet the occlusion remained. I wondered if something was on fire, if I left the burner on when I boiled eggs.

But I wasn't choking. I could breathe—no smoke, no opalesced water. The shape—*the man*—seemed to loom larger in the room, a shadow lengthening up a wall.

Coming closer.

Then there was another movement, smaller. More centered. Tomás stood inside the open balcony doors, head canted down, so his eyes seemed ominous and veiled at the same time. He took five slow, measured paces into the room, staring unblinking at the shape. The cat made no sound, gave no hiss, but the scarred fur on his back rose in hackles. He placed himself between the dark figure and me.

The cat's action snapped me out of whatever it was that held me silent. "Who—" I started. "What do you want?"

I do not know what I expected. For him—*it*—to answer *I'm from the CIA*. Or *I'm an ANI assassin*. To reveal himself in a puff of diabolical smoke as Vidal himself?

To show himself as Cleave?

Tomás took another step, his paw hesitating, as if testing invisible currents in the air. He placed his paw and settled, sphinxlike, on the floor. *Oh, he's resting now? Is this real?* I thought. And then I realized that, no, Tomás was readying himself for a pounce. I turned to face the figure, brandishing the pencil. If the cat could attack, then so could I.

And then the darkness lost cohesion, dissipating. I laughed. Took another drink of vodka. What tricks loneliness and alcohol can play on a person!

Yet Tomás remained there, silent, still, and watchful, for the rest of the night.

6

I bought a military backpack from one of the sports stores that offered hunting and fishing supplies for the adventurous sort and returned to the apartment. I found Claudia pounding on the door, yelling, "Open up! I know you're in there, Isabel! You can't hide from me!"

I said her name and she froze, midstrike upon the door. Her head pivoted toward me on gimbals.

"You," she said. "You—" Words failed her.

I passed her, unlocked the door, opened it. I gestured for her to enter. She looked at me warily.

I am, after all, very much like my mother. When things escalate, I grow cold, distant. I'm sure my face reflected this. Claudia became more and more agitated.

After placing the backpack in the bedroom, I set the kettle to boil as Claudia stared at me and huffed and puffed until she grew calm enough to speak.

"What?" she said. "You were just going to leave? No call? No word?"

I placed tea bags in a cup, poured steaming water over them, and raised the cup in offering to Claudia. She shook her head, vehemently. A little too vehemently.

"I didn't think you'd care, honestly," I said.

"Care?" she said. "I don't just fuck anyone. Of course I'd care."

I shrugged. "Maybe you'd be too occupied to notice."

"Is this about Laura?" Claudia asked. "Laura is great. You'd like her. We asked you to join us."

I opened my mouth, closed it. *It would be so easy just to enter into a spat. A little lover's argument about who said and did what.*

I won't do that. Can't do that.

"There's more to it than Laura. It's Avendaño," I said.

"You told Tilly that your uncle was dying of cancer. She's asking everyone in your department to take over your classes."

I ignored that. "He's gone missing. And I think I might know where he is. But I can't help him if I don't go back home," I said.

"Who cares? He's a relic!"

I wanted to say, *I care! He's Mageran! And the closest thing to family I have,* but it would have been hard to explain, even to myself.

Instead, I said, "It'll only be for the summer, and I'll be back."

"No, you won't. You're going to Magera! I've done some reading up on it. The lunatic who's in charge there tortures and kills students. He 'disappears' intellectuals, or anyone his secret police think could be subversive." She was furious. "And you've got subversive written all over you. I can't imagine that Señor Vidal will spare lesbian professors from his scourging of the country."

"I will not wear a sign regarding those I like to kiss," I said.

Claudia laughed. "You never have," and then she was kissing me and I could not think for a long while. From the kitchen to the bedroom, her hands were on me and mine on her. Oblivion through taste, touch, smell.

When we could breathe again, she said, "I'm glad you recon-sidered."

"Me too," I said. I pressed into her body, glad of the close-ness and warmth. Tomás entered the bedroom, paced around the bed, hopped on the chair nearby, and watched us for a long while.

"Here's a little perv," Claudia said. "Lookin' for a show, buddy?"

I thought about the figure I had conjured, vodka-drunk and translation-fevered, and how Tomás had intervened. How did he know I needed something or someone to play into my imaginary intruder? The alternative was untenable. Could I tell Claudia any of that? She wouldn't understand and I couldn't express it in such a way that she wouldn't want me to be checked out by a psychiatrist.

So I kissed her.

Tomás, bored, blinked slowly once, hopped down from the chair, and padded out of the room.

———

We spent the next five days basking in each other's company. Whatever distance had grown between us was gone during that time. Food, sex, liquor; laughter, lightness, music. We watched television late at night, and I took her to see a Mexican luchador film at the Cinema la Playa, where the masked Toro fought a num-ber of voodoo-possessed zombies who seemed intent on molest-ing Toro's busty aunt, Maria. Claudia laughed throughout the screening, and I couldn't help but compare her sense of humor to Avendaño's. They would like each other, I thought. Or hate each other. But they'd definitely be quite a bit more than I could handle as a pair.

One afternoon, the post arrived and we were just recovering

from a postlunch siesta in which very little sleeping occurred. I roused myself to collect the letters and sat in the kitchen with a cigarette flipping through envelopes. One had no return address.

I opened it and withdrew a torn piece of yellow legal paper.

-19.569912, -70.197901

Rafael

"What's that?" Claudia asked. She stood at the bedroom door, in a T-shirt and nothing else.

I slipped the paper back into the envelope. "Nothing. Just junk for Avendaño," I said.

She kissed the back of my neck. "I might be hungry again," she said.

"You're always hungry."

"This is true," Claudia said, and nothing else. I liked that about her. She didn't feel the need to add *Hungry for you* or quote Police or Rolling Stones lyrics. I put down the mail and returned her attentions.

On the sixth day of our time together, I woke before Claudia, as usual, dressed in jeans, boots, and a black T-shirt, and pulled my hair back in a severe knot. Taking a piece of paper, I wrote:

Claudia—

I have left word with the landlord that you will be staying here for the duration, if you so wish. The Bank of Barcelona will have a 10,000-peseta-a-month stipend for the person who watches over Avendaño's apartment and I'd rather it be you than anyone else. The rent, of course, is already paid. It is a wonderful apartment and I'm grateful for the time we spent together here. I think there will even be enough room for Laura, if you wish. She is very lovely, and I think you'll be happy together.

Do not fret yourself about my departure; I doubt very much you will, anyway. It doesn't seem within your character. Just as my character will not allow me to let Avendaño join the ranks of the disappeared without at least trying to find him.

I will return.

Feed the cat, for your protection.

Isabel

Leaving the note and keys on the kitchen table, I grabbed my backpack stuffed with clothes, manuscripts, photographs, and let myself out into the steaming Málaga morning. In my back pocket, a plane ticket, and in my wallet, two torn pieces of legal paper bearing the names *Alejandra* and *Rafael*.

Within the hour, I was at the Costa del Sol Airport.

By early morning, I was in Madrid, and before noon I was a thousand miles away, over the Atlantic, flying west to Buenos Aires.

7

Green patchwork on copper-brown fields. Brilliant standing water flashing from the sun after the long refraction of blue sea. We had crossed the Atlantic, along with the equator, and more than anything, something about the quality of light indicated to me I was closer to my childhood home. Magnetic fields from the innards of the earth tugging upon my belly; the subtle twinges of the Coriolis effect on the inner ear maybe; the secret calendar that my body kept, all these long years since I had been in Spain, indicated something was *wrong*, that the seasons were off, the sun was in the wrong place, and it was hot when it should be cold. Just as Málaga was heading into the swelter and sway of summer, in Buenos Aires autumnal light filtered into the cabin—ochre, russet, copper, ecru, carmine, blood-red. The stewardesses of the Iberia Airlines flight from Barcelona to Buenos Aires directed us to buckle our seat belts, finish our drinks, and extinguish our cigarettes, and after twenty-four hours, we obeyed all instructions with alacrity. From the window, I watched miniature trucks cast rich dust in long tails on dirt roads veining the fields surrounding the airport, growing larger, growing. Black wheels lowered, pneumatics cranked ailerons into awkward angles, and the dusky land rose to meet the plane with a screeching kiss and shudder.

I had checked no baggage. At a counter, I exchanged half of my money to Argentinian pesos, and the rest to Mageran ones. Moving through the airport, I pressed through the crowds, listening to the rounded syllables and long vowels—the liquid, mellifluous accents of Argentinian Spanish speakers. I had been gone so long, even the same language sounded different. Weary from the flight yet exhilarated—it was just midday—I made my way out onto the street. Hustlers and grifters stalked the shoals of travelers, looking for a score—a shifting school of hawkers, escorts, chaperones, panders, facilitators. Catcalls and propositions, blaring beats from cassette players, cries of salesmen. A deluge of penetrating noise. Beyond the line of men, taxis cruised the surf like sharks. I hailed the most official-looking one, a black-and-yellow radio taxi, but the car just continued trawling for fares, ignoring me.

"Allow me. You might be a little too short to be seen over this crowd," a man said. I found him standing closer than I was comfortable with. I stepped away to get a good look at him and to prevent him from touching me. He wore a black suit that, despite its natty cheapness, fit his lean frame very well. His accent was harsh, his vowels long when they should be short, and short when they should be long; the sum of all the little parts of him—his hair, his nails, his complexion, and his tie, his shoes—told me he was American.

Having read Avendaño's testament, the fact he was American made me very nervous.

"Hey," he said, seeing my expression and body language. He held up his hands, not to hail but to prove his innocence in some way. "I'm just trying to help."

"I'll hail my own taxi," I said.

"I'm happy to—"

I turned abruptly and walked away from him at a brisk pace, not looking back, breath coming fast. At any moment I was sure his hand would fall on my backpack and jerk me off my feet.

It did not.

When I was near the northern end of the platform, I was able to get the attention of a radio taxi and instructed the driver to get us away from the airport and take me to a hotel near any commerce center. He dropped me at a newer hotel, close to the city center, towering twenty-five stories tall. I took a room, paying cash. It was expensive, but I couldn't bring myself to hunt for something cheaper. I drank water from the sink, uncaring if it was safe, and fell into bed. I do not remember closing my eyes.

I woke in the dark, not knowing where I was.

"Tomás?" I said, sitting up.

The cat was not there. He was an ocean—a world—away.

A shadow was, though. It loomed in the far corner of the room, near the dull shark's eye of the television.

"All right then, fucker," I said. Tensing, I reached out and turned on the side-table light . . .

Nothing. White stucco walls, puce-stained furniture a mockery of mahogany, green-and-yellow-patterned drapes. A hideous sfumato landscape above the bed.

I had no watch and the clock near the television was unplugged, stalled on 3:12. The sky, from the window, looked blueblack; morning was hours away. I smoked and flipped through the Buenos Aires telephone book until I found the page I was looking for. Moto Mejor Real, motorcycle and moped sales. I tore the onionskin page from the book, neatly folding it and storing it in my bag.

Afterward, I sat cross-legged on the bed and arrayed the photos and translations of *A Little Night Work* all around me, hoping the sight of them might keep my mind occupied, or, failing that, send me back into a slumber. I wanted some vodka but knew that would be hard to come by at this time of the morning. Other travelers, more prepared travelers, would have had a flask or have taken some of the tiny airplane bottles in preparation for this. I had not. I contented myself with tobacco.

The phone rang, extremely loud in the quiet of the room. I jerked, turning to look at the phone as if it were a rattling snake.

I stretched out my hand, twitching when the phone rang again.

I picked up the receiver and placed it to my ear.

"Hello?" I said.

Silence except for crackling. It sounded like the hiss and noise of an album once it has wound down, needle plowing through the uncharted inner center of vinyl.

"Hello?" I said again. "Avendaño? Is that you?"

Nothing.

Feeling foolish and ignoring all the hairs standing up on my arm, I hung up the phone. A wrong number. It was a new hotel, and the switchboards were automated, I thought. A misfire of electrical impulses, triggering the ringer, dead air on the receiver. Simple.

I spent the rest of the morning at the window, watching for the first light of dawn.

It was a 1981 Yamaha 465 Y2, orange with a blue seat. Racks and webbing for baggage, extra fuel canisters. New, knobby tires and no headlight. An American had ridden it from Southern California to Santo Isodoro in a sort of motorized South American ramble. The salesman—a tall, stubbled man with deep-set eyes and what I had come to think of as a Flock of Seagulls hairdo—wore a nametag that read DUQUE and was ebullient about the machine.

"You know how to ride?" he asked, shifting his weight back and forth. Maybe he had bad feet. Maybe he had too much energy. "Pretty big bike for someone your size."

"I used to ride when I was in—" I started. Stopped. Considered. "A long time ago. I'll need to get back into the hang of it."

"Maybe you'd like to try out this Honda? Or the Suzuki over there? They're smaller and you should have no trouble handling them."

"No," I said. This was the same motorcycle that Marcia had taught me to ride right here in Buenos Aires, when I was getting my doctorate. I could, I thought, abandon all of this. Go to the shore, toss the photographs of *Opusculus Noctis* into the sea, and go find Marcia on this motorcycle, and we could ride north, or south. I had money. Anywhere but west. Anywhere but Magera.

"This is the one," I said.

After a short test ride, we struck a bargain. It took almost half of my money (which was a considerable amount, indeed), but in the end he included a black futuristic, aerodynamic helmet that would totally obscure my face, two extra canisters of gasoline for cross-country travel, some heavy-duty riding gloves, and knee-high black motorcycle boots that had once belonged to a fourteen-year-old competitive rider until he hit puberty and outgrew them. It was cool here in Buenos Aires, and once I was on the road with the wind hitting me, it would be even colder. I pulled on the gloves, zipped up my leather jacket to my throat, and mounted the machine. With the blackout helmet on, and the motorcycle beneath me, I felt the urgency of what I was doing. You can walk through life not thinking about your decisions, moving forward down a path and never considering the different forks and choosing that got you to where you are at any point.

But I was about to very deliberately choose a path.

One that led to a place I both longed and was loath to go.

But I was here for Avendaño.

I kicked the machine to life and moved into traffic.

I rode out, through the winding streets of the city, a single ink stroke moving through a Clorindo Testa rendering into rough drawings of Spanish civil engineers and back again, letting the machine remind me of the shifting of gears, the throttle and brake, as I passed the soaring, elegant fronts of granite buildings, down long plazas and impossibly wide boulevards, past parks and gardens, now brilliantly colored with the change of season, until the motorcycle didn't buck and hitch with every gear change. It moved smoothly under me.

Buenos Aires went on interminably, building stacked on building; the farther I rode, the more destitute and desperate those I passed seemed. Neighborhoods became disordered. Shantytowns and tenements loomed, brightly painted despite their inhabitants' impoverishment, frilled with clothes on laundry lines strung from balcony to balcony. On the sidewalks, plump women in calico dresses dandled infants on their hips, ignoring the traffic passing so close to where they lived out great swaths of their lives. Their older children loitering on trash-littered stoops, or rampant in filthy, packed-dirt lots kicking footballs, smoking, fighting, cursing. All the fret and decrepit pomp of poverty, flashing by.

The city passed away, the bay far behind me, the Río de la Plata a forgotten memory.

North and west, through farmlands still lush, seething, and green, fed by Río Paraná. Combines and harvesters worked fields near mules and sturdy Argentinian ponies. Tawny wheat, green cotton, brilliant sunflower pocked by seed-oil refineries, dense sugarcane drenched in muddy river water. Boundaryless towns flashed by as the sun raced before me, falling westward. A police car followed me at Campana, a single bubble of blue flashing behind me; a small-town officer. I paid his bribe without even removing my helmet and drove on. I had no headlight, so when the pink-and-orange dusk spread itself against the sky, I stopped, spending the night in a picturesque, if decrepit, motel in a town called Cañada de Gómez that had no secure place to store my bike. I waited until no one seemed to be watching and managed to fit the motorcycle through the room's door to sit, still hot and ticking, filling the space with the scent of four-cylinder exhaust. Still vibrating—an invisible quiver thrumming through my calves, my thighs, my hands, my ass—I ate at the local café, receiving strange looks from the patrons, and quickly retired to my room.

When the telephone rang, I did not answer it. I simply let it ring in the stillness of the room and examined one of the photographs—*La dulce bruma del dolor*. The Sweet Miasma of Pain. Cleave had read Avendaño's translation aloud to The Eye when they first met. It held significance for him. Would there be a voice on the other line if I answered the phone? Would it be Avendaño? Or would it be someone else? Someone speaking in a perfectly cultured Spanish?

I left at dawn, rolling the Yamaha tail-first out into the blue half-light of morning. I felt as if there was some great reservoir of pressure building behind me, waiting to spew forth into the world. Full of questions and disassociated fear, I could not fix on any one thing. When I gassed up the motorcycle (I didn't want to deplete my extra canisters while on the road) I noticed a van that seemed familiar from yesterday's drive passing very slowly in front of the motel and wondered if I was being too paranoid. Cañada de Gómez was a farming town, far from the teeming bustle of Buenos Aires and Córdoba, and an unmarked maroon van shouldn't have been reason for suspicion.

Yet . . .

I was dissatisfied. So I took alleys and many turnings down packed-dirt streets to find myself riding, full-bore, on roads rimmed with irrigation ditches and furiously rutted with mud. If someone watched from the town, I would simply be a rising plume of dust, a spray of muddy water in a rooster's tail, a buzzing sound diminishing in the distance.

In the helmet, the Yamaha's body trapped between my thighs, cocooned in droning sound, I felt as though the white noise took shape around me, a trail, a universal vibration, a cascading particle wave, coterminous with the limits of my perception and the forward motion of the motorcycle. I thought I could feel what Avendaño meant when he described the *miasma,* but this was possibly its opposite—the movement of the world toward fulfillment, toward healing itself. The inertia of exaltation.

Possibly it was just the joy of machinery and movement. Of progress.

I don't know.

Never having been there before, I seriously misjudged the size of Córdoba. I thought it would be a remote hamlet, agricultural, some industry. Instead, I found a warren of buildings and what seemed hundreds of thousands of people. I located a *cervecería,* ordered beer and *tortas fritas,* and borrowed the bartender's phone book. It being midday and the place being empty, he placed the house phone on the bar and retreated to the far end to smoke and read a tattered paperback on a barstool in the light streaming in from outside.

There was no Nivia Campos listed, but I hadn't really expected that. Avendaño had said in his letter she had never returned. There were hundreds of Camposes, however. So I picked the first and called.

"Hello," a man answered.

"Hello," I said, and gave my name. "I am looking for the family of a woman named Nivia Campos. She's from here, though she moved to Magera when she married in—" Avendaño told me the year once, in passing, as we were drinking. I could not recall it. "The sixties."

"There money involved?" the man said.

"As in, will I pay you? Um, I had not considered—"

He hung up.

The next listing was a young woman who knew three Nivia Camposes and their families, all under the age of twenty. The call after that got me an ancient woman whose voice sounded like rocks clattering down a hill. I asked her about Nivia Campos.

"There's a Nivia Alvéz on my cousin's side," she said. "But I know every Campos in Córdoba, smacked every bottom, dried every ear."

"This Nivia moved to Magera in the sixties to marry. A man named Avendaño. A Mageran poet," I said.

The phone disconnected.

From across the room, the bartender said, "Avendaño? *The* Avendaño?"

"Yes," I said.

He stood, walked down the length of the bar to stand in front of me. "It'll be a tough day, getting information, then," he said.

"Why?"

He shrugged. "He had a mouth on him."

"What do you mean?"

"The poet Avendaño was never a friend to Argentina," he said.

"It's a big country," I said. "Surely he couldn't have offended all of it."

"No," he admitted. "But let me think. He did call it . . . what was it . . . 'the wine-colored boil on the ass of South America.' Also, 'a desolate nation of whores and drunkards without enough wits to

– 100 –

pour water from a boot with the instructions written on the heel,' I believe." He laughed. *How many other nations did Avendaño offend?* The bartender continued: "I don't care, but a lot of folks remember something like that. And even if they don't remember what, exactly, he said, they remember they don't like him."

"It was probably after his wife had an affair," I said. "Avendaño is always generous with his irritation and tends to overgeneralize."

"Is?" he said. "Sounds like you're looking for the poet and not the woman's family."

"Pardon," I said. "Was." I thought for a moment. "But if Avendaño was alive and had been here visiting the Campos family . . . ?"

The bartender shrugged again, wiping the bar with a gray towel.

I placed one hundred pesos on the bar top. It disappeared.

"Valladolid and Zaragoza," he said. "There's a villa with a dead tree in the courtyard full of baby shoes hung from their laces. Take wine and Old Vesta can help you."

"Old Vesta?"

"Córdoba's grandmother," he said.

"The city has a grandmother?"

"This city does."

I had a momentary flash of a crowned woman standing above a bassinet. The Poisonous Mother Assumes Power.

I thanked him.

"It's nothing," he said. My hand was on the door to leave when he said, "Do not mention me when you talk to Old Vesta."

I turned back to him. "Why?"

"She doesn't like me to begin with, and once you mention Avendaño, she'll like me even less."

8

The tree, a royal poinciana—normally a garish explosion of scarlet blooms—was most definitely dead, though it would be hard to discern its state at first glance. Miniature shoes festooned its scrabbled crescent of branches, each one painted red. "Painted" might not be correct—each shoe appeared as though it had been *submerged* in carmine paint. A plaque nailed to the trunk read *Trae ofrendas a la bruja, lo que proporcionará para el futuro,* which did not instill in me great confidence in either the veracity or the sanity of Old Vesta. The tiny white stucco villa, windows clad in ironwork, showed a small hand-painted tile set in the plaster by the front door: a hand, palm out, surmounted by the stylized representation of an eye. Had I been someone prone to seeing omens in the rising of exhaust smoke, cloud formations—or signs at old ladies' doors—I would have considered the tile to be quite prophetic.

Holding the bottle of wine I'd bought at a nearby market, I approached the front door and before I could knock, it opened and a voice said, "Don't stand there waiting, come in. Come in."

I pushed into the darkened house and found myself standing

before an apple-faced woman of such advanced age, guessing her number of years would be folly. She had merry dark eyes, rugose skin as though she had spent many years of her life outside in the wind and sun, and terrible posture from the weight of age. Her laugh lines were like arroyos carved from a river that stopped flowing a millennium ago, giving her a sort of wounded dignity. Her hair was magnificent. It was ghost-white with no hint of any other color and possessed of a volume and length equal to her age.

She accepted the bottle of wine then went into the kitchen and returned with a single ceramic cup. She sat at a small linoleum table in a dissected spill of light from the barred window in a small, shabby dining area, removed the cork, and poured herself a measure of wine. She stoppered the bottle and tucked it beneath her chair, easy to hand.

"Well," she said. "What do you want?"

"I am looking for a woman," I said.

"No, you're not," she said.

"Well, her family," I said.

She took a drink and smacked her lips afterward. "Who is she, then?"

"A woman named Nivia Campos. She would've been born sometime around the end of the war, early to mid-forties. She moved to Santaverde at some point to marry."

"And you think she might have come back home? Here?"

"No," I said. "But I need to find her family."

"What is the name of the man she married?"

I thought for a while. Finally, seeing no reason to hide it, I said, "Avendaño."

Old Vesta coughed up a phlegmy laugh and jabbed a finger at my chest. "Yes, yes!" Her hands were twisted by arthritis. "I knew that already. I just wanted to hear you admit it."

She drank more of her wine and then looked out the window

at the street beyond. It was a poor area, but clean, the houses and dwellings well tended by owners and tenants.

"You know about the shoes, do you?" she asked.

"No," I said. "I didn't want to—"

"I was married once. Can you believe that? Me?" she said. "Lost five children, the first to influenza, and the rest stillborn."

"I'm sorry," I said.

The wrinkles on her face took on strange contortions. Possibly she was outraged, possibly annoyed. "Why are you sorry?" she said. "You had nothing to do with it."

"I'm sorry that you lost someone you loved."

"Love," she said, ineffably tired. "I don't even know if I have ever loved anything. You can't love what you've never held. And the babies—" She stopped. "I never held them."

"But the one that died of influenza?" I said. *How did I get into this conversation with her? About her long-dead children?* I thought.

"I was fifteen," she said. She waved her hand at the villa's walls. "This city wasn't even here then." Another long drink, her throat working beneath wattles. She took the bottle from the floor, popped the cork, refilled her cup, stoppered the bottle, slipped it back under her chair. "I don't think a fifteen-year-old can love anything but herself. I remember the image of me with the baby, like a photograph. Ernesto. I can see it in my mind, I'm outside and wearing a scarf, there's a sugarcane field behind me. I'm squinting because the sun is bright. Tired. Very tired and look like I haven't slept from the crying. The very picture of motherhood. But I don't remember love," she said. Another slurp of wine, another smacking of the lips. "This world doesn't care for us."

Despite the sun, it seemed colder in the room.

"They started bringing me shoes, shortly after. I don't know who. To torture me, maybe. My husband beat me. I stopped going to church. Because why? Why should I pray? They started calling me '*bruja*' and eventually, maybe, that's what I became." Her face settled into a mask. I saw that her laugh lines really weren't from laughter, after all. Her craggy lips drew back with her next swallow of wine, showing a hint of carious-black teeth. A woman who had let hate fill her as if she were an empty glass with no cracks. "They come at night when I'm sleeping, and put their children's shoes in the tree. I take them down." She placed both hands on the tabletop and pushed herself up, tottered over to a cabinet, opened it, and withdrew two pairs of baby shoes. "I take them down, see? Little shoes for little babies. I hold them in my hands. They have never taken a step. The babies, they cannot walk. The shoes are useless, except for fortune-telling." A drink of wine and then smacking. "When I'm ready, I dip them in the paint and hang them back up, with a fortune inside written on a slip of paper. 'She will marry rich,' I say sometimes, or 'Disease will take her.' Sometimes I'll write 'He will be a disgrace, and break your heart,' or 'Never trust this one, the devil slipped in.' Sometimes I'll just write one word, like 'Police' or 'Whore,' and let them work out what it will mean. The world does not care for us. Why should I care for them?"

Why indeed, I thought. A parent looking at a little girl, thinking they can never trust her. A boy who is always expected to do wrong. An old woman who was hurt, and tortured, and had the capacity for love burned from her. Perhaps just as important, why should *I* care?

And then I thought about Avendaño, when he said, full of good-natured mischievousness, *Misery is a condition that we are all promised. On the screen, painted in light, that misery is very small. Little witches! Next time, we will go see wrestlers fighting vampires and maybe you'll understand.* I missed him then, desperately.

"Nivia Campos," I said. "You know her people? Her family?"

Old Vesta's eyes hardened, and she pursed her lips. "I will give you no answer without knowing one thing," she said.

There are holes in the world, spewing out darkness, covering up hope. One of these holes was Old Vesta's rotten mouth.

"All right," I said.

"Who told you of me?" she asked.

There was no hesitation on my part. To what end? Protecting a man I didn't know? From an old, miserable woman? "The bartender at Piñon Cervecería. Good-looking. Likes books."

She tightened her jaw. "You're looking for Jorge Campos. Nivia Campos's brother. He lives on Boulevard Agustín Garzón, near where it ends at the university. White house, blue shutters. Red tile roof."

White, blue, red. I stood up. "Thank you, ma'am," I said. "I appreciate it." I didn't try to make any more pleasantries. I moved to the door and had it open, the street in sight.

"Don't you want me to tell *your* fortune?" she said, smiling. Her eyes were terrible. "It's very good wine. I like the looks of you."

"I'll make my own fortune," I said. But I didn't turn and flee. Her hard, tight gaze held me in place.

"You will never be happy," she said. Her voice had changed. It was empty of hate, empty of glee. It was simply dead, with less feeling than Odysseus's mother, Anticlea, in the underworld. "Your purpose is folly. But you may find justice."

Avendaño would have sorted this old bag out. But Avendaño was not here, and that's why I was. I set my jaw. "I've got a fortune for you," I said. I walked back into her dining room and approached the table. Standing above her, I took her cup and drained the wine to the dregs. I had paid for it, after all. "When you die, you won't know peace. You'll writhe in your grave. For a hundred years, the sons and daughters of Córdoba will curse your name.

And then you'll be forgotten." I dropped the cup on the table, where it clattered, spattering the surface with a fine spray of wine droplets. It bounced once, twice, without breaking, and then spun to a stop. It seemed so loud in her small dining room. I wiped my mouth with the back of my hand. "Good wine."

Old Vesta began to wheeze laughter, a high, dry sound like dust whipped down roads by wind from the Andes.

"No one ever knows peace, little girl," she said. She pulled the wine bottle from under her chair, popped the cork, and tossed it at my feet. She took a long drink from the bottle. "And every goddamned soul is forgotten." She stood. "Now go. Go find your *desaparecidos,* if you can."

The home of Jorge Campos was a tidy affair, ringed in planters with thick, oily-leaved vegetation I could not recognize. I went to the shop across the street and bought a Fanta and drank it under the awning near my Yamaha. It was so sweet, I felt the fuzzy divergent sensations of a sugar rush and the soporific of a heavy dessert. There was no traffic to or near the house, so I tucked my helmet under my arm and crossed the street, letting myself into the waist-high walled yard through a metal gate, up the steps to the shaded patio with the multifarious and waxy-looking plants, and knocked on the door.

It pushed slightly open, as if it had not been latched properly.

Light washed into the home's interior, revealing a hallway with arched doors and dark-stained wooden floors. On a credenza stood once-lovely purple sprays of lupinus flowers, now flaccid and dropping petals onto the floor.

"Hello?" I said. "Jorge Campos?"

I am as sensitive to situation and intuition as any person. The idea that academics—especially female academics—are cloistered ascetics that retreat from the real world to content themselves only with books is nonsense.

All of that was to say: Something was very wrong here. I pushed open the door and walked inside, listening. I called out again. Nothing. After a few moments, my eyes adjusted to the dimmer light and it was unsatisfyingly cool in the house. My body responded to the temperature change; every follicle firmed and prickled, my hairs standing on end. I tried to concentrate on the ambient noise of the house, if I could discern any movement by sound alone, but I was distracted by the cloying aftertaste of the Fanta I'd drunk outside and the odd scent that hung in the still air. I walked down the hallway, looking into a formal dining room, another room with a television and record player and many seats. The Camposes were wealthy; it was a large house with many rooms. All of them empty. So far.

I pushed through a knobless swinging door into a large sun-drenched area, copper pots strung from a center ceiling rack, wood chopping block. Tile counters and cabinets.

He was maybe eight or nine, lying on the floor of the kitchen, shot in the head. The blood around him had dried and turned black and tacky. His skin, gray-blue. Flies had begun to gather, not too many, but there were enough, feasting at the corners of his mouth and in the wet surfaces of his open eyes. A man lay in the opening of a doorway to a hall leading back into the center of the house. He'd been running, maybe, toward the kitchen. One arm out in panic when he was shot.

I stopped, terrified. It was hard to hold it all in my head. I felt as though I was a water droplet spattered on a hot skillet, the aggressive boil sending it careening around the cast-iron surface until it's gone, evaporated. *I should call the police,* I thought. I could not look at the boy, so I found myself staring blankly at the man.

As he was facedown, his back pockets were easily accessible and the one on the right had a distinct bulge. Avoiding the blood, I withdrew his wallet and identification card. The flies took flight from his face, agitated. Jorge Campos.

They did not even look like people. With nothing animating them—not breath, not the subtle yet very real pulse of blood through artery, vein, and capillary—they seemed carved from some soft foreign material. He'd fallen forward in his bolt for the kitchen—whoever had killed him must have been holding his son—and his head had turned sideways with the death-fall, arm outstretched. His mouth was open, as if he'd been bellowing something. But there was something more, something strange about his mouth.

I bent again and gingerly worked my index finger and thumb between his lips. As my skin encountered the ivory of his teeth, I felt an unreasoning fear that at any moment they would close viciously. A dead man biting. Some malicious chemical spark left in the meat of the fallen. I drew my hand away. A puff of foul air emanated from him. The churning posthumous gas of his gut, erupting. I coughed, gagging.

I knelt carefully, avoiding the blood. There was something there, I was sure. I extended my hand again. From his mouth, I withdrew a piece of torn paper. Yellow, and discolored at the edges from the man's death molt.

-19.569912, -70.197901

Isabel

9

*I*sabel.

Out and back and out, stumbling, into the fresh air of the street. Cars honking as I raced across the boulevard to reach my bike. The smell of the man and boy, all over me. I thought about Avendaño smelling the photos of *Opusculus Noctis,* hunting for that fractional bit of Alejandra's essence. The dead's essence had settled upon me.

Pounding head, breathless and flushed, I reached the *mercado.* I had my helmet on and the motorcycle throttling into traffic when I noticed a maroon van parked down the street, within sight of the Camposes' front door. I felt as though my heart would hammer its way out of my chest. I kicked the machine into life and maneuvered the motorcycle between speeding automobiles, putting as much distance between myself and the maroon van as I could in the shortest amount of time. At the velocity I was traveling I was not able to turn my head to observe if it was following me for fear of wrecking.

The fermata. The stillness of time in acceleration, wind surrounding me, the sound a deafening white noise. Time enough to think. Vibrations thrummed into my body. My ass, my cunt, my hands: all the points of contact with the Yamaha, thrumming. The man and his son. And who else? Was there a woman lying somewhere in the house, eyes open and unseeing? A sister? A baby? And who would have done it? The hushed roar of mechanical speed, hurling me forward. I pressed my breast down, toward the gas tank, making a smaller profile, giving the wind less of me to assault. All the time thinking: Who would have done it? Who would kill just to plant a piece of paper in a dead man's mouth? With a location and *my* name?

Cleave had called Avendaño a poet and himself an envoy from the exterior brigade. Suddenly The Eye's account began to congeal in my mind, taking on firmness and weight it did not have before. *All Magerans are paranoid, Isabel,* Avendaño had said to me, smiling. *With good reason.* I took turns uncounted, clutching up and down gears, until the buildings passed away and I found myself driving madly, throttle wide open, on white packed-earth ghost roads. The dust crackled as it flecked my helmet's visor.

The western mountains drew nearer now, but in my haste, I had not paid any attention to road marker or highway. Just what was immediately in front of me, and what wasn't immediately behind. Outside of Córdoba, I'd been able to see if I had a tail. It was empty, rural roads. What vehicles I did see were purely utilitarian. No van.

I took the time once more to consider the paper. Three pieces of paper, three names, three sets of coordinates. And the last, the one plucked from a dead man's mouth. My name. It was a taunt. It was a hook.

It is a lure, a sweet aroma, the killing and the letting of blood. The pain becomes an offering and sacrifice becomes a beacon.

The sun dipped behind the rim of the mountains faster than I could have believed. The gloaming seeped up around me like a mist, and I cursed myself for not buying a vehicle with working headlights.

I dropped speed, sure every moment a van's lights would appear behind me.

The ride went on interminably, and I found myself ultimately having to stop the bike and dismount. I pissed on the side of the road, in the dark, holding on to the Yamaha's seat for balance. I looked up to the heavens, waiting for the stars to shine through, but high thin clouds wreathed the sky. I could make out the jagged line of the foothills, and the short sparse scrub lining the road. In the distance, a single sodium bulb burned on a pole overseeing a metal barn. Its light made everything else darker.

I leaned into the Yamaha's seat and smoked, waiting, looking up into blank sky, staring into the dark landscape. I sensed movement. A nocturnal raptor, maybe. The distant yips of canines or coyotes, echoing.

When the lights appeared on the horizon, I waited, tensing. I felt as though at any moment it would slew toward me and from it erupt . . . what? Soldiers? Even worse, well-dressed Americans?

The lights passed. A rattling pickup truck full of empty crates, red taillights illuminating the road before me. I climbed back on the Yamaha, started it, and followed the truck as closely as I dared.

We came to a crossroads, where there was a small family-owned gas station and *mercado* still open under brilliant fluorescent lights. The old beater continued on. I turned off, rolling to a stop in the white-gravel parking lot. With the lights buzzing overhead, insects swarming and batting them, the place took on a washed-out, desaturated look. I entered the *mercado* on loose, still-vibrating legs.

A greasy-haired, seriously obese middle-aged woman with a goiter that looked to be strangling her said, "Hello, welcome to Gas y Mercantida Lazaro. Let me know if I can help you find anything." It was one of those stores where they sold everything: hominy, lard, milk, cheese, wine, liquor, beer, chorizo, socks, toothpaste, shortwave radios, boots, hats, transmission fluid, oil, aspirin, tampons, velvet artworks, candles, antennae, condoms, paperbacks, cigarettes, Fanta, pornographic magazines, fireworks.

"I think I've got what I need," I said. On the counter, I placed a South American atlas, an ink pen, two large beers, peanuts, a heavy-duty flashlight and extra batteries, duct tape, two packs of Gitanes cigarettes, a knockoff Zippo with a little poncho-clad figure on a horse and the word "*gaucho*" embossed on the side, and lighter fluid.

"This might sound weird, but . . . where am I?" I asked. She stared at me as if I was a lunatic. And maybe I was. "No headlight on my bike," I added. "Got caught out of town at nightfall and had to follow a truck here."

"Los Gigantes," she said.

"It doesn't seem so big," I said.

She laughed harder than she should have, glad for the nighttime company. The goitered woman, still smiling, began to ring me up, looking at each item for a price sticker and then entering the number she found into the register. "You hear about the visit?"

"The visit?" I said. "What visit?"

"*The* visit," she said. "*Everyone* knows about the visit."

"I'm sure you have me at a disadvantage. I don't know what you're talking about."

"The *Pope*," she said. "In Magera. Where you're from."

"How do you know where I'm from?" I said.

"Look at you. Leather jacket. Big clomping boots. I can pick out a Mageran anywhere," she said. The goiter was painful to look at, a heaving fleshy fist reaching up from the swamp of her skin.

I can pick out a Mageran anywhere.

"The Pope?"

"Love is stronger, you know?" *El amor es más fuerte.* The lady behind the counter waved a fat hand, rings buried in the flesh of her fingers. "To heal Magera. They're saying that Vidal is going to return the country to democratic rule."

I shook my head. "He won't."

"No?"

"Never," I said. "Because we'll kill him if he does."

"But the Pope said—"

"How much is that?" I said. There was a glass case near the register, and inside it were knives of various sorts. Small plain pocketknives, larger pocketknives, even larger knives in sheaths, scenes of *gauchos* and nude women etched into bone handles. The prices displayed became larger with the size of the corresponding weapon. Near the bottom of the case, where the knives became less ornate and more military-looking, was a hooked blade with a crenelated back full of rip teeth taking up the width of the container, nearer to a machete than a knife. The label next to it said CORVO, but did not list a price.

"Why would you want that?" the counterwoman asked.

"A present for my dad," I said.

"It's been there for years," she said, looking into the case. "I don't know how much it is."

"The one above it is seventy-five pesos. It's almost as big."

"One hundred," she said.

"That seems reasonable," I said. "And the whetstone."

The woman added the corvo and whetstone to the tally and I paid. Outside the *mercado*, I sat down on the concrete slab the building was built upon, leaned back into its wall, and drank beer, watching the insects swarm the lights above the gas pumps. I filled the lighter, put the batteries in the flashlight and the extras in my backpack. I smoked and closed my eyes, waiting for dawn. No sleep would come, and dawn was a long while away. From my backpack I withdrew an envelope containing two slips of paper. I took the other from my pocket.

Three pieces of paper, three names. But only two different sets of numbers. Had I had time to look at the paper I took from Jorge Campos's home before now, I might have seen that two were the same.

Opening the atlas, I held the slip bearing *Alejandra* near the map's face and traced the latitude north, to somewhere in the high Mageran deserts, and followed the longitude to a point close to the Argentinian border. I marked it with an *X*. For Avendaño's coordinates, I traced the remaining slips' longitude and latitude to a blip of a coastal village, in the far north of Magera, to a town called Unquera.

If you connected Córdoba, and the point in the high desert, and the coastal town of Unquera, it was almost a straight line, north by northwest.

I dozed some, leaning against the wall, waiting for light. When I finally abandoned the restless half sleep, I withdrew the corvo and spat on the whetstone, running the dull blade over its rough surface, over and over. The rhythmic movement lulled me into a trance-like state, punctuated only by the steaming air brakes of big trucks pulling in to refuel. Goats bleated from livestock trailers, horses nickered, men whistled tunelessly as they walked to their vehicles, checking tires—the cacophony of transporting disparate cargos: livestock, diesel tanks, grapes, sunflower oil, wheat, corn, cotton. Work never seemed to stop in the scrub. The men paid more attention to the bike than they did to me, despite the weapon I sharpened in full view. It was Argentina—no one blinked at a naked blade. At some point the lights above the gas pumps winked out and I was left in the dark. Using my backpack as a pillow, I lay upon the concrete and slept.

When light bloomed in the east, I remounted my bike and rode until late afternoon, covering more than seven hundred miles. The land rose and became more barren—sparse grasses dying away, leaving only bleached rock and dust, passing white at times, and then ochre, then brown, and then back to white once more. The air grew thin. The road-weariness finally settled upon me and I slept in a motel in an unknown and unnamed town for twenty-four hours, my motorcycle sharing the room with me as it had before. The phone did not ring, or if it did, I was not aware of it.

———

The next day, I came to the border. It was manned by soldiers watching the bare road from a small hut. There were no cars. The constant scouring of wind over the million summits of the mountains had softened the edges of the pass. The high salt flats had become shattered rock, like ejecta from some cosmic impact eons before where no plant, no lichen, no living thing grew. The pass was marked by a simple green sign over the highway that read PASO DE MAZABRÓN LIMITE INTERNACIONAL with mile markers to the next town.

I took my bike off-road, and traveled across the scree plains, out of sight of the border guards, passing into Magera unseen, traveling fifty miles an hour, an unsafe speed on the loose rock. When the border guards and their shabby little hut were far in the distance, I returned to the highway. I felt no shock or thrill at my homecoming. No Homeric greeting by a withered ancient. I passed through the same barren landscape as before. But I was closer to the coordinates of the slip of paper bearing the name *Alejandra*.

Every exile dreams of coming home. It's the nature of our loss. Every narrative wants an end where wrongs are righted, where evil is vanquished or, failing that, at least the status quo is returned. I had longed to return for so many years, to be welcomed back with wine and bittersweet remembrance by whatever family I had left or could find. Reuniting Mageran families, after the coup, was like sweeping up the shards of a broken glass and trying to put it back together—there's always less there than before it was broken.

Now, though, I would have been happy simply to find Avendaño, that kind, deranged old poet. He called Neruda the father of us all, but Neruda seemed so distant and foreign to me now—some other small poet lost to some other tin-pot dictator. I didn't think of Avendaño as a poet, I thought of the man, full of beautiful contradictions. In him, some of the wreckage of my mother and father was, if not healed, made bearable.

By late afternoon, I approached Arriate, the town nearest to *Alejandra*'s coordinates. A meager cluster of stone buildings at a crossroads featured a single market, and a church. Up until then, I had seen no official Mageran vehicles, not even at the border—no police, nor army. But now, a handful of green Jeeps and trucks clustered around the church, though I saw no soldiers attending them. I pressed on as quickly as I was able, whipping through the town, stopping a mile or two out of sight in order to pull the atlas out of my leather jacket, lift my helmet's visor, and estimate where the longitude and latitude indicated. It was an imprecise affair, since the atlas did not have either longitude or latitude marked with minutes. I had to make my best guess.

I followed the highway toward where I thought it might be. Within moments, a rutted dirt road cut away from the highway, down a slope and then out on the rocky flats of scree where a far red hill rose above the rest of the land like a cone or loaf of sugar. I took the bike down and then up, casting a great plume of dust into the air. My heartbeat quickened, as I knew that anyone who looked in this direction, for miles, would see I traveled there.

The sugarloaf grew in my sight, rising high, two hundred meters from the rocky flat's floor. I came to the foot of the hill and stopped the bike and dismounted, looking to my backtrail to make sure I had not been followed. I unslung my backpack and left it leaning against the dirt bike's front tire. I could see nothing. The sun stood fingers above the peaks to the west.

I walked around the hill. No tracks, no sign of life, no vegetation at all. Just loose, shattered rocks. It was cold here and I was glad of the gloves and heavy boots. I kept my helmet on, to keep the swirls and lashing tendrils of salt from stinging my face, eyes.

Walking the perimeter of the sugarloaf, I stopped. A bit of blue stood out from the rest of the landscape of scree, flapping, at the top of a rise. An irregularity in the ground, where there was a protrusion of rocks—the berm of a hole that had been dug and then refilled, maybe.

I approached it. A piece of cloth, once bright blue, now faded and washed out from exposure to the elements. I picked it up, pulling it away from the earth that was reluctant to yield it. When it came away, I could see it was the remains of a dress. Looking down, I searched the berm, kicking the rocks with my feet. The light was failing now, long shadows pointing accusingly toward the east, stretching, stretching. A glint of metal. A bracelet. A bracelet that a young girl might wear, full of bangles and charms. A cornicen, a bird, a heart, a shoe, a baby, a fish, a sailboat.

I fell to my knees and began tearing at the hard, rocky earth with my gloved hands, as if I could reveal something just under the earth's crust. After finding nothing I circled the mound like a cat—like Tomás—but far less indifferently than he might. A flash caught my eye, but not on the ground. In the distance, across the salt flat, to the highway. A vehicle on the side of the road, stopped.

A maroon van.

Two small figures stood beside it. One raised his arm in a genial wave.

Stuffing the bracelet into a pocket and the dress inside my jacket to rest near the atlas, I raced back to my motorcycle, slung back on my backpack, and kicked the starter violently until the machine's sound swallowed almost everything, thinking nothing but *madre de dios, madre de dios* in a sort of circular and meaningless chant. It was an empty shibboleth—something my mother would mutter when I was just a girl, before she was taken away. I throttled up the bike and ran parallel to the road for a stretch, watching the figures move back to the van, open the doors, and enter. It began to move. I doubted I could outrun a vehicle on the highway, but they could never catch me out here, on the flats or in the rough terrain. The Yamaha was built for off-road travel, which was one of the reasons I bought it. I had been thinking of the state of Argentinian roads, which were notoriously bad, rather than a chase on the salt flats outrunning—whom? Who were these men? Whoever they were, they were murderers, or at least their proximity to Jorge Campos's home was testament enough that I should be wary.

I hung back from the highway, but soon the maroon van was pacing me. I came to a gulley, where I had to turn either toward the road or away from it, and I opted for the latter. I did not know how long it would take for whoever rode in the van to get tired of the game I played and begin firing. I took the dirt bike out beyond a ridge, out of sight from the highway. The sun had just passed beyond the mountain peaks, and the sky became blue-gray overhead and smeared with orange-pink at the edges. A half-light settled on the flats, giving it that dreamlike air, a luminous darkness; everything dimmed, yet absent of the hard contrast that direct sunlight brought, so that every detail stood clear in my sight, but fading. Caught between states for an instant. Precious but temporary.

It was dark in minutes, and I had to decide. Press on, out here in the waste, or back to the road. If I didn't make up my mind, any possibility of choice would be removed for me and it would be a simple matter of the passengers in the van finding a different vehicle in the night, one that could take the rocks, maneuver in the ruts and arroyos in the shadows of the Andes.

It was not a hard decision. I formulated a plan, knowing it was folly, but lacking any better options.

You will never be happy. Your purpose is folly. But you may find justice.

I waited an hour for full dark; then I took the flashlight from my bag. I duct-taped it to the motorcycle's handlebar axis, so that it shone merely ten feet in front of the dirt bike, and traced my path back, down through the gulley to the point where it rose to join the plateau of salt flat by the road. I extinguished the flashlight and killed the engine. I laid the bike on its side so it wasn't easily spotted if the men had left the comfort of the van and had powerful lights. I removed my helmet—I was afraid its surface or visor might catch the light and glimmer—and unslung my backpack once more. My gloves, I left on.

From there, I crept to the highway. The stars pricked the heavens and a hazy white sliver of moon rose in the east, giving me a weak, tinny light. I could not see the van from where I crouched, but the highway threaded through this part of the high mountains like a silver stream, gleaming with moonlight in the darkness. I approached it and lay on the side of the road, in the dry ditch, listening. I heard nothing. I waited, breathless, and then rose and trotted down the highway where I thought I had marked the van earlier, my breath coming hard. This country was a big space, and bigger in the dark, with rough terrain where every footfall could lead to a twisted ankle or broken leg.

Crossing the road, I hid myself in the far ditch, and waited. Nothing.

I was about to rise and move on when I heard the faint sound of a vehicle. Not the high-pitched whine of an engine at accelerated revolutions, but an oil and steel baritone of a machine barely idling. Lights appeared in the distance. I tried to make myself one with the earth, pressing my face into the rocks. The vehicle approached. Slowly. I did not have to look to know it was the van.

I waited until it drew even with me. Grabbing a rock, I let the van pass—five meters, then ten, away. The red taillights burned in the darkness. I threw the rock. It missed. Stooping, I snatched up another one, took three steps with my arm cocked, and let it fly. I could not see its arcing path in the darkness, but I traced it in my mind's eye.

It hit the van's roof with a hollow *clong*. The vehicle stopped.

I threw myself off the road, in the ditch farthest away from my dirt bike. A door opened, then another. I allowed myself a glance. One man stood in the headlights, looking away from me, to the north, on the other side of the highway. The other crossed in front of the taillights. He said in Spanish, "Get out of the beams if you want to be able to see." I felt as though he wanted to use profanity, but restrained himself. I recognized his voice from somewhere. Flashlights flicked on, and they scanned the north side of the road, methodically.

I had abstractly realized they would have flashlights, but when their beams suddenly cut through the darkness, I was still surprised. The lights bobbed and wavered, searching the scree.

Improvise, I told myself in Avendaño's voice, as if he was saying, *Surely you've shot a gun? A bow and arrow, like Artemis?*

I took up another rock, pushed myself off the ground into a crouch, and threw it as far as I could into the darkness on the far side of the road. It clattered faintly.

One of the men yelped. They both moved away from the vehicle, which was still running. I ran, half-crouched, down the ditch to the van, keeping its body between myself and where I imagined the two men to be. I forced myself to cross the open space to the vehicle. Looking inside, I could see by the green dashboard light the keys dangling there. I could steal the van, I knew. But something stopped me. I cannot explain it other than I couldn't just leave the motorcycle there in the gulley. It had served me well and I had grown to love it in some ways—that dumb collection of metal, plastic, and rubber.

I considered just taking the keys, but the instant the van's engine died, the men would be alerted.

Withdrawing the corvo from my boot, I approached the front of the vehicle. I took the blade's hilt in both hands and jabbed it at the tire. It twisted from my hand and clattered to the ground. I had underestimated the toughness of the radial's black rubber skin.

A man in the dark shouted, and the other man answered. I had only seconds to act.

I snatched up the knife from the ground with both hands and drove it into the tire, which began to hiss violently, wrenched it around until it came loose, dashed to the rear of the van and did the same to that tire, and then fled into the darkness on the far side of the road. Ten meters, twenty, thirty. The flashlights came bobbing and weaving around the van. Forty meters. The lights began searching the scree. I found a hollow among the rocks and pressed myself into it. The lights peered out, passing over and around me, and moved on. I waited.

"Miss Certa," a raised voice said in good Spanish . . . but with the telltale hard sounds of an American. Chemicals sparked in memory: *the man who wanted to hail me a cab at the airport.* A man who restrained himself from cursing in a foreign language. "Very well played."

The other man began to say something and the first man hissed, silencing him. They both remained quiet for a moment, and I felt as though they were whispering to each other. The second man's flashlight went dark. I tensed. He'd be hunting me in the dark, then.

"Step into the light, Isabel," the first man said, giving his flashlight a little wave to punctuate the thought. "This game has gone on long enough. I have an—"

He paused and whistled, indicating something to his partner, but I could not discern what. I rose into a crouch and was surprised to still find the corvo clutched in my gloved hand. I angled south and west another twenty meters, always facing the van. Soon, I would move away from them, following the highway west and crossing back over it to reclaim my dirt bike. Until then, I could not be seen. I dropped back to the ground and breathed as quietly as possible.

"I have an associate who would very much like to meet you. You have in your possession something of his," the man said. His voice was fainter now, with the distance. A flashlight beam darted my way and then passed by. "A very influential man. A kingmaker, you might say," the man said, chuckling. In a lower voice, he said something else I could not hear distinctly, but I thought he might have said, "A kingdom killer."

I had moved far enough away and was angling back toward the highway when the man said, loud enough for me to hear, ". . . questions answered. I can take you to Avendaño. He *wants* me to bring you to him. How else would we know you'd be here?" he said.

It took extreme amounts of self-control not to bellow *But who sent the coordinates? Did you? And why?* But I did not. I could not believe him about Avendaño.

I watched his flashlight beam closely. When it turned to an area of scrub and scree in the opposite direction of where I waited, I made my move, dashing across the highway and down the soft slope to the white flat plain. I could not tell if the gulley was between my bike and me but I kept moving, crouched until I was thirty meters away, and then stopped, to listen and watch.

I could see neither flashlight now, only the red lights of the van. I moved parallel to the highway, angling slightly away when I found the gulley by slipping down the side of it with a tumble of rocks. Things happened quickly then.

Heavy breathing like a dog's approached; I heard the grunt of a man and then his own corresponding clatter of falling rocks. A black shape rose and grew and in the faint light I could make out the second man, his head pivoting about in the dark, his hands raised and misshapen. No . . . not misshapen, holding a pistol.

I made myself small, crouching, gathering myself. I centered my weight, took a deep breath, held it. What happened next would decide my fate. He had to come close enough to me without being alerted. I tried to access that pause of time that Avendaño had talked about, that I felt when hurtling through space on the motorcycle—the collapsed-time, the fermata. I felt as though I might pierce it, and then the man moved forward, close to me, and I launched myself forward and brought the corvo across his face as hard as I could. He fell backward, making a wordless, congested sound, liquid and bubbling. I threw myself upon him, lashing out with the hooked knife again, flailing at his raised hands and, when they fell away, his dim and wetly moving face.

He stopped burbling and gave a long sigh.

I put my face next to the ruin of his. No breath. The eyes gathering moonlight, open and still.

I had done this. Whatever other things I had and would become, I was now a killer.

I spent an eternity breathing into the man's ruined visage, trying to commit it to my memory. *We kill part of ourselves with each loss of innocence,* Avendaño had said once, at the Café de Soto. Earlier, there had been luchadores and vampires, and a girl who went from a white rose to a blood-spattered and befanged virago.

Pushing away, I pulled my gloves off, now sticky with blood, and searched the ground until I felt something hard, with straight edges. Metal. My finger found the trigger and I rose. I tucked my gloves in my belt and moved away from the body of the second man, heading toward where I thought the motorcycle still lay.

I chose the wrong direction, switched back, and searched the other way until I found it, exactly as I had left it. A huge sigh of relief escaped me. If I had a home on this earth at that moment, it shared a point with that machine. How easily we become attached to objects. How easily we become attached to people. How easily we become killers.

I pulled my backpack on, over my shoulders, and righted the motorcycle. Legs shaking, I pushed up the rise, out of the gulley, onto somewhat level earth. The van still sat on the road, some hundred meters away, lights burning.

"Miss Certa!" the man yelled into the darkness. He stood in the lights of the van and was looking in the wrong direction. "Where do you think you're going? We will find you! Step into the light!"

Before I could stop myself, I yelled, "There is no we!" and brought up the pistol and fired at him.

The bullet whanged off the van and the man dropped to a crouch and quickly put the vehicle between himself and me. I had the impression that he'd marked the muzzle flash. I didn't care.

"Your man is *fucking dead*! *I killed him!*" I yelled, rage filling me. I imagined cutting him, torturing him, as if I were Sepúlveda and he were my Avendaño. I thought of opening up his body cavity and seeing what sort of thing might ride out of that red gullet into the world. I thought about the man lying in the gulley, his burbling last breath.

I was as mad as Avendaño.

I needed to leave, fast. I would kill the other man if I had to. But I did not want to.

I started the motorcycle—its roar was like some wild animal's yawp, a vicious creature that prowled the salt flats—and tugged the helmet on, and then I fired the pistol twice more at the van and rode into the darkness.

––––––––

I turned on the flashlight and returned to the highway once the van was out of sight. I couldn't take the road past the van, so I threaded my way through the nearby town, biting my lip, hoping the Mageran army hadn't set up a roadblock. I was a murderer now, in addition to being an exile, and possibly labeled an enemy of the state. Vidal and his regime did not appreciate the educated, and my doctorate labeled me as problematic.

Whatever had driven me through the events of earlier in the night—adrenaline, self-preservation, anger, hatred, the lure of the secrets of the *Opusculus Noctis*—it fled me now and I felt weak, and cold. I shivered. I searched for my gloves but must have lost them somewhere after the frantic struggle with the man I'd killed—*cut to bloody ribbons, Isabel, you left him unfit for an open casket, that's for sure*—along with the weather-bleached blue dress.

Was this location something more than just a lure to get me out here? Was that why it was different from the others? Did they capture Avendaño that way, too? Did they capture him? Was it too much to hope he was alive? Was it too much to hope he was free?

I had no answers. Every part of me with reason, every fiber, wanted me to turn back toward the border. Go back to the comfort and safety of the university. Find Claudia and kiss her and tell her I'm sorry, it was a mistake, just something I had to do, and she'd be outraged but then she'd soften and we could find comfort among Moroccan tiles and Egyptian sheets and drink Avendaño's booze and spend his money until it dried up. We could bring Laura into our bed, that gorgeous tor of a woman, and explore every crack and cranny of her. We could find all the ways smart, loving women can make their lives work.

But I didn't.

I fell into the fugue state of motion. I was alone on the face of the earth, outside of time and light and human connection.

I found a road in the dark. I took it. And the next. And the next.

Until dawn.

10

I woke surprised my skin wasn't crawling with scorpions. I lay in the dirt watching birds circle high above. The sun shone thin and watery and it was cold, a brisk wind ripping at my hands, my face. My lips were cracked—I had slept with my mouth open—and all of my body ached. When I shut my mouth, my teeth ground painfully on silica. Mustering what saliva I could, I spat. Coughed. Spat again.

I pushed myself up, lost my balance, and took two quick steps to correct myself. My body was a reflection of my tumbling thoughts.

Looking around, I spotted the motorcycle, turned on its side. The ground here was too soft for the kickstand. A khaki, dusty soil marked only with stunted grasses. In the distance, obstinate and solitary trees dotted the countryside. A spindly telephone line. Dun-colored hills sloping into dun-colored mountains.

Magera, my homeland. Seeing it now, I wondered why Vidal would commit the crimes he had to rule such a barren and forsaken place. But that was man, was it not? He would water the dust with blood to claim title and rule. I spat again.

I was becoming Avendaño.

I filled the dirt bike tank from the canisters, and in the first town I came to, located where I was. I bought workman's gloves, thin but better than nothing. Tortillas, *carne seca*. I drank water and used the gas station's restroom. I stripped to the waist and washed my armpits, my chest, my neck. I wet my hair and wrung it out. I made pools of water in my hands, sucked it into my nasal passages, and then blew that out too, into the sink, to clear the dust of my fugue state. I pored over the map and memorized my route to Unquera. It was less than a full day's ride.

I reclaimed the road, almost thoughtless. Prudence and discretion were lost to me. This disregard for safety and outward concerns, a form of dumb lassitude. It seemed only moments later when I found myself following highway signs out of the heights and down turning roads to Unquera. From above, the vantage where the highway switched back and forth in its descent, the town looked very small and orderly. An elongated *traza*, planned and surveyed and plotted a century before, when copper was rich in these tawny mountains. A town with a workforce and a wharf on the shore, buried in the curving rind of bay. The sea gave no usable moisture for vegetation, but it was sustaining nonetheless—fish and commerce to a wharf that had seen more prosperous days. At its back, lifeless rocks sloped downward to the shore and their journey was interrupted not by any vegetation, only the construction of man: highway, house, road, wall, breakwall, wharf, pier.

I descended, back and forth on the switchback highway, watching Unquera grow below me. A white-and-blue spear tip of *espadaña* stood sentinel on a hilltop, its bell silent. Closer, an umber park, grassless, treeless, childless; a school, abandoned; a hut, a fishing shack. A narrow dirt path threading through bare-walled shacks. Warmer now, at sea level. Salt on the air. The desert of Magera meets the salt desert of sea.

There were more buildings—dun-colored buildings, like the land all around, *dun and dun and done and Donne,* I thought. *A valediction forfeiting mooring.* Thoughts skittering off into nonsense. I examined the buildings. Some looked industrial, some like dwellings, some looked vaguely military. One, a husk of a hotel, scaling paint and open doorway like the mouth of Pantagruel at carnival. All seemed empty, missing windows and doors. Some appeared to be warehouses, great buglike buildings with hundreds of fractured eyes as windows. There was movement north, closer to the wharf, I could see, where seagulls rode surging air drafts, feathers darkened by the rising dust of vehicles. Diesel exhaust. Soldiers. Green trucks.

I pulled my bike behind a Quonset hut between an industrial-size garbage bin and a wall, hiding it from any casual viewer. I left my helmet on the handlebar and stuffed the atlas in the small compartment under the blue seat. Down the alley where buildings pointed their asses, their most unflattering parts toward each other. I made my way as covertly as possible toward the hotel. I slipped around front, into its gullet. BIENVENIDO AL HOTEL ELENCANTOQUINTAY, a sign read. Wallpaper hung in rotting streamers, in corners piles of broken furniture. All of the light fixtures ripped from the walls. The last vestige of the hotel's dignity was the concierge and clerk's desk, an immovable and immemorial construction of real mahogany now beginning to striate and turn gray from the elements. The sea could strip any finish. It rises up, voracious.

El mar sueña que es el cielo.

I took the stairs by twos. Graffiti here, and the overwhelming smell of mold. I found a room on the third floor with a window that looked out over the northern part of Unquera, where the army vehicles were parked between buildings. I took a position at the window, watching. A barracks, maybe, or an arsenal.

Canvas-tarped trucks surrounded by *carabineros*. Men barking orders. Not many soldiers, maybe fifteen, mostly milling about. From one of the trucks came bound and blindfolded people; men, women, children. The horror Avendaño had documented in his testament went on.

The *carabineros* hustled the prisoners into the building, and the soldiers followed, leaving the streets empty except for an officer and another man I had not seen before. A fat man in a dark suit without a tie, his shirt untucked. He stood near the pier speaking with the officer, gesturing at the ship anchored at the pier. A gray metal boat, with pilot's roost, radar tower, and swivel cannons on the prow and stern. The officer gestured to the building where they had taken the prisoners. He disappeared from sight, entering the building, and then returned, followed by the soldiers who had been there before, plus some who must have been in the building.

I tried counting, but lost track at thirty. They came bearing duffels and weapons, kits and chests, and moved to the ship. Fresh men to man the forsaken outpost, fresh prisoners from Santaverde or Coronada, Mediera or Los Diaz. A changing of the guard. After two hours, they had boarded the vessel and a great horn sounded and the ship retreated into the bay. As the afternoon grew long and the sun fractured on the sea, vanished in the horizon.

A few sodium lights clicked on, buzzing, casting yellow circles of light intermittently on Unquera's streets. The sky blazed with sunset and then darkened. Another streetlight crackled to life, right outside the hotel. I sat on the floor, eating peanuts I had bought and watching shadows grow, and cursed myself afterward, parched. I wandered the hotel, going in and out of empty rooms, bathrooms, looking for sinks or even toilets that might contain a bit of water. There was none. I was just leaving one room, a room very close to where I had observed the ship's departure, when I noticed a handprint on the wall near the door. It was crusted, and brown. Blood.

I scanned the room. Nothing, but—

On the wall, painted in blood, a crude drawing of an eye.

Avendaño.

He had been here.

My thirst was unbearable now. The cascading susurrus of the Pacific's waves maddened me. *Water, water, everywhere, nor any drop to drink.* I waited, staring at the eye. I traced it with my hand. Avendaño. Something about it caused me to shrug off my pack and withdraw the sheaf of photographs of the *Opusculus Noctis*.

A Little Night Work *indeed.*

I pawed through his translations. *La dulce bruma del dolor.* The Sweet Miasma of Pain. I sorted through my own translations. *El señuelo de la inocencia.* The Lure of Innocence. I riffled through the photographs. The words swam in my sight.

In the end, I focused on *Un pasaje a los sueños.* A Passage to Dreams.

It was not the noise that roused me, but the lack of it. The sounds of surf had died away, drawn back from the shore by the tide. My sight could not penetrate the darkness enough to see. But it had quieted. In the sodium light below I could see figures moving. Dark figures, indistinct, walking in a group. A flash of white skin. Bound hands, gagged mouth.

A mist had risen from the bay, it seemed. It hung in the air, still. A clotted artery of air, snaking down the street, between dark figures and their prisoner. Soldiers carrying devices, great packs on their backs, but absolutely silent.

I took the stairs to the ground floor on cat feet. I checked the gun in my belt to see if it was still there. I had fired it three times, and I was sure there were more rounds in it, but as I told Avendaño so long before, I knew nothing of guns. I hoped, if I needed it, it would fire again.

From the throat of the hotel, I waited for the dark figures of soldiers, and the others, the prisoners, to pass and then I followed.

Out, out of the town, past the hill upon which the church bell tower stood, a jutting angle piercing the night sky. The stars a great smear across the sky and the moon just a white haze outlining the mountains to the east. It would take it time to clear their summits and surmount the heavens.

The soldiers did not speak. They did not march in time.

Leaving the road, they followed a packed trail in the dirt, rising up, and up, away from Unquera. Lights winked on the bay from fishermen's skiffs and then became obscured by the thickening haze. I hung back, not wanting to be spotted by the soldiers. I moved, crouching.

A plateau, a mile or more from the town. I skirted its edge, working toward the east, where I could gain a vantage. The soldiers appeared to have clustered near a natural hollow in the earth, large enough for a bus. Breathless, I scrambled upward. Hanging heavy, the vapor wreathing the bay and hillside seemed to pulse and coagulate.

I settled in to wait.

The soldiers arrayed themselves neatly. Two of them took prisoners and forced them into a line. The starlight had grown stronger now, as if whatever particulate matter hung in the air had luminesced. I looked back over my shoulder. The moon swelled and bloomed behind me and I had a sudden sense of dislocation: the soldiers, the prisoners, the plunging hillside beyond, the empty town below, all became clear in my sight. The haze—the *miasma*—wasn't gone, it heightened my perception now. Like some supercharged electron cloud, crackling with light. A swarm of luminous flying insects. The tracers and after-images from looking at the sun.

Soldiers pulled the gags from their prisoners' mouths.

My heart skittered in my chest, as if it wanted to flee my body. I clutched at the pistol as if I could attack these *carabineros*. As if I could free these poor souls lined up on the edge of a pit.

Moving in unison, the soldiers pulled masks over their faces. A boy began to cry, a woman cursed them. An old man sobbed and called out to Jesus, and then his mother.

A soldier—misshapen, with a great cylinder on his back—raised his hand holding a baton. No, not a baton. If he was a conductor of music, it was no composition I'd ever want to hear again. Gas issued forth, merging with the *miasma*. The prisoners began to cough and spasm. The luminous smoke in the air pulsed and grew, sending congealing tendrils skyward. I could not breathe with the horror. The gun was forgotten.

A man pitched over, tumbled into the pit. The rest followed. The soldiers stood still, unmoving.

The *miasma* coalesced, the soldiers stilled to permanent inaction. Time had collapsed. A figure stood twenty paces in front of me. A man in a suit. Handsome. Glasses one size too small for his face.

"Hello, scholar," Cleave said, looking up at me where I crouched. "I am so glad you can join us." Even though I had never seen him before, I was struck with the frisson of recognition—it was as if Avendaño's words had become my memory. He strode forward. At least that is how my brain interpreted the movement. The *miasma* shimmered and coursed around him, eddying in shifting currents. He was a man, yet he was more. *In this man, I could feel my end. I could feel all ends.*

"And you've brought it." He laughed. "Perfect."

I raised the pistol, centering it on his chest. He shook his head.

"You're an initiate, are you not?" he said. "You've read the lines writ in blood? In semen? Of course you read them. You did more than read. You translated them. I could have never come to you if you had not been so invested. You've been at the edges of—" He uttered a phrase I did not understand that nevertheless caused my skin to crawl. "For weeks now."

I thought back to Avendaño's apartment in Málaga, the wading deep into the *Opusculus Noctis.* The growing shadow, the coalescing figure.

"Yes," he said, as if reading my mind. "And then your little sentinel came." *Tomás.* He shrugged. "But despite it all, you did not stop, though any sort of rational thought should have warned you. And now you're here." He extended his hand. "Bring forth the photographs."

"No," I said. "I have a gun and will use it."

Cleave raised a hand. "You can try."

I pulled the trigger, but the hammer did not fall. The *miasma* shimmered around the gun-blued metal.

"Give me the photographs," Cleave said. "The Vatican library has burned, the passage through the girl has been closed now for years. Give me the photos."

Cleave's command of Spanish was eroded, possibly. The mask, slipping. I did not understand most of what he said.

"No," I said. It would be so easy, though. To end it. Shrug off the backpack and sling it toward him and he would go away, surely.

I even asked. "If I give you the photos, you'll let me go? And Avendaño?"

He *tsk*ed.

"We are beyond all that now. Swimming in the ancient air," he said, raising his hands as if feeling a light summer shower. "Look." He turned and looked out over the mass grave to the sea and sky. "See?"

The *miasma* had grown and its coils threaded into the sky in a convolution. Vines eating at the firmament of heaven.

"And look," he said, gesturing to the earth.

The death pit seemed to swell in my vision. I marked the bodies of the prisoners; some were women, firebrands and activists and wives and lovers, some men, laborers and academics who had spoken with miscalculation within earshot of Vidalistas, some children, families wondering where they were. All offered up their misery to the enormous sky. All of them, their last moments were a misery and torment, swelling the *miasma*.

Beneath them, bodies, softened to indistinction—all black and gray and jumbled. Not countless, no. I sensed their number. But some so old there was no telling where one body ended and the next began. Except for one.

Avendaño.

He lay on his back, one arm spread wide, the other trapped behind his back in a painful and awkward position. Both eyes were vacant now. I had never seen him without the eyepatch. He wore the old linen suit I first met him in, tobacco-mottled at the cuffs, now stained and gray with putrefaction. But his face was still his. He looked surprised to find himself in this position. He seemed very small underneath the carious sky.

"No," I said.

"I am afraid you have no choice," Cleave said, and moved his hand in a passing gesture.

The soldiers stirred, still wearing gas masks, turning blankly to stare at me. They moved.

I tossed the gun and stood.

Withdrawing the corvo from my boot, I raised it. The gun might not work in the *miasma,* but the knife would.

Cleave seemed to flow forward, his human face a mask. *Think of me as an envoy from the exterior brigade.* The soldiers began scrabbling at the dun earth, feet and hands, loping forward like wolves.

It had seen too much. So I plucked it out, Avendaño had said.

It's one thing to hold something close to one's eye, the body's seat of perception, and it's another thing altogether different to assault it.

But at that moment I saw beyond now, past the physical world. Cleave was revealed in full, a writhing mass of darkness. His form streaked away in a perverted umbilicus to . . . what? Something else? Somewhere else? The *miasma* lashed and twined about him, sending coils and tendrils to penetrate the soldiers, the corpses in the pit, the sky.

My time had run out.

I drove the point of the corvo into my eye cavity. The pain, outrageous and heart shattering as if I had torn a breach in the levee of my soul and now the torrents of black water could rush in. Yet I worked the blade into my face—my own face!—and dug at the sclera until my eye ruptured.

I wept vitreous fluid and blood.

The corvo was sharp. Sharp enough for what I had to do. The pain, a sacrifice, instructed me on where the blade was to move, what I needed to cut. I required no words. I levered my eye from its seat and cut the flesh that still clung to it. It fell in the ignomini-ous dust.

I cannot imagine what I might have looked like to Cleave. A white light? A hideous creature? An explosion?

From Cleave issued a thin, miserable sound that traveled

through the *miasma* in phantasm vibrations. He had no human mouth to scream, after all.

The luminous haze gathered, coalescing, and entered me. The hollow of my eye contained a vastness where all the *miasma*'s misery could enthrone itself.

"I'm no scholar," I said. "I am memory."

And then, with a single step, I moved out of space and time and walked roads that only Avendaño might have found familiar.

EPILOGUE

The cemetery in Santaverde is almost empty today. It is bright, and relatively warm. A mother pushes her infant in a stroller heading to the ALDI *supermercado* just out of sight, behind the wall. In a place of death, still the tug and fret of the body, the churn of the gut and drive of sex, compels us.

I sit at the bench and stare at the names carved in the memorial, set in stone. Esteban Pávez is there, and Guillermo Benedición. Alejandra Llamos, near the fountain on the south end. Sofía Certa, my mother, there, not too far from The Eye's paramour. Somewhere in Europe, Vidal sits in a cell, waiting for his trial.

Above the names, an inscription reads ALL MY LOVE IS HERE AND HAS BEEN ATTACHED TO ROCKS, SEA, MOUNTAINS.

A poet's words, etched in stone.

But not my poet.

Sometimes, when I close my remaining eye, I can see the luminous and squirming coils of the *miasma*. Sometimes, in that particulate haze, faces surface like pallid koi in a dappled pond. I see them and we recognize in each other something.

But it is never Avendaño.

A group of young men laugh, running through the memorial space, holding a football in their hands. When they see me, dressed in black, sunning myself on a bench, one of them cups his hand over one eye and says, "El Ojo! El Ojo!" and they laugh, sneaking glances at me.

They call me The Eye now.

I have class soon and must return to my office to look over my notes. I never feel wholly at ease this far from the photographs. In this, Cleave was right: I am beyond all reason.

I stand and approach the wall. In a crevice, I place a piece of paper.

It reads:

Rafael Avendaño, champion of the internal brigade.

MY
HEART
STRUCK
SORROW

1

Cromwell: Carbon Monoxide

For a month he sits at home before returning to work. The folklore division's chief has given him leave—a month, but no more. They are so very sorry, but surely he understands. Cromwell reads the Bible, the books at his bedside table. He can't bear to listen to music, though. That part of him seems so unimportant now. So he reads. Bright-colored thrillers and mysteries, more suitable for a beach cottage than his empty house. His gaze passes over the words and they remain with him only long enough to register. Winter has settled, snow hangs in the air and makes those souls with the will to venture outdoors blow brilliant white breath, but Cromwell stays inside. The cat has disappeared; he was never the one to feed it anyway. The heating system has been repaired but he often finds he's cold. It's an old Alexandria home, constructed in the thirties, central heat and air added laboriously later. The lights flicker each time the HVAC unit begins blowing.

"I'll stay with him," he said, looking down at Maizie curled around their son. William. A thermometer and a bottle of children's acetaminophen sat on the bedside table. "If they need you at the office. I have sick days and leftover vacation." He was jealous of the loving sprawl of the boy's sickbed, Maizie so comfortable in it. On the iPad, cartoons danced in primary colors. His wife brushed William's brow. The boy was pale, like a video feed with the picture desaturated. Usually flushed and olive complexioned, like his mother, pumping with energy and bright enthusiasm. Maizie's arms encircled him. She would hoard all the boy's love for herself.

"No, I've called in to Brad and let him know we're sick," she said. "We're comfy cozy here. But it's cold, isn't it? I think it's time to turn on the heat."

"It'll smell funny," he said. He leaned down to kiss his son and wife.

"No," she said, leaning her head away from his lips. "No kisses. We're infected and one of us has to go to work."

"Call me if you need anything. I can stop by the grocery on the way home."

On his way out, he turned on the heat.

2

Cromwell: Vivian

He is oblivious to their stares, their consolations. Eventually, they stop wringing their hands, giving him cards that will remain unread, and allow him to reclaim his office. A blank expression settles upon his features—the caul of governmental vacuity, that wall that he can place between himself and the greater world with such ease. He can make himself other, when he wants, to protect himself.

The halls of the Folklife Center at the Library of Congress are still decorated for the holiday season—it's the dead week between Christmas and New Year's, anyway: *the dead week, the dead, weak* ringing in his head—quilts and rustic paintings giving way to red and green streamers. The main hall's corkboard has a purposefully nondescript and nondenominational banner reading HAPPY HOLIDAYS, careful to give no preference toward Christmas. At the department of American folklife, they are very careful not to offend. Christmas has passed and now it's just a matter of whoever put up the decorations taking them down. But it can wait until after New Year's.

He took William's presents to the local Boys Club and Maizie's sister took hers. He left for an afternoon, when Maizie's family was there after the funeral, solicitous and nervous and discomposed by his composure, and they had removed the Christmas tree by the time he returned, as if getting rid of a body. Cromwell supposed they were, after all.

His office stands cluttered, stacked with printed copies of emails to his notice; beta, VHS, and mini-DV tapes—all legacy formats—waiting to be digitized and ingested into the network, those that Hattie either cannot process or has left to him, since folk music is his specialty. The taxonomy of filing and classification. The rendering of old recordings to melodies, the melodies to sheet music. Sheet music into the computer so it might be cross-referenced. A Highlands ballad? An Appalachian jig? A Low-Country dirge? A Negro field holler? And what tradition? What does the Markov model reveal? How is this modality different from the other? Some relation to French New Guinea lullabies? African wedding songs? Native American war chants? How can he work this into his next paper? How can he transform this melody into a "yes" on his next grant? The song of the department was "Justify Your Existence."

He sits at his desk, turns on his computer, and waits. She does not take long.

"Hi," she says from the door.

Cromwell says nothing. He looks at her and then back to his computer, where he again begins selecting emails to trash. The red notifications bar on his mail client now reads *1,633*.

Vivian enters and shuts the door behind her. Wearing her hair back. He can smell her individual scent; he could never puzzle out if it was simply her or her perfume, or a lotion or cream she used on her skin, or some combination of it all. But her fragrance fills his office and his nostrils dilate involuntarily to smell her. A minor treachery his body commits without his permission.

"I—" she starts.

"Don't," he says. "No need. We're all sorry. I'm sorry. You're sorry."

She sits down in the chair by the door and looks out into the hall to see if anyone has noticed she's with Cromwell now. "I wanted to come by to see you after the funeral. But—" she says. *But how appropriate would it have been for the woman you were fucking to come to the funeral of the woman you married.* She twists her wedding ring thoughtlessly. Or maybe not. He is wearing his as well, even though now there's no reason to except for remembrance.

Like he could forget.

"Not now," he says, and watches her face crumple. In some abstract way, he realizes it took quite a bit of courage for her to come in here and speak to him and he should make some sort of concession to that, but he can't think of what might suffice. "Soon, though," he says. "We can talk."

She looks down at her hands. When she looks back up, her face is more composed.

"Did Hattie tell you?"

"No," Cromwell says. "She didn't. What?"

"Matilda Parker has died. If it's too soon—"

Cromwell waves his hand, dismissing her concern. His wife and son are dead. Yes. This has been established. "Matilda Parker? I'm not placing her."

"Grandniece of Harlan Parker."

There was a time he might have whistled his astonishment, but he can't muster that sort of exuberance now. "And?"

"She has bequeathed all of her estate to the department of folklife." She allows a smile to soften her face. "You've come back right in time."

3

Cromwell: Hattie and Harlan

He's reminded of the figure of Harlan Parker—how could he forget him? But now his mind splits when she says "You've come back right in time" and begins thinking of two things. The olfactory stimulus of Vivian has seeped in, seated itself in his mansion of many doors to remembrance—it triggers a cascade of thoughts and memories: the thrum of her pulse in the hollow of her neck, the taste of her skin so pale, how she wriggled beneath him, above him. The coarse hotel sheets, rough on their skin; her laughter; her mouth on him. The cold pulse of air-conditioning beading condensation on rented windows. The submerged desire during the workday chased by the fear and guilt and shame. Once more his nostrils dilate involuntarily to take in more of her smell. He's betrayed by his body, another insult to his wife and son, another betrayal to their memory. All the doors lead back to not Vivian, but *her*. Maizie.

They married young and he'd always been happy; their future seemed a sun-dappled road with children, and holidays, and playgrounds. Laughter. She had kind eyes and a dry humor and he didn't know when she was joking in half of their conversations, and that made her a source of endless fascination. They had dated for months before they found themselves in a place where sex might even be an option—their natural prudishness, the vagaries of college roommates, their driven schedules. When he entered her the first time it was as if he were an infinitesimal speck upon the ocean of her body. He was overwhelmed at the pleasure of that oblivion.

And still, his mind churns. Away from her. Toward not Vivian but Harlan Parker, born Springfield, Missouri, 1898, son of Frances and Tom Parker. Father died young, and his mother when he was a teen or preteen—Cromwell could not recall exactly—leaving his older, married sister to manage the family home and what little land they had. Trundles east to university at fourteen, a prodigy student at Washington and Lee, quite a hand at music and in particular piano; at seventeen found passage to Britain to join the RAF against his professors' wishes. When the Brits found he was too tall to fit in a cockpit, he joined the men in the trenches of the Somme, crawling over gut-shot dead men entombed in mud and crying for their mothers in English and Dutch, French and German. Hiding from errant clouds of phosgene gas. Fruiting mold on his clothes and in the trenches. Away from the front lines in 1918—two years at war—after being shot in the thigh. He recuperated and, two years after the war was won, tramped halfway across Europe. Wrote a memoir of the Great War and his travels that found some minor success, notable for its fascination with the lot of the common people—the *volk,* from which their department derived its name, the laborers and workers, the downtrodden and disenfranchised—and there took down the words of the German and Austrian folk songs he came across in his travels. Once home, he turned his travel journals into a more scholarly work: *From Cradle to Song: The Teutonic Musical Tradition.* Wrote a series of obscure books on American folk music, and the chautauqua history. Sometime in the thirties, Harlan accepted a commission of ethnomusicology with the Library of Congress to document and index folk music across Appalachia, the Mississippi Delta, and the Ozarks. And there his story ended. He abruptly abandoned his commission. He retired to his sister's Springfield home to live out the rest of his days, never to be seen again.

Viv shifts her legs and observes her movement's registration on Cromwell. It is subtle but still there, and must show on his face. He wonders if his self-contempt also registers.

Parker, a legend. Viv purses her lips, in anticipation or nervousness, he cannot tell. Parker, the folklorist who went mad, who drank himself to oblivion, on the trail of some legendary song. She brushes a strand of hair from her neck. They sit looking at each other, leaving everything to be conveyed wordlessly, with twists of ring and shifting of legs. There is no part of Vivian that does not leave him ashamed. She is eye-sweet and soft to observe, but the guilt that comes with her is an erosion.

"I'm sorry," he says finally. "I don't know what's wrong with me."

Vivian stands and hesitates. She wants to touch him, he can see, but it would not be wise here. He wants to touch her too, but he feels as if his wife would appear in the door, white and openmouthed in silent accusal, gasping for air, holding their son, bleached of all his color. They were chalky white when he found them.

Now. He can't tell if she knows he's hard just talking to her. It has been weeks since he's had any release. He feels terrible for the desire, but he still feels it. But he will never sleep with her again. He can, at least, be faithful in his wife's death better than he was in her life.

"You've been through a lot, Rob," she says. "It's gonna take time."

"Yes," he says. "Of course. Thank you."

"I should go," she says. "I'll let Hattie know you're here." She leaves an invisible eddy of scent churning in the still air.

Cromwell closes his eyes and takes a deep breath, settles himself. He deletes emails, reading some, but mostly trashing automated reports, internal memos, department bulletins. He lets the fascination of work lure him away from the scent of Vivian.

Hattie appears shortly after. She sits in the seat Vivian just vacated. Is it warm still? He thinks of the uncomfortable experience of finding a toilet seat still warm from some other man's use. Women probably wouldn't find the warmth of a chair disgusting. They might find it pleasant. *He* might find it pleasant. His mind shifts, curiously; he's aware of its present disjointed state but can find no way to correct it. Is the seat still warm? Cromwell considers the differences between the two women's posteriors. Of course, he's examined Vivian's quite closely and with more than just eyes—alabaster and lunar, seat of pleasure, framed by rougher hands, worshiped by pink lips and tongue—but he can only imagine what Hattie's must be like. She's trim, though not fanatical about fitness; he sees her eating salad more often than sandwiches in the Library deli, but she joins in when they go drinking and seems to enjoy pizza as much as the next person. Whatever prolongs his callipygian rumination, it was never their bottoms that drew him to either of them. Though he's thinking about it now.

"How are you, Crumb?" Hattie asks. "You worried me after the funeral." She passes a hand over her face like a mime wiping away an expression.

"It's a lot to work through," he says. A single sob comes out of him, and then he stifles it. Where did that come from? Hattie rises and puts her hand on his, her darker one on his pale skin.

Contrast her smell to Vivian's. Easy to parcel out, really. Cinnamon on her breath from candy canes and Christmas so recent, perfume at her neck and lotion tinged with lilac on her hands. Why is it that he can sort out her scent so easily and Vivian's remains a jumble? And Maizie's? He's smelled her clothes, his son William's, trying to take in that molecular residue of them, to keep it with him always. He wasn't sure it worked.

Standing by him, she says, "You know we've got to stick together. I got you, Crumb. Whatever you need."

"Thank you," he says. In all ways but one he's more accessible to Hattie than he's ever been to Vivian. It doesn't make him feel better.

She sits back down.

"So, tell me about Matilda Parker's estate," he says.

"Oh, hell, Crumb," Hattie says, her face transforming. Work is the tether that holds them close. "This job is going to be crazy."

4

Cromwell: Springfield and the Parker Estate

They fly in to Saint Louis to rent an SUV for Hattie's gear. Cromwell watches the land pass beneath them through the airplane's window, the Gateway Arch a raised eyebrow of surprise at their approach, growing closer, and then diminishing as the plane lands at Lambert field. At the baggage claim, he helps Hattie with her Pelican cases full of microphones and cables, cameras and lenses and tripods. There is a problem at the rental car place, and Cromwell argues with the rental car attendant—a kind of centered wildness propelling him—until eventually they wheel a black Chevy Suburban around and load the cases and their luggage.

"This is so us. Feds," Hattie says, patting the hood before climbing into the driver's seat. When they first began working together at the Library of Congress, she was surprised when Cromwell insisted on taking the passenger seat, leaving her to drive. "Most men won't let a woman touch the wheel of their ride," she said.

He shrugged. "I'm your superior. I'm not going to chauffeur *you* around."

"That's racist," she said. "And still somehow chauvinistic." And then she laughed at his surprise and stammered apology.

They head south, watching rolling hills dusted in snow pass stoically by. Hattie searches the radio for music but, finding none to her tastes, eventually drives on in silence. Finally she says, "Thank god the woman didn't live in fucking Ferguson, Crumb," and he agrees with her. Though southern Missouri won't be any better, he tells her. She grunts, an obstinate look on her face, and keeps driving. Cromwell reads Harlan's World War I memoir and German songbook. He remembers mostly Parker's *West Africa to New Orleans: The Story of Jazz*. He's not read them in fifteen years, since he was working toward his doctorate. Miles pass; they are comfortable in each other's silence. Or each other's personal sounds. Hattie sings along lightly to some internal rhythm pounding within her like a dynamo. Cromwell raps his fingers on the back of his iPad as he reads, an unconscious movement. He might have put music aside, but it creeps in, unbidden.

In Springfield, they check into their hotel, an aging Holiday Inn off the interstate. In his room, he calls the executor of the Parker estate, who agrees to meet them at her house in the morning. They walk to a nearby Waffle House and order food, after he gives Hattie her per diem.

In the morning, the executor waits for them at the curb of the Parker home. Hattie wheels the Suburban into the driveway aggressively, grinning, and when they exit the vehicle, the surprise is clear on the executor's face. *Yes,* Cromwell thinks. *Feds.* He wishes he'd worn his sunglasses.

The executor gives a nervous smile as Cromwell introduces himself and Hattie. Her handshake is light, weak, shrinking. This is a strange job, a job where the government is the client and she doesn't know exactly how to act.

The woman—Sarah—leads them to the house. The yard is

neat, flat. The house itself is old, small, and possessed of a certain dignity that only old and well-maintained homes exhibit. The wraparound front porch has been painted in the last decade, as well as the façade. The roof is a stylish red metal, a newer sort that Cromwell has noticed even in his neighborhood in Alexandria.

Sarah unlocks the front door and lets them in and begs off for an appointment. Cromwell holds out his hand for the keys and after a moment's pause and an explanation of the alarm system along with the numeric code, she turns the keys over to him and departs. They enter. It's warm inside. The foyer smells fresh and clean. Sarah informed him in their correspondence that Matilda Parker died of pancreatic cancer, and was a youthful woman in demeanor and outlook, just turned sixty. She had never wed and had no progeny—the last of Harlan Parker's line. But Cromwell isn't concerned with the Parker descendant; the woman who died does not interest him in the slightest. It is her ancestor Cromwell's after.

"What do you bet that if she had an HD television, it's already gone?" Hattie asks him. They've made assays of bequeathed estates before, a handful of times, and there is always something missing once they arrive. A television, a radio or phone, a blank and unweathered patch on a wall. Jewelry, money, pharmaceuticals. Cromwell and Hattie are never the first on-site, and invariably, the baser aspects of human nature become manifest.

He doesn't take the bet.

Hattie sets up her camera and takes three-hundred-and-sixty-degree photographs of each room, moving from the foyer inward. One of her innovations, a photographic record of estates, has proven invaluable when cataloging. Hattie even promises, if they allot her the money for more gear, she can create a virtual reality record of estates, though Cromwell thinks that a bit excessive.

Cromwell wanders through the house. He finds a small downstairs library full of Grisham, Patterson, Evanovich, Connolly hardbacks, some leather-bound classics—Dickens, Faulkner, Hemingway, Maugham, Mitchell, Ruark, Steinbeck—and a nice set of encyclopedias. *I thought the Internet killed the encyclopedia business,* Cromwell thinks. *But those look brand-new.* He opens cabinets, bemused, looking for anything that might be related to Harlan Parker. In a living area, with a bare space on the wall where some sort of HD television used to be—*Hattie will be pleased her low opinion of humanity has been confirmed once more*—he finds what, when he was a child, his parents would have called a hi-fi cabinet. A long credenza-like bit of furniture, bracketed at the ends with tweed speakers, with a turntable seated in the center of the lush-stained wood, a long row of vinyl stored beneath. He flips on the power switch, and the console lights up in a lovely seventies-design user interface—glowing radio tuner, shining indicators for volume and record speeds. The speakers buzz slightly, then subside. He turns it off again, extinguishing the lights. Squatting, he riffles through the vinyl, looking for anything interesting, either personal or professional, but finds neither. He stands, dusts his pants, and moves on.

In the master bedroom, he stops. It's here he feels the weight of the house, its history. A simple enough room, queen bed with a lush, puffy comforter, bedside with elegant if not expensive lamps, a comfy divan in the spill of light from the windows that at Cromwell's house would probably be strewn with laundry but here is empty. It would be empty now at his home too, he realizes. Even a thousand miles away, he can feel it. That thin connection: a breach, an expansion, like gold beat into airy thinness. Mourning. His house stands empty and cold and silent and that's something he'll never be able to surmount. He feels as though he's shrinking, collapsing under the weight of Maizie's and William's deaths.

And the guilt that comes in the shape of a nude woman in a hotel room.

The closet is full of a woman's clothing, from T-shirts to formal wear, coats and sweaters, slacks and skirts and long dresses. In the chest of drawers, underwear and socks, nightclothes and scarves. On the carpeting, he sees the vacuum marks. A sense of dislocation. He's done this before, and recently, the sorting and taxonomy of the belongings of the dead. For Maizie's things, her sister collected almost everything he did not want. And of his son, William, all of his things remained. That was a separation Cromwell was not ready to face.

She lived and died in these rooms, he thinks. The smell of the space is fresh, but there's a hint of decay underneath. Maybe, when the cancer worsened, they moved her to hospice. Or hospice came here to wait breathlessly for her to die. In the trash, there's an empty pill bottle. In the bathroom, the medicine cabinet has been emptied. No one has disturbed her jewelry box on the chest of drawers; its insides glint gold and silver. Behind the bathroom door, a robe, a whiff of rosewater.

Eventually, he'll have to deal with the estate sale planner, to turn all of this, a woman's life and clothes and house, into money for the Library. For now, he moves on.

The kitchen is plain, if well loved. A cacophony of pans and skillets hang from a suspended cast-iron rack over an island butcher block. Potted herbs crowd the windowsill—thyme, oregano, sage. Cromwell plucks a sprig of thyme and rubs it in his hands, letting the smell of spring and warmer times expand in the still space of the kitchen. He closes his eyes, holds his hands to his nose, inhaling deeply. Once when William was five, Cromwell remembers, they passed a towering summer bush of rosemary during a walk through the neighborhood and Cromwell plucked a sprig and rubbed it between his palms like a man using a stick to start a fire and then placed his hands under his son's nose and watched the perception of the scent creep into his boy's expression, a blooming wonder, followed by joy. William held his hand as they walked and kept drawing it to his face, breathing it in. His sweet boy.

Cromwell keeps his eyes closed for a long while. When he opens them, he lets the mangled sprig fall to the floor.

He unlocks the door from the kitchen leading to the backyard. He moves to stand on the grass. Behind the house, a thicket of trees, all denuded of leaves, and beyond, a neighborhood creek. There's still snow on the ground under the bare branches. In summer, Cromwell thinks, the air would be full of noise—the creak and cascading hiss of foliage swaying in the breeze; crickets; cicadas; cardinal songs; the cries of boys playing Wiffle ball in the street, maybe, or touch football, bright voices calling victory or outrage; dogs barking in the distance; the whir of a leaf blower; the diminishing roar of a plane full of people flying far away.

There's a separate garage. More than a shed, less than an outbuilding. Cromwell finds the key that opens the side door on the ring he was handed. An unstained and relatively new lawn mower and Weed Eater, two brooms, various rakes and hoes, a snarl of bungee cords, empty liquor-store boxes, milk crates. A workbench with a toolbox; mason jars full of nails, screws, nuts, and bolts; green nylon rope; a glue gun; shears; hedge trimmers. A Subaru station wagon is in the garage, well maintained but at least twenty years old. His hands find a light switch, illuminating the space. There's another door, with many deadbolts, paint scaling in tessellated patterns, leading to what seems to be a back room.

He opens the door, revealing an empty space with an old desk, an office chair ringed in moldering stacks of handwritten sheet music, yellowed and illegible. On the walls, a guitar, a dulcimer, a banjo. All gray, weathered with time and the corrosive effects of a drafty, uninsulated room. Cromwell takes down the banjo, finds there are no strings, and the fretboard is rough to his touch.

Someone has spent time here, he knows, long stretches of it. Maybe years. But that was many decades before. It has the haunted feel of a living area, forgotten and repurposed to something else.

The desk is empty, covered in dust. He doesn't trust the chair enough to sit, and it would besmirch his trousers, anyway. The far wall is packed high with old newspapers and the offal of an old house. Broken wicker chairs, empty crates, plastic tubs full of moth-eaten clothes, bags of mulch, empty pots, broken and shade-less lamps.

His phone chirrups. Hanging the banjo back on the wall, he shrugs the phone from his pocket and looks at the text—*Found smpin. Upstairs.*

Phone in hand, he snaps a picture of the bare room and goes back inside.

"Crumb, this is a straight trip," Hattie says when he finds her upstairs. "Look at this." She points to a looming armoire of dark-stained wood near flush with the ceiling. Cromwell opens the doors and looks inside. The reek of mothballs overwhelms him. Winter coats spanning decades of styles.

"She didn't have good fashion sense?" he asks.

"Around back," she says.

Cromwell moves to the side of the armoire and places his eye to the gap between the dark, massive furniture and the wall. There's a glint of metal and hinges.

"I was taking three-sixty-degree photographs of these two bedrooms and realized something was off. Looked in the hall for a closet or maybe a door or stairwell to the attic to explain the space between rooms. I'm good with figuring out spaces, you know?" She raps the wall with her knuckle. "There's a void back there with no entrance."

5

Cromwell: Introducing Stagger Lee

It takes both Cromwell and Hattie to move the armoire. The effort leaves gouges in the stained hardwood floor, a negligence Cromwell would normally feel great shame for. But this is why he's come, for whatever is back there.

A door, with a single padlock on a bracket. Cromwell goes to the garage and retrieves a hammer. He rips the hasp from the wall, wondering who might've thought it would stop anyone.

"Why the hell would they just put a padlock on the door?" Hattie asks. "You went through that like shit through a goose."

"Nice," Cromwell says. Hattie's exclamations are always fecund. "Yes, just a padlock wouldn't have stopped anyone who wanted to get in there." He shrugs. "Maybe it was to keep herself out of it."

"That doesn't make sense. Lock up a room just because you don't want to go in it." She brightened. "Maybe this place is haunted." She pats her camera bag. "I'm gonna be rich, Crumb."

He does not smile. "I don't think she wanted to keep herself out of here. I think she just wanted to make herself feel better about whatever was in here."

Hattie shakes her head, not understanding. He isn't sure he understands, either.

There's no doorknob, and at some point in the house's long history, the room—including the door—was painted, more than once, effectively cementing the door shut. Cromwell feels his impatience rise, full-throated. He wedges the hammer's claw into the seam of paint at the edge of the door and applies his strength. The wood creaks, a ripping sound tears through the room, and the door opens. Stale air pours out.

Hattie grabs a lamp from a sideboard table, drags it to its power cord's extent—right in the doorway—and turns it on, illuminating the room beyond.

It's near empty, Cromwell sees. A small bedroom at one time, maybe. A nursery, never used. There are no coverings on the bare walls, nor any pictures or photos. The window has been boarded over. There is, simply, what looks like a large filing cabinet of indeterminate age, a lidded crate, and an oversized wooden turntable with an oddly shaped stylus arm, bulbous at the pivot and the end.

"Smells like an old man's taint in here," Hattie says.

"How would you know, exactly, what an old man's taint smells like?" Cromwell says.

"Crumb, that's a door you *do not* want to open," Hattie responds.

It's an unusual intimacy, but the anticipation of what's to come has him vulnerable to innuendo. With Viv, he cannot exactly piece together all the little moments that led to what they eventually became. He cannot piece together all the little moments that led to what Maizie and William became, either. He thought of himself as happily married. When he looked at himself, in the abstract, he was a good and faithful husband who loved his wife. Their story was a story of faithfulness. Until Vivian. He can't remember all the little pieces falling into place, and then falling into bed with her.

They'd been in Boston, at a convention about using the Markov model to categorize digital sound files. Rooms on different floors. No coworkers other than just them. There'd always been flirtation. There'd always been some attraction, but nothing serious. After all, he was a happily married man. He wore a ring, and so did Vivian, and that made it okay, in ways he didn't understand. She would not leave her husband and he would not leave his wife. It was compartmentalized and separate. She had her George, and he had Maizie. And then they had each other, before he could understand what was happening. It was so easy. *Why shouldn't I have this?* he thought. *It doesn't lessen my love for my wife.* But he didn't think how the betrayal would eat at the fabric between them.

He is at a loss when he closes his eyes or thinks on anything too long. Except for this, this door. The old, rust-colored Master Lock. Work.

Hattie leaves, returning momentarily with another lamp taken from a bedroom. She pauses before plugging it into an outlet, saying, "Let's hope this doesn't burn down the house. These fixtures look midcentury at best."

The light blooms, casting ellipses of illumination on the wall that fold at the ceiling. Cromwell moves to examine the record player. "SoundScriber," he says. He lifts the stylus arm from its cradle. "No needle. Look here." He points to the back of the old device. "Vacuum tubes. And inputs."

Hattie moves around to see and whistles. "Shit, those are XLR jacks. Crazy we're still using the same old-ass tech today as they did . . . whenever the fuck they locked this shit up."

"More important," Cromwell says, "he *recorded* with this thing."

"Cutting discs? Vinyl?" Hattie asks.

"No," he says. "They were either coated aluminum or acetate."

Hattie opens the chest, coughing a little with the rising dust. "Here's why we came, Crumb." Records in white sleeves, each sleeve covered in writing. Cromwell picks up the top one and tilts it toward the lamp.

"'Lucius Spoon, Cummins State Farm. Arkansas. July 13, 1938.' 'Harlan Parker' written at the bottom." He squints at the faint pencil handwriting. "It says, 'Stagolee.' And some lyrics."

"What?"

"Songs," Cromwell says. "Songs."

Hattie picks up a disc, reads the writing after a moment of puzzling out the script. "'Everybody Talking About Heaven Ain't Going There,'" she says. "'Vester White, Alabama.' Different date."

"Careful with that," Cromwell says. "Acetate degrades and the coating on aluminum discs does, too."

"Watch out yourself." Hattie cuts him a withering look. "I'm not going to drop it, Crumb. Chill."

They place the records gingerly back in the crate and shut the lid. "We'll need to get this downstairs, so we can use the hi-fi."

"Right, I'll see what sort of audio outputs it has. If it's something I can route through my mixer into the TASCAM. Failing that, we could just pick up one of those cheap turntables, or I could just mic the room and we get a field recording and then maybe a better one back in DC."

"No cheap turntable. I'd prefer the highest-quality recording here," Cromwell says. "I'll buy it if I have to, on my own dime. The Library will reimburse me." He says this, doubts it is true, and yet really doesn't care. With all the darkness that has come into his life, this death and bequest mean grant money, papers, a lecture circuit maybe. The Library might be the intendee, but Cromwell is the beneficiary. This could be the work of the rest of his life. A hundred, two hundred, bucks on a turntable with a good needle will be nothing in the face of that. He rubs his chin. "I'm nervous even moving this crate downstairs. I have no idea how fragile these discs are."

And there are still the filing cabinets. He opens the top drawer, finds it empty, save for a few brittle, brown accordion folders. One holds what looks like receipts, faded and yellowed. In the bottom drawer, there's a ledger book, blue fabric cover, corners and spine wrapped in leather.

Cromwell opens the ledger. *Harlan Parker, Alexandria, Virginia. June 6, 1938. By commission of the Library of Congress, to make assay of the secular folk musics of West Virginia, Kentucky, Tennessee, including the Mississippi River Valley, and the Ozark Mountains.* Riffling the pages, there's a blur of the same tight, cramped hand that was on the record sleeves. *"Stagolee," or "Stackalee," or "Stagger Lee" has a different modality for every mind and mouth that renders it, I've come to learn. Whatever morphology I've found, I can't help but wonder if there's not some ur-version of the song, without all the myriad variations . . .*

"I'm going to get a turntable. I don't want to risk any loss of music." He makes his decision. "We'll have to record these in here."

6

Cromwell: Smoot Sawyer

By the time he returns from Best Buy with a turntable, Hattie has converted the hidden room into a passable workplace. She's found card tables and folding chairs in a dormer storage space, and a candle from some other part of the house. For the old-man-taint smell, no doubt.

Cromwell unpacks the turntable—he spent more than he intended, over four hundred dollars, enough that his credit card was declined and he had to call the Citibank robots and listen to menu after droning menu until he could talk with a real person and fix the issue. He promised himself that, afterward, he'd ship the turntable home.

He exhumes it from the Styrofoam and plastic wrapping. The odd, unpleasant scent of polymers and chemical catalyzers trapped within the box since its construction in China fill the space, vying with the scented candle and the mold of the room. He keeps all of the packaging neat and in the box for the return trip. The card table is too unsteady for his taste, so he takes the wooden bedside table from the bedroom and places the player on top of that, instead. He lightly grips the device's plinth and gives it a wiggle, as if trying to shake it from its seat. It remains firm. Hattie runs an XLR cable from the rear of the turntable to her mixer, and another from the mixer into her TASCAM digital recorder. She stops.

"Crumb! I almost forgot," she says. "Learned this when those twelve Woody Guthrie acetates turned up in a garage sale." She roots around in her Pelican case. "Two-millimeter sapphire stylus." She holds up a plastic container. "Use the needle you have there and you'll risk delaminating the whole disc." She withdraws something from the case, approaches the turntable, and detaches the current needle and attaches a new one. She returns to her TASCAM recorder. It reminds Cromwell of the old tricorders from *Star Trek* episodes, fitting neatly in Hattie's palm. Hattie withdraws a Bluetooth speaker out of her Pelican case, thumbs it on, and then runs a miniplug from the auxiliary jack to the turntable's headphone port. Her own headphones, she plugs into the mixing board and hangs around her neck.

"Let's play one so I can get levels first, and test the TASCAM," she says.

Cromwell places his seat and the turntable next to the record crate in a bit of proprietary dominance, sits down, and swivels his legs toward the crate. Hattie withdraws what looks like a tissue box, but pulls out a pair of white nitrile gloves and tosses them to Cromwell. He puts them on, his attention focused on the contents of the crate. To his eye, there are at least eighty records within, all vertically stored. He does not know how many might be deteriorated or delaminated, but despite the moldy smell of the room, he cannot see any wear or decay within the crate other than a brittleness and yellowing of the record slips. He pulls a disc from the far end and checks the date. *August 25, 1938.* He replaces it with a level of reverence that scientists reserve for handling sealed test tubes of contagious pathogens and withdraws a second record from the opposite end of the crate. He inspects the faint scrawl of timeworn pencil writing on the white record slip.

"'June 8, 1938. Smoot Sawyer, Buckhannon, West Virginia,'" Cromwell reads.

Withdrawing the record, he feels the faint texture of grooves on one side of the disc, but on the other side, it is smooth as plastic. Unrecorded. Possibly the old acetates were recordable on only a single side. He does not know—he will ask Hattie later. He takes a moment to allow his fingers to absorb that tactile sensation of handling the acetate. Hattie watches him with her earphones on, an eyebrow cocked. He feels good, at this moment. He feels like this is what he's supposed to be doing—he's worked for this, all his life, he endured what he's endured, and now he wants to remember this. Vivian is far away. Maizie and William, quiet now.

When he was young, he listened to vinyl records—Couperin and Vivaldi, Mozart and Beethoven, Debussy and Holst. He listened to Gregorian chants and choirs like Sounds of Blackness. He listened to the Staple Singers and Dolly Parton and musical soundtracks—*Gigi, The Sound of Music, Guys and Dolls, Brigadoon, The Wiz*. He listened to Led Zeppelin, Michael Jackson, Stevie Wonder and Prince, the Fat Boys and the Gap Band. Bob Dylan and the Beatles. The Who and Peter Frampton. All on vinyl. But that was so long ago. A lifetime. Yet the one thing that remained from that jumble of near-forgotten sound was the ritual of vinyl. The hushed withdrawal of the disc, holding the shining object up to the light to examine its surface, fearful of scratches. The placement and setting of the needle. The wash of music and the perusal of liner notes as the first stirrings of sound burst through the speakers.

Cassette tapes started the death of the ritual, and even before digital took over, compact discs had finished the job. But the ritual remains ingrained inside him. Cromwell's hands know it well.

He places the record on the turntable, engages the flywheel, and then carefully—hunched over so that his eyeline settles at record and needle level—lowers the tone arm to the acetate recording.

There's a thin crackling, and sound begins to emanate from the speakers.

That thang takes down mah voice?

It records sound waves and etches those waves into the coating on the disc as it revolves.

Waves. Like the sea? Been there once, got a mouthful of the stuff and was like to die.

Not that kind of wave, sir.

And it hears me?

Every bit of what we're saying now. Any sound this [bamf] picks up—your voice, my voice, the guitar—anything loud enough to be sensed by this microphone gets translated into vibrations and etchings. I will play it for you when we are finished.

And you want singing from 'round these parts?

That's the idea. Secular songs. Local music, not church music. Not religious. Songs that might be typical of this area. They will be stored in the Library of Congress.

Seck-ular, you say? And I'll be famous?

That is not probable, Mister Sawyer. But it's not out of the question, either. Let's try a song and then we'll see about fame and fortune.

Well, I don't know 'bout that, as we're a god-fearin' kind of folk.

Religious music is well documented and formalized, Mister Sawyer. We would like to learn about the songs outside of the influence of the church. [Baying of dog and a woman's voice bidding it hush]

We're god-fearin'.

[Fifteen seconds of silence]

You say you have a little tobacky? Maybe I could remember if'n I had some of that.

[Rustling]

That's better.

So, Mister Sawyer, do you think you could play "Stagger Lee"? We'd like to start off with that.

"Stackalee"? I think I could give 'er a go, but all I got is this here guitar for 'company.

That's fine, Mister Sawyer, just fine.

Cromwell looks at Hattie. She's intent on the mixing board but notices his attention and, raising her gaze to his, gives him a thumbs-up. The audio levels are acceptable. He turns his attention back to the shimmering disc locked in rotation and then to the white record slip. *Smoot Sawyer, Buckhannon, West Virginia. "Stagger Lee," "No More Hiding in the Valley."* Parker's handwriting is a scrawl, but it's strangely quite legible to him.

Faint strains of a guitar fill the room, an atonal buzz steaming from sizzling bacon grease. Smoot—*Mister Sawyer*, Cromwell thinks—plays with an aggressive walking bassline, answered by brisk strumming on the higher strings so that despite the remove of years, the tinniness and crackling of the recording, the song of a man who died decades before is heard once more by the living.

Come all y'all sporty fellers,
Come take a list' to me.
Got a tale here from the tellers
Of that bad, bad man,
Stackalee.

A short flourish of strumming with the alternating bass notes, Cromwell hears, picked with the man's thumb. He went to enough bluegrass performances as an undergraduate to have seen this style of older mountain picking—rough fretting alternating with rhythmic strokes. Cromwell is somewhat familiar with the song, though his familiarity is of the two dominant modalities— the Caucasian bad-man ballad made popular by Pete Seeger and Dave Van Ronk, and the joyous Negro Southern rhythm and blues song popularized by Lloyd Price and countless other sons and daughters of the South. The blues version is preeminent in modern culture, though Cromwell finds himself fascinated by Smoot Sawyer's version of "Stagger Lee," which musically falls in line with the Caucasian traditions but lyrically (from what he can remember from his early days studying ethnomusicology) falls somewhere in between the white and black versions of the song. In his mind, he cobbles together an image of Smoot the man—*What kind of name is Smoot? Surely his parents were not that unkind*—an image that is pure fabrication: overalls over a khaki button-down shirt; a thin, clean-shaven yet haggard face; white but nut-brown from the sun on his neck and forearms; lean from the daily toil of growing corn, or mining, or any of a hundred other demanding physical labors a man named Smoot in West Virginia would be heir to.

Sawyer begins singing once more. The old story, Stagger Lee and Billy Lyons gambling—not playing dice in this version, but playing cards in a sporting club, oblivious to the "perfumed ladies" all around them, focused on the game. Stagger Lee loses his money and his hat; Billy Lyons taunts him, wearing it. Stagger Lee goes home to get his "forty-one"—not a caliber of gun that Cromwell is aware of, though it's within the realm of possibility, as he's not much for firearms. Billy Lyons begs for his life, telling Stagger Lee about his wife and family and how they're waiting at home. Stagger Lee laughs; they are in a house of prostitution, and he's talking about his wife and children? He shoots Billy Lyons through the gut; the bullet passes through the man and shatters the glass in the barkeep's hands. The whores scatter.

The sheriff and his deputies come to arrest Stagger Lee, but they're too scared and argue among themselves as to who should go into the sporting club to get him.

> *The big ole Sergeant Frisbee come into the bar,*
> *Saying, "Stackalee, you done killed a man,*
> *We ain't going to go too far.*
> *Come on down to the station,*
> *You better come along with me."*
> *That bad, bad man,*
> *Stackalee.*

They take him to the station, and in the collapsed-time of music, by the next verse he's before the judge. And by the verse after that, he's to be hanged. *Not too far off from how the judgments of black men happened back then*, Cromwell thinks. *Things haven't changed much. We're not far from Ferguson.*

> *Standing on the gallows,*
> *His head held way up high,*
> *Twelve o'clock they kilt him,*
> *We was all glad to see him die.*
> *That bad man,*
> *Stackalee.*

It's curious, Cromwell notes, that at the end of the song—a song that has been sung from a remove—Smoot inserts himself in the last couplet. *We was all glad to see him die.* We. Glad to see a black man put to death. That bad man, Stackalee.

There's silence on the recording and then Harlan Parker's voice sounds amid the crackle and hiss.

Very good, Mister Sawyer. Do you know any other verses of this song? Verses after the last one?

Don't rightly know what you're talkin' 'bout, mister.

Verses that continue the story of Stagger Lee?

Continue the story? We're a god-a-fearin' people, we don't sing no songs 'bout that kind of trash.

But you have heard other verses of "Stagger Lee"?

You ain't got enough shine or tobacky for that. How 'bout "No More Hiding in the Valley"?

All right, Mister Sawyer, that sounds just fine.

Smoot Sawyer launches into another song, very similar in structure to the first, about a boy chasing a girl all over the "holler." Once he catches her, they go and pick flowers from her mother's grave. Cromwell scrambles for a notepad and pen from Hattie's case, and takes down the name of the song and the key and a rough guess at the chord progression. He writes, *"No More Hiding in the Valley." Unknown song and verses.* Then: *"Stagger Lee," extra verses?* At the end of the record, Cromwell uses the lever that lifts the tone arm. Hattie thumbs the TASCAM's menu, retrieving the audio file. She hands him the headphones, he places them over his ears, and the crackle and hiss come through. The recording is not perfect, but it is a perfect capture of the degraded audio of Harlan Parker's recording. Cromwell knows either he or Hattie can batch-process the files once they are back at the offices, removing some noise, and play with the levels. But they definitely have it.

"What was all that about continuing the story of Stackalee?" Hattie asks. "They hanged him."

"And were glad to see him die," Cromwell says, shaking his head. He lifts Harlan Parker's field journal and opens it. "Hopefully, this will give us more answers to what Parker was looking for."

7

Harlan Parker: The Field Journal

Property of
HARLAN PARKER
If found please return to:
212 KENMORE LN
APARTMENT 2
ALEXANDRIA, VIRGINIA

*By commission of the Library of Congress, to make assay of
the secular folk musics of West Virginia, Kentucky, Tennessee,
including the Mississippi River Valley, and the Ozark Mountains.*

JUNE 6, 1938

The commission has begun, and not a day too soon; I was desperate short of money. The advance on my last book is long gone and there are no royalties forthcoming. I have not had letter or telegraph from my agent in months. I am worried that he's closed up shop and moved on to some other profession selling something that people actually have the money to buy. Nowadays, most folk don't have the extra income to spend on print unless it's a newspaper.

Everywhere you look, there are bedraggled and sad men, down on their luck, hand out for a dime. Without my good fortune in securing this, in a month I would be much like every other Joe, destitute in the breadline or waiting for a tin of cabbage soup.

Even with the money from the Library of Congress, I will have to camp and sleep under the stars more than sleep under a roof. I have sent letters to friends in Knoxville, Memphis, and Greenville and to the administrators of the Federal Writers' Project in hopes I might be able to bed down in comfort. The Darcy Arkansas Folk Society has promised quite a hospitable stay.

I have also made contact with Edmund Whitten, who will be coming with me. Indeed, when I saw him and mentioned that I would require a driver and all-around assistant (and there was a stipend allotted for the job) he jumped at the opportunity. A good man, Bunny, and one who deserves a better shake at life than he's got since we returned from Europe. The hard erosion of time and fortune should have a wearing effect on ideals, I would think, but Bunny remains as loyal and enthusiastic as the young man I knew so long ago. There was a time we did not think we would see our twentieth birthdays, as his is very close to mine. We are of an age. In the Somme, scurrying through the trenches, caked in mud, mold growing on our uniforms, he often was the only voice that kept me from going mad, throwing away my Enfield, and squirming out and up through the mud into the light, in the sights of the Germans. Why I should have fared better since the war than Edmund remains a mystery to me. Maybe because he tends toward red—an admiration of Trotsky and having worked for the *Daily*

Worker—which concerns me. I wonder if I can steer him away from that on this trip.

I've settled my affairs the best I am able and tomorrow morning we shall meet at the Library of Congress to collect our vehicle and recording equipment. Just today, I received a letter from John Lomax, the senior fellow at the Library of Congress, instructing me to ask each subject to record "Stagger Lee"! As a point of commonality, since it spans both white and black cultures. As if that were not my goal to start with, though they hardly could know that.

I am quite eager to begin and shall have trouble sleeping tonight. I have never relished the idea of remaining in Washington, DC, too long. Bad memories from my youth, after Mother died. There are ghosts here. Ghosts of myself. Ghosts of people I knew. Ghosts of memory, of my time at the Harrow Club, a performing servant for rich men. I am happy to put its humid streets behind me.

I need a drink and now that I have the money, I shall find one. It has been too long.

8

Harlan Parker: A Dream of Mother Chautauqua

JUNE 7, 1938

This morning, we collected the recording device—the Sound-Scriber, as its small metal plaque bolted onto a wooden side proudly proclaimed—along with its inordinately heavy Edison batteries, the microphone, the mixer, and the gas-operated generator, the "genny," or so the khaki-clad technician at the Library of Congress called it, as he demonstrated its usage and the process of charging the batteries. All of this we managed to fit within the used Studebaker that Harold Spivacke, our direct superior at the Library, had procured for us for a mere ninety-seven dollars (which is unsurprising, considering its condition: its interior worn and smelling of cigars and grease fire, its Motorola radio silent and unusable—the tubes blown out, the technician tells us). The recording device, however, fits easily in the massive trunk, and the batteries and crates of virgin acetate discs take up most of the backseat. There is room to spare for our personal bags and varied and sundry other gear.

We were on the road before noon.

More than two hundred miles before dark.

Hot, even in June. Sweat beading in the interior of the car, Bunny cursing at the stiff gears and clutch. The Studebaker has a definite pull to the right. Bunny and I discussed the current state of affairs, and caught up.

"After my divorce—" Bunny said.

"Divorce? I didn't know you had even been married!" I said.

"Evelyn was too radical even for me," he said.

"How so?"

"After I was canned from the *Daily Worker*—can you believe that? The mugs, laying off workers from a Communist rag! Well, Evelyn was hot to go to Michigan to rally the black workers outside of Detroit in unionizing efforts. I was not as hot."

"That doesn't sound good."

"It wasn't. So she found another fella that had the same sort of vim and vigor for Dostoyevsky."

I laughed. "I much prefer Pushkin," I said. He smiled but kept his eyes on the road.

"And you?" Bunny said eventually. "Lost track of you for a while."

"Traveled some. Living off the money I made from one book, trying to write another book."

"I heard you were in North Africa. Morocco," he said, chuckling. "Your love of the tribal rhythms of the dark continent and all that." He waved his hand, as if indicating a small thing and not the massiveness of Africa, its vast and disparate peoples, and their innumerable cultures and musics.

"Don't call it that," I said sharply. "You're showing your ignorance. It's not something I'd spend years studying if I thought it a trifle."

"I don't have any problem with it. I love swing," he said. "And your time in New Orleans?" He was asking about my trip to the delta. This is how Bunny talks—a bright but restless mind, hopping all over the garden of thoughts. He laughed. "Never had absinthe. You ever try that down there? I hear it's the only place you can, in all of the States."

"Drank a whole bottle trying to bring on the hallucinations. The Green Fairy. All I got was a bad hangover and an empty wallet."

"I hear the women down there are not to be believed."

"It's hot, and everything is sticky," I said, and left it at that.

It is lovely being with Bunny again, and too easy to fall into the patterns of soldiers' talk. Together we have faced horrors, and so together we are used to normalcy in the face of the strange, the bizarre. Even the hostile.

We drove on into the night, until we found a remote barn somewhere around Morgantown, West Virginia, and it is there I write this, by the light of an oil lantern. It's comfortable in the Studebaker's cabin, and I can stretch out here and sleep on the front seat if I draw in my feet some. Bunny is sacked out in a sleeping bag on the ground in a moldy and graying pile of hay, which, at least, is dry. I must join him in slumber soon. Yet I am keyed up and want a drink. I overindulged last night and the only thing for it is more, but there are no bars or liquor stores I know of within a hundred miles. Tomorrow, we will have to find a town large enough for one. The Lomaxes, in our correspondence, inform me that tobacco and liquor are a necessity for the getting of recordings. It will take whiskey to pry the songs from them. It will not hurt me at all to join in, I imagine, once the SoundScriber is cutting.

I cannot sleep.

I tried, truly I did. And I did nod off and dream, for a short while. The same dream. I was just a boy. Mother and I were at our last chautauqua again and there was a festive air and she had already drunk a bottle of wine and we entered the mouth-shaped entrance at the tent grounds, a Rabelaisian touch that some organizer whimsically threw together. Mother was arm in arm with her new beau—the tall, pale Matthew Insull—and he gave me a dime to spend however I wished. I ran off to watch the Negro minstrels and dancers. I had grown up attending the Mother Chautauqua in New York, and that tradition had continued and spread all over the country into massive affairs with multiple tents, some featuring speakers conversing on the history of agriculture, theology, philosophy, the natural sciences. Finding myself there in the landscape of dreams did not surprise me. All emotion was blanketed, lethargic. I moved like I would swimming through molasses. Or sinking in water.

The minstrels arrayed themselves on the rough pine-planked stage and sang and danced by inconstant kerosene light and gave me peppermint candies after I clapped and offered up my dime. They played "Precious Lord" and "Take My Hand" and "Let My Heart Catch on Fire," and when they saw I was becoming tired of spirituals (for I have never, even as a lad, been much fond of organized religion), they launched into more bumptious and robust songs. It was night and couples swayed in the darkness, some kissing immodestly, but most holding hands. White people, white faces, come to see the Southern minstrels. The songs swelled. Some made me blush. Some made me want to dance. Some of the black men and women came down from the raw pinewood stage past the kerosene footlights and surrounded me, laughing. The women clasped me to their breasts and kissed me and pulled me onto the stage, where they danced and held my hands. I was just a boy. Moving through song after song, they laughed and imitated Bill Monroe's twang, as he was the featured artist. It quieted and a kind black man sat me down on a bench on the side of the stage as if I were some prince—an honored guest—and then from somewhere behind him came a simple voice ringing out.

A guitar joined him, then a tambourine. And I heard it for the first time.

"Stagger Lee."

I do not know his name, the man who sang it. But I remember his abject face as he came into the kerosene light of the stage, his voice rising and falling. He had burnished skin and bright eyes and was dressed in a dapper suit. As he sang, somehow in the fabric of dream, I knew my mother was drowning, swimming drunk in the nearby lake. She sucked water into her desperate lungs as the story of a bad man played out.

And in my dream, I became Stagger Lee. I shot a man and was hanged. I *have* shot men, though. Bunny killed men as well. At Reims. At Ypres. We both wore uniforms when we did and that guilt does not weigh me down so heavy. Yet I have bad dreams. As I gasped for breath, my mother went below the water. As I thrashed at the end of a rope, she clawed toward the surface of Lake Chautauqua, the moon a sliver of shifting refraction above her. Was that the silhouette of a man? Was Insull with her?

Stillness and then cold. An inhuman hand pressing down, holding me there, below. A voice.

I found myself in Hell. I have seen its mark on the living world, I know it well: The wrecked and body-strewn warrens of the Somme. The muddy battlefields of Europe. When I walk in dreams, I can recognize it. Hell is not full of fire and burning pits like you usually hear. Hell is cold, a maze of rotten trenches.

But Hell is also brightly lit, an office, and tastes of bitter coffee while some man, a man in a uniform, puts his hand on my shoulder and says, "I'm sorry about your mother. We've contacted your grandparents and they are coming for you. Can you describe this man? His name is Insull? Can you tell me what he looked like, son?"

I woke, sweating. This summer it will be too hot to sleep without corn whiskey or drink. I will find some today.

It's been years, obviously, but the dream haunts me.

I think about that song all too often.

Maybe I can sleep now, in these few short hours before dawn. Today, I will find alcohol.

And another version of "Stagger Lee."

They say every day is a new beginning. But I think they mean there are no endings, just beginnings. And that is a comforting thought.

JUNE 8, 1938

We found a man named Anderson who sold us a hay-filled croker sack with ten mason jars full of moonshine, far back in the overhung hills. It came dear enough, despite prohibition's end—the Twenty-First Amendment does not quite yet have even distribution across West Virginia. Once the money was exchanged, Anderson was quite content to take us to Mister "Smoot" Sawyer.

Smoot Sawyer was a thickset older white man, stout and ruddy faced, with arms like trees. He had the sort of solidity that comes with a highly physical life of manual labor. I feared that if he gripped my hand and squeezed with some intention, I might be handicapped or rendered feeble.

He sat as if waiting for us on the front porch of his log cabin in a thick copse of the unkempt forests of "West Virginny," a rifle close enough to grasp, smoking a corncob pipe. A nervous female hand pulled back calico drapes and let them fall quickly. A spotted hound lay near him, and I soon realized the dog's back legs were paralyzed.

Anderson, who was slightly intoxicated at this point from drinking some of his own stock, said, "Mister Smoot, got some fellers here from the gubmint, want to record some songs."

"The gubmint?" Smoot said, hand subtly but surely reaching for his gun. "The gubmint's gettin' into the music business?"

I slowly explained to Mister Sawyer the mission of the Library of Congress, and the Division of Music, and gave a perfunctory overview of its history. He seemed to have trouble understanding that we wanted regional or songs more recently crafted, outside of the public purview. But once we presented a mason jar of moonshine and a pack of cigarettes, he readily enough played for us.

It took an hour to move the SoundScriber to the porch (Sawyer would not allow us to record inside his cabin), attach the batteries, and cut a test acetate—our first!—and prepare another twelve-inch for the songs.

I played the man back our test acetate, and the faint sounds of our conversation emanated what the SoundScriber had recorded. Smoot whistled, eyes large. "I ain't never heard a ghost before!" He laughed. The man had many questions about the device, and unfortunately took some of the short recording time asking them, on the first disc. I will transcribe them later, once I have world, enough, and time. Sawyer did, however, know a version of "Stagger Lee"—or "Stackalee," as he called it. He played an up-tempo version of that song and followed it with a colorful local ballad, "No More Hiding in the Valley."

It was an interesting modality of "Stagger Lee." When pressed about the later verses, the verses more infernal in nature, Sawyer begged off, proclaiming a sort of rustic righteousness that did not sit well with me, though I made no indication of it.

I played back the recording to Sawyer, who hooted and laughed and dusted his leg with his hat. "I'm fixin' to be a danged radio man, Lord help me!"

When asked if he knew other musicians we might record, he listed a couple near Pineville. I took down the names and Bunny and I made our adieus, dropped a very drunk Anderson back at his barbershop, and drove south.

We camped on the banks of the Guyandotte River. There was enough timber on the shores for a merry fire, and both Bunny and I sampled a fair bit of the moonshine to be tight enough for easy sleep, though my companion fell into slumber far before I did.

I write this now, weary, drunk, and ready for bed. Still, Smoot Sawyer's rendition of "Stagger Lee" peals in my head. But the forgotten verses sound as well, indistinct and veiled, and lead me on.

9

Harlan Parker: High Rank Summer

June 11, 1938

The people of Pineville were helpful and open about their local musicians and we recorded three men and one woman today. Jim and Mae Coats, a threadbare young white couple, more bone than meat, and newly married. Lovely harmonies, together and singly—both with the earnest, open faces of the young, though. With some regular meals, the brace of them would be very handsome and could turn some heads, but now, their complexions are sallow and they look unhealthy. Pellagra, maybe, though I saw no affliction of their skin. Neither knew any sort of verses of "Stagger Lee," but they sang a local song called "Mabel the Mule" and went on to render "No More Hiding in the Valley," "Buck Brush Parson," and "Thirty Silver Dollars." A stout fellow named Wilson Neale performed a quite lewd and bumptious song he called "Motter Fotter," though I'm unsure on the spelling. And a colorful character named Bash Bunks sang another version of "No More Hiding in the Valley" and an interesting version of "Mockingbird" that sounded more like an incantation than a lullaby (see acetate notes). Bash also gave us the names of five musicians "that knowed enough pickin' to be worth-a-while, I reckon." A good day and a good find was Mister Bunks.

It is hot, so very hot, and still early in the summer. At the five-and-dime in Burnsville, the thermometer read ninety-eight degrees. No telling how much water had already evaporated into the heavy, thick air. I've bought a metal five-gallon container for potable water, as we're likely to get dehydrated due to the physical labor of moving the SoundScriber to wherever we record. The device is quite unwieldy and weighs at least two hundred pounds; the Edison batteries, each of which is a hundred pounds; the folding chairs; the microphone; the cables; the whiskey—setting it all up is a labor and in the rising temperature, sweat not only beads, it pours. Bunny and I were absolutely sodden after setting up the SoundScriber first in a back room of a general store that I think doubles as a speakeasy and then in a barn. My shirt was drenched down to my trousers and undergarments. We'll have to stop somewhere tomorrow for laundry, unless we can camp near a creek.

I've also spent more of our money on tins of sardines and cans of beans, cigarettes, matches, soap, cloth towels, rope, clothespins. The vehicle is getting tight.

Now we're camped in a barn for the evening, with the farmer's permission. Bunny has walked into town; he was restless and possibly had a bit too much of the shine. I am with the Studebaker, as all of our gear is in it. Slept poorly last night, in the steaming darkness. Hopefully, I can sleep better tonight.

And not dream.

10

Cromwell: Remembrances of a Hotel Room

Crumb," Hattie says, looking at him. She's wearing a slightly worried expression. He looks up from the field journal, shaking his head. "Another record. It's getting late."

"This is bizarre. Parker's all over the place," Cromwell says, tapping the journal.

"How so?" Hattie asks.

"He goes from describing recordings to discussing his dreams. I knew his mother drowned when he was young, but it really did a number on him."

Hattie takes the journal and begins reading, her brow furrowed.

Cromwell stands and stretches. He exits the secret room, goes to the bathroom, urinates, and then washes his hands and face. He wipes his hands on a towel and blankly wonders who will wash it now that the inhabitant of the house is dead. Should he wash it? He holds it to his nose and smells the ghosted scent of detergent and thinks about the humdrum minutiae of a living house. Laundry. Trash. Dirty sinks and toilets. Leftovers crowding a refrigerator. The detritus of a family.

Maizie insisted on doing laundry; cooking and the management of the kitchen fell to him. "You don't know how to fold clothes," she said, smiling. "And you'll burn down the house with an iron." She took care of the bathrooms; he was tasked with the yard, the gutters, the windows. She dusted and fed the cat. He cleaned the litter box. The division of labor sorted through twelve years together, through college and after, during their young professional life, from apartment to condo to house. It was an undeniable progression, one his parents approved of. Cromwell was a man who would always do the right thing, whose life would unfold in predictable ways.

She would do the laundry but wanted him to help make the beds. The rustle of sheets ballooning over the mattress with a pop, caught in light from the window. A white bedroom, the color of purity. They would sleep with William between them, when he was younger and sick, baby breath sweet in Cromwell's nose, Maizie's gaze searching his face. "How did we deserve this?" she whispered.

"I don't know. Who deserves anything?"

"We do," she said, kissing her son's head. "We deserve this. *He* deserves this."

There are no endings, just beginnings, Parker said. That phrase sticks with Cromwell.

In the bedroom, he notices that the sun has fallen and realizes he's hungry. They worked through lunch. So easy to forget the demands of the body when the mind is otherwise engaged.

"Let's call it a day," he says to Hattie. She raises an eyebrow but doesn't protest. She sets down the journal and removes her earphones from her neck and places them in the Pelican case's padded interior. She sets the TASCAM to charge in the outer bedroom.

"It's bizarre," Hattie says. "These two men driving around,

sleeping in their car for the government, recording folk songs. Everything's so different now."

"Not that different, really," Cromwell says. "We're just better funded. At least this year."

Something bothers her, Cromwell can tell. He waits.

"No, this dude is weird. Like, he's got a hard-on for 'Stagger Lee.' And you know, Crumb, there's some super-racist versions of that little ditty."

"Sure, but that's what makes it an interesting study in ethno-musicology," Cromwell says. "There's always some dirty origin to most songs." He shrugs.

"No, that's not what I'm talking about," she says.

"What are you talking about, then?" he asks.

"I don't know. This room, the locked door, Parker's weird-ass dreams—something ain't right."

"You're right, I'm sure. Let's get some dinner, and then maybe we'll work on more of the acetates. Hopefully the journal will let us understand *what* exactly isn't right."

Her face is tight, lips pursed, but she nods and they stand and go downstairs and out to the car.

"How long do you think it'll take to get all the acetates digitized?" Cromwell asks.

"Couple more days, I'd say." She shrugs, climbing into the Suburban. "We can take as long as you want, if you . . ." She stops to think. "Need to draw it out. Can't be good going home to an empty—"

"No," Cromwell says. "Taxpayers' money and all that."

He didn't say that he was pretty sure there was no amount of time or distance that could change how he felt.

At the hotel, after a cheap dinner at the nearby Denny's, they agree that returning to digitize more recordings can wait until the morning and retire to their separate rooms.

For a long while, Cromwell lies in bed, silent, thinking of the oncoming springtime chores around their Alexandria home: Pruning the lilacs, cutting back the crape myrtles, mowing the yard. Weeding. Picking up the deadfall of winter. The long heat of summer rising, the distant sounds of people working on their lawns, the soothing buzz of mowers and the smell of cut grass. But that is a long time away. Summer used to carry the promise of birthday parties and Fourth of July celebrations and then, when the heat died away, the carnival atmosphere of the fair. But not anymore. William would have been seven. They would have walked hand in hand down the fairway and laughed on the Ferris wheel. They would have eaten corn dogs and funnel cakes and breathed in the confectioner's sugar and returned to Maizie wound up and happy and exhausted. At night, after William had gone to bed, straining against each other in the dark, his mouth heavy on hers, fearful their son might wake and appear in the door, asking to sleep with them.

He rises and paces the room. A room not too dissimilar to the last one in which Vivian and he often stayed. He thinks about her body now, how they fucked in the cheap prefabricated shower and then, falling over each other, moved to the bed to let the moisture cool on their skin. How he looked down at his cock entering her and then back to her face as if there was some great significance in that rather than simple adultery.

How easily he transitions from thinking of Maizie to Vivian.

Something in his stomach churns and he fumbles to the restroom, where his dinner comes up in a chest-racking, clotted mess. He does not feel better afterward. He rises from his knees and looks down on the swirling mess in the white porcelain blankness and flushes. That easy, it's just gone.

It's late when a knock comes to his door. He rises from where he lies on the bed and goes to it, peeks out the peephole, which is curiously dark. For a moment he thinks it's Hattie, messing with him, her finger over the peephole's outer lens. She has that sort of sense of humor. So he opens the door, saying, "All right, very funny—"

Empty hallway.

He's on the second floor and he looks back and forth down the length of hall, seeing no one. Flipping the bolt so his door doesn't lock, he walks to the elevators to see if there's any inconstancy to the digital floor numbers, revealing a moving carriage. Nothing. Numbers still on 2 and L. In the hallway's canned air, there is the faintest hint of . . . smoke? Alcohol? Sex? He cannot tell. He has the impression that someone just passed his room and walked the corridor only moments before but now they are gone.

He returns to his room and shuts his door and looks again through the peephole. Clear now, a fish-eyed view of patterned carpet. He thinks no more of it and returns to his bed, but he's fully awake now.

It's near midnight when he leaves the room and returns to the Parker house.

In the secret room, he places a record on the turntable and opens Harlan Parker's field journal.

11

Harlan Parker:
Bear Henstead, Amoira, and Gramp Hines

JUNE 17, 1938

On June 12 in Mallow, we recorded Hiram Randolph Burkes, a cherubic little man with no hair on his head, playing "Stagger Lee," almost word for word matching Smoot Sawyer's version, though his chord progression was different—and the bass-string obbligato was a bit more jubilant and meaty. The day after, we found one of the men Smoot Sawyer had told us about, a gentleman by the name Bear Henstead. The directions were vague: "He lives down thar by the confloo of New and Greenbrier Rivers, fellers. Ask for him." So Bunny found where the Greenbrier and New Rivers met and we drove there, backtracking some, and the first person we asked at the Bellepoint Five and Dime directed us straight to Henstead's home, a tidy little house outside of town in a field of withered tobacco, brown leaves hanging like moth wings.

Despite his name, he did not resemble a bear, but was a small, clean-shaven white fellow in overalls and a starched white shirt who greeted us on his porch and told us he'd been expecting us. I do not understand how knowledge moves among the hills of these mountain folk faster than the car drives, but it seems to nevertheless, without the benefit of telegram or telegraph. He indicated we should set up in his barn, among the horses, and I fancy you can hear them making noises in the background as we recorded. Henstead also required a mason jar of moonshine before he would open his banjo case.

It began like this.

"Mister Henstead, we like those we record to start with 'Stagger Lee,' if you know it. It's a good bellwether song."

"Don't rightly know what that means but I knows the ballad of that damnable Stack Lee," he said, smiling. "Never a n—— been born blacker."

The word—which gives me such a loathsome feeling that I will not commit it to writing here—was said in such a nonchalant manner, it took me aback. I saw a great fury pass over Bunny, and felt it mirrored in myself. We had not fought and killed and watched our friends and companions die in a far-off country so that men such as Henstead could set themselves over others.

Hatred constantly reinvents itself. Prejudice against one's fellow man is rampant and omnipresent, but I had not expected to witness it without some object of animus present, apropos solely of a song.

"All right, then, Mister Henstead," I said, determined to move on—sparking a loathsome feeling now, this time in myself, thinking on my cowardice in not confronting the man on his bigotry. "I will signal you when to begin once the device begins cutting the record. All right?"

He waved me off, though, and unscrewed the mason jar instead, taking a long pull. He hissed like an adder afterward. Henstead stuffed his cheek with tobacco, and only then picked out an arpeggiated chord and slapped the banjo's sounding board, and then began singing.

It was a version of "Stagger Lee" that closely resembled much of Smoot Sawyer's rendition—which follows logically, since they are not divided by any gulf in geography, culture, or station in life. Between Smoot and Henstead, the latter was a far more proficient player, his right-hand picking technique adroit and fluid. His bright tenor voice sounded like a choir bell, which I found an irony, considering the baseness of its source. He ripped into "Stagger Lee," and it was all well and good.

But then, at the end of it, he sang this verse:

The devil saw Stack a-comin'.
He hollered out, "Now listen to me,
Get ready them ropes and pitchforks.
We gone lynch ole Stagger Lee,
Gone lynch him for eternity."

After he finished, I asked him if he knew any other versions of "Stagger Lee," other than the one he just sang. He indicated that he might, but he did not like them as much and they were more of the Negro persuasion, though—again—he did not use those particular words.

I recorded the rest of Henstead's songs without much enthusiasm (noted on the acetate sleeves: another version of "No More Hiding in the Valley," which more than likely is the real find here; a rousing version of "John the Revelator," despite my indicating the Library's desire for secular songs, rather than spiritual; "Up Near Boochy Holler," another unknown song; "Half a Jar of Moonshine"), using up three twelve-inch discs in total, and packed up the SoundScriber without any small talk. I had intended on follow-up interviews with musicians where I might discuss a player's musical influences, training, favorite tunes, whatever regional themes and variations of popular music might be prevalent for a fuller understanding of their art and heritage. But the neat, starched Henstead emanated such a negative air— and his casual bigotry left me so discomposed—we left as quickly as we could to find Sawyer's other recommended musician, a man named Gramp Hines.

Gramp Hines was not so easy to find. Smoot had been vague about his whereabouts: "Ole Hines used to run the chautauqies way back in the old days, but now he likes to keep to himself 'round about Leatherwood. Might find him near one of them mountain lakes down there, in a big ole tent for Sunday-mornin' congregatin'. Or Saturday-night carousin'. But he's a strange one. He knowed fifty-two more songs than anyone else."

Bunny and I laughed at that recurring phrase and returned to the Studebaker and the back roads of West Virginia. We had come out of the folded land of the more mountainous regions, into the softer foothills. The woods around us canopied the road, dappling the cab of the Studebaker. With each turning of the sedan, it was as if the old forest, drowsing in the early summer sunshine now lengthening into afternoon, had its own gravity drawing us to it.

"That old son of a bitch," Bunny said softly, around his cigarette. "If he was on fire, I wouldn't piss on him." I laughed at that. We had removed our jackets and rolled up our shirtsleeves. Sweat discolored our armpits, pooled at our backs. Bunny had removed all the contents of his pockets and placed them in his hat, upturned on the seat between us: pocketknife, handkerchief, Zippo lighter, some silver change, Pall Malls, a flat and exhausted wallet. Beyond those items, I doubt Bunny owned much more. After returning from overseas, he'd never stayed in one place too long. He had the clothes on his back, and in his kit. A sleeping bag. And the memories. We both had those.

At a gas station in Leatherwood, we asked the attendant about Gramp Hines.

"Why the hell you want to find that loon?" he asked. He was a gaunt, ill-looking man, about my own height and size and coloration, though his hair was dirty blond where mine is black when it is not gray. His white Union Gas uniform was oil stained at the waist and on his trousers, around the pockets. The only clean part was his cap. I explained what our commission was and he scratched his head. "Most of the time, you don't find Gramp Hines, he finds you. But last I heard, he had his tent up near Gooseneck Lake."

Bunny went to the Studebaker and returned with the map, brow furrowed. "I can't seem to find Gooseneck Lake. Can you point it out?"

The man went inside the Union station, rummaged around behind the cash register, and returned with a grease pencil and marked a large X on the map and handed it back. "That's where it was last time I was there, oh, maybe in twenty-two or twenty-three."

Bunny chuckled. "You make it sound like it might've moved."

"Might've, gents. Might've."

"How so?" I asked.

"Crick dries up, changes course. Water pools someplace else. Lake moves from one side of a holler to another. Disappears. How it happens 'round here."

We thanked the man. He finished filling the Studebaker and I paid, buying us both cigarettes and bottles of Coca-Cola from the icebox. We drank them in the fading summer day, enjoying the sweetness of the soda. The sun had lowered in the vault of sky, and Bunny squinted his eyes and said, "We better get a leg on, Harlan, if we're gonna find this mug." He hopped back in the car and I took up the map.

In an hour, we were hopelessly lost. We had followed an un-marked road off the highway at the point where it might've led to the greasy mark on the map the attendant had pointed out, but that dirt road became a switchback up a small mountain; we were halfway up the skirts before we stopped. The sun had dipped below the far rim of hills, turning the sky blue, striated with pink clouds. We turned around and went back down, retracing our route, but due to some errant turning, we found ourselves riding along a dry creek bed deeper into the hills. In the half-light of evening, the sound of insects began to rise, their fat bodies im-pacting like intermittent raindrops as they splattered against the windshield. The light faded, and Bunny turned on the headlights.

"I'm hungry. We could just find a clearing and camp for the evening. I still have some peanuts and a can of beans," Bunny said. "And I could use a drink." I had been thinking along the same lines.

"That sounds just fine," I said.

We drove until the sky had totally darkened. By the head-lights of the Studebaker, we found a camp at the side of the dry creek bed we'd been following. It was a wide grassy area, settled among oaks and horse chestnuts on springy, dry soil. Bunny was pleased, as he was—of the two of us—the one who would sleep on the ground. We set to building a fire from deadfall and soon had one burning brightly, fragrant hardwood smoke wreathing the clearing. We shared a jar of shine—a sip, a hiss, then a shak-ing of the head like a dog snakebit on the nose—and waited for the fire to render enough coal to set the can of beans to cooking. On a whim, Bunny suggested some music and it wasn't too late in the night when we drunkenly set up the SoundScriber and listened to what we had already recorded.

There, in the woods, we set up the device near the fire, attached the batteries, and played Smoot Sawyer's recording of "Stagger

Lee" and then "No More Hiding in the Valley." Then on to Bash Bunks, and the others. The sound echoed up and into the darkened foliage. The air had cooled from the heat of the day, and there was a light breeze. In my mind, I pictured a fox halting his nocturnal haunt, hushed and inactive, his ears twitching, listening to the music rising up into the night air. The insects stilled, the night creatures listened.

"Let's hear 'Stagger Lee' again, boss," Bunny said. He lay with his hands behind his head, his sleeping bag as a pillow. "I like 'No More Hiding in the Valley' better, but there's more meat to 'Stagger Lee.'"

I knew exactly what he meant. I withdrew the first disc I had recorded, placed it on the turntable, and was about to lower the tone arm when a voice said, "That's a fine song, but I could do you fellers one better."

Bunny was up in a flash, despite his drunkenness. A woman stood there, right at the edge of the firelight. I rose to face her.

"Ma'am," I began. "Are you all right? We're far away—"

"I know where I am," she said. "Do you gents know where you are?"

When she stepped forward into the brighter firelight, I could make out her features. At first glance, I thought she was an old woman, due to her lustrous white hair, but after the first shock of it, I saw her shining, unblemished skin, and her straight posture and unbowed figure. She wore a simple, modest dress of blue, a white woolen sweater. It took a moment to register she wore no shoes. Her feet seemed wild, dirty, animal—there is no other way to put it. As if her soles had never known shoes. But her legs were well formed, as was the rest of her. An amused, expressive mouth, and intelligent eyes gazing back at me.

Bunny said, "Well, now you mention it, not exactly. We know the general area, you might say."

"But not yet how to get out of it," I added.

She moved near to where I stood next to the SoundScriber.

"What's this? Quite a sight, a couple of city boys out here playing music in the dark," she said, turning her head to examine it. "I've seen ole hand-cranked Victrolas before, but nothing like this thing." *This thang.* Her voice had a musical quality to it, the lilting rise and fall of country folk. As she neared me, I could smell lilac and jasmine and honeysuckle—odors I'd been catching whiffs of all day with the windows down and the summer rising, but more discernible now.

"It's for making recordings," I said. "Of regional song."

I hastily went into the Library's mission. "My name is Harlan Parker," I said, extending my hand. She took it in her warm, firm grip. She had thick calluses on her palms and fingers and a deep strength in her grip. "And my companion is Edmund Whitten."

"Amoira Hines," she said. "It sure is a pleasure runnin' up on you two. How 'bout offering a lady a drink, Mister Whitten?"

"Bunny. Everyone calls me Bunny."

"Sounds 'bout right, Bunny." She reached out and touched his cheek as he handed her the mason jar. Strange seeing a man I've known as long as Bunny, and through all of it—war, women, whiskey—stalwart and unblinking, blushing.

I finished explaining what we were doing in those parts, camping in the woods, and she nodded her head as I spoke. "You should find Gramp. He could sing you a doozy or two," she said.

"That was who we were searching for! His tent near Gooseneck Lake, but we ended up here."

She smiled. "He's packed up and moved on, down into Tennessee."

"You know him well?" I asked.

She nodded. "I ought to." She paused and looked at me with a bright eye. "He's my husband."

Bunny spluttered. "But, but—"

I said, "We were under the impression that Gramp Hines was—"

"Was what?"

"Older," I said.

She laughed. "I imagine he's 'bout a hundred and a day. But still spry."

"But you can't be more than—" Bunny said.

"More than what?" When he didn't answer, she chuckled and moved to sit down beside him.

As Bunny scrambled to make room, I said, "Where did you come from? I didn't see any houses or cabins nearby."

"I hail from Cidersend. Hoo, I could sing you a song from back home that would have you stiffen in your britches!"

"Would you sing it for us?" I asked. "I'd like to record it."

"Maybe in a little bit, eager boy," she said.

"Where's Cidersend?" Bunny asked. "Is it around here?"

"Naw, it's back up in the Ozarks, a far piece west. Now I live up the holler," she said. "Been there for many a year now. Can remember when this crick ran high."

"And Gramp," I said. "Your husband. He's gone for good? Or—"

"He makes his rounds and then meanders back 'round autumn," she said.

"At his age?" I asked.

She shrugged. I was under the distinct impression that age in this part of the world was purely arbitrary.

Bunny handed her the mason jar again and she took a long swallow and then hooted, casting a bright gaze about. "When I was a girl," she said, "I'd strip naked and swim in the creek."

Bunny took a swallow of the moonshine himself, fascinated by her and her words. It had been a while since either of us had enjoyed the company of a woman. And she was quite a handsome woman, if one discounted her ghostly white hair and her gnarled bare feet.

"Time was, I might get up to some trouble with a coupla young fellers like yourselves on a night like this, when the moon and crick were high." She laughed. A luxurious, indolent sound.

"Do you know any songs from around here?" I asked.

She slowly turned her head to me and wetted her lips. "I figured you'd never ask."

The woman and Bunny remained sitting close together, smoking cigarettes. Bunny making sure that Amoira drank enough shine to feel comfortable being recorded. I busied myself preparing a fresh acetate disc for cutting.

"We like to start with 'Stagger Lee' if we could, should you know it. It's a good indicator of—"

"I know it, course I do," Amoira said. "Who don't? It's like my very own shadow."

I nodded and readied everything—writing down her name on the sleeve of the acetate disc, followed by *"Stagger Lee."*

"Whenever you're ready," I said. She nodded. I placed the cutting arm on the blank acetate disc, watching the brittle coating peel away from the virgin surface of the record. When I was sure it was recording well, I turned back to Amoira to watch her performance.

She opened her mouth.

And screamed.

12

Harlan Parker: The Morning After

When I woke, it was dawn and the campfire was dead, sending a faint ribbon of smoke skyward. I pushed myself up from the ground and felt a moment of dislocation—*Bunny sleeps on the ground, not me,* I thought—and looked around. Morning filtered down through the canopy, a flowering of light that flooded the dry creek bed and painted the forest in bright greens.

Bunny looked as if he'd been poleaxed. He stood and said, "What the hell happened, Harlan?" He turned around in a circle. "Where's the woman?"

The events of the night before were muddy in my mind, indistinct. I remembered placing the cutting needle on the SoundScriber, and then Amoira opening her mouth and her face becoming hideous for a moment, racked with either pain or hatred or some other overwhelming emotion I could not fathom.

"I don't know," I said. Bunny, disheveled, began buttoning his shirt. "But it looks like you had a good time." I gestured at him. There were love bites and scratches and suckling marks all across his torso.

He pulled off his shirt and looked down at his chest. "What the hell? If I'm going to roll around in the dirt with a country girl, I'd like to be able to remember it." He looked at me, bewildered, as if seeking some sort of explanation. He stopped. "Looks like you had a fine time yourself."

All the aches and pains of the night settled upon me then. A million little wounds surmounted by a great one: my throbbing head. I went to the Studebaker, sat in the front seat, and adjusted the rearview so I might look at myself. Haggard, unkempt, bloodshot. Near my collarbone were suckling marks, too.

I returned to Bunny, who stooped in the clearing, gathering up our things. I took the mason jar of shine—there was only two fingers left in this one—and drank half of it and handed it back to Bunny, who drank the rest.

"Where's that raccoon?" Bunny said.

"Raccoon? What raccoon?"

"The one that shat in my mouth," he said. He puckered and spat. "Don't know if I signed up for this business, Harlan."

We hastily packed up the SoundScriber and batteries, and I carefully re-sleeved the twelve-inch acetate labeled *Amoira Hines*—"*Stagger Lee.*" The rest of the disc cover was blank. As I held it, there was a pause from Bunny and we exchanged glances before I placed it carefully in the case with our other discs, those few scrawled with song and the others, unmarred.

In the light of day, it was a simple matter finding our way back out, to Leatherwood, where we visited the restroom at the same Union station, drinking our fill from the hose on the side of the building and running our heads under the stream. How many mornings, in those times away from the front, did we spend like this in France? In Belgium?

Between us, we decided to put West Virginia behind us, and head south and west into Tennessee. There was an unspoken yet great relief when we passed over the state line, the sign WELCOME TO TENN-O-SEE! whipping by at seventy miles per hour. At the back of my mind was Gramp Hines and his wife—we were, in some ways, on his trail. It was something I did not linger over very long.

The land's undulant hills and fields became greener, and I saw shotgun shacks now near parcels of land. Negro men and women working fields behind mules, sitting on porches, standing by trucks. The farther south we traveled, the heat seemed to grow more intense, the sky became hazy, and the country became flatter.

At noon we stopped for hamburgers at a roadside diner outside of Nashville. Afterward, Bunny and I felt almost normal, considering the strange events of the night before. We arrived at Ramsay Schweitzer's home, one of the men in Tennessee on the Federal Writers' Grant, and he welcomed us warmly, poured cold beers, and brightened our stay with conversation about the area. His wife, Anne, seemed bemused at our disheveled state and openly smiled at Bunny's wild hair. Liszt, Rachmaninoff, Debussy filled their house with strains of music from the Victor Electrola record player, sounds very far away from those one might have heard in West Virginia.

Aware that we resembled hoboes from days and nights spent on the road, Bunny and I kept our collars buttoned and ties firmly in place, as if in an effort to convey some respectability, even when the day's heat did not subside as night deepened. Schweitzer poured generous glasses of good bourbon for a nightcap and led us to our room—an enclosed sleeping porch, with two cots and a single black General Electric fan that oscillated back and forth between us—and we fell into dreamless sleep.

I was acutely aware of the acetate disc labeled *Amoira Hines* sitting nearby, unlistened to and unheard in its crate.

13

Cromwell: Amoira Hines

Cromwell closes the ledger and delicately sorts through the acetate discs until he finds the one labeled in faint pencil *Amoira Hines*.

He removes it from the handwritten sleeve, places it on the turntable, and lowers the tone arm. A faint crackling begins to sound. The familiar preamble of vinyl.

Then the sound of a woman's voice.

What first sounds like a scream becomes . . .

Laughter.

It's an indeterminate voice—not with the rough gravel and distress of the aged, but not a youthful timbre, either. Closing his eyes, Cromwell can see her white hair, her gnarled feet.

Deep feminine laughter, laughter that goes on and on, unstopping for what seems like forever. It has a manic power to it. Cromwell checks his watch. Two minutes. Three. Five. Seven.

The emotion behind it, the wellspring of the sound—the song, really, Cromwell thinks, a wordless song—isn't joy, or mirth, or humor, but something else Cromwell cannot place. Abruptly the laughing ceases.

There's a grunt, and some subvocal noises, another grunt, a moan, heavy breath. At first it sounds like a slap but then it occurs again, and again, picking up speed. A faint *yes* from a female mouth, and then it's repeated by two male voices. Cromwell has watched enough porn to know what he's hearing. Then, softly: *Ogdru tulu handria agga rast benthu hasi tulu on aggrom nung delendu* and more nonsense that the woman says over and over again until the men repeat it after her. Moans and the slapping of flesh.

The acetate ends.

Cromwell finds himself hard, clutching his cock through his trousers. He considers masturbating then, in a dead woman's house in the small hours of morning. He rises, unzips his pants, takes his swollen member in hand, and is about to spit upon its head—*comme il faut*—when his iPhone begins to vibrate madly in his pocket.

He withdraws his phone to see an Alexandria number displayed and for an instant he thinks it might be Maizie calling and he fills with shame and answers it. His cock wilts in his hand, and he looks down on it in a dismayed acceptance of a personal diminution. *I will diminish, and go into the west,* he thinks, picturing Cate Blanchett's smooth, androgynous face. *To the gray havens, where sap does not rise in trees, cocks stay soft. Where spouses stay dead.*

He places the phone to his ear. The overly cheery prerecorded voice on the other end says, *Hi, I'm Allison! Please stay on the line to learn how you can refinance your home,* and Cromwell responds, "Go fuck yourself, Allison," and hangs up.

He slips the phone back in his trousers and zips his pants. He removes the acetate from the turntable and gingerly replaces it in its sleeve.

Cromwell recovers the journal and opens it once more and begins to read.

14

Harlan Parker: Tenn-O-See

July 7, 1938

I've lost Bunny, and the SoundScriber has been destroyed. By fire. I'm distressed by Bunny's departure, but I fear the destruction of the SoundScriber will be a harder obstacle to surmount.

Thankfully, none of the acetates were lost, save one, and that one I have thought on solely since its burning. I am now checked in to the Hotel Gayoso in Memphis, and as I try to sort and settle my mind, I will recount here the events leading to its destruction to the best of my memory, but I fear that is indefinite and flawed.

We found Gramp Hines in Tennessee. I do not know what to make of the experience, or of our bizarre evening with Amoira, and I am still puzzling out all that has happened. I fear that these two things are the cause of Bunny's departure. He left me in Tennessee, abruptly, and under mysterious circumstances.

No matter the catalyst, the result is I am here for the next few days. I intend to spend that time taking down my notes of the last week, transcribing some of the more interesting—and disturbing—songs, and resting. Living on the road, sleeping in the

Studebaker, has taken its toll upon me. I have broken out in a rash, either from the heat, or from the stress of travel, or from insect bites—or all of the above. The corner of my mouth bubbles. My ankles and legs are riddled with itchy, angry welts. I need days indoors with decent food for both my mental repose and my physical well-being. A few nights of uninterrupted sleep would not go amiss, either. The hotel is an extravagance, I know—but I have been exceedingly frugal thus far.

I have telegraphed Spivacke requesting more funds, a new SoundScriber, and sapphire cutting styluses for the device. I am more depressed than I care to admit about Bunny's abrupt departure but console myself with the fact that it does mean the money will last longer.

I will continue on without Bunny, but I'm forced to head now to Arkansas, where I will at least find comfort and respite from the kind people of the Darcy Arkansas Folk Society. It will be there I shall await the new SoundScriber.

On June 18, we spent the day restocking our larder, and performing maintenance on both the Studebaker and the SoundScriber. Bunny made sure the vehicle was well oiled and its tires in good shape. We bought more alcohol and cigarettes, since it's obvious these are necessary to woo songs out of our subjects. I am in a quandary as to how to notate the purchasing of alcohol on expense reports. I am quite sure Spivacke will understand, but his masters at the Library of Congress may not.

The next morning, we drove south near the Alabama border, to a farmstead near a church, in Ardmore, Tennessee, to record that afternoon a group of men, all Negro farmhands. Their names were, as marked on the acetate sleeves: Otis Steck, "Big" Mike Battle, Vester White, and Jimmy James.

When we arrived, late in the afternoon, we were greeted warmly by the men and their hangers-on: pretty women in flowered hats and calico dresses, teens in Sunday church garb, and children scampering about, their high-pitched voices cutting through the dust cast up by the Studebaker's wheels. Life on the road had left me in a daze, and it took some counting for me to recall that today was a Sunday, and so most of these gathered folks would've been here since midmorning for a church service and now a recording with the "gubmint" men. They welcomed us inside the church house, a one-room affair, and the preacher, a thickset, dapper man with dark skin and a lovely deep voice, bowed out to let us "young folk sing and dance in ways not entirely for the lord's benefit, but for the community's, I'm sure," and I thanked him heartily. It was a rare open-mindedness he displayed for a country preacher.

After setting up the SoundScriber, I gathered the musicians behind the church, sharing some of the whiskey and cigarettes I'd brought. Of the four men, Vester White seemed the leader. He was a man of raw physicality, high and noble cheekbones, and indeterminate age—and I've known since my days working at the Harrow Club that it's a common joke among blacks that white men can't tell the age of Negroes—but I would have known Vester was eldest if only from his demeanor and not the halo of gray threaded through his hair. He seemed to me ineffably tired, and I could understand that reality due to the Southern situation and his place in it. Scars ran up his arms and he was missing the tips of his fingers on his right hand. "But I can still pick a guitar just fine, sir."

"Let me ask you a question," he said, after taking a pull of the whiskey bottle.

"All right, Mister White, ask away," I said.

He stopped. "Best if you didn't call me that, sir," he said.

"What?"

"Mister," he said. "'Nother white man hear that, 'round here, they won't be too pleased, that's for sure."

"Calling you 'Mister'?"

"That's the size of it," he said.

I nodded. It was their world I was trying to enter. I had to be open to what they chose to tell me. Even the ugliness of it. Which, I was afraid, there would be quite a lot of.

"What is your question?"

"Why do a prim and proper white man come down here wanting us black folk to sing for you?" he said.

The other men chuckled, and Bunny snorted, but I could tell Vester White was utterly serious about his question. I considered giving him the spiel I had nearly memorized already, the mission of the Library of Congress and so forth, but I didn't think that was what he was asking.

I said, "The world is changing, Vester, and if we don't take down your songs, they might be forgotten."

"No, sir," he said. "Big Mike and Otis and Jimmy know all I got to sing."

"That might be true," I said. "But Big Mike might change a verse, or a word, or a chord, and then the song changes some and it's not wholly yours anymore. Then someone learns it from him and changes it some and suddenly it's not anything like Vester White's version."

Vester mock-raised his hand as if to strike Big Mike, who cowered dramatically even though he was a foot taller and heavily muscled. "Ain't gone steal nothin' from me, Mike!" he cried. Once their bit of jovial theater was finished, Vester said, "I thank you for answerin'."

"You're very welcome," I said.

When the bottle was finished, and a number of cigarettes had been smoked—"It mellows my voice considerable," Otis Steck informed me—we entered the church. Some of the congregation had grown bored and left, mostly those women with children in tow, but many of the younger folk had remained.

Vester chose to go first. I positioned him in front of the microphone, instructed him on the best way to sing into it and still get the sound of his guitar.

"We like to start with 'Stagger Lee,'" I said. "Since both white and black folks know that one."

"Never been that fond of Stacker, but I imagine I could give it a round," Vester said.

I readied the SoundScriber's stylus and set it to cutting.

"We begin recording with Mister Vester White," I said, and pointed to him.

He leaned in and said to the microphone, "Hello, President Roosevelt."

I looked at Bunny and he shrugged.

After a few moments I said, "Mister White, you can start now."

"I'm waiting for the president to hello me back," Vester said.

Bunny laughed. I smiled with him. "I'm afraid this only records, it does not transmit," I said.

"Shame, I'd like to tell him what we think of him down here," Vester said, and then winked. I did not know if that would be praise or criticism, and with the stylus curling away at the acetate, I did not ask.

He began to play. It was a wholly new version of "Stagger Lee" to me, familiar in structure and theme, but with a different chord progression and an introduction I had not heard before. In this version, Vester told the story in a speaking voice of Billy Lyons (or "Billy de Lyons") and Stagger Lee gambling in a coal mine, with the intimation that Billy is white and Stagger Lee is black, an interesting variation made more interesting by the fact that, through cheating at cards, Billy Lyons steals Stagger Lee's Stetson hat. I have seen men, both white and Negro alike, inordinately proud of their hats—such that someone taking one would cause great umbrage and wounded pride. So, Stagger Lee is justified (as much as one can be) in the murder.

However, in this version, it is the story of a black man killing a white man. As I looked out at the listeners, none of them would meet my gaze.

From there the song went down predictable paths but ended in the refrain of "he's a *bad* man, Stagger Lee," the same phrase so heavily featured in the Caucasian version. It occurred to me that this refrain of "he's a bad, bad man" could be protective coloration, like dun-colored grouse in the field—an appended chastisement of Stagger Lee's behavior in order to avoid accusation of promoting violence against whites. Yet, the music was jubilant, joyful.

Understandable. I wished I could express to those listening that I am not as the white men they know, they live under the rule of. That I fought for them, and even now, on this commission, I fight still so that their culture—so maligned and denigrated by the larger white world—does not fall away, ground into the dust of history without remembrance.

But I am too outré, and there is too much bad blood—every day a litany of outrages and ignominious diminutions—for me to ever be more than an outside observer. You can live all your life on the outside looking in, never from the inside looking out.

The outside looking in. I imagine that's how Vester and his companions feel, too. Their whole lives.

Once Vester had finished the song, I removed the cutting arm and delicately swept away the acetate rinds that had curled away from the surface and replaced it with the tone arm, and the sounds of Vester's voice filled the church. His eyes grew large and he laughed and the rest of the congregated Negroes in the little wooden building laughed too and murmured about the marvel that was the SoundScriber for a long while. When they had settled, I placed a virgin acetate on the recorder.

Vester went on to render a version of "Ain't No Grave Can Hold My Body Down," then on to "Buzzard Lope" and "Ain't Going to

Rain No More," followed by "Soft Bed and a Half Dollar," which had copious mentions of the anatomy of women, especially their legs and feet. I have appended the transcriptions to my report. His songs spanned multiple twelve-inch acetate discs.

The next two men were eager to perform, once they saw how the SoundScriber worked. Big Mike Battle and Jimmy James, neither of whom played instruments, simply sat down in front of the microphone and began singing in strong, unadorned, but mellifluous voices—delivering rousing but shorter versions of "Stagger Lee" and then progressing on to "Rock Island Line" and "Cornfield Holler."

The last player, Otis Steck, was physically much smaller than the other men, but he held himself with such poise that when he borrowed Vester White's guitar and sat in front of the microphone, the church stilled, the observers quieted.

"Sir, I know a good piece of that ole ballad of Stackerlee."

"Well, that's just fine," I said. "I'd love to hear it. Is it considerably different than Vester's?"

"I'll say. But the thing is," he said, shifting uncomfortably, "I'm a mite nervous singin' it in here, under the cross."

I will not lie, at his words my pulse quickened.

"Well, that's fine, that's quite all right," I said, suddenly verbose. "Sing what you want to sing, and maybe afterward, we could move our recorder out a ways in that nearby cotton field and you could sing it there. Would that be all right?"

"Sounds fine to me, sir," he said. "Though it's coming up on dark."

So I set the SoundScriber to cutting acetate and Otis Steck sang "Take This Hammer" and "Boll Weevil" and "Bottle Full of Scotch" inside the church. He had a bright, penetrating tenor voice, and toyed with the longer phrases, dancing around the root notes in a sort of *cante jondo* style that came down, through the years, from

French Guinea and Barbados, Martinique and Jamaica; further back still, down the generations from West Africa, but coalescing in this man as a pure and intimate expression of the American experience.

When we played them back to him, he smiled and said, "This mean I'm gone be a radio star?"

"Maybe," I said. "But that's not our purpose here."

"Shame," he said. "I could use a new suit."

Vester said, "A new one? Gots to have a suit before you can need a new one." Laughter, then, except from Otis, who smiled but did not let it touch his eyes.

Bunny and I moved the SoundScriber out of the church, into the field, with the help of some of the men. As Otis had said, dusk was rising up around us in a half-light, and the sun hung over the far tree line by a mere finger's breadth. Our shadows moved as loping and distended figures with the aging day, our feet casting up dust.

The SoundScriber we placed on a point of hard-packed ground near the furrows, and I quickly attached the Edison batteries and readied a disc. I did not want anything to stall or dissuade Steck from his decision to sing his version of "Stagger Lee." As the sun went down, and the sky beyond suddenly bloomed with streaks of color, bruised purple and orange, we watched the rest of the observers leave, either by foot, or wagon and mule, or farm truck. I explained to Steck and Vester—the only two who remained behind—the ambient noise could ruin a recording, outside. In all honesty, I did not know that this was true; however, the engineer from the Library of Congress had lectured me earnestly that it was best to record in the quietest of surroundings, and that made eminent good sense.

As we came to a point where we were ready to set the cutting arm to etching, Steck said, "Way I figure it, you really want to hear this song."

I was sweating heavily, as was Bunny, from the effort of setup.

Both of our breaths came in heaves. Otis Steck and Vester White, though, were both dry and mildly amused at our discomposure. I nodded to Steck.

"I figure, lemme get some of them squares from you, and a bit more whiskey, and maybe a dollar or two, and I can run through everything I know again."

"Squares?" I asked.

"Them smokes," Steck replied.

Bunny trotted back to the Studebaker and returned with a fresh pack of Pall Malls and a bottle of whiskey, both with unbroken bonded stickers. He handed the cigarettes to Steck, cracked open the bottle and took a long pull, handed it to me so I could follow suit. Steck laughed at the order of things.

"Getting dark," Vester said, passing over his guitar once more. "Let's roll this thang."

I handed the bottle to Steck, whose bobbled throat worked up and down three times in long, deep swallows before he set the bottle down. He sat down in the folding chair, at the edge of the field, in the lubed and woozy way of someone who just felt a wallop of alcohol hit their bloodstream.

"Ole devil Stacker Lee, then," he said.

Otis looked to me and gave a significant nod and I moved the cutting arm into place and started the SoundScriber recording.

He moved through a version of "Stagger Lee" that was less bouncy and jubilant than Vester White's. He hung on a single chord for a long while, before moving to the fourth and fifth chords, and back again. The fretting was slurry, indistinct, and his fingering of the strings twisted the sounds into more of a minor lilting melody.

In Steck's version, both Billy and Stagger were black men, gambling in the dark on some lonesome street corner. Billy wins and ultimately takes Stagger Lee's ten-dollar Stetson hat. Stagger, in a fury, goes home and gets his forty-one and returns to kill

Billy Lyons. He finds him in a bar, and "shoots him so bad" that the bullet goes through Billy and shatters a glass in the barman's hand. Billy pitches over, gouting blood. When Stagger reclaims his lost Stetson, it's drenched in crimson, but he places it on his head anyway. The sheriff arrives and there is a bloody gun battle. Stagger Lee is killed in his scarlet Stetson hat.

At this point in the song, most versions I'd heard reiterated, over and over again, what a bad man Stagger Lee was and ended. But Steck continued on:

> When the ladies heard they shot him,
> That they shot old Stagger dead,
> They came to his funeral dressed in black and
> Some was dressed in red.
>
> Stackerlee came to the devil
> To identify poor Billy's soul,
> But the poor boy was absent.
> He had burnt down to charcoal.
>
> Now the devil heard a rumblin',
> A mighty rumblin' under the ground.
> Said that must be Mister Stack
> Turning Billy upside down.
>
> But ole Stagger heard him talking,
> He had named him by his name.
> He jumped up by the devil and
> Killed him, just the same.

If this had been the extent of the verses of Otis Steck's rendition, I would have been happy, as I'd heard them before but without this exact phrasing. I was very pleased and surprised when Steck continued on:

Now old Stagger, he was kingly,
And they set on him a bloody crown—
He stood up in the dark there,
In the darkness underground.

But they kept him from Billy Lyons
And Stagger craved for Billy's soul.
His eyes burned like yellow lanterns
And mouth burned like charcoal.

And across all them fire pits,
Across that burning plain,
Old Stacker grew so angry
He called out each soul's name.

They twisted, and they rolled,
And they thrashed they souls around,
But King Stagger knew their secrets
And burned their candles out.

He's a bad king,
He's a bad king,
Stackerlee.

Something grew in me as he sang in the failing light. Some sense of order, descending. It's said that music is a ritual with the power to transform both the singer and the listener. As he sang, Steck's stature grew in my mind, his mouth became cavernous and dark, and I felt a heaviness descend on me. Hairs stood up on my arms, and I looked at Bunny and Vester, who both seemed enthralled by Steck's music. When he finally let the song die, I raced to the SoundScriber to make sure the acetate had cut properly and played it back.

It was such a small sound compared to what had come before, echoing out above rows of cotton. A flight of crows erupted from the far tree line and wheeled in unison, passing overhead and then diminishing into the west for what seemed like an eternity, their caws drowning out the sound of the disc playing. When their avian vocalizations finished, the recorded song ended. *He's a bad king, Stackerlee.*

"If you don't mind me asking, Mister Steck," I said, "where did you learn those verses?"

"Aw, back in Arkansas," he said. "I'll tell you something true. Made some mistakes in my days and spent some time at Cummins farm."

"Cummins State Farm?" I asked. The correspondence I'd had with Jack Darcy of the Darcy Arkansas Folk Society had mentioned I could record numerous field hollers and secular songs there among the inmates.

"That's right," Steck said, and took another drink. He leaned back in the folding chair at an angle—the whiskey was obviously doing its work—and thumbed a match into life and lit a cigarette. He drew on it heavily.

Bunny went to the Studebaker once more and returned with our camp lantern. It wasn't fully dark yet, but would be soon, and I slapped at my neck and my exposed forearms where my shirt cuffs had been rolled back, leaving streaks of blood.

"Them skeeters like the white meat," Otis Steck said. Vester hooted, slapping his knee.

"That seems true," I said. "Though I do not know why they'd discriminate in this manner."

"Discriminating!" Otis said. "Ain't that rich. They picky eaters but it's a matter of freshness, if you catch me, sir."

I ignored the laughter. "So you learned it from a man in Cummins? What was his name? Had you ever heard verses like that anywhere else?"

"Naw," Otis said. "Never heard nothin' like it, if you don't count some older folks' verses of 'Ole Hannah.'"

"Who did you get it from? These verses?" I asked again.

Steck raised an eyebrow at me. "Feller by the name of Honeyboy."

"Just Honeyboy?" I said.

"Naw, his Christian name's Lucius, but everybody call him Honeyboy."

"Why?"

"One time, ladies liked to kiss on him, I reckon," Steck said. "Get a little sugar. But he got a head on him. Blue eyes, too, the devil. Some white man was bucking in his momma's stall."

"Can you recall what he was in for?"

"What you think?" The whiskey had gotten to Steck, and his deference to me had disappeared along with the liquid in the bottle. "Kilt a man. Maybe more. Least that what he said."

"Did you believe him?"

"Sure. Hell yes I do," Steck said. "Honeyboy in for life and nobody fucks with him."

"He sounds—" I searched for the word. "Formidable."

"Ain't knowing that business, if you catch me, but he's one baaad man, Honeyboy is."

That put me in mind of Stagger Lee.

"You mentioned 'Old Hannah,'" I said, and I guess the interrogative was clear in my voice.

"Yep," he said. "Ole Hannah the sun. She gone down now." He began to sing in a quieter voice.

Why don't you go down, ole Hannah, well, well, well,
Don't you rise no more, don't you rise no more.
Why don't you go down, ole Hannah, Hannah,
Don't you rise no more.

Rise up, dead man, and help me plow my row.
Wake up, dead man, and help me turn my row.
Go down, ole Hannah, don't you rise no more.
If you rise in the morning,
Set the world on fire.

"Apocalyptic," Bunny said softly. He lit a cigarette, took up the bottle and drew on it, and then chased that with a deep inhalation of smoke. I took the bottle and drank some myself.

It was simple enough to understand; a people persecuted and ground down within a system constructed and maintained to ensure their subjugation would logically, at some point—when change looked hopeless—dream of a cleansing, overwhelming fire. To end their own misery. For justice against their oppressors.

I felt a great shame and anger spill over me. *These are my brothers. These are my brothers. We are all connected.* The hopelessness I felt in that moment was overwhelming. Not just for these men's continued suffering, but for the fact that their suffering made the wall between us even harder to surmount.

"Thank you, thank you, gentlemen," I said, busying myself, uncomfortable with the welling of emotion. I withdrew my wallet and gave each man two dollars—such a puny gesture. I cleared my throat. "Can we get a recording of 'Old Hannah'? And then I'll leave the rest of the bottle with you and we'll be on our way."

15

Harlan Parker: Rosalie Davis

Bleary, slightly drunk (once again), we were back in Nashville before it was too late, and Schweitzer and his wife had prepared a cold meal of bologna sandwiches and milk for us, which we fell to with great gusto. There truly is no hunger as ravenous as one spurred on by a long fast and exacerbated by whiskey. Afterward, we brought in the SoundScriber from the car and played our day's recordings for both Anne and Ramsay, who, I think, understood intellectually what we were trying to accomplish—preserving the culture of the folk of the South—but emotionally were not in a place where they could accept that these black voices could have the power to move them. They would rather remain in the safe, sanitized halls of Liszt, Chopin, Debussy.

On the twenty-sixth, we drove into Alabama following the directions of Ramsay.

The following day, we drove south and west to record a woman named Rosalie Davis—a real prodigy of the guitar with a voice like a horn of Jericho—who knew "Stagger Lee" but refused to sing it for us and instead insisted on presenting us only spirituals.

Her ability with the guitar made the performances a pleasure, but the Library of Congress has quite enough versions of "Amazing Grace" and "Swing Low, Sweet Chariot" for this century.

I am not concerned with matters of salvation.

If not the opposite, then rumors of it.

JUNE 28, 1938

A day of rest. Slept until almost noon. Woke to find Bunny gone, Anne and Ramsay gone, alone in a foreign house.

Spent my time indexing and cataloging the acetates; transcribing the dialogue and lyrics of the songs. By evening I was recharged.

Anne and Ramsay returned from visiting her parents, and after a light supper of tuna casserole, we listened to their lovely burnished-wood Coronado radio—*Russ Morgan and his orchestra presented by Philip Morris, Horace Heidt's Brigadiers brought to you by Chevrolet, Fibber McGee and Molly sponsored by Johnson's Wax, Jimmy Fiddler's Hollywood Gossip sponsored by Drene shampoo.* I grew tired of the endless cheeriness of the programming and constant reminders of sponsors and advertisers and borrowed a novel from Ramsay, thanking them for their hospitality and retiring to the sleeping porch. I read some of that gentleman Faulkner's *Absalom, Absalom!* and found the prose labyrinthine and his fixation upon a certain class of men—the planter class—odious in its worldview and treatment of his fellow man. For Faulkner to linger so lovingly on the doomed fates of the Southern aristocracy while ignoring almost half the population—the black community teeming with life, song, love, hate, violence, longing, and all of the raw emotion of creation and most definitely fiction—he must've been a very myopic and shuttered man.

Late that evening, Bunny returned. He walked with the loose, happy gait of a man who'd recently been vigorous. Wherever he'd been—I'd imagine a whorehouse, though I have no idea how he had the money for it, his per diem surely would not cover that—he'd been drinking.

"Heard some news," Bunny said, pulling off his boots and sitting down on his cot on the porch. "They say there's a feller in a big tent out on Obion River who's doing an old-time chautauqua. Going by the name of Hines."

"Gramp Hines!" I said, sitting up.

"That's right," he said. "We going to find him?"

"I feel like we are bound to," I said. "He falls within the purview of this commission. And . . ."

"We messed with his good-time gal."

"I feel like that's a misnomer," I said. "Rather, his wife."

"If Amoira—what I can recall of her—if she's his wife, I'll eat my hat." Bunny had stripped off his shirt and lay back heavily on the cot. I winced, hoping the canvas wouldn't tear. We had both put on some weight since our days overseas. "Rather, his good-time gal," he said, mimicking me.

"No call for that."

"For what?"

"Getting personal," I said. Bunny laughed.

"So, we going after him?" he said.

"Of course we are. 'He knowed fifty-two more songs than anyone else,'" I said, doing my best West Virginia mountain dialect impression.

"Well, that's just beneath you, Harlan. You'd never do that to Otis Steck," Bunny said, shaking his head. As he closed his eyes, I realized he was right. It was easier for me to scorn poor whites for what they are than poor blacks. What does that say about me as a man? "And that was Smoot, not Gramp Hines, anyway," Bunny said, voice thick with slumber.

Soon he was snoring and I followed suit.

16

Cromwell: Morning and Exploitation

What the hell, Crumb," Hattie says. "I've been calling. Had to Uber over here." She places her hand on my forehead as if checking for a fever. "You been here all night?"

"I couldn't sleep and wanted to listen to the acetates and read Parker's field journal. Didn't think I should wake you."

She looks at him closely. She's younger than him, and his junior in the hierarchy of the Library. Yet, her concern is apparent. "You should've woke me. You're not up to—"

"The journal. It's fascinating," he says. "Listen to this." He reads to her the section with Amoira Hines and then plays her the recording.

"Well, there's definitely something going on there. Sounds like two dudes going at it. Course, back then, they never could've admitted it. 'The love that dare not speak its name' and all that," she says. "Never had moonshine before, but apparently, that shit is like tequila but on steroids."

"There's a woman's voice, too. The laughter is remarkably unnerving."

"I'll say. There's some weird shit going on there. But the men grunting and knocking boots. I'm thinking this guy is closeted."

"Doubtful. From the journal, I get the impression that when they were soldiers, both Bunny and Parker frequented whorehouses in Europe," Cromwell says.

"That doesn't mean anything. But lemme see that," Hattie says. She holds out her hand, impatiently. She takes the journal and reads for a long while. When Cromwell gestures for her to return the journal to him, she shrugs him off. "Go get us some breakfast. I didn't get any since you never showed. I need time to read this shit—damn, his handwriting is crap."

Dismissed, he leaves. Using his iPhone for directions, Cromwell drives to the nearest Starbucks and buys them both breakfast sandwiches and large coffees. He sits outside the store in the predawn light under the glowing green-and-white sign, staring abjectly into traffic. Cars hissing past on the wet street. It has rained lightly, melting the snow, breaking down the begrimed ice drifts like dirty sugar cubes in black tea. Bare trees mix with power lines, cutting geometrical silhouettes into the gray sky. He goes back to the house.

Hattie eats her sandwich and drinks her rapidly cooling coffee as she continues to read. At some point, she shuts the journal with a snap. There's a slightly disgusted look on her face. "Dollars to donuts, Parker had syphilis rotting his brain. Thanks to his time overseas. Or in New Orleans. They might not have been closeted, but Bunny calling the woman—Amoira, what kind of name is that?—a 'good-time gal' tells me neither of them had a high opinion of women."

Cromwell had not thought of either of those things and says so.

"Of course you haven't. You're like Parker two point oh."

He doesn't know how to take that, so he waves it off. "I don't have syphilis, if that's what you're saying. Whatever the case, if you look at the appended transcripts, it's quite an addition to the Library," he says. "Many new songs, the unheard-of versions of 'Stagger Lee.'"

"Sure." Hattie sniffs. "But this is the part of the Library's mission I've always been a little uncomfortable with. All his protestations of love for the black man. Their brotherhood."

"You don't buy it?"

"Maybe. Was a different time and woke white dudes like Parker and this Bunny fella were rare. But doesn't mean their false protestations of love for the Negro weren't—"

"False? What do you mean?"

She holds up her hand to silence him. "Doesn't mean their false protestations of love and brotherhood weren't justifications for their exploitation of these poor folks. Both black and white."

"Exploitation? I don't see where you're coming from."

"Of course you don't," she says. "You're a part of the same system they were."

"If I'm not mistaken, you get your paycheck from the same place I do."

She tilts her head. "It's a matter of perspective, Crumb. I see this shit for what it really is and you've got your blinders on. Ever think that, back in Parker's day, the mission of the Library was coming from a race-based viewpoint? That these fine, upstanding, woke-as-fuck dudes from 1938 were collecting for the archive, but the archive itself was geared toward a white audience? Academic circles were almost wholly white. And all these fellas would go back from collecting and make the speaking circuit to audiences full of white faces wanting to hear 'primitive' music and stories of the proletariat."

Cromwell shrugs. "Whatever else it is, or represented at the time, it's data, to be interpreted how it's interpreted. You're here now."

"And you're lucky as fuck I am," Hattie says. "Look, I appreciate what he's doing, what John and Alan Lomax did, capturing and preserving the culture. But don't tell me part of it wasn't exploitative, Crumb." She pulls out her phone, scrolling through the data displayed on-screen. "Reminded me. Richard Wright said that John Lomax's treatment of Lead Belly was the greatest cultural swindle of the twentieth century."

"I believe Lead Belly successfully sued John Lomax," Cromwell says.

"Damn right he did! And took back the rights to his songs," Hattie says, a triumphant expression on her face. "But he was one of the lucky ones. The Lomaxes, I think, really weren't in it to exploit black folks consciously. At least Alan wasn't."

"I agree there," he says, thinking of Lomax's writings. He was a fan, pure and simple. The hardships the man endured for his love of race music were remarkable, especially in the face of the frowning white society—

"But still!" she continues. "What happened because of his work is unforgivable. You listen to all the rock-and-roll white dudes in the sixties and seventies discovering Lomax's recordings. 'Midnight Special,' 'Sloop John B,' 'Black Betty,' 'Going Down the Road Feelin' Bad,' 'Motherless Children,' and of course 'Stagger Lee' . . . Shit, Crumb, every longhaired dude with a guitar had a part in strip-mining the black experience. Men like Harlan Parker and John and Alan Lomax made that possible."

"Your definition of 'unforgivable' and mine are quite different. So, better to leave all that history and culture unrecorded?" Cromwell says.

"No," Hattie says. "Better to acknowledge up front the inherent exploitative nature of collecting it."

"Seems to me that the exploitation comes from the listener, not the person who records," he says. But Cromwell also slumps into the chair he's been sitting in all night. "I don't want to argue about it."

"Of course you don't," Hattie says, echoing her earlier statement.

"I'm tired, Hattie," he says.

An angry word leaps to her mouth and her face contorts, and then she seems surprised for an instant and she unclenches. As if remembering.

The ghost of his wife and son stand even here.

He hates her pity then. He asks, "What did you think of the Amoira Hines stuff? Didn't you find it bizarre?"

"Not really our concern. But, yeah. The whole thing is strange, Crumb," Hattie says. She looks at the walls, at the hidden and locked secret room. "This house is fucked up. This room is fucked up. Why lock all this stuff away?"

"If Parker did have syphilis eating his brain, maybe his sister had to lock away all this stuff to help control him."

"Maybe." Hattie shrugs. "Why not just destroy it? Maybe his particular stripe of crazy was catching." Yet even as she says it, she moves to her seat near the TASCAM and looks at Cromwell expectantly. "Well, let's get this party started." She presses the power button on the Bluetooth speakers. They make a small digital noise to let her know they've powered up, and she connects the miniplug.

He's tired from a sleepless night and for a moment Cromwell lets the thought of his hotel room and its bed distract him. He rubs his face and drinks the last of his coffee. But then Cromwell places another acetate disc on the turntable and sets the tone arm on the spinning surface. The room crackles into sound. Harlan Parker's voice says, "Gramp Hines, accompanied by his family, recorded July 5 on commission by the United States Library of Congress."

He opens the field journal.

17

Harlan Parker: Chautauqua on the Banks of the Obion

JUNE 29, 1938

Goodbyes are always like contrary motion in music—the rising melody of being on the road, and the descending notes full of the sadness of leaving friends behind. I thanked Ramsay and Anne for their hospitality vehemently and vowed to fête them if they ever came to Washington. I just hope my pocket is flush enough to do so if they ever come to call.

After our departure, Bunny remained cranky and unresponsive to my efforts at conversation—his hangover had seated itself in the flesh—and he smoked and grunted at all of my directions. With each shifting of the map, I could tell I was irritating him and decided, since he was here due to my benevolence and would assuredly have his hand out for his per diem before long, to make sure I folded the map with crispness and often.

After we'd eaten lunch, and Bunny's demeanor had softened, he said, "I know what you tell the subjects, but what's the score on your fixation for 'Stagger Lee'?" He lit a cigarette and pushed himself back in the Studebaker's seat. "You're really hot under the collar for all this devil malarkey."

How could I say it? "Stagolee," or "Stackalee," or "Stagger Lee" has a different modality for every mind and mouth that renders it, I've come to learn. It is a distinctly *American* song. And like this fair nation, it is impoverished and wars with itself. Its myriad verses contain the stress of inequality, the iniquity of plenty versus want. "Stagger Lee" is a mirror that reflects the desires, and sometimes the shadowy animus, of every man or woman that gives it voice. But with every morphology I've found, researched, and documented, I become more convinced that there's an ur-version of the song, when it first divorced itself from real human events— the sad story of Lee Shelton and William Lyons—and became the upwelling of American cultures before its popularity shattered it into a million scintillate shards.

But there was more. A beyond to my landscape, a horizon to the fields and lakes of my waking, and slumbering, mind.

How could I tell him about the dream of Chautauqua? How could I tell him about the surface of the water, shimmering, the warmth of black faces, black hands comforting me, black voices singing to me? Me, a child? Arrested in forward movement, still caught in an eddy. There are currents in the Mississippi and the Arkansas and the Ohio that turn upon themselves forever, pockets roiling, where fish live their whole lives without escape. The man Insull, holding my mother down, grinning. That maybe I'd never been happy, and never could be happy, unless I could get back to that place where my mother wasn't dead and a Negro minstrel's song swaddled me.

The high, rank summer foliage passed by us, dense and green and dark as an ill intent. A water moccasin curled upon itself on the macadam shoulder, taking in the heat for the coming night. Bunny did not alter the Studebaker's course to kill it, and for that, strangely, I was grateful. The hazy sky burned near white, pushing the blue to the edges. I sweated heavily.

"It's a fascinating song, and it's always drawn me, especially the infernal bits I've heard," I said. Even to my ears, it rang hollow.

"The opiate of the masses," he said. "I thought we'd agreed upon this, long ago. You might not be as red as me, but you've got a mind that works, and eyes to see, and enough war behind you to know—"

"The only devils are men," I said.

Bunny nodded. "That's why I just don't understand why you're all stuck on this 'Stagger Lee' business—"

"In a purely sociological sense, it's important to understand all the different morphologies of a—"

"Spare me the lecture, professor." Bunny waved his hand as though dismissing everything I had said, as if it were smoke from a particularly noxious cigar. "And you're no theologian, or man of the cloth. You're a veteran like me. We came home with enough sense to see the world as it really is. No benevolent god, no prancing imps. Just men. Bad men. Good men. Poor men. Stupid men." He rubbed his face as if coming to his senses. "I'm sorry, Harlan. Holy hell, I've got to lay off the hooch. Not as wet as I used to be and the drink makes me mean-spirited."

After that, Bunny fell silent and continued driving. But I could hear his voice, echoing my words back to me.

The only devils are men.

We drove north and west and found the wellspring of the Obion River in the hills, a wide, fast-moving body of water, very shallow, and followed it as best we could west, where it would eventually flow into the Mississippi somewhere north of Memphis, stopping in the small flea-bit towns to find rumor of Gramp Hines's traveling chautauqua. We spent the week moving down its course and camping on its bank. During that time, we had sparse success with our mission, finding only three subjects to record—George Markus, Mary Goodwin, and Wilhelmina Gipps. All fine musicians, if unimaginative. So when we were not recording, we hunted for Gramp Hines's chautauqua. Independence Day passed without fanfare—though we found a tonk that served cold beer and whiskey and drank enough to be unsteady. Many of the tonk's patrons had heard of Hines's chautauqua, but none had seen it or knew exactly where it might be located. Yesterday, in the midst of high heat, we pulled the Studebaker down a side road, came as close as we could to the banks of the Obion River, and stopped in a sort of wordless agreement. We had grown tired from the heat, and each other's company, without respite from either. The summer had grown unmerciful, and often the hypnotic words of "Ole Hannah" would come to me at odd moments—*Why don't you go down, ole Hannah, well, well, well*—and its lolling, rolling melody would fill my head for hours on end. As long as our vehicle moved, the sweat cooled on our skin, but the farther we drove down diminishing back roads, into and out of Kentucky and Tennessee, the more stultifying the temperature of the Studebaker's cab became. At rest, engine off, the Studebaker hissed and ticked, as if allowing a great anger to subside. When we exited the car, the thick growth and foliage pressed around us, the forest in a summer trance. The rushing water was heard, not seen. The cacophonous discord of cicadas pealing, chitinous. We pushed through the brush and undergrowth to gain the shore. It was shallow and quick water, with brown, current-smoothed rocks. Turtles, surprised at our appearance, plunged in a line back into the flow. We walked downstream, to a soft, placid pool. A water snake cut its path away from us across the still surface. We stripped naked and dove in. It was blessed cool and kept the mosquitoes from us.

Back at the Studebaker, we both took pulls off a bottle of whiskey and smoked. We did not speak.

Dressed, we traced our way back down the dirt road and continued on, Bunny in a much better mood. Whether it was the hooch or the swim, his demeanor had righted itself and he was joking in a short time.

At a roadside store, we topped off the Studebaker and underneath a Nehi sign we found an old man to give us directions to the last place he'd heard that Gramp Hines had been.

"That odd tent revival over near old Mills Ferry? Take yonder highway until you come to the fork and keep right." He looked at the fading light of day. "Should see the fires soon enough."

"Fires," Bunny said. "All right, old-timer."

"Hot, but they got pinewood fires burning near the tent to keep the skeeters outside and music and storytellin' inside."

"Have you been?" I asked. "Seen the show?"

"Naw, but my daughter told me about it. Got a guitar picker, and a banjo man, and a lady that plays the dulcimer. Real family affair. Singin' and dancin'. Spinnin' tales."

We thanked the old fellow and drove on, following his directions as best we could, though we were soon almost completely lost. Another dark night on a dirt road, surrounded by steaming dark forests, insects flashing in the headlights. Bunny drove, hunched over the wheel, a pained expression on his face, illuminated only by the faint light coming from the Studebaker's dashboard. I could feel his agitation rising. I was the one who spotted the faint firelight flickering among the dark bristle of tree trunks, saplings, underbrush in the distance.

We found a small side road—something that more resembled an overgrown wagon trail—and followed it to a spot where the trees withdrew and the light from the stars made the brown, sluggish waters of the Obion silver. A towheaded white boy in overalls and a grass hat stood near a wood fire, and the smoke wreathed his figure, though he did not cough. Two kerosene lanterns burned, past him, illuminating the front of a large canvas tent, the like of which one might see in rural come-to-Jesus revival meetings from Vermont to western Texas. Outside of the tent stood a tractor, a twenties-model Ford truck much the worse for wear, and a mule-driven wagon. We parked, careful not to startle the animal transportation.

"Hello," I said to the boy, exiting the car. "I hope we're not too late for the show."

"Ain't a show," the boy said, without looking up. "It's a shadtalky." He spoke with a mealy-mouthed indistinctness, as if there was too much saliva in his head for proper pronunciation.

"Can we go in?"

"Coster dimer piece."

I gave the boy two dimes and we passed the lanterns. In more rural chautauquas, there was always a heightened salacious and carnival bent—tents emblazoned with their attractions in gigantic letters, DEVIL CHILD! BEARDED WOMAN FROM BORNEO, TATTOO ART, CANNIBAL PYGMIES, and so on, all in the guise of education, to lure in the provincial, the bored, the untraveled. They had fallen off in popularity, drastically, since the end of the war and now that radio was so popular. But most people in the rural areas of America, the forgotten fields and riversides, those small towns with a lot in which a carnival might set a pavilion—they still remember the chautauquas. Music and education and storytelling—possibly a little proselytizing—and mostly good, wholesome fun for the whole family (though I daresay many a country girl found herself in trouble months after, and hastily married).

Hines's chautauqua was simply a single canvas tent, no signage, quite large, with at least three center poles. I could hear no music from inside, just the hushed voices of conversations. The wall flaps had been dropped, no doubt to fend off the mosquitoes. Pulling back the lip of the tent, we entered.

There were more lanterns burning inside the tent, placed at regular intervals. A cluster of wooden folding chairs stood mostly empty at the far end, but there were ten or fifteen men, women, and children clustered around three seated figures—a white-haired man holding a guitar, a boy without eyelashes and with a port-wine stain on his neck cradling a violin, and a wisp of a woman with a dulcimer in her lap.

The white-haired man—Gramp Hines, I was sure—spoke softly to the gathered people. "Now, let me instruct you, since you so kindly asked: Never step over a fishing pole or another man's fishing line. Nor your own. If'n you do, you'll catch no more fish that day. Understand?" There was murmured assent and some of the gathered folks' heads bobbed in agreement. "They bite best when the light of the moon falls upon the water's upturned face. But if you pull them danged fish up, and the moonlight stays on them too long, they'll rot in a'hour unless you wrap 'em in walnut leaves."

"Walnut? I heard oak when I was a girl," a woman said.

"You misheard. Or listened to the wrong man," Hines said, shaking his head. "Don't bother with spoonbills, they ain't wholesome for eatin' and can't swim downstream. If you catch one, hang it high in a tree in an offering to the birds of the sky, because birds themselves swim in their own right. Swim in the currents of air." He held up a finger. "Catch you a mud turtle, and you'll feast on seven kinds of meat straight from the shell—pork, beef, chicken, duck, fish."

"That's only five," a boy said.

"What did I forget?" Gramp Hines counted his fingers and the gathered laughed. "Mutton and venison." He struck a chord on his guitar, a jangling discordant sound. "Spoonbills'll eat pawpaws, which is why they ain't good for people eatin', because everybody knows you always find a pawpaw next to a dogwood."

"Why's that matter?" the boy asked. Gramp Hines seemed to focus on the lad, peering at him.

"You got a mouth full o' questions," Hines said.

"He don't mean nothin' by 'em," a man said. "Just powerful curious, he is."

Hines nodded sagely. "Everybody knows—everybody except Junior here—that the dogwood was the tree they made the cross our lord and savior was crucified upon from, and all sorts of black things are drawn to them. Why, I once saw a dogwood with its boughs heavy with black serpents a-hissin' and spittin'—"

He stopped.

"Well, what have we here? You there in the back, come join us. Say hello, introduce yourselves."

Bunny and I moved forward into the light and began to introduce ourselves.

"Oh ho! It's the boys from the government," Hines said loudly. "Did you bring your record maker?"

"How—" I said. "Yes, we did. We hoped you'd allow us to record you."

"Well, of course!" Hines said. "Part of every good chautauqua involves some learnin', and I'd like everyone to see this newfangled technology at work."

Closer, I allowed myself a moment to take in Hines. He was a compact, solid man, with a jaw like an anvil and heavily muscled arms. Like Amoira, his age was indistinct, but I placed him at near sixty years old. Still hale enough for life on the road but waning in physical prowess. Maybe.

"How'd you know who we are?" Bunny asked.

Hines smiled. "Little bird told me." His answer did not sit well with me, though I did not allow my face to show my displeasure.

"Bring in the record maker! Gents, help the government boys out. They look like they could take a load off."

Bunny sat down and I managed the men who went to the Studebaker and trucked the SoundScriber into the tent. They were as solicitous of its well-being as I was—no lord or lady from Achæan past rode in a gilded palanquin with more careful bearers. But I sweated anyway. It was blasted hot, and the fire made the night hotter. I felt as though my blood boiled and all the water in my body wanted to evacuate through my pores.

We set up the SoundScriber and I gave a perfunctory lesson on its design and usage. The locals looked on with interested, if not too bright, faces. Happy to be spoken to, happy to be entertained.

Hines reasserted himself. "All right then, let's play a song for you," he said.

"We like to start off with 'Stagger Lee,' since it's such a—"

"We might get to ole Stack Lee, son, eventually," Hines said. "But I've got a few doozies up my sleeve these fine folks might want to hear. Might want to send the young ones out, though," he said, winking at an unaccompanied mother of two boys. Even in the low light of the tent, I could see her blush.

I readied an acetate disc, set the SoundScriber to recording, and lowered the cutting arm.

"Gramp Hines, accompanied by his family, recorded July 5 on commission by the United States Library of Congress, Harlan Parker, archivist."

Hines wasted no time before he started playing. He called out, "'Cotton-Eyed Joe'!" and the young man with the port-wine stain began sawing madly at the violin—or fiddle, as these roughspun mountain folk would call it—and Hines and the woman with the dulcimer joined in a rising crescendo until Hines called out, "'Granny, Does Your Dog Bite'!" and the tempo shifted, the melody pitched upward with a single minor interval, and the music trundled along for a while until Hines bellowed, "'Hot Time Down Below'!" and the tumult of instruments repeated a single tritone through an ascending scale—*diabolus in musica*—and so forth and so on for four or five more instrumental songs, filling the acetate.

The crowd clapped and exclaimed when I played back the recording, and even Hines chuckled at his own voice. "Damnation, Hank, that fiddle really cuts through the guitar and harmonium!" He turned to me. "Why, I thank you for the pleasure, Mister Parker, was it? It ain't often a man gets to put on a performance for his own self." I made notations on the disc's sleeve with a grease pencil, stored it in its carrying case, and withdrew a virgin disc for the SoundScriber.

Hines and his children did not hesitate; they quickly began strumming once the SoundScriber was cutting and began to play a happy melody. The fiddler boy opened his mouth and, in a pealing voice, began singing.

Big Tom, Little Tom, Big Tom Bailey,
He had a wife and three little babies—
One got sick and one got drownded,
One got lost and Grandpap found it.
One in the corner grave, the other in the cradle,
The other'n in the soup pot up to its ladle;
I love my wife and I love my baby,
And I love my biscuits sopped in fresh gravy.
Climb up, little boy, climb up higher,
Climb up, little one, your foot's in the fire—
Poor little Bailey—poor little fellow.
Poor little boy, he died in the cellar.
Big Tom, Little Tom, Big Tom Bailey,
He had a wife and three little babies.

It was sung in such a spritely and jovial manner, with such a youthful timbre, it took a moment for the words to register on me. What a morbid little tune. The next song was "Jump Jim Crow" and I won't bother with transcribing those lyrics here, but I've made note of them on the liner notes and will file them with Spivacke and the acetates once we've completed our assay and had a chance to transcribe them.

Hines played for an hour or more, and we used six acetate discs for that portion of the night. When I indicated that the last acetate was about to exhaust its available recording surface, Hines brought the song he was singing—"My Ship Is on the Ocean"—to an abrupt close. The dwindling crowd clapped, and he bid them good night. The few lingerers were shooed away. Once the tent was empty, Hines placed his hands on his knees and said, "Hoo-eee. All this singing sure brings on a powerful thirst. Martha?"

"Yes, Pa?" the wisp of a woman said.

"We got anything to drink?"

"Just a bucket of river water," she said.

"A powerful thirst," Hines said again.

A simple request would have sufficed. Instead, a telegraph. A performance. I looked to Bunny, hoping he'd take the hint and retrieve a bottle of whiskey from the car, but he was slumped in the folding chair, his legs stretched out in front of him, arms crossed, and head down. As a soldier, he could sleep while the Hun shelled our trenches in a downpour. Civilian life had not changed him. The excesses of his previous evening had caught up with him.

The package of blank acetates I'd brought in with the Sound-Scriber had been exhausted, so I took the fresh recordings out, went to the car and stored them in the lidded box provided me by the Library of Congress for disc storage, and placed them with their brothers. I took a fresh packet of paper-wrapped acetates and retrieved both a half-empty bottle and a full one, and a fresh pack of Pall Malls. I will not deny I was ready for a drink myself. I took a long pull from the open bottle before returning to the tent, the liquor worming its burning path down into my belly as I walked back. The boy guarding the front of the tent was gone and the fire had died down to seething coals. I reentered the tent and handed the bottle to Hines, who tilted it up and killed it. I broke the bonded papers on the fresh bottle, twisted off the cap, and passed it to Hines, who took another long drink. He in turn handed it to his son, who sipped daintily, then over to his daughter. She wiped the mouth of the bottle with the hem of her skirt and then tilted it up and nearly retched with the shiver of alcohol.

"So, Mister Hines, you seem to know quite a few songs. A man in West Virginia told us you know fifty-two songs more than anyone else."

"Just fifty-two?" Hines said. "I knowed more than that. They taught us well back in Cidersend."

"Cidersend?" I asked. That strange word rang a bell. "That's where you're from? A town, correct?"

"Never been a town, you can't rightly say. No electricity, no telegram, no highway. Was a track right through it where the wagons would come. Time was, there were orchards and children. But all that's gone now." His right arm was cradled over the hip of the guitar, and in his left he held the bottle. I lit a cigarette, reversed it, and offered it to him. He set down his guitar, took the cigarette, and narrowed his eyes, looking at me. "Just fifty-two songs?"

"That's what the gentleman said," I responded.

"Ain't no gentlemen in West Virginia," Hines said. "And ain't no gentlemen in this here tent either. Is there, Mister Parker from the Library of Congress?"

"I don't quite know what you mean. It's simply an honorific—"

He held up a hand to quiet me and I ceased speaking. I had an uncomfortable feeling that he was well aware of whatever liberties we might have taken with his wife, though I, myself, would be hard pressed to recount them and could not explain the feeling if I had to.

"You come for a song," he said. "That ole 'Stacker Lee.' But that ain't the real song you seek. I don't know *that* song." He drank from the bottle. "I might know another *shadow* of that song, though. Just like the ballad of ole Stacker is a shadow of a shadow of that song."

"What song?" I said. "What do you mean a shadow of a shadow of a song—"

Hines blew smoke and said, "Stacker got his hat, covered in blood. But it ain't a hat the song's about, it's a crown."

From his overall pocket he withdrew a tuning fork and held it up.

"You ever sat real quiet and still, Mister Parker? Maybe in the mornin' with the sun washin' over your bed, or in the wee hours of the night when you're all by yourself?"

"Of course," I said.

"In those quiet times, you ever felt the thrumming of the world?"

"I'm quite sure I don't know what you mean," I said.

Hines slapped the tuning fork upon the open palm of his other hand. A bright tone filled the interior of the tent, pulsing in waves. As the fork vibrated, its tines became blurry, indistinct. Hank and Martha began making slight adjustments to the tuning pegs of their instruments.

"The whole of human existence just like this here fork," Hines said. "A-frettin' and strivin' and castin' about." He grasped the fork in his hand, snuffing out the sound. He slipped it back in his pocket. "This ain't a song you can unhear."

He turned his head to his daughter and said softly, "We'll run through 'Think on Death and Judgment,' you hear me? Listen for the turnaround, and we'll hang on that to a—" He made his face into the mummery of sadness. He began strumming his guitar in a circular, hypnotic rhythm that was dissimilar from most mountain music I'd heard before—a three-quarter waltz time maybe, but there was something slippery about it and I couldn't count the beats to verify its time signature. Mountain music, and folk music in general, are simple distillations of more complex melodies and chord progressions: Much of it falls within the major scale and often, in my experience, working around the C chord. This progression lingered on minor chords, though—A minor to C, C to a strange diminished chord I could not place as guitar is not my specialty and Hines's fretting was slurry and indistinct. He continued on, moving from majors to minor falls easily, arpeggiating the lilt and sadness in his rough manner of picking, causing a haunting effect. Soon Martha joined, strumming the dulcimer lightly. Hank kept his violin cocked and plucked intervals, pizzicato, holding down a soft rhythmic melody that might have been filled with a more basso instrument.

Hines began to sing.

Come think on death and judgment,
Your time is almost spent.
You've been a wretched sinner;
Time has come to send
A word of your black bargain.
Lost in the days of youth;
A soldier red in slaughter,
Both words and deeds uncouth.
For lesser men are foolish
And hide by Christian names.
Come think on death and judgment,
Come think on what he'll claim.

He picked his guitar, keeping his eyes focused on its fretboard. Hank's and Martha's eyes too were fixed upon their instruments. There was a marked difference in their demeanor during the performance of this song and those they had played before. Before, Hines had focused his attention on the crowd, watching for whatever reaction or emotions his music might stir within the audience. But during this song, it was as if their eyes were lowered in deference, humility.

The music churned and swirled, Hank opened his port-stained mouth, and a low sound emanated, like a subtone from an organ or the drone of a hurdy-gurdy, and persisted, vibrating, shivering the air. Then Martha opened hers and another tone emanated from the hollow bell of her mouth, finding a harmony with her brother's. I felt a bizarre shiver run through me, and my skin rippled in goose bumps, as if a frigid draft of air had blown through the tent, though it was still sweltering hot in the still air.

Come think on death and judgment,
Your words have all been said.
A soldier home from warring,
His hands and heart stained red.
No water flows will clean you,
No ocean wash away
The stain that now corrodes you
Until your dying day.

The wind must have shifted. The tent's canvas walls rustled and flapped for a moment. A haze rose in the tent, stinging my eyes. The pinewood smudge fire to keep the mosquitoes away. I reached for the bottle and drank from it, rubbing my eyes. The music churned. In the shadows behind Hines and his children, I made out two figures: silver haired, feminine.

Amoira.

And her twin? They came forward, swaying with the music, long silver hair loose and wild, obscuring their faces, wearing simple white dresses. Feet gnarled, hands sharp. I would have stood, but my surprise, mingled with guilt and fear, arrested me. I could not move.

Hines and his children continued, eyes lowered.

Supposin' you'd lie down this night,
A-thinkin' all was well,
Your eyes would then be closed in death,
Your soul awake in Hell,
To make your case before him,
How you have sown his seeds.
Pray he'll grant power and mercy,
Give mercy, my lord, on me.

The two swaying women—*Amoira!*—began a series of bizarre yet elegant genuflections and hand gestures as the music pulsed and churned. First stretching down to the ground, then rearward, toward the gathering shadows and smoke at the back of the tent. In a syncopated movement, they slipped off their white dresses and stood naked in the shifting kerosene-lantern light.

The darkness behind Hines swelled, movement within it. At first I thought what I saw was a horse, a white horse, and then the thing grew and shifted to a shoulder and haunch of an ox, leached of all color. A pale muscular animal in dim light. But the darkness shifted once more and from it came forth a man, alabaster white.

He was nude, and enormous, at least seven feet tall, bald head brushing the canvas of the tent's roof. I tried to look toward Bunny, to see if he was joined with me in this towering spectacle, but I found I could not move; a sickening paralysis had settled upon me, and even my eyes were fixed in their sockets.

The great man stepped closer, out of the shadows. Utterly devoid of hair and bone white. A tremendous phallus swung between his legs. He seemed powdered with talcum, a great amount of it, sloughing off his body like grave mold from a revenant. The shock of his manhood alarmed me in ways I could not express. A challenge, a lasciviousness, a disease. There were bloody cankers on his member, and at his mouth, bubbling sores. Though, visually, his first impression was of whiteness, beneath the powder—the talcum caked upon him, every inch—beneath that sloughing veneer, there seemed rot, a discoloration. A sweet-sickly odor assaulted my nostrils.

Raising his arms above his head, he began to drag a foot, and then the other, back and forth, until I realized that he danced. *He danced.*

> *Raise your eyes to heaven,*
> *Behold this vault of ground.*
> *Give praise and supplication,*
> *Shuck off your fleshy gown,*
> *And take up dev'lish raiment,*
> *And crimson become crown'd.*

As Hines's words rang out, over and over, turning upon themselves, the alabaster man began to shift and sway in a writhing torsion. *Music, a ritual with the power to transform both the singer and the listener.* His hands and body traced courses in the air as if he was both in pain and mocking it, simultaneously. The music continued, with Hines singing over and over, *Take up dev'lish raiment, and crimson become crown'd.* Notes coursing and turning and devouring each other.

The man diminished; I cannot explain how. One moment his bald pate brushed the ceiling of the tent, the next he was as a normal man. He waned, like the moon. He shrank, a refraction. Falling away, *tempo ritardando*. The two Amoiras had disappeared into the smoke.

A writhing gavotte, a shivered drag. The alabaster man moved with unctuous and sliding grace. Talcum (or was it ash?) fell from him in a constant flurry. He was a small man. His penis had withered and collapsed, so that it appeared as small and puny as some Renaissance statue's. He was the size of a boy, shrinking. *And crimson become crown'd, and crimson become crown'd.* A vile infant now, squirming, twitching. A wail pierced the music, the child's cry. A writhing serpent.

A worm.

A pallid maggot.

Gone.

Smoke billowed inside the tent. The song ended, stretching into silence.

A moment's pause and then a voice crying, *Fire! Fire!* The illumination shifting, growing. Heat.

The sound of glass breaking and then a wash of yellow-orange light overcame me. Heat, intense. And close. The tent was on fire.

I found I could move once more. I pushed my way up and called out for Bunny, but there was no response. The tent was shrouded in black, oily smoke, tearing at my eyes, scratching in my lungs. Behind me, at the entrance, the tent's canvas was awash in flames; one of the support poles stood uncertainly in a pool of fire—the ruins of a kerosene lamp.

The roof shifted and lowered, flames racing along its surface. Panic rose in me. Arms above my head like some long-deceased Pompeian in a Roman mosaic, I pushed toward the back of the tent, where the two Amoiras had entered and the powdered, alabaster giant had made his way into this world. Hands grabbed me. A great cacophony of voices rang out, even though I felt as though I were alone. Hines, his progeny, their instruments. All gone.

Blind, I pushed out of the rear of the tent, where the cankerous man had entered. Reeling, stumbling into the hot darkness, my arms outstretched before me, feeling. Hands struck at me, ripped at my face. The world tilted and I felt myself toppling forward. I tumbled, ass over head, and felt myself pitch into water. There was a dislocation; I did not know which direction was up, under the surface. I felt hands again.

I lashed out at whoever gripped me. Their clutch tightened.

That shadowed form, indistinct in the warp and shifting prism of the water's surface. Cruel hands holding me below the surface. The Mother Chautauqua.

Rage then, like I knew from old. The loss of my mother. The great pounding heat of German guns and British artillery. The stench of the dead and blood and bowels and shit, steaming in the air. A wet snarl of a man's intestines. My hands traced the arms back to the body. I lashed out with my fists, intent on harm, the panic of self-preservation rising in me. I felt a blow connect and someone's weight plow into me, dragging me down. My feet found the river bottom. I breached the surface, water streaming. But a frenzied blood haze rose in me and with one hand I held him and the other I thrashed and struck out viciously, violently, over and over. I caught glimpses of Amoira's face, mouth open in ecstasy as I thrust against her; Hines's face, singing, mouth an open bell; Bunny's face, hands up, screaming.

A slackness. Fingers slipping to float away.

I slogged forward, my clothes tugging at me with the current, and pulled myself onto the shore on my hands and knees. I lay upon my back and took draft upon draft of air, staring at the rising smoke. I coughed. I retched. The Obion flowed beside me.

Faintly, I was aware of the sound of a truck, maybe, or the roaring of some infernal engine. But my senses were playing tricks on me.

I do not know how long I lay there, in the smoking dark.

I might have passed out of thought, for a while at least, into the blessed release of oblivion.

18

Harlan Parker: The SoundScriber

The trees, the brush, the interlaced canopy of life stilled. The river called in a low murmur. I opened my eyes.

I was alone. I pushed myself up on unsteady feet. The night sounds had quieted except for my labored breathing; I stood there panting in the dark, broken only by the light of cinders from the fire. A coughing spell overwhelmed me and I stumbled away from the river, hacking heavily. Tripping, fumbling, I found myself back at the Studebaker. There were no other cars around, though plenty of tire tracks mired the semisoft ground. The fires—both the smudge pit at the front of the tent and the tent itself—smoldered in the dark.

I called for Bunny but there was no answer. Where could he have gone? I toggled on the Studebaker's headlights. Maybe he thought I was dead and he went with the Hines clan, in their truck? I was chilled with a thought: Maybe he did not make it out of the tent. Within the narrow window of light cast by the car's headlights, I saw a smoking shape in the sooty ash of the tent's ruins. I ran forward. All I could taste was smoke and ash.

I approached the blackened shape. The SoundScriber. There was no saving it. The fire that had torn through the tent had left it charred and unusable.

"Bunny!" I yelled, turning about, cupping my hands around my mouth. "Edmund!"

There was no answer. I searched the area, hoping against hope that I would not find any bodies, but it seemed I was the sole remainder of this particular chautauqua. However long I had been passed out, they must have lost me in the darkness. But why would they—why would Bunny—leave me? It didn't make sense.

I checked the contents of the car. Nothing was missing, not the acetates, not my gear, not the box of whiskey or our supplies of tinned food. Nothing except Bunny's bag. He'd gone.

How long had I been unconscious?

I drank some more whiskey, and waited, hoping they would return. They did not. With much effort, I moved the ruined SoundScriber into the car and by morning, I left.

As far as driving goes, I am not proficient at it and do not have the knack of switching gears easily. By the time I had arrived in Memphis, the Studebaker had become more familiar to me, but I fear I might have done some damage to the transmission during my acclimation period.

And now I am here, in this hotel. I would transcribe acetates—*thank heavens I brought them to the car!*—but I cannot until I receive a new SoundScriber. So, I must content myself with writing this, and filling out expense reports.

The Gayoso is luxurious. Normally I would be relaxed. The bed is soft and sleep should be restful. But I have terrible dreams and wonder where Bunny might have gone.

In the morning I will go to the police and report the fire. And Bunny's disappearance.

19

Cromwell: Edmund Whitten

Cromwell pauses between recordings. The music has become a crackling drone and he is weary. It's afternoon now and the day drags on. He's gone back and forth, splitting his attention between the audio and Parker's journal. And now something bothers him.

"Crumb, why don't you go on back to the hotel," Hattie says. "We've got twenty-three acetates left. I can record ten or fifteen more and then we can finish the rest in the morning." She looks at him with a kind but stern expression. Her phrasing might be as a question, but her demeanor indicates she's not interested in his arguing with her.

"No, I need to be present for the recordings."

She places her headphones on top of the Pelican case and stands. "We can call it a day. And I could use some coffee. I'll drive you to the hotel."

On the way back, she remains silent, but he can feel her glances. He holds Parker's journal in his lap.

"You really need that? I can—"

"I'm just tired, Hattie," he says, before she can start.

"Seem to be really digging into his journal," she says, gesturing.

"It's fascinating," Cromwell says. "My sleep's been off. Reading'll put me to sleep. And there's something I want to investigate here."

"What?" Hattie asks.

"Edmund Whitten. Bunny, Parker's driver and friend." He taps the journal. "He made an abrupt 'departure' from the trip and I need to get back to my computer and see what I can find on him."

"What do you think happened?"

"No idea, but there is at least the possibility that Parker might be losing his mind," Cromwell says.

"Insert joke about working for the ell-oh-cee here," Hattie says. "But all this stuff happened eighty years ago, so it's not like there's a huge rush. You need to get some sleep. I got some Benadryl in my bag, I think. Poor folks' Ambien. You want some?"

"Sure," Cromwell says. "It always used to knock William out when he—" He stops.

Hattie says nothing. The rest of the ride is silent. At the hotel, she ducks into her room and returns with a pink pill. He thanks her and retreats into his room.

Cromwell doesn't take the pill, though. He puts down the journal and from a black bag removes his laptop. He opens it, uses his forefinger to clear its security. In a browser window, he logs in to the Library of Congress archives, both the outward-facing databases and those not yet (if they ever would be) made public. In the advanced search tab Cromwell enters the name Edmund Whitten, specifies the year 1938, and initiates the query.

The Library of Congress servers are notoriously slow, especially from remote access, but eventually his search results populate the browser window.

A record of Harlan Parker's contract, where Edmund Whitten is mentioned as a subcontractor. Another mention in a telegram from H. Parker to Harold Spivacke—*I have a driver, veteran of the Great War and old friend, Edmund Whitten. AKA Bunny.* A missing person's report from the *Memphis Register,* dated early August, filed by Harlan Parker in July 1938.

That is all.

Cromwell searches for Edmund Whitten, with no date range specified.

An FBI file, declassified in the seventies and digitized in 2006, showing Whitten to be considered a Communist sympathizer, if not agent. The report is dated February 1934.

No other mentions.

No death certificate, no obituary. But the Library's archives are incomplete. Whitten could've lived to a ripe old age and unless the appropriate newspaper had been digitized, Cromwell would never know.

Rubbing his chin, he enters *body found in Obion River, 1938.*

One hit. A paragraph in the *Dyersburg Clarion,* dated July 22: *The Dyer County assistant sheriff issued a statement to the press, declaring that the body of a man was discovered on the shores of the Obion River, only three miles from the confluence of that river and the Mississippi, and remains unidentified due to advanced decay. His body has been interred at the Dyer County morgue and will receive a pauper's funeral. Any information regarding his identity should be reported to Mike Hanson with the Dyer County Sherriff's Department.*

Cromwell reaches for the phone and calls Hattie. His call goes to voicemail. He calls again, and she answers. "What? I just lay down."

"There's something I need you to see."

"Crumb, this better not be—"

"Goddamn it, Hattie," he says. He thinks about Vivian, he thinks about Maizie. "I think Harlan Parker killed his driver."

"Really?" Hattie sounds skeptical.

"Yes."

"Gimme a couple of hours, I'm gonna go to the hotel gym," she says. "Keepin' it tight."

"Right. Just whenever," he says. "Not like he's going to get more dead."

Cromwell retrieves ice from the humming machine down the hall. He feels dislocated, from either lack of sleep or the oneiric quality of Parker's journal, he cannot tell. The impersonal, bland hallway clad in industrialized carpeting and lit by evenly spaced economy sconces seems to stretch on and on in his vision, as if he's caught a glimpse of himself in an infinity mirror. It is not the repeated image stretching off into oblivion that is the disconcerting aspect of that particular optical effect, he knows, it's the barren and empty focus on whoever is caught between the mirrors. He returns to the hotel room, dumps the ice in the sink, and fills it with cold water. He plunges his face below the surface, allowing the cold to prick his skin. He opens his eyes, as if in rapport with Parker, but there is nothing there, no insight, no understanding. He lifts his face from the water when his lungs swell in his chest, outraged and starving for air. He thinks about Harlan Parker, and what the man wrote of the events at the Obion chautauqua. He thinks about Parker's mother.

Dripping, he stands in the room, unsure for a long while of what to do, opening and closing his hands. He dresses slowly, puts on his overcoat, and goes to the door. Just a quick walk to clear his head. The long day hunched over the journal listening to acetates has taken its toll.

He wanders out of the hotel. It's still cold and now dark. He finds himself trudging along a thoroughfare, a wide empty highway leading away from the brightly lit Holiday Inn's environs toward an area that has seen better days. He passes an empty strip mall, and a large square building with broken windows and a faint industrial cast—he recalls Missouri used to have a booming industry, but for the life of him he cannot think of what that might be—then continues on past a neighborhood of dark houses. Through a very quiet industrial park full of metal buildings with signs like VERNOR BROS. UPHOLSTERY, MEGAWATT A/V RENTAL, CENTERVIEW MINI-STORAGE. Very few cars move on the roads, and the sky is overcast, so the stars are gone and the spaces between streetlights are very dark.

As it does on many walks at night, his attention becomes focused downward, on his own feet, minding his steps, feeling the movement of his body as his heart rate rises.

It's a moment before he realizes he's beyond the neighborhoods and industrial park and on either side of the road are two fields. *You get this mix of urban and farmland in the Midwest,* he thinks, *where neighborhoods run right up and kiss these vestigial fields. What could they have planted here? Where's the farm?* He looks back over his shoulder to the last streetlight. It is a small speck burrowed in a dark tree line. *Am I still in town? How did I wander so far?*

He looks out in the dark over the stubble of last summer's furrows and stops. A dim white figure stands motionless.

"Hello?" Cromwell says. "Hello? Are you all right?"

A breeze ruffles the figure's clothing. Is it a child? A woman? He cannot tell. He leaves the road and tumbles forward, a misstep in the dark. The ground is hard, and frozen, and when he stands back up, his outraged shin and scraped palms where he arrested his fall burn in the cold air. His breath comes in white plumes.

The figure is gone.

He feels a shrinking sensation. A tear in the cloud cover above passes overhead and a spray of stars appears above him momentarily, brilliant and casting a blue light about. He hears a laughter far off, faint, but then a dog barks in the distance, obscuring the sound.

He looks up to the sky and feels the yawn of the tear and the stars beyond and his infinitesimal place in the world, standing at night, in an unknown field, far from everything he's ever known or loved.

He turns slowly. It takes him an hour to get back to the hotel.

Entering his room, he moves to the bed and lies down, thinking of sleep, the empty, emotionless release of it. He doesn't take the Benadryl. He used to nap—even at work he used to be able to sneak to the parking lot, kick back his seat in the Toyota, close his eyes, allow his breathing to slow, and let sleep take him for a short while. Until he was refreshed. But that was before the affair. It was then he lost that ability. In a hotel room very much like this one. The moment his prick slipped into Viv and she rolled back to give him better entry, the life behind his closed eyes had become clouded, threaded with guilt.

He picks up the journal and begins to read once more as he waits for Hattie.

20

Harlan Parker: Darcy, Arkansas

July 8, 1938

Western Union Telegram—Harlan Parker

Will have recorder and discs shipped to Darcy, posthaste. Transferring operating funds to Darcy Bank & Trust. Expect them within week.

Harold Spivacke, Division of Music, Library of Congress

It was hard passing Greenville—the emerald of the Mississippi River—to travel on to Darcy. H. L. Mencken, that onerous, brilliant man, wrote of the miasmic jungles of Arkansas, and as I drove on, the heat growing intolerable, sweat discoloring my clothing, I understood what he meant. I have spent enough time in the South and I fear he meant the unnamed jungles in the hearts of men.

Darcy is a quaint little town on the shores of the Mississippi. It is but thirty miles from Helena, and fifteen from Rosedale, Mississippi—though on the wrong side of the river—but it seems removed, in some ways, from the rest of the world. No major highways connect it to other towns, and the dry lakes that ring it—watershed areas for the Mississippi—seem moatlike in the steaming heat of day.

I found a ferry at Rosedale, a great diesel contraption that accepted the Studebaker without problem as two roustabouts placed chocks under its wheels. It carried a family of weary farmers in a Model T truck—held together with wire and scrap metal—and two mules hitched to a wagon. For two bits, it took me across the Mississippi. The ferryboat captain was no Charon, simply a drunken and grizzled old river boatman, pistol at his waist, looking for all the world like a farmer who decided late in life to become a river pirate. The ferry barge seemed tiny on the face of the great river. It was somewhere around here that Hernando de Soto's body had been secretly dumped into the Mississippi, to not alert the native population that the great Spanish god had died. We landed on the far shore in a stand of old-growth trees, cottonwoods and oaks. Mosquitoes teemed by the trillions. A fat, black moccasin slipped into the water from the brush of the shore, and I watched it with fascination. The barge captain whistled, patted his pistol, and winked at me.

Darcy suffered heavily from the Great Flood but there were no rills on Main Street, no water stains on stately homes lining docile streets named after trees—Oak, Poplar, Birch—many of the houses replete with Ionic columns and cast-iron lawn jockeys for horses. I felt a heaviness press on me as I passed these manicured dwellings—I was much easier in the pomp and blare of the city, or the wild, unkempt sprawl of tenements and the poor. I was ill at ease in the idylls of landed gentry. But, like some goliard in ancient days, I needed patrons, and it was here I could find them.

The Darcys are a family of farmers who built this town from the alluvial soil of the delta, draining the brakes and sloughs for farmland, felling the giant old trees lining the Mississippi, piling earth between berm and barrow to make levees to hold back the wrath of the river—all on the backs of the Negroes that lived here in tenement shacks south of the rail line to the river port. Once I entered the town, I simply had to ask at the Chevrolet dealership the location of the Darcy home and was directed there straightaway.

At the door, I was greeted by a black housekeeper who led me through the ornate interior of the home into a sitting room where a white man a few years my junior sat with a whiskey in hand, next to a very pregnant woman—obviously his wife—who had her face near a humming, black General Electric fan.

"Mistuh Parker," the housekeeper said in introduction, and was moving away before the people in the room had a chance to respond.

"Thank you, Sophie," the woman replied, breathless.

The man stood up, came forward, hand out. He was dressed immaculately in a tan suit and crisp shirt and tie that had not had the opportunity to wilt in the heat yet. He was a small, compact fellow, quite handsome. We shook.

"Jack Darcy, though everyone around here calls me Jackdaw," he said, smiling. "Forgive Persephone for not getting up—"

"I am hot and bothered," Persephone said, hand at the small of her back, damp hair stuck to her neck, though the Darcy home, with its electric fans and heavy curtains, garlanded in oak and cottonwood trees and capped by crape myrtles, was as cool as any building could be at this time of year. "No, that didn't come out right. I am hot and *intemperate,* and fixing to burst."

Jackdaw winced and then said, "We're expecting our second child here, in the next few weeks."

"I would be fine if it happened today," she said. "Fix me a drink, Jackdaw, and one for our guest. Mister Parker, come sit. Tell us all about yourself. Entertain me. Anything. I need distraction."

I did as she wished and sat down next to her on the couch. Jackdaw brought us scotch, with ice. Persephone lit a cigarette and looked at me brazenly as she smoked it. "So, Harlan," she said. "Can I call you Harlan?" She went on without waiting for a response from me. "Tell me about your folklife studies. Jackdaw has given me a little information, and we have your books, though I must admit they're a little dry for my tastes."

"No heaving bosoms," Jackdaw said.

"That is unkind, husband," Persephone said. "Though not altogether untrue. Jackdaw says that in addition to being a scholar, you are rumored to be quite a pianist."

Jackdaw smiled at me, taking a seat nearby. "My uncle attended Washington and Lee around the same time as you and told me how you spent your weekends in Georgetown. At the Harrow."

It had been many years since I thought about my time at the Harrow Club in Washington as a performer: there, I swung like a metronome between the respectable Mahler quartets, piano adaptations of Strauss and Ravel, and then pivoting to the other extreme with Irving Berlin's romps, performing for the rich, pampered guests of the gentlemen there. I was paid well, and treated very much like some carnival sideshow oddity, this embeggared yet brilliant fourteen-year-old stick figure with spindly fingers, more at ease in the kitchen with the Negro help than in the library at the grand piano. A child of two worlds: During the week, I lived at Washington and Lee, but on the weekends, I slept in an attic room of the Harrow Club and wore a tuxedo not my own yet tailored especially for me, spending every free moment either working on my studies or walking in the city. My grandparents, who took me in after Mother died, were sad to see me go, yet proud of my acceptance to Washington and Lee at such a young age. Their wunderkind, their prodigy. And no prodigy can remain static in this world. But university, they could not afford it. I was a young man of ability, if not means, so the Harrow welcomed me and I could leave there with my time rewarded. Possessed of a degree.

And something more.

During that time, I searched for a man. Insull. My mother's lover. My mother's killer. I was just a boy, and angry. I knew where he came from. I remembered the dime, hot in my palm, when he sent me away from her to watch the Negro minstrels.

I remembered how I never saw her again.

Possibly it was there I began my interest in the "rougher" musics, the songs crooned by Sibyl, the Harrow's head cook, the call-and-response work songs belted out by roustabouts down on the wharf.

I told Jackdaw and Persephone of my studies, and my trip so far, glossing over much of the hardships and focusing on the bright, entertaining parts. But Jackdaw expressed real dismay at my recounting the loss of the SoundScriber. "This is terrible!" he exclaimed. "Where can you purchase one? Maybe I can expedite things."

"My superior has already purchased one, and it will be sent here," I said. "But until then, I am unable to record."

"Well, you can do some scouting, then," he said. "I have just the man to help you."

"Who do you have in mind?" Persephone said, turning her face this way and that in the flow of the fan.

"Big Tap's Augie," he said.

"Oh ho," Persephone said. "The perfect Virgil to Mister Parker's Dante."

Jackdaw chuckled. "Quapaw isn't so hellish as all that."

"That is very true," Persephone said. "Hell is cold."

"Don't talk like that, darling," Jackdaw said. "It's morbid. What will Harlan think?"

"He'll think that the heat is driving me mad," Persephone

said, looking at me strangely. "Do you think I'm mad, Mister Parker?"

"Discomfort can drive anyone batty. You have ice for your scotch," I said, taking a large swallow. "It's very good."

"That's the last of it until this afternoon. I cannot tell you how much money I spend on the stuff. More than on gasoline for the automobiles and farm equipment!" Jackdaw looked at me a little sheepishly. "It was costing me so much, I ended up buying the whole icehouse. Who knew selling water to hot people would become so profitable."

"I have them place hundred-pound blocks in my bedroom in a washtub and place the fan by it," Persephone said. "Sometimes I strip down and climb in there with it. It's quite scandalous, I assure you."

I imagined her belly pressing against the ice. Jackdaw said, "It's not a scandal if you tell everyone you do it, darling."

Persephone sniffed. "Allow me my scandals, dear," she said, lighting another cigarette and taking a sip of the iced scotch. "My assignations with blocks of ice are one of the few vices left me."

"My name's Augustus Franklin Hughes but everyone 'round these parts just calls me Augie on account of their piss-poor memory," Augie said in introduction. He was a tall, lean black man with gray in his beard, the white of it in sharp contrast to his skin. He dressed neatly in khaki pants and khaki shirt, with a pistol at his side and a proud Stetson hat, putting me in mind immediately of Stagger Lee. Jackdaw had driven me out to a town called Howard, a few miles south, and brought me to the front door of a columned plantation home. The home's owner—a man named Tap Howard whom everyone in the county called Big Tap—was riding his fields on horseback, but his right-hand man, Augie, was happy to guide me. "They say you work for the government."

"Not full-time, but I am contracted with them currently," I said. "I record folk music."

"That right?" he said, though the way he said it, it made me think he did not understand fully my purpose. Or, more likely, he just didn't care.

Augie nodded. "Well come on, let's go. Got someone I want to introduce you to."

"Really?" I asked. "Who's that?"

"Finest musician in Quapaw County." He laughed. "Finest musician in all Mississippi, Arkansas, Tennessee, and maybe even Louisiana."

"Truly?" I said, interested.

Augie nodded. "There's something uncanny about the boy. Not all right upstairs," he said, tapping his temple with a long forefinger. "But shoo-ie, can he play."

He led me to his work truck and we both got in. He removed his Stetson and placed it on the seat between us. "Mind the lid, Mister Parker."

He started the car and drove with a practiced hand, left arm hanging out the window, patting the truck's door.

"Is every town around here named after planters?" I said.

"Funny, ain't it?" he said, smiling. "The men who own the land want to put their name on it, too." He chuckled. "Most of 'em would get down in the mud and do the old bump and grind with it if there was half a chance." He looked away from the dirt road for a moment to gauge my reaction to what he said. "You're different, if I might say."

"How so?" I asked.

"Most white folks would tut-tut and act all offended. But not you."

I shrugged. "Spend most of your life on the outside looking in, nothing really surprises you."

Augie nodded and looked back to the road, his face a study in thought. "That might be true," he said. "But a man that thinks he can't be surprised is like to get a big one."

We rode in silence for a while. The summer sky had turned white with haze, and the umber fields and cotton dashed away from our vehicle, growing more indistinct in the distance. The far tree line, the levee beyond, and past that, the Mississippi flowing south in its indomitable course, past Greenville and Vicksburg, until it reached the gulf, dumping countless tons of silt and alluvial soil into the sea—all moved in slow progression.

"Lemme ask you a question," Augie said after a while. "The Great War, was you?"

I indicated I was. Augie whistled in response.

"Damn shame when men die. But I read an article that said that over six million horses died over there, and I liked to cry when I saw that." Augie paused, thinking. "You a religious man?"

I thought about the sodden French and Belgian countryside. The ruins of buildings, steaming craters in the mud, the bodies of both men and horses in great rotting tangles, bodies indiscriminate, mired in the wreckage of food, water, and munition wagons. War is but the throwing away of life—the lives of men, horses, animals—at the other side until one nation, one army emerges victorious. How willing are you to let men die? How much life can you pump at that bunker, that embankment, that fortification? Throw more life at it than the other side has, or is willing to expend, and the day is yours. Will you give a thousand lives? Ten?

Horses die. Men die. Mothers, brothers, sisters. We live down in the mud and there we run the course of our lives with very little hope of an end to our pain, or a release once the pain is gone. Our lives spin out, unraveling, and we have to live them.

"No, I'm not a religious man," I said.

"That's good, because we going to di Tonti's and I didn't want you to get all righteous. It's just Friday."

"Di Tonti's?"

"Indian mound. Rising up out of the Old Bottoms. French Indian family, pretty black girls all living together with a big parlor and rooms to their selves."

"Ah," I said. "And in the parlor . . ."

"A piano. Ozzie's there, most days, or at the Whitmore. Ain't no way Mister Darcy can take you to di Tonti's himself, no, his reputation wouldn't stand the storm that would blow in then. But he owns it, the land around it, and some of his walking-around money comes from di Tonti's. Every time one of them girls opens her legs, a silver dollar pops to life in his pocket."

I was surprised, though nothing in my personal experience would have run contrary to the idea that Darcy might have points on a house of ill repute. It seemed that like Persephone, he had his own scandals quick to hand, though he was far less willing to speak of them than his wife.

As he'd said, it wasn't nearly so scandalous if you could freely talk about it.

We continued on, entering a thick, wooded slough with old-growth oaks, easily ten feet wide at the base and towering above. The shade offered by the trees was at first welcome until Augie began cranking up his window. "You'll be a gallon short of blood soon if you don't watch out," he said, indicating I should roll up my own. I reluctantly followed his instructions.

Once, in Germany, after the war, I slept a summer night at a river's brim, and when I awoke I was pocked with angry, swollen bug bites—the tenacity and voraciousness of Old World mosquitoes. Old World mosquitoes do not rush. They watch and wait until you are asleep. They devoured me through my clothes. But those insects, millions of generations after supping on their first human blood, had grown contemptuous. New World mosquitoes were still in love with the blood of man, still thrilled and drunk from its novelty, desperate for the taste of it and not full of the wiles of bloodlust. In the shade of the old growth, they make bee-lines for your waking face, your wrist, your ear. With the windows up, the truck's cab became stuffy and hot quickly, and I began pouring with sweat. Augie, like many men who live their lives outside, seemed utterly indifferent to the heat.

We came upon a rising mound of earth, crowned in trees, at least as high as the levee that kept the Mississippi at bay. Trees grew on the earthen flanks, and at its summit stood a house, gray in the dappled shadows, verdigrised with moss around its skirts where the rain fell and wetted the wood around the base. It had a wraparound porch with an upper floor whose tiled roof might have been clay found on a Tudor manse or a Spanish villa, it was hard to tell. An offshoot looked for all the world like a shotgun shack appended as an afterthought, with a thick brick chimney from some other, more substantial building style. It was a bizarre conglomeration of looks, and sprawling, two—maybe three—stories, occupying the whole crown of the mound.

"Call these mounds the Quapaw Indians, like the county, and I've heard them named as Toltecs, but some professor came down here and said that was a made-up name. Only Indians I know about 'round here are Choctaws and Chickasaws, but I'm not really educated on Indian issues." Augie sucked his teeth for a moment, then continued on. "You'll have to pay your respects to Fantine di Tonti—she's the lady of the house—and then you'll be able to talk to Ozzie, have him play a bit, if you want some of the finest music you're like to hear in this world or the next."

I nodded as we came to a graveled area where two cars were parked, and he stopped his truck and we climbed out. It was cooler in the shade, but almost immediately the mosquitoes began to whine and press in at every bit of exposed skin. We trotted up to the house, and the main doors, constructed in a French style you might find in any bar or social club in New Orleans, opened before we could knock, and we were welcomed in by two large bearded white men who obviously stood as enforcers. It was dark and cool inside: Heavy drapes trapped in the cooler air from night and there was a fountain merrily tinkling away somewhere. Fans hummed and rotated back and forth, and the house smelled of women, and tallow, and perfume, and fried food.

One of the bruisers led us into a salon to the side of the main atrium and a woman sat at a small rolltop desk and wrote in a ledger. In the sprawl of her area there were novels, newspapers, letters, and telegrams. A Victrola stood in the corner playing Holst's *Mars* with all its pomp and blare, yet turned down to a soft level. When we entered, she stopped her writing, blotted the page, and then stood and welcomed us both.

"Augie, you're back," she said, a smile playing about her lips.

"Aw, Miss Fantine, don't you be teasing me. You know I have to check up on young Ozzie, as he's dear."

"It's good to see you," Fantine said. Her attention shifted to me. She looked at me with wide, clear eyes. She had a light brown complexion, indicating some sort of mixed race I could not discern, and an open and unlined face. She was younger than I thought a madam might be, but there was a mottled look to the skin of her neck, dashing away into her blouse. She'd been in a fire at some point and burned badly at that. "And Mister Harlan Parker, of the Library of Congress." She smiled openly then, at my surprised expression. "Darcy is a very small town and we now are on the telephone switch with Winslow Corner. With Cathy Downing at the switchboard, there are no secrets anymore."

Augie snorted and shifted his Stetson from hand to hand.

"I brought Mister Parker to meet young Ozzie. He's gonna record him, if that's all right with you."

"I think that will be acceptable, as long as I receive a recording as well."

"I can arrange that," I said. "Though I won't have a new recorder until early next week. But I would love to meet Ozzie."

"Well, we won't keep you from him, then," Fantine di Tonti said. But she held up a hand and looked at Augie, who bowed his head and stepped out for a moment, leaving us alone. "I don't know what you know about him, Mister Parker, but he's an intelligent boy, and a brilliant musician. But he has . . . difficulties."

"Difficulties? Of what sort?" I asked.

"You know of the flood?"

"Yes, the Great Flood of twenty-seven. It changed the South."

"More than the South," she said, a very intense look upon her face. "There was a levee breach south of here. It was like god himself released his wrath upon us for our sins."

You a religious man? Augie had asked. I waited for the rest of it from di Tonti.

"Ozzie lost both of his parents during the flood and, in doing so, gained something."

"Gained something? I don't understand."

"More than just the levee was breached. He was transfixed across the veil."

"I don't understand what you mean, I assure you."

"He's ghost-haunted, Mister Parker. He sees them everywhere."

I thought about what she was saying. "So, he suffered a blow to the head, maybe?" For a moment, the giant white-powdered man from Hines's chautauqua tent danced in my mind, sores at his mouth and cankers along his prick, diminishing. "Or his sanity has been tried?"

"The boy is sane, sir, I assure you. He can see the dead," she said simply, "his own and others'."

I laughed, looking about for Augie. "Surely this is a joke."

Di Tonti shrugged, disinterested in me then. "All right, Mister Parker. You've been warned. I'll grant you some time today with Ozzie and then after your interview, possibly a recording session. But that depends."

"You are . . . serious?" I asked. "The boy possesses some sort of phantasmagorical sense?"

Fantine di Tonti returned to her desk, picked up the *Commercial Appeal,* and opened it. It was clear my audience with her had ended. "A pleasure to meet you, Mister Parker," she said, her voice devoid of any pleasure. "Frontenac will lead you to Ozzie." One of the bearded bruisers appeared at the door to her salon and led me away, down a hall to where dark-wood pocket doors stood closed. The man, Frontenac, opened them, revealing a luxuriously appointed salon with multiple divans, a Victrola, a dry bar, and an upright player piano against the far wall. Low electric lights gave the room a yellow, cheery atmosphere and Augie sat near a young black man at the piano. The boy was saying, "And how's my auntie?" A pause. "I miss her."

Augie said, "The reverend is a hard man, not like to forgive." The boy bowed his head. Augie said more quietly, "But she did give me this here letter for you." The boy took the letter and opened it, reading it closely. I remained between the doors, not wanting to interrupt their conversation. Eventually the boy sniffed and tucked the letter away in his back pocket.

"Want to introduce you to a Mister Harlan Parker, Oz-man. He works for the government," Augie said.

The boy—young man, really—turned on the piano bench to look at me and his eyes widened and he cocked his head. I looked behind me and back at the boy. He was maybe sixteen or seventeen, and very thin, with long, articulate hands and an exceptionally large head, closely cropped, with protruding ears. His lanterned green eyes took me in, and the area around me, as if I were a group of men rather than an individual. He stood, approached me, and extended his hand.

In the South, shaking hands with a white man was something reserved for other white men. Luckily, I am not a Southern man. I shook his hand happily. The boy said, "I'm Oswell Bishop Munk, but everybody calls me Ozzie or Oz-man. Easier to remember, I reckon."

Augie laughed and clapped him on the back. "Let you two get acquainted," Augie said. "Mosey over to see if there's anything happening with Miss Chloe in the kitchen." He winked.

I sat down at the piano and the boy sat next to me. I blocked out a chord and then another and soon I was playing Béla Bartók's piano sonata *Sostenuto e pesante,* from memory, its jangling and aggressive chords, unexpected and atonal melodies. I could feel the boy become quite still as he sat beside me and I worked through the piece. In many ways, I would not be here if not for Bartók—a Hungarian, he was the first comparative musicologist and the father of ethnomusicology, interested in folklore and folk musics of the peasants of Hungary and Romany. He translated that into his work, channeling the rougher, simpler musics and making them palatable to the wider world.

As the music went on, the boy turned to look at me, and I stopped playing. It had been a long time and I had flubbed some notes, it is true.

"You got lots of company," he said. "I know they told you about me, and what I see. They don't like to talk about it, but they do, all the time."

I didn't know what to make of that, so I played another bit, this time moving to one of Bartók's sonatinas, brighter, happier. The boy stilled again and watched my hands as they moved across the keyboard. When I was done, he easily repeated the last few measures, replete with trills and scalar runs. It was quite remarkable.

"Didn't like that first one," he said. "It reminded me too much of the . . . the *silence.*" He shook his head. "But that second one was nice. Who is it?"

I told him about Bartók and promised to mail him some sheet music, which I was happy to learn he could read quite well. I learned, after some conversation with him regarding his playing, he had lived with other people—a reverend and his wife, where he went to school and was taught piano and musical theory—until the last year or so. "But, I needed more music than what they was willing to let me have and Miss Fantine wanted me here," he said, shrugging. "The music, it drives off the silence and keeps the—"

He stopped.

"Keeps the what?" I said.

"Not really a word for *it*. For *them*. Music keeps them away and lets me rest."

"You said I had lots of company," I said. "What did that mean?"

"The drowned lady, the soldiers, so many dead men."

"The drowned lady?" I asked. "What do you mean?"

"She's there and there's a mighty sadness on her and she watches you."

I looked at the boy closely. I am no expert on the wiles of mankind, but there was no subterfuge or deceit in his voice. "And the soldiers?"

He swallowed and looked at me. "Men you done killed, ain't they?" His accent had slid back to a simpler tone, rustic. "They hate you and would see you dead." His face became puzzled. "There's a gray man, with his hair burnt away and water pouring out his mouth." He patted my knee. "But look! Right here." He placed his hands upon the keys and began to play a rollicking, bouncy song that sounded like something I had known all my life, yet I'd never heard it before. It was both simple and complex, sad and exultant all at once, with blocked chords and fast runs between them. It had the musical density of a piece of Mozart, yet rendered with bonhomie and down-home charm. The room seemed to lighten.

"That was wonderful," I said. "What was that song called?"

"Noodlin'."

"The song was called 'Noodling'?"

"Nah, that was just what I was doing. Noodlin'."

"Will you play something else for me? Do you sing? Can you play 'Stagger Lee'?" I asked.

"Nah, I don't like 'Stagger Lee' much, never cared for the words. But I do like some Scott Joplin!" He worked through a flawless "The Entertainer" and "Maple Leaf Rag" and then said, "Wrote some that were like his, but not his, if you know what I mean," and then played some pieces of his own that sounded like Joplin yet weren't. Compositions of his own that people in Washington and New York would flock to in droves. He could play in Carnegie Hall if he was of a mind. Part of me wanted to drop everything, abandon this contract, and take this young man somewhere his talents could be realized. The Lomaxes had taken Lead Belly under their wing, led him to notoriety and what fame a black man might find through "sinful" Negro songs. But something held me back. The memory of Hines's abject gaze as he sang, the doubled Amoiras, the dancing giant diminishing to nothing. The delirium of sickness that passed over me, lying bedridden in New Orleans once, echoed here, now, in the vaults and chambers of my body. The way of all flesh.

A gray man with water pouring out of his mouth. The drowned lady. There's a mighty sadness on her and she watches you.

I sat and listened to the boy work through his pieces. Once he stopped, and we'd discussed Joplin and jazz, I asked him if he'd ever been to Memphis or New Orleans and he allowed that he had been to Greenville once, but not to play, to get hot tamales for a church picnic.

"Do you know the song 'Crowned in Scarlet'?" I asked him, as it occurred to me. I began to tell him about recording "Stagger Lee" in northern Alabama, and the man named Lucius Honeyboy in the Cummins State Farm, but the boy stood up and backed away from me, horror filling his face.

Puzzling. To explain I sang a line, hoping that he'd catch the lyrics and melody: *Come think on death and judgment, your time is almost spent.* And: *Give praise and supplication, shuck off your fleshy gown, and take up dev'lish raiment, and crimson become crown'd.*

The boy's back hit the wall and his eyes opened wide as if taking in some vast presence that had filled the room.

"No, no, no," Ozzie Munk said. "Music should've driven you away. And what's that with you—" His eyes rolled back in his head and he began to thrash, saying, "Ain't opening that door. Ain't gonna open that door for nobody. No no no no no no. Not for nobody."

He slumped to the floor and closed his eyes tight and covered his ears with his hands and remained that way until a voice behind me said:

"Mister Parker, I'm afraid I must ask you to leave. Now."

Fantine's face blazed with outrage and anger and even some fear, I think, now I've had some time to reflect on it. She called for Augie and he rushed in, hat in hand, as Fantine went to the boy. Augie looked discomposed and hustled me out of the building and back into his truck. The afternoon was getting on, and the shadows under the thick trees had shifted, and summer cloud cover had darkened the sky—the air felt dank and heavy with moisture.

The man Frontenac called from the porch for Augie, who turned back. They exchanged a few words on the front steps of di Tonti's and Augie returned to the truck, face tight. He got in the truck, placed his Stetson between us, started the engine, and backed the truck out and drove it from the slough, past the brakes and cypress stands, until we were running beside cotton fields.

"Well, Mister Parker," Augie said, after filling his cheek with tobacco. "Congratulations. You managed to get yourself kicked out of Fantine di Tonti's, the finest whorehouse in this state and possibly the whole South, in a matter of just under three hours." He worked the tobacco in his jaw and a look of disgust came over him. "I believe that is a record."

"I just asked the boy if he knew—"

"I don't care. Ain't nobody around here will care. 'Cept Fantine. You're just some carpetbagging Joe working for the government. But di Tonti will not lift a finger for you, ever again, and I suggest you not step foot in the Old Bottoms, for fear of your life."

"Surely, it can't be so dire. I did not threaten or strike the boy, I simply asked about—"

"Don't matter. And that's all the conversing I want to have on the subject," Augie said. He shook his head, masticating the tobacco chaw. "Fantine didn't like me much beforehand, goddamn it, and here I go bringing your silly ass to her," he muttered. "I'll drop you in Darcy. Got some tractor parts I need to pick up at the machine shop."

And after that, Augie would speak no more.

21

Harlan Parker: The Whitmore

JULY 10, 1938

The Darcy House is sprawling, amply appointed in furnishings and servants, but my thoughts chase me through the corridors of the mind back to the boy, his abject horror at the mention of "Crowned in Scarlet," and my prohibition from di Tonti's. A Negro servant of the Darcys', a stout man named Georgie, has mentioned (at my prodding) that on Sunday nights Ozzie Munk sits in at the Whitmore and I might catch him there.

So today, a Sunday evening, after supper but with an hour or so before sunset, I mentioned I might stroll about the town, and look upon the Mississippi River from the summit of the levee on the eastern part of downtown, and Jackdaw, having had a scotch, hopped up and begged to join me. I could not say no.

Once out of the house, I had to inform him of my true purpose, hearing and speaking with Ozzie Munk once more.

"That's not a good idea," Jackdaw said, shaking his head.

"And why not?" I said.

"I'd rather spare you being turned away from the door."

"Surely you must be joking," I said. "Di Tonti cannot have that much sway here, at a hotel, among—" I did not know what to call them. We walked down Poplar, as idyllic a little street as any that might pop up in a confectioner's American dream: neat lawns, automobiles in most drives, pecans heavy in boughs, crab apples falling, ripe blackberries running rampant on fences, the towering hedges crowded with children and matrons, filling buckets for cobblers. Fingers stained with juice. Bright voices and dogs barking. "All this."

"There's not a man from Quapaw County that hasn't, at some point, come within her grasp, Harlan, surely you understand that. A small town is like a cauldron, you only see the surface and not what bubbles underneath."

"In that sense, it's also like a river, or a pond, or a cup of coffee, for that matter," I said, but halfheartedly.

"Except for the roil," Jackdaw said.

I had not the urge to dicker. So instead we walked and looked at the Mississippi, the blue herons and gulls that had traced its route from the Gulf and found the shores here good hunting: great slicks of mud broken by turtle-strewn logs. Summer clouds piled on the horizon, towering pink superstructures in the sky. Our shadows grew long.

I convinced Jackdaw to at least walk down Main Street past the Whitmore on our way back to his home. He reluctantly agreed. As we drew near, past the boys out front yelling *Boiled peanuts! Sody pop! Newspapers! Coca-Cola! NuGrape! Cigarettes!* I could make out a piano plinking crazily from the mezzanine, a tobacco-smoothed voice crooning "Darktown Strutters," which segued into "Ain't Misbehavin'" and then on to some more modern popular tune I was not familiar with.

"That's not Ozzie," I said. "The boy doesn't have quinine jitters."

"Hmm, that's strange." A proprietorial air seemed to come

over Jackdaw and he pardoned himself and ducked into the hotel and then returned a few minutes later as I was smoking a cigarette.

"It's Burr Saddles playing," Jackdaw said. "Ozzie did not show up. It seems that the Munk boy has disappeared with one of Fantine di Tonti's girls and fled south. Probably to New Orleans."

At the look on my face, Jackdaw chuckled.

"You are the harbinger of doom, Harlan," he said. "Di Tonti has been known to punish men for far less than losing her the boy and one of her girls."

"I am at a loss to understand how I am the cause of all this," I said. "And do you not have some interest in di Tonti's endeavors?"

Jackdaw's face clouded. "No interest other than I am her landlord and she my tenant. But she won't harm you." He became sour. "Let's get back."

I am now typing this in the room I sleep in on the second floor with its own private, if small, gallery looking out over the town. The room seems to have once been a boy's—lead soldiers and cannoneers lined up in phantom and miniature formation on shelves, a baseball bat and glove hung on a wall like some rifle from the War Between the States. An oil painting of some unknown Southern general on rampant horse, sword drawn, glowering at a far tree line, men rallied behind him. The books are expensive and copious and smack of a good education: gold-embossed *Encyclopaedia Britannica* occupying two rows on its own; texts on nature, hunting, Audubon; and *Naturalis Historia*. Histories from Greece to Rome, Egypt, the Middle East, Persia, and beyond, but stalwarts of Latin and students of it: Herodotus, Xenophon, Livy, Sallust, Caesar, Suetonius, Tacitus. An older radio. Jackdaw informed me this was his older brother's room, and that unfortunate soul had drowned in the Great Flood, swept away as one of his friends watched.

Just as Ozzie was swept away by whatever currents brought me here.

22

Harlan Parker: Return of the SoundScriber

JULY 11, 1938

The SoundScriber and my funds have arrived, courtesy of Spivacke, and consequently Jackdaw and Persephone today arranged for members of the Darcy Arkansas Folk Society to come for dinner and drinks at their home to see an exhibition of the use of the recording device and to listen to some of the acetates from my travels.

It was a merry occasion, with many interested and educated questions. The gathered crowd—full of Darcys and McDonalds and Howards and McHughs and Rheinharts—seemed delighted when I recorded a young woman whose name I don't remember singing "Goodnight, Irene" and played it back for the crowd. We worked through many of the acetate discs and I gave a small lecture on the meaning and value of the song "Stagger Lee" that I think made some of the people gathered understand how music can express the desires and wants of a larger society than the singer. Or maybe not. For these gathered, race music is a curiosity, a glancing thought, of no seriousness. This society is, I've learned, good for a nice dinner every few months with drinks.

However, I signed some books presented to me: *West Africa to New Orleans* and *From Cradle to Song*. The alcohol was copious and of good quality. In the end, attention drifted away from Smoot Sawyer, Gramp Hines, and Steck, and the Victrola began spinning Gershwin, saving me from speaking any more. It would not have done for the crowd to insist on hearing all the acetates—one in particular might be dubious to play in front of a mixed crowd. The one with laughter. Screaming. The sounds of flesh slapping against flesh.

I felt uneasy and smoked too much, drank too much. I could not sleep. I cannot sleep.

When I returned all the discs to their case, and packed away the SoundScriber, the loss of the last recording of Gramp Hines—the disc of "Crowned in Scarlet"—dealt me a small, private, and wholly unnoticed blow.

I leave tomorrow for Cummins State Farm, where I'll find Honeyboy, and get the "shadow of a shadow" song that might well lead me to "Crowned in Scarlet."

Can't sleep. This Darcy manse shifts around me, creaking, moving. Off, unseen in the distance, the Mississippi flows, inexorable.

It's said you can't enter the same river twice. It's like music in that way. A constant flow of no rests, no stillness. There are no endings there, only beginnings.

When I close my eyes, I see the Amoiras, and the dancing canker man, and the burning tent, and Bunny's face. I hear the sound of Hines and his children's voices, and that other tone layered on top of their pained melody. There are no rests, no fermata. A river in music.

Notes upon notes.

We are sound waves crashing against the shore with no Sound-Scriber to take down our likeness, our facsimile. Words like these are just echoes of that original sound. We are but small vibrations on the face of the universe.

In the dark, I went downstairs and found a drink. A decanter of whiskey left out from the night's earlier gathering. I gulped down a glassful, and then poured another tumbler to the brim, and now I'm smoking and decidedly not sleeping. Every bit of me itches, but I cannot find any mosquitoes in my room. I am uncomfortable and wonder if I should visit a doctor—could it be malaria or some other insect-borne illness?

I don't know.

I lay in bed earlier and felt my ribs and my prick and balls. The muscles of my thighs. The rush of blood to my member something I needed to address, even if just for clarity of thought. There was a soft woman in New Orleans who had a bright voice and attentive eyes and spoke to me like I was part of her circle of friends, confidants, rather than some lost man. I thought of her, gripping myself in the dark. Her face, her breasts. The round curve of her unblemished cheek.

Can't sleep.

On the gallery, in the cool of the night, I look to the river, hidden behind the levee and the rooftops of the houses of planters' sons. It's out there, churning in the dark.

With no silences, no rests.

There are no endings there, only beginnings.

23

Harlan Parker: Cummins State Farm

JULY 12, 1938

It would look like most other farms if not for the fences and gun towers. But beyond the fences, green fields. The Negroes worked the rows in squads—mostly cotton, some beans, but no corn, too easy for a convict to disappear in—while white inmates or trusties watched them on horseback. From the towers, men with rifles watched the trusties. The rows of cotton disappeared into the distance and wavered in the heat.

The Studebaker had begun belching smoke with every gear change and making strange noises as I left Darcy and put Quapaw County behind me. I did not have the way with it that Bunny had, and it was rebelling at my ill use of it. With the Mississippi behind me, I had my regrets. I wished I could have had more time with the Munk boy. An amazing musician. But it was not the music I thought on the most; it was what he said. *The drowned lady, the soldiers, so many dead men. A gray man, with his hair burnt away and water pouring out his mouth.*

I pulled up to the Cummins farm gatehouse and introduced myself to the trusties there—two ill-kempt inmates with snaggled teeth and sallow complexions stinking of stale tobacco who had no record of my impending visit and would not let me enter the penitentiary grounds without the say-so of their "whippin' boss," a white man named Captain Crossley, who appeared disgruntled and disheveled, like a man awakened from a hot summer's nap—which he very likely just was.

"You that gubmint man?" Crossley asked, tucking in his shirt and strolling up from the stockade. The Cummins farm spread out behind him. Austere two-story buildings painted white, evenly spaced. There were no trees, no shrubs. No shade or shelter from the pounding sun. A water tower of galvanized tin shone in the light. The ground was packed dirt and scrub grass.

"Yes," I said. "I should be expected."

That satisfied Crossley but judging from his gut spilling over his belt and his slovenly appearance, he was a man easily satisfied, if you discounted the dinner table. He waddled around the Studebaker and got into the front passenger seat and directed me through the farm to one of the white two-story buildings. Inside, it was infinitesimally cooler than the summer inferno raging outside. We entered through a simple wooden door—if a bit heavier than normal—passing into the plain, bare penitentiary constructed of heavy cinder blocks and poured concrete. There was no woodwork to speak of with the exception of signs and desks and chairs, and the high ceilings held electric lights behind cages to protect the tungsten bulbs. There were many kerosene lanterns hanging in various places, easy to hand, which made me think that the electrical power was irregular at best. In the outer holding area, a single sleepy-looking guard stood watch, and seemed alarmed at my appearance but diligently took my name and marked it down in his ledger. He unlocked the metal door leading to the interior of the building, and pulled it open with a squeal. Another holding area inside the first gate—where a table of white men in state uniforms smoked, drank coffee, and held hands of blue Bicycle playing cards. There was loose change on the table. The jailers did not rise from their card game.

"Will I speak to the warden?" I asked.

"Hell naw," Crossley responded. "Warden don't concern himself with the ins and outs of the farm. But the assistant warden will be through here on the evening rounds, to make sure our darkie squads are healthy enough for another day in god's country, chopping cotton." He wiped his nose with his sleeve. "He'll let you know who to record and where you'll be set up."

"Could I get some help moving the SoundScriber from my car?" I asked.

"We'll get some boys to tend to that," Crossley said. He kicked at a leg of the card table, rousting the guards, who shuffled off and returned with a gang of workers from the barracks, many of whom had bandages on their arms and hands, some on their heads. Crossley said, "Sick squad, can't chop cotton for one reason or another. But they can still tote shit back and forth." I accompanied them back to the Studebaker with the guards and managed the transfer. On a whim, I grabbed a couple of bottles of whiskey from the trunk and brought them in with me, offering them to Crossley and his guards. He said, "Can't have none of that in here, this is a state-run penitentiary. 'Fraid I'll have to confiscate it," and made the bottles disappear quickly to accompanying smiles from the other guards.

They offered coffee, and cigarettes, and I drank and smoked until the afternoon grew late, judging from my watch. There was very little natural light in the building. I felt it would be easy for time to slip away here—which is probably exactly what the architects of prisons want.

"Mister Parker."

It was a hard country voice. There are those who think Southerners soften their vowels, and maybe in South Carolina they do, but in very few other places will you hear them speak in such a way. In Mississippi, in the delta of Arkansas and northern Louisiana, they speak in harsh tones, clipped syllables, as if their entire morphology of communication were angry and inflamed.

"That's me," I said, standing.

In contrast to the guards, Assistant Warden Horace Booth was clean-shaven, with a neat suit and oiled hair.

"Join me in my office, will you?" he said, and took me up a small set of stairs to a cubby of a room, with a set of double windows looking out over cotton fields and a sky striated with pink and purple clouds as the sun dipped toward the rim of the world. An overhead fan stirred the air, and another General Electric fan hummed behind Booth's desk, wafting the scent of the man at me. Pomade and dirt and tobacco and sweat—none of them displeasing smells. He sat, somewhat heavily, and withdrew an envelope and tossed it in front of me.

"That's a letter from Jack Darcy. He sits on the board of trustees for the Arkansas Department of Corrections. He says I'm to let you make recordings of the boys here." He crossed his hands in front of himself. "Says you'll want to record the n——, too. Them most of all."

I remained silent, as I couldn't discern a question in his words.

"Darcy's got friends, that's the only reason you're sitting here. But I need to know something first . . ." He fell quiet. I could not tell if he was thinking or just pausing for dramatic effect. He was obviously a man used to being in charge, and men like that often have the need for the theatrical.

When I did not rise to his bait, he rummaged in his desk and withdrew a crisp, neatly typed letter and placed it before me. He finally continued on. "Let me see your government credentials, and I'll need you to sign this affidavit swearing and affirming that you will conduct only the business of recording of music and make no other report or write any sort of government description as to the conditions you find here."

"And if I don't?" I asked.

"You'll have to find yourself another state farm to record n——, Mister Parker. And it won't be in Arkansas. Word tends to travel fast around here." He gestured to the telephone hanging on the wall, its cord in a messy snarl below it.

I quickly read the letter—there was nothing in it that could bind me—and signed it, readily. That seemed to satisfy Booth. He withdrew a bottle of whiskey from his desk—I was startled to find it was one of the ones I had brought to the guards—and Booth broke the bonded papers and poured us two generous measures in smudged glasses.

"Can't imagine why the hell you'd want to record these darkies. I'm more of a Benny Goodman or Bing Crosby man, myself. Darcy's letter said you wanted to record Honeyboy in particular. That is one baaaad n——. A straight-up killer."

"I can only imagine," I said, thinking about "Crowned in Scarlet."

"No," Booth said. "You can't. He killed three men on the outside with a straight razor and he's surely killed more than that on the inside."

"Would have thought you'd have hanged or electrocuted him by now," I said.

Booth smiled. "Jury was kind to him and you'll see why. On top of that, he's a useful man in here. He runs the row squad in the day, and after hours he's the night yard man."

"Night yard man?" I asked.

"Honeyboy doesn't sleep but maybe an hour or two a night,

and being the meanest son of a bitch on god's green earth, he'll shoot any man that makes for the fence and fields."

"He's given a gun?" I asked.

"Of course," Booth said. "Trusties that aren't in for murder can have guns under guard supervision and if they shoot a man escaping, they'll get paroled. It's 1938, bud, and this is America!" He took a drink and lit a cigarette. "But Honeyboy, he knows he ain't gonna get paroled, however many men he shoots. On account of the murders. He just likes the guns and the shooting." A thought occurred to him. "Once we take you into the barracks to record, can't do much to assure you of your safety. Can't drop everything to make sure you don't get your throat cut."

"Surely a guard will accompany me?"

"I'll have Crossley see if there are any volunteers."

The sun had gone down, but the sky had lightened in those oblique moments when the sun's rays cast the land in shadow but lit the clouds from below, creating a titanic spectacle of pastel hues. Lines of dust were raised in the failing light, against the dusty green of cotton. "Looks like the mule plow squad is heading in, and the water wagon, and the rest. Give them a half hour and I'll take you down." He stood and went to the door and called down the stairs for Crossley, who soon appeared. He gave him orders to find a guard to accompany me into the barracks.

Soon, two black inmates in striped garb were trucking the SoundScriber into the barracks of the Negro inmates, two buildings over, near the grain dryers and motor pool. It was a shabbier building than the one the guards and Booth loitered in, and hotter. There were no fans here, just stale air and the smell of sweating bodies. Crossley led me through the guard area into a main room that looked like a hospital ward more than a penitentiary—rows of beds all together in one large room, with no partitions or privacy. Crossley bellowed, "Big Head! Big Head!" until a tall, lanky black inmate trotted forward and said, "Yes suh, Mister Crossley."

Crossley pointed to me. "This man's from the gubmint and wants to record you lousy sons-a-bitches for a library or some such. You make sure he don't get kilt, you hear me?"

The man called Big Head nodded—his head *was* of inordinate size—and Crossley said, "Mister Parker, how long do you figure you'll be?"

"A few hours, at least," I responded, checking my watch.

"These boys need to get their grub and wash their nasty asses and then, when that's all done, there'll be time enough for your recording. I imagine you could use the time to set up the contraption," Crossley said. "Bentley here will keep an eye out for you." The fat man gestured to a younger, hard-faced white man who had a hungry disposition and lean frame, wearing an ill-fitting Arkansas Department of Corrections uniform with a pistol at his side. As Crossley moved to leave, he stopped for a moment near Bentley and murmured something in the other man's ear that I did not catch, but as the words were spoken, the younger man's eyes moved in their sockets and his gaze fixed upon me. I felt as though it was not a kind gaze.

I spent my time setting up the SoundScriber and readying the acetate discs. Inmates began to fill the barracks, forty men, sitting on beds in threes, looking at me curiously. In some ways, I felt far more at ease with these men than I did with the guards.

When it seemed as though no more inmates would be returning, I stood before them and introduced myself. "My name is Harlan Parker, and I work for the Library of Congress. I've been tasked with recording songs of the common man—"

"Ain't nothing common 'bout us, man," a voice said to a spatter of laughter.

I went on, explaining the mission of the Library, and I think the inmates understood my purpose. The gathered men, however, stared at me blankly and did not ask questions. I decided an example of the workings of the SoundScriber might be the best way to break the ice.

"Do any of you men have songs you might want to perform? I will record you and then play it back so that you might listen to yourself sing."

Near the back of the room, a black man—bald and sleek and very good-looking, with blue eyes and a muscular physique—sat with his arms crossed. He said, "Clyde, get yo ass up there and sing something for the man."

Another man, Clyde apparently, popped up and positioned himself before me. I asked his name, and wrote it down—Clyde Bush the Third, a man from a long line of bushes, he assured me, a hedgerow even—and he, unasked, said, "In for armed robbery, five years."

"That's fine, Mister Bush, no need—"

At the word "mister" the inmates fell out, laughing, holding their stomachs, slapping knees, until the sleek man who had originally volunteered Clyde whistled and then everyone fell silent. He said, "Ain't no misters in here, mister." He sucked his teeth for a moment and then said, "Go on, Clyde."

Clyde, who had been looking back at the sleek man, turned back to face me.

"Do you know 'Stagger Lee'?" I asked, explaining why I usually started off with that.

"Naw suh," he said. "But I do know 'Midnight Special.'"

"That will be fine, Mister—" I said, stopping myself. "That'll be fine, Clyde."

I set the cutting stylus to record, and the man intoned a sonorous version of "Midnight Special" full of the woes of being a black man incarcerated, and when he had finished I asked him to sing another since there was room on the acetate and he began "Ole Hannah," entreating dead men to rise up and help him hoe his furrow and voicing his hopes the sun would never rise again. When he was through, I lifted the cutting stylus and blew upon the fresh-cut acetate. The light caught its surface nicely and shone in the barracks. The men were hushed.

I placed the record back on the turntable and, using the tone arm, set the acetate to play. I looked out at the gathered men's faces. The sound emanated from the speaker and I saw the words of Clyde Bush reflected in every man's face. At first they smiled, amused with the technological wonder of captured music, and then their faces became somber, thinking about their lot, possibly, or affected by the song, I could not tell.

Afterward, many men queued to sing their songs. And I recorded until the guard came in and said, "Trusties, get up, you flop-eared sons-a-bitches. It's lights-out and you got cotton to chop tomorrow." He withdrew a billy club and began striking the gray metal bars with it. Men lumbered into their beds.

"Can I get someone to help me move the SoundScriber?" I asked the guard.

Bentley opened his mouth to speak but the sleek fellow said, "Naw suh, don't you worry 'bout that none." He approached me and I was able to get a better look at the man. He was almost perfectly formed, with white teeth and a pleasant face, bright blue-green eyes that shone against the rich color of his skin. His scalp was oiled and smooth and I suspected he shaved his head, rather than allow whatever hair nature had left him to grow.

Standing by me, he turned out to the men, readying themselves for bed. "Ain't that right, fellers. Ain't none of you gone touch this contrap, is you?"

"Naw," a man said. Others joined in.

"Because if you do, we'll have to have a little conversation out in the yard, and that kind of conversing you ain't gone come out of without some leaks."

"That's right!" a man said.

"Yes suh, Honeyboy!" another called.

And then I realized who had been talking to me the whole time. Lucius Honeyboy Spoon, the man whom I'd come to see. I began introducing myself again, telling him how I had learned of him, but he interrupted me and said, "I know who you is, Mister Parker. You just introduced yourself."

Embarrassed, I said, "I look forward to recording you, er . . . Lucius."

"Errbody calls me Honeyboy, ain't no reason for you to be different."

"I look forward to recording you," I said. "I want to hear your version of 'Stagger Lee.' I've heard a part of it and would love to hear more."

"We'll see about that," he said. "Got some conditions and the mood has to hit me right."

"The mood?"

In a lower voice, he said, "Them bulls put a goddamned damper on music, if you catch me."

"Ah," I responded stupidly. "I think I do."

He turned to Bentley. "Gone get some sleep, boss, but I'll be up in an hour or so for the yard detail." Bentley nodded in response and brusquely ushered me out of the barracks.

They have given me a cot to sleep on for the night, in the guards' barrack, a smaller, much nicer affair than the quarters of the black inmates. I've commandeered a spot on their mess table and set up my typewriter, poured myself a glass of whiskey (I still have some of my own supply left, thankfully), and typed this. Had I the SoundScriber, I would transcribe some of my recordings of the past days, but the thought of listening to the music from the banks of the Obion and Hines's chautauqua depresses me and makes me uncomfortable in ways it is hard to put into words. It's become a jumble in my mind, and as if it's some festering wound, the more my waking mind picks at it, the more inflamed and aggravated the memory becomes. I would forget much of it—Bunny, the canker man, the two Amoiras.

Better to write and work.

And drink until sleep takes me and hope I have no dreams.

24

Harlan Parker: Honeyboy

JULY 13, 1938

I slept restlessly last night, and so was tired throughout the day. The penitentiary never seems to still or quiet—guards moving; men crying out in their sleep; sounds of unknown machines, either farm equipment or motorcars, I could not be certain; a buzzing; metal doors being opened and shut; the baying of a dog in the middle distance, filtered through concrete and cinder blocks; yips of coyotes in moments of silence in the small hours of morning; calls and responses and the jangle of keys; the whine of a mosquito; the low rumble of a freight train impossibly far away; a bell ringing somewhere out above a darkened cotton field. It was a constant and persistent demand upon my senses. I felt as though I had a fever and found myself in the guardroom lavatory, washing my face and wetting my clothes to cool myself. Even with the ceiling fans in the guards' quarters, the air was still, heavy, oppressive. By morning, I welcomed the weak coffee and cigarettes and ate the prison farm scaugh—slabs of corn bread, a hunk of gelatinous fat and gristle most likely harvested from porcine feet, and a mess of greens cooked until near tasteless. Bentley was kind enough to give me a powder for my pounding head that I chased with coffee, but no amount of joe or cigarettes would relieve the throbbing pain. So, when I saw a guard withdraw a flask and take a belt, I rummaged through my belongings for the bottle and drank a long draft. The rasp of alcohol smoothed out the worst of the rough edges.

Booth was gracious enough to give me a tour of the farm. I know now far more than I had ever wanted to know of the life of Southern prisoners. I had come into this endeavor thinking they were in cages and locked away, working the fields in shackles and chains. That was untrue. There was a remarkable amount of freedom—many teams working the fields were supervised solely by trusties, with guards watching on towers. I saw countless opportunities for inmates, both black and white, to flee into the high, rank summer growth around the farm.

But they did not.

When I asked Booth about this, he shrugged and simply said, "You run, you die. That's the beauty of paroling trusties who kill any man who attempts to escape. They *want* the other inmates to try, because it means their own freedom if they kill them."

Another reminder that the millstone of the state is made to grind men to dust, setting us against each other.

There were a few inmates wearing tin cups around their necks on twine strings. Booth explained they were "bell cows," which puzzled me until he went on to describe the lamentable situation in prison: There were some men who were discovered to be homosexual or were forced into being so, and the cup was a marker or punishment. Or both.

As in any environment in the South—and America—mankind within the Cummins State Farm had separated into layers of sediment, with the black man at the bottom. White inmates had better jobs, better food, better access to the commissary. White men made up the majority of trusties and worked the easier farm jobs: the water wagon, the vegetable fields, the motor pool. The black inmates chopped cotton and cleared the swampy edges of the camp of timber, scrub brush, canebrakes, the air swimming in mosquitoes and horseflies, the water thick with cottonmouths. They sang in groups, call-and-response field hollers, hoeing the line, turning the soil, cutting the timber. Booth kept me far enough away from the black teams working the fields that I could not pick out Honeyboy—all the men wore grass hats to protect their heads from the merciless and beating sun, making most indistinguishable from their fellow inmates.

It was a relief when Booth brought me back to the stockade and barracks, and I spent the rest of the afternoon dozing in a near delirium from the heat and my pounding head.

As evening drew on, Bentley came and kicked the leg of the cot. "Honeyboy's asking after you."

I followed him out of the guard quarters and back to the barracks, where there were the cell block's inmates, but now Crossley and Booth and a passel of other guards sat on benches nearest the bars separating the sleeping floor from the guard area.

When he saw me, Honeyboy said, "We thought you expired from the heat. And you ain't even hoeing rows or chopping cotton."

"I must admit," I said, "I have felt better."

"Ain't we all," Honeyboy answered.

"I was hoping I could get you to perform the version of 'Stagger Lee' that I had from Otis Steck in Alabama. It was quite a ballad," I said.

Honeyboy cocked his head and regarded me with electric blue eyes. "Maybe you'd prefer ole John Henry."

This was new. In my experience, not many black balladeers

sang, or even held the barest interest in, "John Henry." That song was found in the Ohio River Valley, mostly, though the location of Henry's titanic struggle against the steam drill moved west with each version with our country's Manifest Destiny. "Why do you think that?" I asked.

"Ole Stack is a bad n——. So why's a white fella like you so interested in him?"

Many things went through my head all at once, but none of them made it into speech. "Why does *anyone* like the ballad of Stagger Lee?"

Honeyboy slapped his knee, laughing. But the humor didn't touch his eyes. "White folk like John Henry because he a n—— that did what they said to do until he died. He worked with them. He was a democratized man."

I did not correct his usage. I said, "And Stagger Lee?"

"Black folk like old Stack because he sharp, he got a smart-ass mouth on him, and he don't run by white man's rules. He jump when he want, he fuck when he can, and he'll kill you dead as sure as the sun gone rise."

It was an interesting contrast, one man working within the white man's system and dying because of it, the other outside the system, living by his own rules. I said, "But they both died."

"Hell yes, they did, but at least Stack died with his Stetson fucking hat, you catch me?" A grin cracked across his face. "Ole Stack a bad, bad man. But he's a *man*."

"Does this mean you'll record your version of it for me?"

"I reckon so," Honeyboy answered.

Honeyboy was as good as his word regarding the SoundScriber. It had not been touched since the previous evening's recording session. I placed a fresh acetate on the turntable and readied the cutting arm. Counting it down, I began the recording and indicated to Honeyboy he could start when ready.

Honeyboy leaned into the microphone and said, "My name is Lucius Spoon, and I'm in for life for three counts murder in the first." He smiled, and this time it was wholehearted. "When I was a boy I always wanted to be warden and when I got in here, they told me I had to work my way up."

Even the guards laughed at this, and for a while the barracks were full of the laughter of incarcerated men. They sounded like any group of men gathered together. Each full of his own particular sorrow, his mirth, his guilt, the comet's tail of his existence pulling wreckage after him.

With no further preamble, Honeyboy launched into "Stagger Lee." He had a fine tenor voice that could rumble and soar up to surprising heights, rich with vibrato. Had he been anywhere else, with his good looks and ability, he might have gained fame and fortune. And that is the world's loss. Yet he had killed men, and from what I could tell, not in defense or in revenge for some injury. Like Stagger Lee, he was a bad man put to use by the state.

He ran through the verses, very much the same as Otis Steck's, up through the gates of Hell, where Stagger Lee kills Lucifer himself and supplants him. Here's where Honeyboy went on.

He's a bad king, Stackolee.
The king gots his kingdom.
He goes through every bit,
From the fountains of the palace
To the edges of the pit.

They's a black wall he can't figure;
They's a black wall he can't break.
They's somethin' movin' beyond he can't see
In the shadows, Satan's wake.
He's a bad king, Stackolee.

He ask, "What behind this wall here?
Ain't I king of Hell?"
And the devils all around him answer,
"You is, but well well well . . ."
And Stack don't like they answer,
So he shoots them as they plea.
He a bad man, Stackolee.

But somethin' moves beyond the black wall,
And Stack takes off his bloody hat,
Listenin' at the black stones, listenin' for a call.
"What is you? Ain't you scared? Ain't I king of Hell?"
And the black wall whispers, "Yes you is, Stack,
You is, but well well well,
King ain't but a man, and I'm a thunderclap."
And Stagger sat down heavy,
Landing on his back.
"I am like a mountain, and need no crown on me."
He's a bad man, Stackolee.
"I am an ocean, a black and churning sea."
He's a bad man, Stackolee.
"I am like a mountain, ain't need no crown on me."

It was a long song, and as the cutting arm made its progress across the face of the acetate, I worried I would not get the full rendition of Honeyboy's version of "Stagger Lee." But still, as worried as I was, I felt the hairs on my arm prick up at the final few lines of the tune. I obviously had not heard this before, but neither had I expected it to turn in this direction. To cover my befuddlement after the music had died away, I busied myself marking the acetate sleeve with the pertinent information.

When I had finished my task, I looked up at the gathered men and a number of them had expressions of horror, looking at me and Honeyboy as if two cottonmouths had suddenly slithered in among them. No griot would get such a response. When I played back the recording, to check its levels and integrity, damn me if some of the men in the audience did not plug their ears with their fingers to keep out the sound.

"Never heard those verses before," I said.

"Might be I should sing something with a bit more swing to it," Honeyboy said.

"Did you come up with those lyrics on your own?"

"Lyrics?" Honeyboy asked. "Them words? Hell naw, I didn't make them up. Who'd have made up shit like that?" He gave a short, barking laugh. "White folks, most like."

"So, if you didn't make them up, how did you learn them?"

And then, for the first time, I saw Honeyboy's self-assurance leave him. "That ain't a story I want to tell right now."

"But I feel like it's important. For historical and—"

"No, sir. How 'bout 'Take a Whiff on Me'?" Honeyboy said. He leaned in closer, voice low. "Later, Mister Parker. Get Crossley to let you talk to me in the yard and bring that bottle I know you got."

I wanted to press but knew it wasn't going to work. I'd have to wait.

We continued recording. Honeyboy Spoon was a real player, and he moved through a whole songbook's worth of tunes as fast as I could change discs. "Where Did You Sleep Last Night" to "Sally Walker," "Rock Island Line" to "Pine Bluff Blues," "Pick a Bale of Cotton" to "Hot Springs Ladies," "Whoa Back Buck" to "Little Sugar My Coffee" and more. As he played, I found myself leaning back into my chair, my head pounding and my pulse thrumming in my neck, my chest. Dislocated, as if I were there and not really there all at once—almost as if I were the tinny and scratched acetate recording and all the inmates listened to me. When I looked at them, often they would be regarding me with cool eyes—both the prisoners and the guards. Sometimes they would laugh and stomp their feet with Honeyboy's rhythms; other times they would call out "Hell yes!" and "Sing it!" when he was particularly hot. I swooned in the heat, pouring sweat. When Crossley called for lights-out, it was a relief. Slowly, I packed away the freshly cut acetates and retired to the guardroom to smoke and pour myself a drink. When Crossley entered at the end of his duty, he found me blurry and slightly drunk. And in a negligent rush to change clothes and leave Cummins farm to reach home, he instructed a guard I only knew as Gene to allow me to talk to Honeyboy in the main yard while the trusty was on watch during the night.

I dozed, passing in and out of consciousness until Gene kicked the cot I slept on, saying, "I thought you were gonna have a little talk with Spoon?" and I rose, shaky. Light-headed, I made my way down and out into the yard, carrying a whiskey bottle in a paper bag. The guards smiled and raised their eyebrows at the package but said nothing: Trusties were pampered here, like gladiators willing to kill in ancient Rome.

Rules were rules, until there weren't any rules, and then *that* was the rule.

25

Harlan Parker: The White Woman of the Wood

I passed into the main yard, walked through the parked vehicles. My watch read three thirty A.M., and most of Cummins State Farm was silent. It was a clear night and thousands of insects swarmed the electric lights at the corners of the yard.

Honeyboy stood in a pool of light near the far fence, looking small in the large open space. I crossed the packed dirt and approached the man. He held a shotgun with the breach open, hanging over the crook of his arm, the brass of two shells shining in the artificial light.

He noticed my looking at the weapon. "Only time they let me close the breach is if I see some fool making for the fields or fences," Honeyboy said. "Lemme get at that bottle."

I handed the package over and Honeyboy spent ten, maybe fifteen minutes alternately drinking and smoking cigarettes and saying softly, "Hoo-ee," and "Ain't that right, goddamn," and hissing with alcohol as it hit his stomach.

Finally, when he had had enough to sate himself, he said, "You ain't so bad, is you? Fit right in here."

"I don't know about that," I said.

"Naw," Honeyboy continued. "You ain't so bad because you just as bad as me." He passed the back of his hand across his mouth and spat into the dirt. "Ain't no innocent babe asking after them parts of 'Stackolee,' I can tell you that true."

"I've done my share of bad things, I guess," I said. "Over there."

"Naw," he said, "that ain't it. But it's your business."

"I imagine so," I said. "About this song. The verses at the end of 'Stagger Lee.'"

Honeyboy raised his hand. "I'll tell you. But it ain't something I've thought much about these last twenty years. Ain't something I wanted to think about." He lit a cigarette with a match and then gestured at the bottle, which I'd been holding, dumbly, and then took one last, great swallow and launched into his story.

"It was in Blytheville. They had us clearing the swamps and paid good money, five dollars a week to chop lumber and kill them damned snakes that was everywhere. This was before the flood of twenty-two, and way before the big boy five years later, when not everywhere was all leveed up." He thought for a moment. "I was just a young buck, but the farm manager saw I knew how to handle the horses and mules, and I lived with my momma nearby so I guess he knew I weren't going nowhere. He picked out me, Rabbit, and Jofuss, to ride out west past Crowley's Ridge and Newport and into the hills to pick up a head of cattle and bring 'em back to Blytheville. I rode point, Rabbit rode swing, and Jofuss was to ride flank—only three men to bring back twenty head—only their most trusted n——. Maybe that was why it went wrong, I don't know. Just three men. But we getting out there where the roads got small, heading west, and the land rises. Ain't no n—— wants to head up there, because them folk don't want the sun to set with us sleeping in they towns, or in they barns, or bunking down anywhere near they water or women or children.

"Anyhoo, I find the Hodgson farm and the farmer—he don't like having to talk to a black man like me, ain't no doubt about that—but he tells us how to get to the field he's pasturing the cattle, and we ride out. It's up the skirt of one of the first hills of the Ozarks and them woods is dark and the light is falling, you know? There was this big . . . I don't know . . . big old ball of dark clouds coming at us, blottin' out the sun, catch me? Dark as my daddy's ass. It was like ole Hannah gone dipped behind the mountains and gone away, leaving us in that nowhere light before full dark.

"The mule I was riding fell, tossing me. Don't know if she just stepped in a hole, or her foot slipped on a rock, but her leg was broken. Horses scream like people, but a mule, she'll holler. Awwoooo. And boy, I ain't never heard nothing like that mule hawing and panting, and god save me if I'm lying, that damned thing was crying."

He paused, thinking back. "You know, I'm a bad man and they oughta write songs 'bout me, but I ain't a man without love. I love the women. And I ain't never had a bad thought about a dog. Can't abide cats, though. But a good dog, a good dog is love through and through. But that mule, I felt a powerful sorrow listening to it. Jofuss and Rabbit realized we weren't gone be able to bring back the cattle with just three men, and I told them to ride back to Hodgson's farm and ask the man if we could bunk down in his barn for the evening and in the morning we could figure out what to do about the cattle. I waited until they was far enough away before I took out that old forty-one and put it to the mule's head and stopped the poor thing's misery. Sound of the crack, and then the silence . . . something you don't forget real easy.

"I was about to turn back but the sky opened up and damned if the lightning and thunder didn't make me hunch over, it frightened me so, and I took myself away from the dead mule and into the tree line to get out from the storm and it was there I saw the white woman."

"White woman?" I said, amazed.

"When I say white, I mean *white*. White hair, white dress and everything. She was gesturing to me with her fine hand, you know, like 'come here.' So I did, though there was a powerful fear startin' to eat at me. But the rain was beatin' down and it had turned cold and to be honest, maybe I weren't right in my head because it seemed like it was dryer by the lady. So I goes up to her and says howdy, and she laughs and says hello and puts her cold hand on my arm and starts humming and then says, 'I can sleep you, and I can eat you, but you have to come with me aways up in the trees,' and right then I was hungry and tired from the trail and her voice held the warmth of blankets and the smell of good food, pork and hominy and greens and corn. So I follow her up into the trees, you know?

"We walk a good long while and when I say, 'Where we going?' she says back to me something that sounds like 'Cidersend' but it weren't quite that if you catch me and I found out later what she was saying. She says, 'You like music, don't you,' and I admitted that I could pick some on the guitar my daddy left me before he took off for Texas. So she starts humming and singing about kings and crowns and that ole black wall that whispered and over time, walking and listening to her, that music seeped into me. I could feel it come in me, if you catch my meaning."

I said I did not, fully. So Honeyboy drank more whiskey and smoked another cigarette and thought about it.

"You know how a real stomper is, don't you? Like that song gets in your head, and you can't get it out. Little snatches of it keep churnin' in you, like you got a river you never meant to have running through you."

"I think I understand," I said. "Can we sit down?"

"Naw," Honeyboy said. "Ain't no sitting in the yard." Honeyboy waved a hand toward the towers at either end where the electric lights shone over the rows of cotton. They appeared as obsidian hedges, flecked with white, in the dim illumination. "Them guards will bust me down from being a trusty and take my goddamn shotgun if I did that, so naw, ain't no sitting. But you look like five pounds of dog shit hammered flat, that's for sure. You want to go back to the big house?"

"I'll be fine," I said. "Please, go on. You were talking about the music. The song, 'Crowned in Scarlet.'"

"That its name?" He chuckled mirthlessly and then spat again into the dirt. "Damned thing didn't just get into my head, like a good boogie-woogie number, it kinda came in sideways. The melody floated around and the woman, she played with the time, you know? The rhythm? I'd be thinking the beat might fall one place, and she'd trick me and it would fall in another, while that black wall was talking to us. And that song came inside me, in my body, if you catch me. Like I'd got the clap all of a sudden, just from listening. But I was also wanting more of it, you know? The music, just like the white lady, was leading me on and on.

"Don't know how long we walked. I'd like to pass out or eat a whole hog by the time she stopped singing. We was in a grove of apple trees, and the ground was covered in them, and they was all brown and splotchy and worm-eaten. The white woman took my hand and led me through them trees and them rotten apples squelched under my feet and I looked down and realized I didn't have my boots on. No pants neither. And my dick was out there for this woman and all to see, just swinging in the breeze. And that made me scareder than almost anything else, my nakedness under the sky. Where'd my clothes go? How'd I lose them? What if some white man saw me walkin' with this white woman with my prick out? They'd lynch me for sure.

"We came through the trees and there was this big-ass old metal gate, and beyond the gate I saw all these tombstones and at the top of the gate, they was the words 'Idyll's End'—"

"What? Can you spell that?" I said, wondering if he could read.

"Hell yeah, I can. I never forgot the look of it, if you catch me. And they taught me to read in here." He spelled it for me. "Ain't likely to forget something like that. I can close my eyes and see it right now. I can hear her words. And that's what she had said, Idyll's End and not Cidersend like I had first thought. And this woman—I saw she was naked too—and she looked real old and real young all at once. I remember looking at her caboose and thinking all the bad things I could do to that ass and right when I would think it, she would smile real big like she knew what I was thinking and I guess my dick was holding its own apple if you catch me, and I think you do."

"I do," I said. "Not leaving much to the imagination."

Honeyboy shrugged. "You asking the questions, I'm telling the story. I ain't shitting you."

It was my turn to shrug. The admission of nakedness and sexual intent toward a white woman alone might get him in trouble in Cummins. Might find him tied to a tree. But it wouldn't happen because of me.

"We head into that graveyard, and she starts singing the last few verses over and over, about the black wall whispering, and she goes to a grave that has this big old statue standing over it, an angel with a sword and a long crooked finger pointing to the ground, them wings folded up behind, and I look at the standing stone and there ain't no name on it. A gravestone with no damned name. This woman lies down on top of that grave and spreads her legs and puts her hands down there to open herself up to me on top of that grave and the only thing not white is the pink of her center and it darkens to red like blood and the whole time out her mouth the black wall is talking and my dick drops that apple. She says all I need is to drink the wine of her body, and eat the rind of her cheese, kiss the crust of her bread. How 'bout that shit. Talking 'bout food with that pussy spread open for me. Hundred white motherfuckers with forty-ones could tell me grind that white lady but ain't no way I'd do that, and I ran. I ran so far and so fast that my heart was like to give up, come up and out of my chest through my mouth in a big ole bloody mess. And behind me that lady laughing and singing and telling me in the voice of that wall that I would come to her someday and the wall would open up and take me in."

He stopped. The shotgun lowered and he looked out into the darkness of the fields.

"Came out of them woods, cold and hungry. Naked as I was born. Farmhand saw me and ran and got other men and for a while I was figuring they was gone string me up on account of being a black man running around with his tallywhacker just swinging around but they didn't. I told them I worked for the Stephensons out of Blytheville and about the white lady and the grave and they shut up real quick and wrapped me in a horse blanket and put me in a wagon and when I got back to Momma's I found out that my momma was dead and I'd been gone for two months. Momma had come down sick, sick of grief that her boy had died. That's how she was thinking. That's how everyone was thinking. But there I was. That woman took me into the forest for two months, though it seemed like a single goddamned day."

Under my breath I said, "Jesus Christ."

"He couldn't help me." Honeyboy placed the knuckle of his free hand to his forehead and twisted, as if he were taking a corkscrew to his temple. "That goddamned song was eatin' at me. And eatin'. And it wouldn't go away unless I sang a little of it and it wouldn't feel right unless they was someone to hear. I could go into the corncrib and sing to myself but that wouldn't do nothing. So, in the end, I had to take up that guitar and go out and play that motherfuckin' song. I could play whatever I wanted, but that song would seep in, like floodwaters. Seepin' and risin'. I be layin' in bed at night hearin' that song running in my head. I close my eyes and that woman opening herself up to me. So I have to sing it. I might try to push that shit away and play some barrelhouse, a stomp, and the music would change as I played it and before I knew it I'd be talking 'bout that black wall and whispering to come to me. Wasn't sleepin'. Wasn't eatin'. Drinking all day long. Got real sick and then finally, I had an idea. I worked a little magic of my own. I built a goddamned black wall myself. And that wall was ole Stackolee. I put that cursed song inside *him*. After all, he's a *baaad* man.

"After that, song didn't eat at me so much. I sing it once in a while. Taught it to that boy Steck and he took a big ole chunk of the burden from me. Maybe in a hundred years, ole Stackolee will be forgotten and ain't nobody will sing that song. It's like drinkin' poisoned whiskey, share it around enough folks and it won't kill you."

Honeyboy, having uttered the word "kill" and allowed it to sound aloud and fall away, stood thinking. Throughout this revelation, he did not look at me. "Maybe I killed them men so I could get in here, with all the other bad men. We all Stackolees in here." He raised a hand and gestured at the dark fields. "Wouldn't take nothing to get over them chain fences and I could be gone. Larry's up there sleeping with his carbine or jerkin' himself. That fool'd never see me. The world is spread open before me and I could slip into it easy as you please. But it's better if I stay here," he said, and patted the shotgun.

I felt as cattle come to a slaughterhouse, hammer-struck in my forehead. I felt the world tilt and sat down heavily.

"Here now," Honeyboy said, grasping my arm and pulling me back to my feet. "You white as a sheet." He drew me back to the ward where the guards had their quarters and I can remember falling and the blurred faces of men, white and black, muscling me through the hot, humid confines of the penitentiary. I must've moved out of time and mind, for I saw Bunny's face and my mother's swimming in my blurred vision. Honeyboy and Steck and Smoot. The loathed man, Insull, and the faces of Negroes, either inmates or minstrels or field hands, I could not tell.

I fell into blackness, as I always have.

There are no endings, just beginnings.

26

Cromwell: Hattie Judges Harlan

The knock comes as a surprise. He's nodding at the cheap desk, Parker's journal open in front of him. He rises, opens the door.

"This better be good," Hattie says, entering the room. She doesn't seem sweaty but she's still dressed in workout clothes. He can smell food on her breath, as though she's been in a restaurant with a fryer or an open grill. "I'm about ready for my pajamas and some HBO. You know they got HBO here, don't you?"

Cromwell murmurs assent and retrieves the journal and his laptop. "I need you to read this," he says. "It's quite a bit, but it's important."

Hattie looks at the journal and back to Cromwell and sighs. "Can I take this back to my room?"

"Yes," Cromwell says. "But I'd like it back before bed. I need to see if I can follow up on what I've found."

"Shit," Hattie says, and instead of leaving, moves to his hotel desk and sits down. Cromwell remains standing, not knowing what to do with himself. It seems weird to just watch her as she reads, so he sits on the bed and that seems just as awkward, so he stretches out his legs and leans back into the pillows and looks at his phone.

"Cromwell," Hattie says after what only seems a moment. But the light has changed. It's darker now, though it was early evening before. Something's different. He's kicked off his shoes. "You're snoring."

He shifts his position on the bed and in a moment of self-indulgence—or so it feels to him—allows himself to drift off once more.

"Goddamn this motherfucker," Hattie says, a while later.

"Who?"

"Who else? Harlan Parker. This guy's a piece of work."

Cromwell stirs, pushes himself into an upright position. His eyes feel crusty and he fears he's drooled as he slept while Hattie has been reading. He excuses himself and goes to the bathroom to splash water on his face and returns.

Hattie shakes her head, with a sour expression on her face.

Cromwell says, "His writing is disjointed, surely, but it is a private journal. I plan on a comparative read of it with all of the documents filed with Spivacke at the time. And his other writings from the period."

"Nah, it's not that." He sees she's filled the book with strips of folded hotel stationery. "It's bullshit like this." She flips to a page. "'I felt a great shame and anger spill over me. These are my brothers. These are my brothers. We are all connected. The hopelessness I felt in that moment was overwhelming.'"

Cromwell rubs his eyes; he is very tired. "What's wrong with that?" He can't understand why she's not focused on the events at the Obion chautauqua. The canker man and Bunny's disappearance.

"It's a load of bullshit. It's the 1938 version of white folks virtue signaling. 'Oh, look at how much I love black folks and fight for them.'"

"He did spend a good portion of his life studying jazz music, traveling from New Orleans to the West Indies to Africa and back to learn of its roots," Cromwell says. "The study of jazz is the study of African Americans. It was a different time and what he was expressing was—"

"Spare me the 'different age' or 'it was a cultural norm' horseshit excuse for a white man's holier-than-thou behavior." She stops, closes the book. "But you know what gets me, Crumb? It's that he's a damned coward."

"How so?" Cromwell asks.

"He refuses to use the word. *The* word. 'Nigger.' Makes a big self-righteous deal about never having to write that word again. But then—" She gives a short, disgusted laugh. "But then Mister Delicate writes *N* and a series of dashes to indicate it. It's a fuckin' private journal, Crumb! The man cannot even be honest with himself."

Cromwell thinks about what she's said. "I think it's worse than even that," he says.

"Yeah, you think he killed Bunny." She shrugs. "I mean, his brain is for sure rotting from late-stage syphilis. That fucked-up 'canker man' might actually be a hallucination embodying the disease. Like, somewhere, inside himself, he knew he'd been infected and couldn't bear to actually look that in the face. For a dude who went to war and had to kill men as a soldier, he's surprisingly finicky about a hard examination of himself."

"I'm a bit dubious about the armchair syphilis diagnosis, Hattie," Cromwell says.

"I actually took the time to Google some of the symptoms and nothing he describes falls outside of that."

He opens his computer and Googles "syphilis" and reads the Wikipedia entry. It's inconclusive, like just about everything else relating to Harlan Parker. He calls up the article on the body found on the Obion River in 1938 and says, "Read this."

He waits as Hattie scans it. She whistles.

"He damn sure has got some mental health issues," she says. "But nothing about this could be proven without an enormous amount of detective work and a deep fucking dive in historical records. And maybe not even then."

"True," Cromwell says. "But I've got nothing better to do with my spare time now."

Hattie opens her mouth, shuts it. There she is, Maizie again, a presence in the room. You can be haunted without ever seeing a ghost.

"You know, for a second there, Crumb, I thought you were gonna try to put the moves on me," Hattie says. "When you called."

He realizes, as she says it, that she knows. About Vivian. "How long have you known?"

"A while now," she says. "Can't imagine how you—"

"No, you can't. Maybe that's why this Parker thing is eating me. Guilt, maybe." He thinks about what they must be saying at the office. "And everyone at work?"

"No, I don't think so. There are a shit-ton of junior archivists who'd have let a higher-up know about it in hopes of getting your job if they knew about it. It's DC, after all."

He sits on the bed and allows his shoulders to sag from the weight of it all. Hattie sits beside him and places her warm hand upon his. "We all fuck up, Crumb. We all do. And all you can do is forgive yourself and go on."

"Easily said for someone who's never fucked up like—" He stops. "I can't even make it up to her. To them."

"No, that's true." She pats his hand and stands, goes to the hotel door. "And you'll just have to figure out some way to move forward, anyway. But I know you, Crumb. Your brain is working. Thinking about a book, maybe. Thinking about a lecture tour. You're gonna exploit this dead-ass hypocrite just like he exploited those black folks, aren't you?"

Each word feels like a physical blow, leaving him nothing after-ward. He looks at her and feels only desolation.

"Get some sleep. We'll be done tomorrow. Don't let this Parker motherfucker get to you. He's not worth your time. Don't let him get at your ambition. Because maybe your ambition and pride is what fucked you up in the first place." She shrugs and he can tell she's absolving herself of his grief, his adultery, his *fucked-up-ness.* "You're gonna do what you're gonna do."

She leaves without saying goodbye.

He doesn't sleep.

27

Harlan Parker: Sickness and Escape

I awoke in a cell, in an echoing hall stinking of mildew, vinegar, and lard soap. A voice called, "The fish. The fish is up and at 'em, boys. Hey, fish, hey, fishie, you got any smokes?"

I sat up, every fiber of my body outraged and sore. My head pounded and there were needle punctures in my arms, carelessly bandaged. A thick smear of black, crusted blood on the bare, gray-striped mattress where my head had lain. The inside of my mouth was abraded, as if I had nearly bitten through my own cheeks, and the pain was outrageous.

Looking around, I saw that they had placed me in a prison cell but had left the door open. In a pile in the cell's corner sat my box of acetates, my suitcase taken from the Studebaker, the SoundScriber, my various notebooks and journals, my Dopp kit. I struggled to standing and wandered out into the hall, searching for water.

"Hey, fish, you got some smokes?" a voice said again. I looked and a bloated pink face leered at me from between scaling metal bars. Rough hands protruded into the open space of the cell block.

"I need a square, man. Cummere, willya? Help a brother out." The rough hands gestured to me to come closer. I would not. Down the length of the hall, other hands emerged from the cells—inmates coming to attention at the doors.

Unsteady, I shifted, and the man reached for me, grasping. "Cummere, willya? I ain't gonna hurt you. Just give you a little squeeze is all."

I stumbled down the block, to where two guards looked alarmed to see me coming toward them. I said, "Help me, I shouldn't be here, tell—" and tried to remember any of the guards or the warden's name, but couldn't dredge up those memories. What ended up coming out of my mouth was "Honeyboy" and the guards looked at each other.

I found myself on the floor, again looking up, and then Crossley—I think his name was Crossley—lifted me up and put me back in the cell and forced water on me, which made me cough and splutter. Eventually I slept again.

In dreams, things never come unbidden. The silty bottom of the river churns to the surface, dead things arise.

It was a hot day, in 1914, and I was sixteen years old. I knew where I was from the quality of the sun, the pressure of the light on my skin and clothes and back, the heaviness of the water-laden air. Washington, DC. Past storefronts, the clangor of an oncoming trolley and the rattle of a motorcar, the sulfuric stink of its exhaust. A wood fire burning somewhere near, scenting the air. Uncollected garbage, night soil dumped from an upper window into an alley. Sizzling meat and spiced stew. A cacophony of noise: infant cries, dogs barking, the industrious sounds of hammer-falls, a mule braying, a man calling to workers, a woman wailing. Storefronts in procession: a tailor, a dressmaker, a cheesemonger, an open market in an empty lot like some Anglicized Moroccan souk passing on my right; on the left, the street filled with dray-drawn wagons and motorcars. My gait that of a young man with some urgency spurring him on. Light, arms swinging, sweat at my brow, beneath my arms, and at the small of my back. In my hand I held a scrap of paper, moist with either sweat or the sodden air or both, I could not tell. An address written upon it in my own hand. I had very little time. I was due back for the dinner performance at the Harrow Club, and the internal clock within me wound itself down. Liszt's *Liebesträume* ran through my head, as I had been rehearsing it all morning, as I would debut it that evening for the well-to-do men with their scotch and whiskeys as the Negro servants moved among them, lighting cigarettes. Their pampered, flushed faces all turned to me, to these hands. I flexed them. They were strong. Very strong for someone so young.

I had something to do. Something dire. As pressing as the music, as insistent as the rise and fall of the fingerwork on the keyboard. I had someone to see.

There are no endings, only beginnings.

I awoke two days later, with a doctor looming over me. He was saying, "You shouldn't have him in here. He should be hospitalized, somewhere they can put some fluids in him, and get to the bottom of this illness—"

"This ain't the Peabody Hotel, Doc," Crossley said. "And he ain't got any money on him."

I struggled to rise, to speak, because I did have money. In the back compartment of the SoundScriber. I had stashed it there for the occasions when I did not want to walk around with the whole amount. Just for a moment like this.

"Here, drink," the doctor said. "Drink all of it."

Warm lemonade. Sweet and tart enough to curl one's tongue. I drank it down. The doctor did not give his name and his eyes were dark and his skin nut-brown and he had rough, calloused hands as if he worked more with farm implements and livestock rather than the sick, which I found strange for a physician. The doctor gestured for more lemonade and Crossley shuffled off, a sour look upon his face, and returned with another glass, which I gulped down.

"Whoa, now, mister," the doctor said, standing and packing his bag. "That'll all come up in a mess if you don't watch out." He moved to the barred door. "Eat some toast. Some oatmeal. Something mild. Don't just wade into a big old steak."

Afternoons passed into steaming evenings, lost in delirium, where long darknesses were filled with the cries and profanity of prisoners, then the nights lightened into the half-light of dawn and once again through the heat of day. I woke and slept and woke and slept, racked by dreams. Over and over again. Those times I was awake, whatever light there was in my eyes dimmed and I found myself staring blankly at a bit of scaling paint, or the point in the cell's ceiling where the corners met in a puzzling bit of architectural geometry. When I was well enough to stand on my own without fear of falling, weak-kneed and gaunt, Assistant Warden Booth came himself with a gang of Negro prisoners to collect my things and the SoundScriber and escort me off the farm.

"I need to speak with Honeyboy," I said, as we exited the main block of the prison, heading toward the Studebaker. "I have unfinished business."

"Honeyboy?" the warden said. "We don't have any prisoner by that name here."

"Lucius Spoon. Honeyboy. The man I recorded."

"Mister Parker," Assistant Warden Horace Booth said. He did not look at me while he spoke. Instead he turned his head toward the men who placed the SoundScriber in the backseat of the vehicle. When they had finished, he said, "We have no such record of any prisoner by that name." He coughed and dipped a hand inside his jacket pocket. He withdrew an envelope and handed it to me, a blank expression on his face. I opened it and read. It was an invoice for food and lodging and medical care to the amount of $67.25.

"A bill?"

"I'm sure you can have the Library of Congress compensate you for the expense." He sniffed. "I personally do not care if you pay it or not, but this is how Mister Darcy—and the board—instructed me to deal with this matter. Should you not be able to pay, it will be no matter. We can have the sheriff here in a few hours and you will then be his problem. Either way, your time at our little home is over."

He had hard, shiny eyes. A man with one hand on the lever of the gristmill. I felt myself precariously teetering on the edge of falling between those millstones.

"If you'll wait a moment," I said. I went to the trunk of the Studebaker and opened it. I quickly made inventory. My bags were all there, as was the box of acetates. The Underwood. The crate of tinned food and sundries. The case of whiskey was gone and I was unsurprised at that bit of larceny. I opened my suitcase and found my wallet and opened it. It was empty. Either the guards or some industrious prisoners had taken the money I had there. If I had enough money to bet, I would place it on the guards. Booth watched implacably.

"Hold on," I said. "Let me get at my stash."

I got in the Studebaker's driver seat and, leaving the door open so that I was in full view, with my left hand I felt around underneath the steering wheel as if I had something secured there. With my right, I slipped the key in the ignition. Pressing the clutch in, and giving the gas a brief pump, I twisted the key in the ignition and the Studebaker—that wonderful old faithful girl—coughed into life immediately and I slammed the door and ground the vehicle into gear and accelerated the car in the open space of the farm's main yard. The rear tires shifted and slewed, spitting a plume of dust to swallow Booth and his prisoners, and the Studebaker fishtailed into another vehicle, crumpling its side door, but the wheels caught, the car lurched forward, and I was heading for the main gate without a look back.

I had every intention of barreling through any barrier before me, but there was none: the crossbar was raised and the guard watched me pass through in a blur. In moments I was on the open highway, the Cummins State Farm diminishing in the rearview.

When I could get my bearings, I drove east and north, putting the Arkansas River between me and where I had been for so long. At a roadside Union Gas station I opened the back of the SoundScriber with some difficulty and withdrew the envelope that contained the last of my money—little more than a hundred dollars. I opened the trunk and ran inventory of the acetates, making sure I had all of them. On Amoira's moaning, Steck in Tennessee, the Obion chautauqua. They were all there, even Honeyboy (I was scared I had perhaps invented him in my delirium).

Near Blytheville, I found this motel and took a room and it is here I commit all of this to paper. I am still so very weak. The land here seems miasmic in its bloom and heat, and the haze occludes the far fields beyond my window. I keep watch, worried that Booth has notified authorities of my escape. I could be wanted by the state police, I surmise. Somewhere there might be a bench warrant for my arrest for an outstanding debt, but there will be no wanted posters for a sixty-seven-dollar bill and a crumpled automobile door.

I would leave Arkansas, never to return, but there is something I must do here first. I must remember. I must recall everything Honeyboy said, if I'm to complete what I must.

I thought "Stagger Lee" was my goal, those infernal verses, but I was mistaken. I *will* hear "Crowned in Scarlet" in full.

I look in the mirror and see a changed man. Blood-colored eyelids and a shaggy, haggard face. My belly is gone and I find I have no appetite or thirst for liquor anymore.

The world of flesh falls away, after all. It's but a wincing prick, so very small. Who said that? William Bless?

I will rest now. For tomorrow I will go west to the White River and find someone who can take me to Idyll's End.

28

Harlan Parker: Dethero and the Bargeman

We are come to Idyll's End. I now put down this testament to our journey here before I enter the stone garden. The girl and her father watch me expectantly, trying to hide their interest. They will not have to wait much longer.

I have found the grave.

The man was named Mike Dethero and I came across him in a town in the Ozarks called Guion. He was wolfish, with long yellowed teeth and a five o'clock shadow at nine in the morning, and looked as if, given half a chance, he might run about on all fours when no one was watching. But at each town I came to, he was the only man who had ever heard of Cidersend.

"Mah wife, god rest, was from around there, weren't she, Mollie?" he said to his daughter, a plain-faced girl in braids. It was evening and they both sat on the porch of their small cabin in front of a field of corn. It had rained in the night but now the sun was out full, the bugs whirring in the tall grass, and the whole earth steamed. Dethero and his daughter looked not affected at all by the heat.

"Up where all them apple orchards are, off Hell Creek."

"Hell Creek?" I asked, slightly bemused at the name.

"Yep, comes pouring cold out of a cave somewhere in the holler. Cold as hell. Cidersend ain't much farther beyond that."

"Can you take me there?" I asked. "I'm trying to track down the origin of some folk songs—and all signs point to that town."

Dethero looked dubious. "Harvest coming on and I'll need to be here with the boys."

"I can offer you money," I said.

The man brightened. "What're we talkin' about here?"

"I can give you fifty dollars. Surely that's enough for a couple of days."

"Might take more than a couple of days, you hear?"

"Fifty is all I can afford," I said. It was true. After my motel stay in Blytheville, I was down to seventy-five dollars, though there should be money waiting for me at the Blytheville Trust if Spivacke came through. "I could get you twenty more, possibly, afterward, if you have some patience."

"Naw," he said. "Ain't no easy way up to Hell Creek except by boat on the White, and what? You said you got to take equipment up there?"

"That's right."

"That means a mule, and gear, up into the holler? Seventy-five and no less, and you pay for the boat."

"How about a hundred? Fifty up front, and the rest on return when I can get it from the bank?"

Dethero thought for a long while. *He a bad king, Stackerlee.* "Michael!" he yelled. "You and your brothers can mind the farm for a few days while I'm off on an errand?"

A young, strapping teen came onto the porch from somewhere within the cabin. Most mountain folk I had known ogled every stranger with some intensity, but the Dethero clan seemed strangely unfazed by my appearance.

"Sure, Pa. Goin' somewhere's with this man here?"

"Up to where yer momma's from," he said.

The boy whistled and shook his head. "Ain't no accounting some folks," the boy said.

Dethero laughed. "Sure as hell ain't," he responded, as if I weren't there. He turned back to me. "You'll leave that motorcar over there with my boys as collateral, while we're upriver." He stood. "Let me pack a bag. Mollie, you fancy a trip?"

Mollie hopped up, bright and smiling, and said, "Sure I do, Pa. Sure," and ran inside the cabin.

In a short time, they both reappeared with loose bags hung over their shoulders. Dethero carried a lever-actioned rifle. At my request, he lent me a shovel for the journey. His sons appeared and from an outlying barn brought forth a sturdy mule and coaxed it onto the flatbed of an older Ford truck—where it hawed and then promptly sat down, having performed the maneuver before, obviously—and we all drove to the river ferry, a diesel barge run by a man who stank of catfish and cigarette smoke and who agreed to take us across the river and as far upstream as he could, on his boat, the *Sleepy John*, for five dollars. My wallet had become remarkably flat. Within an hour, the mule, Dethero, Mollie, and the SoundScriber and its batteries and related accouterments—and of course me—were slowly motoring up the White River. It was cooler here, and Mollie lay on her stomach near the prow of the barge with her hands in the flow. *They's a black wall he can't figure; they's a black wall he can't break. They's somethin' movin' beyond he can't see in the shadows, Satan's wake.*

I remarked on the temperature change and Dethero shrugged. "Spring fed, mister. Comes out of the ground barkin' cold." He moved to the railing. "Look over there."

I followed him and looked where he pointed. The river was remarkably clear.

"See?" I followed the line of his finger. "See 'em move? Trout. They're good eatin', if you don't mind all them bones." He grinned, showing some gaps in his yellow teeth. "Brought some onions, a tin of lard, and my small skillet for us, if you're of a mind."

In all honesty, I don't think I'd had thought of food, or alcohol, since Cummins State Farm. "That sounds just fine, Mister Dethero. Just fine," I lied, and turned back to the river to watch the current flow and the steaming land pass.

29

Harlan Parker: Up White River, Up Hell Creek

We watched the land, the shore moving by in a stately and graceful slide. The mountains grew larger—soft, ancient mountains sanded by the rasp of wind and atmosphere passing roughly over the face of the earth for eons, wreathed in old-growth forest with very little evidence of habitation of man. Few lines of blue smoke from cabin fires unspooled toward heaven. A startled congregation of deer dashed into the brush. A line of turkey glided across the river, wind loud over their coarse wings. Dethero laughed at my surprise that turkeys could fly, at least for short distances. A bear looked for all the world like a large dog, lurking on the shore. Rabbits, doves, quail. Turtles, snakes. The air swarmed with mayflies and mosquitoes and dragonflies. Animated particles strewn in the refulgent light of afternoon, gleaming on rock smoothed by centuries of river flow *the king gots his kingdom, he goes through every bit, from the fountains of the palace to the edges of the pit* the sweet scents of honeysuckle and hay mixed with diesel exhaust and cigarette smoke. It was evening by the time the barge began shuddering and the bargeman brought us to the far shore, many miles upstream from where we began. We disembarked and, since night was drawing on, made camp at the shore of the river, on the rocky bed. Mollie gathered firewood and Dethero arranged for the *Sleepy John* to return here in three days' time to recover us, though the bargeman decided not to leave that evening for fear of running aground and remained with us there until first light. I used the gas-operated genny to charge the Edison batteries and the captain was kind enough to allow me to let it remain on the boat until he was to reclaim us—I was there to collect only one song and a single charge should be ample for that.

I shared some of the tinned food I had, and we had a meal by the fire Mollie built and slept on the barge's deck, beneath the stars.

In the morning, I double-checked the fastenings on the wooden lid protecting the tone and cutting arms of the SoundScriber, and then Dethero deftly balanced and attached the device and its batteries and acetates and related gear on the mule, which hawed and grumbled but soon grew accustomed to the load. It was packed ingeniously, I must admit, and I found myself considering the luck I had running across Dethero, who, in addition to knowing the location of Cidersend—the village and not its graveyard—also had the rough-hewn skills and knowledgeable hands to bring me there.

We set out, following the river up and up, on game trails and old camp roads cut lifetimes before by settlers and the Quapaw Indians before them, before Hernando de Soto came and western man, with blood and whiskey and gunpowder and steel, to take away the land and claim ownership. I leaned heavily on the shovel as though it were an oversized walking stick. I was tired from my sickness, yes, from the constant hooch and cigarettes these many years; from the war; from the weariness of living orphaned so young by murder; from the heat. From loneliness. I could not keep up with Dethero and his daughter, and lagged behind, much to his dismay and irritation.

The mule—named Bess after Mollie's least-favorite aunt—hawed and complained when it grew tired and insisted on rest, and there was no amount of coercion or cajoling that would get it to move when it was of a mind for a break. I found my disposition often matched the beast of burden's exactly, and Bess would begin her lamentations the moment I felt I could go no farther without rest.

By the end of the first afternoon, as the shadows grew long, we made an early camp on the White River's banks and Mollie retreated into the old growth with a slingshot to hunt squirrels while I stripped nude and fell into the river to wash the sweat and lingering stink of sickness from me. The water felt luxuriously icy. The moss-slick stones shifted under my feet, treacherous. The current took me for a bit, drawing me under. I dreamed then, waking, of my mother and the man Insull, his hands on her shoulders, at her throat. I was for a moment three people: a man lost in a river; my mother, being drowned; a man—*that man*—holding her beneath the surface. A silly song from when I was a child came to me, as the White River washed me downstream.

> *I am you and you are me,*
> *Though we always disagree.*
> *You are I and I am three.*

Alarmed, I thrashed in the frigid water, flailing for shore. I pulled myself onto the bank downriver and had to march back to the camp as naked as when I came into the world, moisture drying on my skin. As I walked back, in the shadows of the trees, I heard a rustling and stopped, not knowing whether to cover my prick and balls with my hands for propriety's sake or raise my hands into fists to defend myself.

"Mollie?" I called. "Is that you?"

The rustling sounded again and from the underbrush, a single black figure emerged, spread its wings, and landed on a small tree near the riverbank. A raven, black as coal, blade-beaked. A small green snake twisted and writhed in its obsidian rostrum.

The bird considered me for a moment, then swallowed the serpent in a single large gulp. It cocked its head, blinked its shiny black eyes, and then cried, launching itself into the air, leaving me puzzled as to what its cry sounded like—*flee? Flee?*

At the camp, I dressed and threw myself down on the ground in an exhausted stupor until Dethero awoke me in the dark. "Got some squirrel and trout left, fried up nice with some onions. Come to the fire if you want some, mister," he said, and moved away. But inside me, I could find no hunger, nor thirst. I joined him anyway and when he placed the cooling skillet in front of me, I went through the mechanical motions of ingestion: Picking morsels, lifting to my mouth, the tentative feel of lip and tongue, mastication. Swallow. I could not say now what I ate or how it tasted. There were many bones. When Dethero brought forth a flask with shine, and I drank, it did not burn and I could not say if I became drunk. Everything is veiled. Everything is old and worn away. I felt ancient in my bones and flesh.

"Should come to Cidersend in the afternoon," Dethero said. "Ain't but a mile to the mouth of Hell Creek, where it empties into the White. Then a hike up the holler, till we pass what folks in these parts call 'Needle's Eye.'"

"And then," I said.

"And then you'll be able to do whatever you came to do. We'll get to Cidersend, and the old black orchards there."

"Black?"

"Some disease got into the trees there, black spots on the apples. They were supposed to burn the orchards to keep the disease from spreading, but it's said they couldn't bring themselves to. It was a garden once, and beautiful." He sighed and stirred the fire with a stick. "So they left it all and moved on to Mountain View. Down to Guion. Over to Batesville. Calico Rock. All over the place. It was just a few families at a farmstead, after all."

"The Hines family?"

"Yep, them Hines. Showboats, one and all. And the Loves. The Saylors. Evensons and Briers. All gone." He looked lost, the yellow light of the fire shifting in his eyes. "My Olive was a Saylor. I miss her dear." Mollie reached out a hand and grasped his and squeezed. Such a simple gesture, and immediately I felt an interloper at a family moment. "You ain't looking so well, mister. You might want to rest."

I fell back into a restless sleep, with dreams of Insull and my mother. Château-Thierry and the Somme, the chatter of gunfire and burning horses. West Africa and Austria and French New Guinea, new spices and cinnamon and scented oils upon the air. All my experience collapsing on itself, my own personal acetate caught in an endless loop.

—*he ask, "what behind this wall here? ain't I king of hell?" and the devils all around him answer, "you is, but well well well . . ." and stack don't like they answer, so he shoots them as they plea. he a bad man, stackolee*—

I recall the morning. The light rising in the east, sky lightening over the rim of earth. The White River moving with only a whisper of falling glass, of gurgling, of the endless churn of water, blue-white until it reaches the Arkansas River, where the mud seeps in.

We rose. Dethero was not much for talking and he did not restoke the fire. I took up my satchel—containing only a few things, this field journal being one of them—and we began the hike.

Finally we came to the black orchard, where the trees still grew. Hell Creek was left behind. The orchard trees twisted in misery, blackened and discolored with the disease that choked the life from their roots and darkened their leaves but could not kill them. A smell rose from the ground, thick and sweet and cloying, and with each step the dark, mulched earth released fruiting spores, rising upward. Black, molded husks of farmhouses, barns, outbuildings—a grain dryer, a ramshackle silo, tin sides gone to rust and ruin and standing like lost sentinels at the edges of the trees.

"This is where she was from, Mollie," Dethero said. "It was falling down before she left and came to us."

Mollie walked with a tight expression on her young face. Distaste and some dread, I think.

"There's the stone garden, Mister Parker," Mollie said, gesturing to the west.

The apple trees, for all their spots and litterfall, stood in military rows, dashing away. As I walked among them, at times they would fall in diagonals to my eyeline, so that at any forward step, the world would take on the illusion of divine order, as if everything had shifted and arranged itself exactly so, specifically for my arrival. Then with the next step, it would disarrange itself. Tension and release. Crescendo to diminuendo.

The columns of trees stopped before me and there was a cast-iron gate beyond, crowded with growth, saplings and young trees mostly, springing among the graves. Wrought in simple ironwork were the names of the families to each side on the supports and an arch over the entrance to the graveyard reading IDYLL'S END.

Cidersend. Idyll's End.

I walked among the graves in the slanting late-afternoon sunshine, a million particles strewn on beams of light, across the dappled and overgrown brushwood. If it had ever been a well-tended cemetery, that had been years—decades—before. Now the forest had reclaimed the land, and only the lichen and moss-covered gravestones and the iron gate were any reminder that this was a place where a township had buried its dead.

WILLIAM OGDEN LOVE, AGED SIXTY-THREE YEARS. I RAISE HIM UP ON ANGEL WINGS AND BRING HIM UNTO ME. JAMES AND LORENA EVENSON—IN DEATH, BOUND IN LOVE. SULLY SAYLOR, A GOOD FATHER AND HUSBAND.

The names began to deteriorate, becoming illegible without some closer examination. I ignored them.

There was the figure I had come for. Fifteen feet tall, beautifully hewn from granite, the cloaked angel stood on a pedestal, its wings furled but heavy behind it and its face hidden within the shroud of a cloak. It was carved with such delicacy the softness of the fabric seemed real. In one hand the angel held a sword with lichen for blood spatter down the blade, and the other hand pointed at the earth before it with one bony index finger. There was a sorrow hanging around it, something about the shoulders, the cant of head.

"So what now, mister?" Mollie asked.

"I wait until after midnight, and ask the questions I need to ask," I said.

"Ask who?" Dethero said. "Midnight in the graveyard? I don't want no part of this, mister." The man began shaking his head. "Me and Mollie will just wait out in the orchard for you."

"I've paid you good money. I require you to bring the Sound-Scriber here, help me to set it up, and then you may do whatever you wish."

Dethero looked from me to his daughter. She shrugged.

She seemed unfazed by it all—me, Idyll's End, the ruins of her mother's hamlet—all of it was just another bit of information, it seemed, she would file away.

I sat before the angel, looking up at her, and withdrew from my bag the bottle of wine, the wedge of cheese, and the loaf of bread I had purchased in Blytheville. Both the cheese and the bread had suffered during the journey and were misshapen lumps, with spots of blue-green mold blooming on them, but I ate most of them anyway. My spectral distance from food and taste was gone and I could taste the totality of the food. Each bite of bread held the grit and dirt of the wheat that grew it, the salt of the sweat of the baker, the imperceptible exhalations of every man, woman, and child who came near it. The cheese held the lowing of the heifer that gave the milk, the bacteria that spoiled the milk in a contained burn. The decay of all things. The taste of the mold curled and blossomed upon my tongue. The devil crept in.

I left only a rind of the cheese and a crust of the bread. I opened the bottle of wine and drank heavily until there were only a few swallows left. By this time, Dethero had maneuvered Bess into the graveyard, and between us, we took the Sound-Scriber off her and I set the Edison batteries near the recording device but did not attach them. I did not want anything, even a dormant connection, to drain the reservoirs of their charge.

"We'll piddle around in the farmhouses, I reckon, maybe see if there's a stove or fireplace. Looks like it might rain," Dethero said.

"That's fine. You do that," I said, focused on the task at hand. I took up the shovel. The wine and food had given me a preternatural strength I had not felt since . . . since I cannot remember when. France? Belgium?

"Diggin'?" Dethero said, agog. He looked bewildered. "Who in the hell you gonna dig up, mister?"

"I do not know," I said. "Someone who can give me answers."

"Let's get the hell out of here, Mollie. Don't want no part of this."

Mollie looked reluctant to leave, though. She opened her mouth as if to say something. But Dethero made a chopping motion with his hand and she stopped abruptly. Soon I was alone in the graveyard. Silence returned. The grave and SoundScriber waited.

I placed the shovel blade in the loam, set my foot upon it, and drove it into the earth.

30

Harlan Parker: A Rind, a Crust, a Kiss

Night falls sometimes without your knowing. That is the way of it. There are no endings, just beginnings.

The soil was loose and sprung from the clutching grip of earth as if it wanted to be free. There were few rocks in the barrow clay, and a rich, opaline scent rose from it. I fell into the rhythms and syncopation of digging, my own private and onanistic percussive composition, fretting between movement and expectation, excitement driving me on. The rise and fall of breath and an invisible melody—a threnody—pulsing within and around me. It took on the shapes and contours of Honeyboy's song. There was no room for anything else but the black wall and his melody. I moved in time with it. My head felt as though it were the seat of some infinite pressure. My nose ran freely with blood. My hands burned and rose with fat blisters from the shovel haft, suppurated, raw, wet. I felt strong and reveled in the strength of my body. I felt untethered from the earth that infused my pores, infested my mouth, lived in the cracks and crevices of my body.

It became too dark to see, so I lit the candles I had brought with me and placed them at the foot of the nameless stone angel and was waist-deep in the earth when my shovel hit wood. It was a matter of an hour more to clear the lid of the coffin and open it wide, revealing the figure within. There is no figure as disappointing as the withered husk of man. Clothes returned to gravesoil and dust, all the bones pushing through the remains of the flesh— scraps and parchment pieces drawn tight at the jawline and cheekbones like leather and in other places like vermin-chewed cloth that once held the stuff of life. He yawed, dramatic, in my vision. I moved the candles and sat and smoked and examined the remains. The mandibular bone leering and askew, cocked in a silent bellow, maybe. He had worn down his teeth in life, or they had rotted away, a diet rich in the sugar of apples. A *he*, surely, for the gravesoil gave the impression of a suit. By candlelight, I looked at my watch. It was only eight o'clock.

I rose from the grave and wandered out among the gravestones and through the wrought-iron gate to find Dethero and Mollie and rest before doing what I had to do.

It is late now, as I write this. I have reread what I have written in this field journal by candlelight. I have searched these words and recollections for some indication into the nature of Amoira, and the story of Honeyboy. The nature of "Crowned in Scarlet." *Couronné en écarlate.*

A piece of music draws you on, leading you places you've never been. You'd never think of journeying to. Would that I had a hand-cranked Victrola. Once more with Mahler, Stravinsky, Liszt to wash away the melody that has infected me. Once more into the wheeling music of the heavens and spheres. I do not know where I will go from here. *Preludio a Colón; L'amour, toujours, l'amour; Ce qu'on entend sur la montagne; Totentanz; Années de pèlerinage; Grande messe des morts; Das Lied von der Erde; La damnation de Faust; Scheherazade.* I remember that hot day in Washington, walking with such purpose. I would hear *Liebesträume* once more. My fingers twitch in sympathetic response to the melody in my head.

But it is not *Liebesträume*. It is only "Crowned in Scarlet" that draws me onward.

Dethero and Mollie have made a fire, and we have eaten the last of our food—save for a crust of bread and a rind of cheese—and now I use the firelight to take down these thoughts. The girl and her father have gone to sleep and it seems that the whole world of night calls to me in its silence. The yellow firelight shifts on the old timbers of this rotten house. The heavy odor of moldering apples fills the air, and I have seen a variety of wildlife come into the moonlight of the black orchard, noses held high, scenting the litterfall, and then return to the darkness of the woods without eating—a deer, a raccoon, a possum, a fox.

He a bad man, Stackolee.

This world corrupts me and its sweetness—its impoverished and unthinking vice, its careless and unfeeling death—makes me carious with rot. I intend to go to the grave and hear "Crowned in Scarlet" in full. The girl and her father sleep, oblivious to the wonder that is soon to be revealed.

I go now. I go.

31

Mollie Dethero: A Testament of the Events at Cidersend

My name is Millicent Olive Dethero and my daddy told me to write everything down that I can remember about Mister Harlan Parker because neither him or my daddy have any letters. Mister Parker did, of course, since he wrote all the words in this here journal, but he doesn't have them now—that's for sure—and my daddy never had any so it's just me to tell you what happened. Daddy thinks it's important, too, so that the lawyers and government men don't think we did something to him. Which we didn't. So I've got to give my testament here before it all fades away.

I have read what's in this journal and can't say I understand very much of it but the parts of it that I did take in . . . well, it's a real doozy, a whopper. The man is certifiable, as Ginny Haskins would say. "Absolutely certifiable, put him in the booby hatch," she would say. "Lock him in the nutcase. Cat and tonic," she would say. I know because she said the same thing about me when I shot her brother with my slingshot. I guess I should say now, since I wrote that all down and lawyers and government men will read it, that the only reason I shot her brother was because he kicked my dog, Flutterby, when they came onto our farm at the first of summer to swim in the creek. And I only shot him in the caboose as he ran away. Both Ginny and her brother were lucky I didn't decide to shoot out their teeth, because I could've if I wanted to since I'm the best shot in Stone County. That isn't a lie, it's the simple truth, and anyone around here will tell you so. I thought about it, though, shooting out their darned teeth. I was gonna yell, "*Hope you two like soup!*" and then bust their choppers but I thought about the time I put the snake in Mikey's bed when he was sleeping and it bit him something good and then he put all the poison ivy in my clothes and I spent a month oozing and itching. So, I didn't bust their choppers. But I wanted to.

Mister Parker. He was a strange one.

When I think about him, it's not about how he is now, but when he first came to our house asking about Cidersend, and not how he was on the trip back downriver. I could tell Daddy was going to go with him even before they talked money because he gets restless after a long summer and he once was a rover before Momma made him settle down.

So I knowed he was gonna bargain.

But Mister Parker. He was a big man, tall and gangly really, and he seemed like he could be old and young all at once if that makes any sense but even as I write it I can see it doesn't. Maybe I should say that there were things about Mister Parker that were young, and there were things about him that were old.

His skin was pale and loose, like he'd dropped some weight, and his shoulders sloped down like he was a man who had carried too much of a burden for too long a time. His eyes sunk into his head, like he'd seen too much or had been sick for a long time away from the sun. Or he had what Grandmam called the "sorrow-sickness." His voice cracked and croaked when he talked

and sang. He was always singing, and I don't think he even knew
he was doing it himself, like my grandmam, who's always humming. Old folks don't know what they're doing all the time, I
guess, and they lose control of their mouths. Or maybe, over the
course of a lifetime, they get too full of thoughts, and music—
music is a thought, ain't it? It's something someone thinks up,
isn't it, and then lets free into the world? Like a turtle. Or a baby
bird, I guess. Music really isn't like a turtle, is it? I don't know.

But he was young, too. He had this really fierce gaze, if you understand what I mean. Like in the Bible in the Song of Songs when
that Shulamite woman says "Set me as a seal upon your heart, as
a seal upon your arm; for love is strong as death, passion fierce as
the grave." He had a look that made me think of those words from
the Bible, if that makes any sense. I don't take much from Bible
studies, most of the time, but that sits upon me and comes to me
at times when I don't even want it.

So he had a fierce gaze, full of love. For things and thoughts
and ideas. And music. Which is a thought, as I said before. Music is a thought that becomes sound. Mister Parker searched for
music and so he searched for thoughts and maybe he picked the
wrong thought to search for, in the end. But that made him seem
far younger than he was, in my books. Also, he respected my
daddy, even though they were from two different worlds, and
only a young man from the big city would do that, not a man of
his age. I guess I'd put him around forty, if I was guessing, but
Daddy says younger and Dr. Crowley says older, judging by the
state of his body. But the more I got to know him, I realized, he
was even younger than his body really—isn't your body really a
thought too? Daddy says you are what you eat, and you choose to
eat hard candy and peppermint, or you choose to eat vegetables,
and so your body is just a mirror's reflection of all your choices,
right, so it's the song that your mind makes. Does that make

sense? Reverend Owens says we're souls at sea riding on ships looking for a lighthouse. We're candles in the dark.

But he was younger than his years, really, because he respected me too.

I liked him right from the start.

Maybe that's not right.

I was interested in him from the start and the longer I spent with him, the more I liked him.

So, I was happy when Daddy asked me if I wanted to go a-roving with them.

I'll admit here that I did see Mister Parker in his birthday suit when he came out of the White River. I'd been hunting squirrel, and I killed a couple and was looking for another in the wood by the shore when I heard Mister Parker's singing and he came up out of the water on the shoreline. He was singing, "He's a bad man, Stackerlee," over and over in a croon, under his breath. And he was naked and dripping.

I've seen a man's privates before—I've got brothers—so I wasn't about to go hiding my eyes like I have curls in my hair or wear dresses and flounce about. It's just regular business. And Mister Parker's business wasn't anything to get worked up over anyway. What I really noticed wasn't his tallywhacker but the scars running down his back and legs, and the hollowed-out husk of his chest. He looked like a man who hadn't eaten in a month and just got punched in the gut. Bowled over and reeling.

"Is that you, Mollie!" he cried out, and I nearly jumped out of my shoes thinking he might see me. When he covered his privates with his hands, I nearly laughed. I wanted to holler, "Why you covering up now, when I've already seen everything you got?" But I didn't.

Then he did something strange. He cocked his head and looked at the leaves in front of the trees where I hid as if he was seeing something. I craned my head so I might see what he was looking at, but I couldn't see it. And now, having read his journal, I can tell you for sure there was no raven with a snake in its mouth. And at the time I did not understand what he was doing but I was eager to get away, so that I wouldn't be caught. So, when he walked on—and boy does a man's buttocks look funny shifting back and forth as they walk, lemme tell you—I went back up in the woods and looked for another squirrel.

But I guess I should get to the part that you probably want to know about. Him making that recording at the grave.

It was obvious he had dug up the grave under the pointing angel. My daddy might not have figured it out, but I knew the moment he sat down and started eating that moldy piece of bread and that green cheese. He seemed different then. Happy maybe. Like he was where he wanted to be.

So, I waited until he came back. Daddy and I set up camp in the least run-down of the houses and made a fire in the fireplace. If it rained, we would've been drenched—I could see the stars through the rafters and there was a hoot owl blowing noise into the night somewhere in the house above us. When Mister Parker returned, he was filthy with dirt and he floated like a ghost made of soil into the house and sat down and ate food, humming and muttering all the while, rocking back and forth. He smoked and drank some coffee Daddy had brewed for him—I love my daddy because he's a good man who believes he is his brother's keeper—and then Mister Parker bowed his head and wrote in his journal for two, maybe three hours. He could've been a priest or one of those robed monks like they have out west, near Subiaco.

I lay down near Daddy, who was snoring away—he'd had a nip of the shine, for sure, and ate two tins of sardines by himself and smoked many cigarettes, so he was cutting some lumber, let me tell you. Sawing and sawing. I closed my eyes but only barely and watched Mister Parker work in the failing firelight. He rocked back and forth and at some point his nose bled even though I didn't see him pick at it and he simply wiped the blood away in long streaks down the length of his forearm and sang to himself in a circle, "I am like a mountain, and need no crown on me. I am an ocean, a black and churning sea. I am a mountain, ain't need no crown on me, I'm a bad man, Stack-o-Lee," and the way he sang it seemed as though he was talking to somebody, in the same way my grandmam does sometimes, having conversations with people she knew in different places and long ago. And that scared me some. What could have happened that even after a person is long gone—maybe even dead and in the ground—you still want to keep talking to them?

Maybe I fell asleep. I think I did, because I remember being startled that the firelight was gone and the whole house was lit up blue and ghostlike in the moonfall. Mister Parker was gone. So I pushed myself up and, making sure I didn't wake Daddy, walked out into the orchard and then to Idyll's End.

It's here I should say I ain't much afraid of anything, not boy or girl, not man or woman. If there's such a thing as a ghost, it seems like a pretty poor and meager thing to get all worked up about, since all they can do is maybe make faces at you or remind you of something that was done long ago. No reason to be scared. I have snatched water moccasins out of the creek and I've stared down a pack of wild dogs once with only my slingshot to protect me. I wouldn't mess with a bear, though, not because they aren't deserving of fear—they most definitely are—but because all the bears I've ever seen were content to just go about their own business and want more than anything to just be left alone. I'll give them that.

I don't have no truck with geese, though, other than eatin' them. They're mean, evil birds and I kill every one of them that comes within reach of my shot. I do.

But I forget myself.

Idyll's End and the grave.

I came in on cat's feet, like when I hunt. I can move silent as hell when I'm of a mind but even if I'd waltzed in, singing at the top of my lungs, I doubt Mister Parker would have heard it.

He'd lit some candles, a couple at the base of the vengeful angel and one he put at the side of the grave. He went to the recording machine and connected it to the batteries and then carefully withdrew a record—just like one you'd put on a Victrola, except without the grooves, if you understand—and placed it on the recorder and flipped some switches and buttons and levers and then moved away. He said, "This is Harlan Parker in Cidersend. I don't know what day it is." He stopped like he'd forgotten what he was saying and then looked up at the sky for a long time. "Close to the autumnal equinox, I think. Idyll's End. Somewhere in Arkansas. God help me."

There was a heaping mound of dirt at the statue's feet and Mister Parker climbed down into the grave like he was sore all over, which I imagine he was, having dug it only hours before.

When he was in the grave, he placed the candle down under the ground level where I couldn't see and then grabbed his bag and said, "Kiss the crust of my body," and put something in his mouth.

Then: "Eat the rind of my cheese." And he ate that too. Finally, he uncorked the bottle with a pop and said, "Drink the blood of my body," and he drank the rest of the wine.

His head tilted back and he flopped forward into the grave where I couldn't see him.

Now, this is where it gets a little different, I guess. All of this is true and we brought back his records and the SoundScriber, so if you don't believe me, listen to the recording and you'll see— you'll hear—that everything I have said is true. Maybe I didn't notice the mist coming up from Hell Creek, but I noticed then

- 343 -

that the air was hazy and all around us the forest had gone silent again.

I crept forward. There were a thousand things in my mind running around like foals in spring or puppies or a mess of snakes. My imagination sparked, I guess you could say, and I could see in my mind's eye a dead body down in that hole, a woman maybe, all in white like she had died at her wedding. I don't know. But as god is my witness, I heard a creak like a door opening and in my mind it was the woman's black mouth and a wind came up and blew into the world a cold, cold breeze.

"Ask," the wind said. "*Ask.*"

"I would hear 'Crowned in Scarlet,'" Mister Parker said.

The wind howled and moaned. Don't know any other way to explain it. The mist was thicker than milk now, and I crept forward so I could get where I could see and hear better.

The wind laughed at Mister Parker, and it was a bitter sound. From where I crouched, I could see his back and shoulders, he was hunched over whoever was in the grave with him and for a moment I thought he was the voice of the wind.

"*Baby,*" the wind said. "*My baby. It's been so long.*"

"Momma?" Mister Parker said. "Momma, I've missed you so much. I've done—"

"*Sssssshhhhh,*" the wind said, its voice coming from so far away. It sounded like two tin cans connected with string. It sounded like someone speaking softly in a big house in a different room from where you are sleeping late at night when everything is quiet and still. "*Don't think on all that now,*" the wind said.

"He killed you. I couldn't rest, I couldn't sleep until I found him. And I did," Parker said. His back hitched when he said it, and I realized he was crying. "I killed him," he said.

"*What are you saying, my son?*" the wind asked.

"It was in Washington and I saw him. Insull. Matthew Insull.

On the street. I followed him home and watched him. And then, one day, I went to his house and wrung the breath out of him."

"*What what what what what,*" the wind said.

"My hands found his throat and I did to him what he did to you, Momma." Mister Parker's voice sounded like car wheels over gravel. There was so much pain and misery there I liked to cry. But I didn't.

"*No no no no no no no no,*" the wind said. There was something rising in that sound as well. Terror, yes, and agitation. In my mind the white woman writhed in the grave. "*You lie. You lie. You lie. If not to me, then to yourself,*" the wind said. "*Bunny is here. Bunny is with me, at your hand.*"

"Bunny? I would never have hurt him," Parker cried. "I would never have hurt *you.*"

"*My son. My son. My son. Insull did not drown me. I was drunk and foolish. I stripped naked to swim, having drunk so so much, and slipped. The world flashed and flipped and went white. My head struck the dock, my body struck the water, and my lungs filled. And then I found myself here. Matthew was a good man,*" the wind said.

"Why did he flee?" Parker asked.

"*He's a man, just like you, and scared and small, like all men.*"

"I killed him," Parker said back. "And then to hide, I went to war. And killed again."

"*No no no. Please no, I do not have much time. It is coming,*" the wind said.

"Momma, I'm sorry, I thought—"

"*I cannot help you now. There is no succor for murderers. It is coming,*" the wind said.

"What's coming, Momma?"

"*The crowned man, the scarlet king. The black wall,*" the wind said. And then: "*Goodbye.*"

Then there was a sound, and I don't like to think about it too much. You can hear it yourself on the recordings. There was a sound. I cannot say whether Mister Parker made it, or the wind, or something in the ground. But it rose up and shattered my ears and I ran away into the dark and got lost in the woods. Behind me I could hear Parker or the wind singing words over and over again and they became huge, taller than the trees, taller than the sky. I glanced back once, and there it was, a black wall of night and a tall man standing in front of it and beyond it nothing.

Daddy came to find me in the morning. He was scared, I could tell, and very frightened by my hair. It's all white now.

I don't mind it, really, and I think it looks like a queen's hair— "royal" is the word they use in advertisements—especially when I string together red mountain flowers in a daisy chain and wear them as a crown. I feel beautiful then, and any boy or man would find me that way too.

But I can still shoot out the eye of a sparrow on the wing with my slingshot.

My daddy found Mister Parker still in the grave, gibbering. He said Mister Parker had lost his mind, and from what I could see on the way back, he surely looked to be cat and tonic, just like the doctor said about Grandmam before she passed.

Daddy put the SoundScriber in the house we made camp in, and we put Mister Parker on Bess, and went back down Hell Creek to the White River where the bargeman waited. He couldn't stop looking at my hair, nor Parker in his mute and dumb state. He drooled, Parker did.

I never saw him do or say anything else. Except once.

Daddy had someone contact the government. Daddy, who was worried about the government and their lawyers, went back upriver and collected Mister Parker's SoundScriber and all the records that went with it. He did not keep the Studebaker, but held it in waiting for the government men. But the government men did not come. Eventually, they sent a telegram saying Mister Parker's sister would collect him, and his belongings. It was a long while, waiting for her to come, and in the meantime, we had to take care of Mister Parker. He could eat, and he could sleep—it seemed like all he did was sleep and sit out on the porch in the sun, staring into the cornfields, drooling. Sometimes, Daddy would roll a cigarette and light it and put it in Mister Parker's lips and he'd smoke it, never using his hands. But if you didn't watch it, it would burn down to a nub and blister the poor man's lips. I never had to wipe his backside with a corncob, but Daddy surely did, and did not enjoy that one bit. Daddy hated that part so much, he said we weren't to feed Mister Parker but once a day, and then only a little bit. So that's what we did.

My brother Michael came home with a cigar box, CORONATIONS DE LUXE it said on the wooden lid, and with a bit of wood and some of Daddy's tools, he made a three-string guitar for himself. He always wanted a fiddle but Daddy said they cost too much, so he made himself something he could pick a tune with. When he brought it in our house's main room down from the attic where he kept his workshop, and struck a few notes, Mister Parker appeared in the main door from the porch, a wild look in his eye. He moved to Michael like a wolf and snatched up the cigar box in one hand and began fingering it madly, producing a weird, disjointed melody. His hands moved like spiders across the strings. Michael and Daddy just stood there, poleaxed.

Mister Parker began mouthing words, whispering at first and then growing louder, "Ain't I king here, well well well, Ain't I a good man, well well well, Ain't I lord and where's my crown, well well well, Ain't I belong here, well well well, I'm a bad man, I'm a bad man . . ." Over and over and then he opened his mouth like a bell and a sound came out so black that I stretched out and my hand reached into my pocket as if it had its own mind and found the rock I had there for my slingshot and I threw it as hard as I could and hit Mister Parker between the eyes. He fell backward and the cigar-box guitar went a-clattering across the floor.

Mister Parker never spoke again.

His sister came a couple of days later and collected him.

My name is Millicent Olive Dethero and that is my story. I swear every word of it is true.

If you doubt me, come touch my hair and listen to Mister Parker's acetates. And then maybe you'll believe.

He was wrong, though. Some endings are final.

32

Cromwell: He Cannot Sleep

Cromwell closes the field journal. It is morning now and he's read through the night. He rises, showers, brushes his teeth. When he opens the blackout curtain, a woman with shocking white hair stares up at his window from the parking lot. She's dressed in her shift and the wind tears at her clothing. *Dementia, maybe,* he thinks, *grief is like dementia,* and barrels down to the lobby and out into the parking lot to help her but she's nowhere to be found. The hard, cold asphalt of the lot hurts his bare feet and he realizes he's standing beneath the clotted sky in his nightclothes. He returns to his room slowly, rubbing his face. He sits at the glowing screen of his Mac, vacant, and pecks at the keyboard. He answers emails, he looks at his direct messages on social media accounts. The Realtor, the estate sale planner, the lawyer, the inspector, his bureau chief. A high school friend expressing belated condolences. A woman who has heard he is newly single. Viv has not contacted him. She won't, he knows. He must be the one to reach out to her and that will never happen.

Hattie texts him and they meet in the lobby to check out. They eat prepackaged Danishes and powdered eggs with hot sauce from the continental breakfast as Hattie asks which continent as a joke and it takes Cromwell a full ten minutes to catch it.

"You all right?" she asks, by rote now. Purely habit. His work wife, as if there ever can be such a thing without work sex. He thinks of Vivian. Her remarkably strong hands insistent at his body. He thinks about Maizie, the curl of her stomach against his son, breathless, the house still. The carbon monoxide detectors had beeped in the night—he doesn't remember which night—indicating the batteries were low, and he'd pulled the nine-volt to stop the beeping and shuffled off back to bed and did not think of them again, ever. And now he's here, in Springfield. *Did I want them to die? Did I? So I could be with Vivian? Am I that sort of man? A monster? I cannot remember.*

I cannot remember who I am, he thinks. *Who I am supposed to be.*

"I've arranged the flights."

"I look forward to getting back. Hotel life sucks, man," Hattie says, observing him. "You?"

"Yes. The recordings will be my work for a long while," he says.

"You gonna follow up on the Bunny angle?" Hattie asks.

"Maybe," he says. "I don't know yet. Let's just get the acetates in the system and then I can move on to the next part."

She seems dissatisfied. "So that's it?"

"If I did write something, I don't think I could do it without you working with me."

She's still for a long while, and her gaze searches his face for what, he cannot tell. Honesty, maybe. She shakes her head.

"No, man," Hattie says. "You can't write that book."

"Why not?"

"I think you know. You've got other business to attend to."

He says nothing.

"And right now, you're a fucking hot mess, Crumb," she says. Her face is hard as she says it. He meets her gaze. In some ways, it's a rejection that hurts more than anything he can think of. He needed her acceptance and not getting it makes him bitter. Angry. That grubby spark of ambition burning in his chest. "But ask me again, later."

He nods. It's like a lifeline. Possibilities indicate a future, a road that can be followed.

"I'll probably still say no," she says. "Writing isn't really my bag. But you never know. I'm probably as good at it as you are. Can always give it a shot." She stops, thinking for a moment. "What was that phrase that Parker kept saying?"

"There are no endings," Cromwell says.

At the Parker house, Hattie cues up the TASCAM and they work through the remaining acetates, slowly. Hattie decides to go get some Starbucks, and takes Cromwell's order, and he wanders down through the house, to the front lawn. It's sunny today, with a bright, moistureless winter sky. The Realtor has placed a sign on the front lawn. He finds himself returning to the backyard, and the room in the back of the garage. The deteriorating instruments within.

Here they would place Parker, with the banjo, the guitar, the dulcimer, and lock the door. They'd flee, he knows, out of earshot. Whatever music Parker played, he played solely for himself.

They finish by noon. But Cromwell, for reasons he cannot wholly explain, takes the last acetate, the one marked *Cidersend*, and files it in the middle of the records without presenting it to Hattie to digitize. It's a subterfuge that will most likely be found out, but not today, and not by Hattie. All he can think when he does this is *I am not ready, I am not ready*. Hattie smiles in relief when he tells her they are through. Carefully, working as a team, they load the acetates and the SoundScriber into the back of their rented SUV and bring the items to a USPS, where other government employees take the cases and equipment and pack it under Hattie's supervision. By evening they are home.

33

Cromwell: Mollie in Mountain View

Winter: The house is cold and remains so. In the mornings, Cromwell rises silently, dresses somberly, and returns to work. He does not listen to music on his new turntable. He does not cook. His commute has changed. He does not drive to DC, but goes west to Culpeper, in the shadow of Shenandoah and the Blue Ridge Mountains, passing fields and markers for Civil War battle-grounds and farmhouses and new real estate developments. What sort of songs do those hills contain? A song is a thought the heart gives expression. He does not miss the office in Washington, with its political struggles and jockeying for position. He does not miss wearing the suits and ties.

In Culpeper, there is a hole in the ground, and in that hole the American government stores all of the audiovisual records of the country's history. The climate is controlled; it's a tomb, a sepulcher for the nation's film, its acetates, its microfiche and wax tables and deliquescing paper history. Through its halls walk technicians, curators. They're young people, bright faces downturned to glowing device screens. It is there where Harlan

Parker's recordings have gone to live, deathless. The National Audio-Visual Conservation Center campus looks to Cromwell like the site of a Roman amphitheater, covered in ivy and decay. Surely the architect must've intended this, he thinks, each time he enters. It's the ruins and remnants of a dead culture. Why do this?

His days are spent indexing the recordings. Listening to the voices of Smoot Sawyer and Lucius Spoon and Gramp Hines and all the rest. He works on papers and writes, as he listens, taking notes. Notating key, tempo, structure. He transcribes each acetate. He's accompanied by a young technician who wears forensic latex gloves and who does not let him touch the acetates. She is young, and blond, and plump, and smells good, and Cromwell cannot stop himself but he often thinks about what it might be like if she opened herself up to him, thick legs spread. When these thoughts occur, the hurt feels like a palpable thing in his chest, his stomach. *I'm a bad man, Stackerlee.* It becomes a litany. In time, Stagger Lee has ceased to be the villain and is now Cromwell's confessor. Her name is Bethany March and she has a gaudy and large diamond wedding ring that distends the latex gloves and a vapid laugh he does not like but still he thinks about her spreading herself. But he cannot come, even at his own hand. He thinks of Parker, near the end, when no food could sate him. Liquor and smoke did nothing. At night Cromwell will thumb through the worst sorts of porn the Internet has to offer, his hot prick in hand, and cannot reach completion. That part of him has been walled away.

One day, after winter has passed into late May, they listen to the Amoira Hines acetate together. He watches the technician as it becomes obvious what is occurring in the recording, the sex, the demented laughter, arcane and unknown words, the slapping of flesh together. With her gloved hand she touches her neck, brushes an errant bit of hair from her face. Eventually she rises and leaves the climate-controlled listening room. The next day, she offers Cromwell instruction on the care and handling of acetates and does not remain with him again during his work.

He requests the acetate labeled *Cidersend.*

It is as Mollie Dethero described it, though it is not clear whether it was Parker, in his dementia, speaking for himself and the "wind" or if it was Mollie who was speaking. A jape, a trick she pulled on a poor sick man. A snake in the bedsheets, poison ivy in the clothes. Surely it was not the wind. Not a voice from the grave. The sound at the end is like a tempest in a tin can, full of words and jarring melodies, full of sound and fury. You know the rest. It's a small sound, full of the crackle of recording and seemingly very far away. There is no intimation of the black wall.

On a whim, Cromwell turns to his computer, opens a browser, and keys into a search bar *Millicent Olive Dethero, Arkansas.* A single hit. Her name became Millicent Dethero Tackett at marriage. He is glad it is not an obituary. An article regarding gardening, dated 2002, in the *Stone County Register.* In her byline, it mentions her husband, Richard "Buddy" Tackett, and a search reveals his death in 2009 at the age of ninety. He is survived by his wife and two sons, George and Lester Tackett. It takes two phone calls to contact her oldest son, George, and discover whether she lives and where she is.

He's on an early-morning flight the next day to Little Rock, Arkansas. By late afternoon, he's in the parking lot of the Stone County Retirement Home and Assisted Living Complex, a drab, run-down affair. *This is where people come to die,* he thinks, *those too tenacious to let go on their own. There's always pleasure to be found somewhere. In a television show or vanilla pudding. In an OxyContin or a foot rub. Isn't there? The world still contains pleasure, does it not?* The voice of Mollie that lives in Cromwell's mind is thousands of miles, and eighty years, away from this poor place.

He gets out of his rental. Already, he can feel the summer. There'll be a long procession of days like these, hot and bright and golden. It's Arkansas, and the heat is rising in the hills and the air is full of moisture and the sky teems with columns of clouds.

The nurse will not let him see Mollie Dethero, so he leaves a note asking permission to speak with her, indicating he'll return tomorrow. He takes a room at a motel and has an urge to have a drink, to have many drinks, to see if something still churns in his depths, but Stone County is dry. A pocket of prohibition that has hung on to life since Mollie Dethero was a girl.

In the morning, he returns. The queen has granted an audience, he finds.

Her room, when he enters, is simple and cheap and smells of disinfectant and sickness. A bed, a walker, an ugly couch. A big expensive high-definition television set in contrast to the cheapness of everything else—there is pleasure to be found in something, isn't there? Here it is the mind-deadening glamour of Fox News set to mute. She sits in a chair by the window, looking out at the soft mountains rolling beyond the parking lot. Majesty framed in the humdrum. Cromwell has done the math in his head. Mollie Dethero is ninety-five years old.

"Mrs. Tackett, my name is Cromwell, and I'm from the Library—"

"I always knew someone would come," she said. "I just didn't think it would take this long." She's withered and unlike how Cromwell pictured her. Fatter, and softer. Wobbling skin slack at her neck and on her forearms. *Aging isn't like desiccation,* Cromwell thinks, *where the flesh is drained away, leaving only the bones. It's the baggage of life hanging from your frame, it's the fat, it's the fused vertebrae, the skin full of scars and tears and liver marks.*

He sits down near her. She says, "This is about Parker, isn't it?"

"Yes," Cromwell says. "Of course it is."

"What do you want to know?"

"Did you ever listen to the recording?"

"No. How could I?"

"You had the SoundScriber for weeks. It's a simple enough machine."

"No," she says. "I didn't want to hear it all again." She looks away from Cromwell and out the window. "Once was enough."

"The recording was not very revealing."

"Young man, you sound like you're accusing me of something."

"No," Cromwell says. "Of course not. I am just curious. Could you have been playing a trick on Parker? Speaking for the—"

"The wind?" She laughed. "God help me, I wish I had played that trick on him."

"Why did you call it the wind?"

She remains quiet for a long while. "It was eighty years ago. I was just a girl and full of myself and scared. Calling it the wind was easier than saying *death.*"

"Death? What—"

"What isn't about death, mister? It's all about death."

"When you ran away, you wrote you saw a man standing before a black wall," Cromwell says.

"I don't know what I wrote," she says. "It was a long time ago."

Cromwell stops, examines the woman. She breathes through her mouth and he can see, on the parchment-thin skin on the back of her hand, she's had an intravenous drip recently: blue and purple bruises bloom around a white bandage. Her head is wrapped in a multicolored floral silk scarf, and she's a riot of different fabric patterns on her dress, her sweater. Her feet outrageously swollen and painful for Cromwell to look at.

"All right, Mrs. Tackett. I just have one more question for you," Cromwell says. "What do you think happened? Was Parker crazy?"

"He most definitely was that." She laughs. "But, just because you're crazy doesn't mean you're crazy."

"So, the second voice. Was it him?"

She reaches up and unpins the scarf around her head. Slowly she unwinds it. Her hair has been pressed to her skull in a misshapen and ugly clot. It's a garish shade of red, and not white.

"Curl up and dye," Mollie Dethero says. "That's my motto. Ever since I was a girl."

Cromwell stands. He has wasted his and her time, and she does not have much left. "Thank you, Mollie, for talking to me." He turns to leave.

"It ain't far away, Mister Government Man," Mollie says. "Cidersend. All you gotta do is use one of them computers and find Hell Creek. Ain't more than ten miles away. You can ask the angel all the questions you've got. All by yourself."

"Thank you," he says, and leaves her. In the car he wonders when was the last time her hands held a slingshot, the last time she shot a squirrel from a bough or a sparrow from the sky, as she bragged in her testament.

He opens his phone and brings up Google Maps and enters *Mountain View, Arkansas, Hell Creek* and as easy as that, his phone begins to give him directions.

In thirty minutes, he's at a home on a ridge. It's a stone house, made from local rocks nested in a copse of pine trees, and there's a large antenna scrabbling at the sky and two satellite dishes. A truck sits on blocks, and there are ATVs and Polaris vehicles in a grease-stained cluster by a garage. A thickset man leaves the motocross bike he's working on and wipes his hands on a shop rag and approaches Cromwell's car with a wary and questioning expression on his face.

Cromwell gets out of the car and introduces himself. "I'm looking for Hell Creek and a place called Cidersend," he says, adding, "For governmental records."

The man looks puzzled. "Don't know why the government would need that, but Hell Creek ain't but a half mile that way. Ain't never heard of no Cidersend."

"It's a place where there's an orchard of apple trees," Cromwell says.

"Aw. Right. My girls call it Applesauce on account of the smell."

"Could you take me to it?" The man looks dubious but brightens when Cromwell says, "I'll pay you for your time."

"What're we talking 'bout here?"

Thinking of Harlan Parker and the Detheros, Cromwell says, "Fifty dollars okay?" The man smiles.

They climb aboard a rattling Polaris ATV and drive down raw-red trails recently cut into the mountain. The man is dressed in Carhartt, with thick mud boots, and stinks of stale tobacco and sweat and petroleum. Within minutes, they're deep in the woods and moving away from any paved road or house. He can smell it before he can see it. They're in a steep gully, climbing a switchback trail, when Cromwell scents apples on the air.

"We're on government property now, I reckon. National easement," the man says. "We hunt deer around these parts. And turkey. Ain't nothing in that direction for twenty miles but trees and rocks."

This astounds Cromwell—Cidersend belonged to the government all along. They reach a plateau that's heavily wooded with deciduous trees. A single stone chimney remains standing;

all the wood is gone. "Here we are," the man says. "Crisscross Applesauce."

"Give me a moment, will you?"

"Sure, no problemo, mister," the man says. He lights a cigarette and opens his smartphone, leaning back in the Polaris's cushioned, mud-spattered seats.

Cromwell leaves him and approaches the chimney. Here was a home; he can see the faint outlines of a foundation, but a mature oak stands where there might've once been a kitchen or parlor. There is no orchard, though the smell of apples fills the air. It's pure forest here, full of thick undergrowth and crowded trees. Cromwell looks up at the sky, observing the crown shyness, and then moves on.

Black apples at his feet, releasing their smell. And farther, two brick bases with rusted wrought iron jutting upward. The arch that once read IDYLL'S END is gone. Mosquitoes swarm him, and he slaps at his neck.

A little farther, he stumbles, his foot catching upon an overturned granite stone.

He brushes away the litterfall. NADINE HINES, SHE KNOWED FIFTY-TWO MORE SONGS THAN ANYONE, DIED 1861. And farther on. EMANUEL EVENSON, SUFFER THE LITTLE CHILDREN TO COME UNTO ME. BORN 1831, DIED 1899.

Before him rises a thicket, strewn with heavy vines and thick brush, in the shadow of an oak tree. He is not dressed for this excursion, he realizes, but cannot stop himself. He reaches forward, pushing aside the vines and brush—a hundred bloody pricks spring along his arm, tearing through his button-down— and his hand encounters stone. He traces the stone upward, and rising up, he finds a face with his hands. *The vengeful angel,* Mollie called it.

Cromwell returns to the man at the ATV and offers him

more money. By nightfall, the angel gravestone will be cleared of all vines and detritus, the ground around it bare, and the man will be three hundred dollars richer. They are both pleased with the bargain.

He has to drive to a town called Fifty-Six on the county line to get the wine; the rest he buys at a local grocery. The shovel he buys at Walmart, along with cheap work clothes. He's amazed at the prices. He rests in his motel room, letting the air conditioner belch out frigid air to condense in droplets on the windows.

The man with the Polaris—*my name's Dexter Reece but everyone calls me Dex*—greets him at sundown, looking happy but exhausted. He's drinking a cheap light beer—"Natty Lite, you want one?"—and Cromwell finds that he does and they begin drinking in the machine shop.

"If I'd knew there was an angel statue out there in the woods all these years, I'd have been taking folks out on tours."

"It's a piece of historical value, Mister Reece," Cromwell says. "Just a reminder."

"It's one helluva statue, that's for damned sure," he says.

They drink a twelve-pack of beer between them. It reminds Cromwell of his youth, killing time with cheap alcohol, waiting for life to begin. Out on the edges of fields and away from anything that happens. But no more.

"I guess it's time. Take me out there."

"You on a schedule?"

"I am," Cromwell says, and laughs. For no reason, Reece shakes his head and joins in.

They take the Polaris once more, and the journey has changed in the darkness. The headlights move in small patches of illumination through the woods. The darkness deepens.

When they arrive, the wheels of the vehicle churning in the mulch of fallen apples, Cromwell disembarks with his bags and shovels and asks the man to come get him at dawn. Reece is being paid enough he doesn't question but gives Cromwell his cell phone number in case he changes his mind.

The night is full of mosquitoes and biting insects but Cromwell ignores them and sets up his lantern at the foot of the angel's gravestone and begins to dig.

Digging a grave is much harder than it seems on television and takes much longer. He is glad for the gloves and mouths a silent thanks to Harlan Parker for taking the time to describe the state of his hands at the end of things.

The earth does not come easy. It is three in the morning when Cromwell realizes there is no body buried here. Whatever soul lies interred at his feet, it has returned to dust.

He sinks to his knees, exhausted. The wine is cheap. The backwoods liquor stores of Arkansas are not known for their selections of Malbec. It is a pint of fortified port wine. Cromwell says the words anyway and drinks it all down. From the bag, he removes the bread and cheese and eats them down to rind and crust. And then consumes them.

"I've drunk the wine of her body. I've eaten the rind of her cheese, and kissed the crust of her bread," he says.

The oaks and birches, the cedars and apple trees, shift in the night breeze. A dog barks far away in the distance. A branch snaps. And then nothing.

"Let me speak to my wife!" Cromwell cries. "My boy!"

There is nothing. No wind, no sound.

"I'm sorry. I'm sorry. I'm sorry," he says. On his knees, he bows his head until his forehead touches raw earth. His tears mix with the grave mold. "I'm a bad man. I'm such a terrible man."

He stays like that until the dawn breaks against the sky. He unfolds himself painfully from the grave he's dug with his own hands. He thinks about his end, his wife's and son's ends, all ends. There is nothing left him except guilt. There is no more story left to unspool. He is empty.

There are no endings, only beginnings.

Like this one.

THE END

ACKNOWLEDGMENTS

Thanks are due, of course, first and foremost to my agent, Stacia Decker, who agreed to represent me so long ago and more recently agreed to try to sell a weird little novella, *The Sea Dreams It Is the Sky*; my thanks to Stacia again for her fine and steady hand as my first and most trusted editor; also to David Pomerico and his team at Harper Voyager for buying the novella and trusting me to write *My Heart Struck Sorrow* and work on its development. At every turn, David and his team have shown their support and enthusiasm for this book and I'm so grateful to work with a publisher that understands what, as an author, I'm trying to do. I'm grateful to Chuck Wendig for agreeing to write the foreword and Laird Barron, John Langan, Daniel Kraus, Daryl Gregory, Michael Moreci, Michael Patrick Hicks, and all the other folks online who supported *The Sea Dreams It Is the Sky*'s ebook release.

I'd like to thank my favorite artist working today, Jeffrey Alan Love, for providing the striking cover art. His workups for this duo of tales blew my mind. I have lectured online and elsewhere about the importance of cover art for genre books, and I am extremely pleased Jeff was able to contribute to this. I can scratch one more thing off my bucket list.

~~Have Jeff Love do your cover.~~

My thanks to Todd Harvey of the Library of Congress Folklife Center. Todd curates the Alan Lomax collection and his guidance and works—especially his wonderful multimedia book *Michigan-I-O*—provided a surfeit of granular detail for *My Heart Struck Sorrow* and my story of a demented, insane Alan Lomax–like character.

I am deeply indebted to Eduardo Arias and Mónica Ramón Rios for reading *The Sea Dreams It Is the Sky* and to Kwame Mbalia for reading *My Heart Struck Sorrow*, with an eye toward any sort of issues of cultural insensitivity. Without them, I would not have been confident enough to see this book to publication.

Thanks to Dave Oliphant for helping me deal with some rights issues. Thanks to M. L. Brennan for information about the ins and outs of faculty at university. And to Fabio Fernandes for advice regarding South America, and how Americans speaking Spanish (or Portuguese, in Fabio's case) sound to native speakers.

My thanks to Duke Boyne for information regarding motor-cycles—I have ridden one, and enjoyed it (I didn't die, or peel all the skin from my body), but I know nothing about them.

Any mistakes of culture or language, or any detail that is amiss regarding Argentina or South America—all my fault. Should you feel strongly enough about any of my errors to want to inform me of them, please feel free to contact me at me@johnhornorjacobs.com.

Of course, thanks to my wife and kids for understanding the demands of the day job and the night and weekend job and tolerating the ghost-haunted life of a writer.

SOURCE BOOKS AND INSPIRATIONS

The Sea Dreams It Is the Sky

Allende's Chile and the Inter-American Cold War, by Tanya Harmer

Chile History and Pre-Columbian Civilizations: Wars of Independence, 1810–18, Civil Wars, 1818–30, Constitutional History, The Society and Its Environment, Economy, Tourism, Government, Politics, by Henry Albinson

The Condor Years: How Pinochet and His Allies Brought Terrorism to Three Continents, by John Dinges

My Invented Country: A Nostalgic Journey Through Chile, by Isabel Allende

A Nation of Enemies: Chile Under Pinochet, by Pamela Constable and Arturo Valenzuela

The Pinochet File: A Declassified Dossier on Atrocity and Accountability, by Peter Kornbluh

Salt in the Sand: Memory, Violence, and the Nation-State in Chile, 1890 to the Present, by Lessie Jo Frazier

Where Memory Dwells: Culture and State Violence in Chile, by Macarena Gómez-Barris

The works of Roberto Bolaño, Enrique Lihn, Pablo Neruda, Jorge Luis Borges

My Heart Struck Sorrow

Alan Lomax: Selected Writings 1934–1997, by Ronald D. Cohen

Alan Lomax: The Man Who Recorded the World, by John Szwed

Confronting Southern Poverty in the Great Depression: The Report on Economic Conditions of the South with Related Documents, edited with an introduction by David L. Carlton and Peter A. Coclanis

Hammer and Hoe: Alabama Communists During the Great Depression, by Robin D. G. Kelley

The Land Where the Blues Began, by Alan Lomax

Michigan-I-O, by Todd Harvey

Ozark Magic and Folklore, by Vance Randolph

Prejudices: First, Second, and Third Series, by H. L. Mencken

Rising Tide: The Great Mississippi Flood of 1927 and How It Changed America, by John M. Barry

The Southern Journey of Alan Lomax: Words, Photographs, and Music, by Tom Piazza

Stagolee Shot Billy, by Cecil Brown

Stories of Survival: Arkansas Farmers during the Great Depression, by William D. Downs Jr.

A Treasury of American Folklore: Stories, Ballads, and Traditions of the People, by B. A. Botkin

Library of Congress website

ABOUT THE AUTHOR

John Hornor Jacobs's first novel, *Southern Gods*, was short-listed for the Bram Stoker Award for First Novel. His young adult series, The Incarcerado Trilogy, comprised of *The Twelve-Fingered Boy*, *The Shibboleth*, and *The Conformity*, was described by Cory Doctorow of *Boing Boing* as "amazing" and received a starred *Booklist* review. His Fisk and Shoe fantasy series, composed of *The Incorruptibles*, *Foreign Devils*, and *Infernal Machines*, has thrice been short-listed for the David Gemmell Awards and was described by Patrick Rothfuss like so: "One part ancient Rome, two parts wild west, one part Faust. A pinch of Tolkien, of Lovecraft, of Dante. This is strange alchemy, a recipe I've never seen before. I wish more books were as fresh and brave as this." His fiction has appeared in *Playboy*, *Cemetery Dance*, and Apex Magazine. Follow him on Twitter at @johnhornor.